Futuristic Romance

Love in another time, another place.

AWAKENINGS

He kissed Calla then, the hard pressure of his lips making her feigned sleep a torment. Was he testing the depth of her unconsciousness? She wanted to match his passion and return his kiss with all the passion she'd experienced only in her dreams. She wanted to call out his name and beg him to hold her in his arms.

Logan felt an answering quiver when he obeyed the dictates of his heart and kissed her with abandon. During all the adult days of his thirty-two full-cycles, he'd accepted celibacy as an inconvenience, a lifestyle compensated by his honors and success within the Order. Now it felt like a great length of iron chain crushing his chest, squeezing out his life forces.

He caressed her face with his lips, bolder now because she'd shown no signs of waking.

Moon of Desire

Pam Rock

LOVE SPELL ✦ NEW YORK CITY

LOVE SPELL®

November 1993

Published by

Dorchester Publishing Co., Inc.
276 Fifth Avenue
New York, NY 10001

The name "Love Spell" and its logo are trademarks of Dorchester
Publishing Co., Inc.

Printed in the United States of America.

To Ralph

Moon of Desire

Chapter One

"Push, Ede! The baby won't come without your help," Calla pleaded, tenderly wiping her young sister's brow with a scrap of yellowed flannel.

The sheen of perspiration on the girl's wan face made her look even younger than her fifteen full-cycles. Silky blond hair was damply matted around her face, and her eyes were violet pools of anguish.

In spite of the intense heat in the small bed chamber, she shivered convulsively and clutched at the thick blanket bunched under her chin. Her fingers were like white sticks against the dark green wool, and when a contraction racked her body, she clutched the covering with a desperation born of countless hours of fruitless labor.

Although Calla was wearing the thinnest of her muslin night garments, she could hardly endure the suffocating warmth of the room. Yet she continued to build up the fire on the stone hearth by adding chunks of quick-burning fuel cut from the gnarled phage trees on their farm, hoping to relieve the constant chattering of her sister's teeth.

Outside the long, low clay-block farm home, the night wind continued to howl through the dense grove of phages, poignantly reminding Calla of what her mother used to say about Calla's childhood fear: "Children born in the Mars cycle will always be wary of the wind."

She still dreaded the times of the high wind when gale forces battered the coastal village and their out-lying farm. Legend had it that the roar of the wind was always fiercest and most destructive before the eclipse of the three moons that orbited Thurlow. Even though this occurrence, which happened every sixty-six full-cycles, was still several moon cycles away, the fisher folk were disturbed by the drasti-cally high tides and hurricane-force storms at sea.

"Help me," Ede pleaded, tears filling her eyes.

"I'm here, darling," Calla murmured, covering her sister's icy hands with her own hot palms.

Never in the many full-cycles since her mother's death had Calla missed her more. She dearly loved her younger sister and tried to take their mother's place in her life, but she was tortured by her inad-equacy. Ede's agony was almost unbearable, and Calla hated more than ever the term of servitude in the mines that had forced their father and Ede's young mate to be absent at this crucial time.

"Doran—" Ede called out weakly.

"I sent a lad to the village to fetch her," Calla said.

"Taking so long—"

"It only seems so because vou're anxious for her to come," Calla lied, wondering for the hundredth time what was delaying the midwife. Had age made her too feeble to respond to their urgent appeal for help?

Calla had often been present at the birth of a foal to one of her cherished equests, but the sturdy, massive beasts rarely required human assistance. Old Doran had several times urged Calla to apprentice herself to a midwife, but her heavy responsibilities on the farm left no time for learning the ancient arts of birthing and healing.

In truth, Calla admitted to herself with a pang of guilt, she loved the family's herd of equests so much that she thought of little besides their care and training. If Ede or the babe died because she lacked the skills to save them, she would never forgive herself.

"Oh!" Ede screamed, half rising as she fought a pain that seared through her.

"Darling, don't fight it!" Calla urgently counseled. "I've watched our woolies give birth. They relax, go limp, and the little lambs come easily."

Ede fell back moaning, too weak to respond to her sister's oft-repeated advice.

Hot tears stung Calla's eyes, and she walked to the room's one window to hide her face while she savagely wiped them away. Where was the midwife? There was no sign of her on the dark cinder path that led to the house, and Calla had to fight a

11

desperate urge to ride a swift equest to fetch her. Had that foolish boy neglected to summon her? If he had, she would see him apprenticed to a stern fisher captain!

The baby wasn't coming! Calla was terrified that her sister would die with the child still within her. The light of day had come and gone, and still her labor continued. There was nothing Calla could do to hasten the birth or save her sister, and more bitter tears coursed down her cheeks.

Did this long and agonizing labor mean that the child was a defective? Calla clutched her head between her hands, fearing that the family's urgent prayers would be denied.

"E-e-e-e!"

Ede's chilling shriek sent shivers of dread down Calla's spine, and she rushed back to the bedside, trying to conceal her terror from her suffering sister.

Damn you, Doran, where are you? she silently cried, again patting Ede's damp forehead with a bit of cloth.

She knew Ede was long past the normal birthing span, and her fear grew with each excruciating spasm. She held her sister's hands, willing her own strength to her suffering sibling. The pains were close together now, but Ede's grasp grew more frail with each contraction.

Calla blinked back tears and wondered if her beloved sister would see another dawn.

Six hooded figures moved silently in the darkness, the sound of their equests' massive hooves muffled by the storm. The men rode stiff-backed, disciplined by their calling to be oblivious to the hail pelting their heavy woolen cloaks and chafing the exposed areas of their faces.

Logan shifted in his saddle, willing away his weariness and the dull ache in his spine that radiated down through his buttocks and thighs. He'd lost track of the number of days spent in travel, riding over countless kilometers of Thurlow's hostile terrain, stopping only to rest the equests and snatch short naps.

The men rode single file along the cinder road to the village of Luxley, the Elder Warmond leading as he had since they'd left the Zealotes' Citadral. Logan was there because the Grand Elder himself had decided he must serve as Warmond's lieutenant, an appointment the Master of Apprentices greatly resented.

Logan shifted uneasily, his mind full of questions about Warmond. Did he suspect that Logan was the Grand Elder's spy, commissioned by the exalted head of the Order to learn if the rumors that had reached him were based on truth?

Behind Logan the four Youngers appointed as guards were as silent as their leaders, but Logan sensed that their enthusiasm for the venture had been drained by hardship. Chosen for their strength and devotion, the four young men were among the very few ever permitted to journey beyond the boundaries of the Order's territory. They'd ridden forth with great zest for adventure and pride in their appointments, only to discover that nothing in the outside world matched the splendor

13

of the Zealotes' domain.

He heard a muffled cough behind him and hoped the faint sound hadn't reached Warmond. The Master of Apprentices was in a foul mood, and Logan didn't want one of the Youngers lashed for such a petty breach of the silence.

Clenching and unclenching his jaw, Logan struggled to control his anger at their leader. The Order taught that negative emotion was unproductive and self-destructive. Logan had been chosen for this mission because his self-control exceeded that of all his peer group. He hadn't expected his dislike of Warmond to escalate into a black hatred that tested his self-discipline, but the man's casual cruelty was a betrayal of the Order's sacred purpose: the brotherhood of men. There had been too many punishments on this trip: denial of food and sleep, the bite of Warmond's rope on exposed flesh for the most trivial of offenses.

The future of the Order depended on missions such as this one. For many years Warmond had led all the expeditions, but increasingly of late, the Master of Apprentices failed in his quests. It was Logan's duty to learn why.

Disappointment was like a pall over the riders. They had long ago lost count of the number of villages they'd searched without success.

The dwelling ahead was a rude hovel constructed of the chunky clay blocks used in coastal villages. Unlike most of the thatched roof homes in the small settlement, this one showed a light in the window. Warmond signaled a halt under the twisted branches of a clump of trees.

Logan and the Youngers shook off their lethargy and sat tense and alert, waiting for Warmond to advance on the hovel. The four guards fanned out at his signal. Their duty was to ward off unwanted interference. They were allowed to enter an outsider's dwelling only if the life of their leader was in jeopardy. At all other times the youths had to be spared the sight of females, even elderly ones. When the group passed one of that gender on the road, Warmond gave the sign that they must cover their eyes and trust their mounts to convey them safely past. Logan needed no such command; he automatically averted his eyes, even for creatures bundled from head to foot in bulky quilted garments. Ten full-cycles older than the guards, none of whom had lived more than twenty-two full-cycles, Logan felt nothing more than a slight unease in the presence of the females who were crucial to their mission.

Countless dwellings had yielded disappointment, but the light in this window gave them all new hope. Warmond dismounted and secured his reins on a low branch. Logan needed no command to do the same. Silently the two men approached the door.

By the Grand Elder's express command, Logan was permitted to enter any dwelling in Warmond's company. Much to Logan's surprise and displeasure, the Master of Apprentices gave him a curt order to remain outside.

"Guard the door," Warmond said, "and see that those fools keep a sharp watch."

Logan knew he could disobey; his commission from the Grand Elder made him Warmond's equal, but he didn't want to challenge the Master of Apprentices over a minor matter. Warmond gained entrance by forcing the door with a blow from his shoulder, and Logan wordlessly took a stance with his back to the opening.

How many midwives had dashed their hopes, shaking bowed heads in denial? The roar of the wind drowned any words that passed between Warmond and this crone, but Logan's heart pounded in expectation. As an empath, he could neither read minds nor predict the future, but he could sense emotions. The exchange between Warmond and the midwife sent out vibrations that warmed him like a roaring fire, and for the first time in many long days he hoped for success.

One of the Youngers slipped from his mount to relieve himself, a breach of duty Logan would have reported if Warmond were not so heavy-handed in his discipline. Instead the prospect of good news made him smile indulgently and hope the youth would be quick about it.

The hail had abated, but the wind screamed around the dwelling. Logan pulled his cloak tighter around his lean, powerful frame. He couldn't remember ever hearing such violence in the wind, but it wasn't loud enough to drown out another, more disturbing sound. The crone was shrieking, her distress jarring all his senses.

Something was drastically wrong. No midwife should recoil in fear in the presence of the Master of Apprentices. His mission brought honor to any crone who aided him. It was a great privilege to assist the Order, and any midwife who contributed to the success of a mission earned the reverence and respect of the people. Logan's cynical side reminded him that she could also command a higher fee for her services if she delivered one of the summoned ones.

The midwife screamed again, the mortal terror in her voice unmistakable. Logan rushed into the hovel, even though it meant a confrontation with Warmond. The Grand Elder must be informed if the Master of Apprentices was misusing his power by terrorizing a midwife.

"What's wrong? Is there a babe?" Logan asked.

Warmond, his long pale face contorted with anger, stood over the hysterical woman securing her with strands cut from the rope all members of the Order carried as their only weapon. Their law forbade the use of steel to harm any human. The short dirk they carried in their boots could only be used to cut rope or other objects.

Not looking up from his task, Warmond tore a strip from the crone's skirt and stuffed it in her mouth, gagging her with another rag from the same source.

"Why are you doing that?" Logan demanded to know.

"Would you have this hag alerting the whole village?" Warmond asked, his anger filling the room like a poisonous vapor.

"There is a babe then?"

"Not yet delivered, but this hag was preparing to go to the woman. She refused to lead us there."

Logan saw a boy cowering in a corner, his face contorted with fear. His clothes were the soiled, shapeless garb of the lowest class, but his cheeks were full and his limbs looked solid, signs that he served a well-intentioned master.

"We mean you no harm," Logan said, speaking softly to reassure the lad. "You know who we are, don't you?"

The lad barely managed to shake his head in the affirmative.

"Then you know we're here to bring honor to one of your own. We won't stain our reputation by harming you."

"If he doesn't lead us to his master's home, I'll string him up," Warmond threatened.

The boy began weeping, a blubbering sound of sheer terror that brought an icy smile to Warmond's face.

"This isn't the way," Logan protested.

"No, and how many moon-cycles do you expect to wander before we find what we came for? Did the Grand Elder send you to hasten the end of the Order?"

"Treat the lad more kindly," Logan insisted, uncomfortable because Warmond had used the one argument he could never refute: the welfare of the Zealotes.

"I'll do him the kindness of letting him keep his miserable life if he leads us to the woman who's birthing."

Logan reached out with his mind, finding only terror and an abject willingness to obey in the youth. Risking a quick probe of Warmond's emotions, he discovered nothing, only the cold, passionless armor of a guarded psyche. It was what he expected. The Master of Apprentices was too wily to open his heart in the presence of a known empath.

Warmond grabbed the boy by the arm, his grip tight enough to make his victim wince with pain, and forced him out into the tempestuous night. Logan paused just long enough to speak a reassuring word to the midwife and loosen the gag so she wouldn't choke or suffocate.

"I'll watch out for the lad and send him back to free you," he promised. "No harm will come to either of you."

She moaned, her dark, red-rimmed eyes wide with fear, but Logan sensed that her concern was for the mother and baby, not herself.

"No one will come to harm," he said, then hurried after Warmond.

The Master of Apprentices was taking no chances with his prisoner. The lad's wrist was tied to a rope before he was allowed to mount the broad-haunched white equest that had brought him to the midwife's. The beast was a magnificent creature, as sturdy and well-bred as any in the Grand Elder's stable. A servant boy entrusted with such a superior mount could only mean one thing: The master and all the adult men were away serving their time in the mines.

Gustaf was trembling even before the torrential rain soaked through his many layers of tattered clothing. Mistress Calla had trusted him to bring the midwife, and instead he was leading members of the Order to her doorstep. The rope was biting into his wrist, and he didn't for a moment doubt the horrible consequences of not obeying his captor. Never in his twelve full-cycles had he been so terrified, but for her sake he had to deceive these evil baby-stealers.

Tears filled his eyes even though he was much too old to blubber like a babe. Ahead the black rain obscured the roadway, but Gustaf knew it well. Once they passed the mill and crossed the plank bridge, the road would divide, the right fork narrowing into a trail that led to the cliffs. He didn't have a plan, only the compelling need to bring honor to his name by serving his beloved mistress.

So far he had failed her miserably. Old Doran had been away when he went to her hovel, and he had wasted precious hours searching for her. When he did track her down, she was treating a fisher-wife's malady. Gustaf had allowed himself to be persuaded to take hot milk and fish cakes with the family before leaving with the midwife. Worst of all, he had allowed Doran to return to her home for her special bag of birthing potions before starting off for the farm, not that anyone could stop her from doing as she wished. Folk said her hair had been flame-red before it paled with age, and no man could master her temper.

Gustaf took the right turn, so frightened that he leaned forward to hug the equest's neck for comfort. His captor tugged on the rope, nearly pulling him off the mount and sending searing pain up his arm.

"Let me talk to him," one of the men insisted. "This trail leads only to the sea."

Gustaf froze, expecting some horrible punishment for attempting to mislead the Zealotes. Ahead the path climbed upward, curving and disappearing in the curtain of rain. How long could he hide the location of the farm if the rumors about the Order's diabolical use of ropes were true? He was trembling so violently he didn't know if he could force words from his mouth.

The second man rode up beside him and freed his wrist by quickly untying the complicated knot in the rope.

"I know you're trying to serve your people," he said in a soothing voice, "but your efforts are misguided. If the babe is a girl, we'll leave immediately and no one will be harmed. If a boy, we can give him a life of honor, rich in purity and knowledge. Think of us as givers of a great gift."

Gustaf shook his head, mutely rejecting the consoling words.

"Halt!" Logan gave the order, ignoring Warmond's angry protest.

"I'm an empath, lad. I know you're trying to deceive us, so the other road must lead to your farm. I feel your pain too, and you must believe there's no betrayal in taking us to the babe. We will find it if we have to visit every house in the countryside, but the delay will make our leader very angry. I can't protect you from his wrath unless you help us now. Nothing you can do will thwart our mission."

Logan felt the lad's resistance collapse, but it didn't bring him any satisfaction. This weak child's courage brought honor to his people, and Logan vowed to see that he came to no harm.

Wet and weary, the band retraced their way, not trying to communicate over the howl of the wind.

Logan scarcely noticed the battering rain; his own inner turmoil made the storm seem inconsequential. He had never heard of an anointing ceremony performed without the assistance of a midwife. Was this part of the puzzle the Grand Elder had sent him to investigate?

Ahead of him Warmond was erect in the saddle, his hood thrown back and his coal-black hair plastered to his scalp, impervious to the buffeting gale. Logan tried again and failed to pierce the guarded psyche of the Master of Apprentices. Uneasily he followed Warmond and the lad through the darkness.

Calla hovered over her sister, leaving her side only to peer anxiously through the black rivulets of rain coursing down the window. Ede's screams were growing weaker as each contraction drained her remaining reserves of strength. She still reached for Calla's hands, but her grasp was frail, nothing like the painful crushing grip during her early pains. Even though Calla's fingers ached from the long hours of encouraging her sister, she welcomed the feeble grip, reading more into each weak squeeze than was warranted.

"Where's Doran?" Ede gasped.

"She would be here if she could," Calla sadly admitted, giving up hope that the midwife would come to her sister's aid.

Gustaf was a loyal and reliable boy. Doran was true to her calling and a faithful friend to the family. Both must have fallen prey to some terrible mishap, or they would have been there hours ago.

22

If the midwife were anywhere near, she would sense the seriousness of the situation. She was one of the very few people in the village gifted as an empath, and the anguish pouring forth from the two sisters was strong enough to reach across the neatly tended fields to Doran's home.

"Calla!" There was a new note of fear in Ede's voice.

"I'm here, precious. I'm with you." She pushed away the lank strands of hair clinging to her sister's forehead.

"It's coming—" A hoarse cry of pain cut off her words.

"You can do it," Calla urged. "I'm here, sweet. Don't give up!"

"Can you see it?" Ede asked, her tone begging for reassurance.

"Yes, I see the head." Calla was trembling with excitement. "Bear down. You must push your child into the world."

"Hurts!" Tears of agony gave a watery sheen to her deep violet eyes, making Calla fervently wish that she, the stronger sister, could bear this burden of pain.

"Oh, no . . . no . . . I can't—"

"Do it!"

Ede's inhuman shriek paralyzed Calla, but only for an instant. She reached for the wet creature emerging from its mother's womb, easing the last harrowing moments of separation.

"Tell me—" Ede pleaded, desperately summoning enough strength to speak.

"He's perfect. A boy. Flawless!"

23

"Show me."

Calla deftly cut the cord and held the squirming newborn by the heels until a feeble cry reassured her that he was breathing.

"Here." She held him near his mother, then laid him on a soft towel and gently began cleaning him.

When the baby was dressed and securely wrapped in a blanket warmed by the hearth, Calla again showed him to Ede, then placed him in a basket lined with a down-filled quilt that stood ready beside the bed.

"I was so frightened . . . You're sure he shows no sign of affliction?" Ede asked.

"No, darling! How could he, when his father had never been to the mines at the time of mating? Your child isn't a defective. His head is beautifully round. His skin is as smooth and pink as a piglet's. He's perfect—truly perfect!"

Ede's fear evaporated, and Calla thanked the Great Power over and over in her heart as she ministered to the needs of her exhausted sister.

Their family was blessed by the most wonderful of gifts: a healthy child. It was the only normal child Ede would have. Now that her mate had started work in the mines, he would only father defectives: deformed babies with elongated heads, few of whom survived the first moments of life outside the womb. It was the curse of Thurlow: only young lads scarcely past puberty could sire babies who lived. Calla's mother had died giving birth to a stillborn defective, and Calla was eternally thankful her parents had mated young enough to give her a sister.

Calla's eyes flooded with tears of gratitude. Her beloved father had a grandson. She thanked the Great Power again, pledging her own life if need be to ensure that the baby would grow up strong and healthy, a priceless blessing to their small family.

Once she had hoped to have a child herself, but the mate her father found for her didn't give her that privilege. She was barren when he was forced to begin his annual six moon-cycles of servitude. He was sent to work in a new tunnel and lost his life when faulty pilings caused a cave-in at the mine.

"Fane," Ede said, opening her eyes and weakly smiling. "We decided to call him Fane."

"A fine name," Calla said, then urged her sister to rest.

Calla's heart ached with pride and happiness as she hovered over the precious newborn. The few hairs on his little round skull were like fine strands of gold, and his eyes were a deeper, darker violet than his mother's. She couldn't resist taking the tiny hand in her own, touching the top of each little finger, astonished at his miniature perfection.

Her eyes were wet with tears, but she'd never in her life been happier.

Sitting in a bentwood rocker, Calla kept watch over the mother and child. As exhausted as she was from her long vigil, she was too excited to nod off. Her only regret was that her father and Tadd, Ede's mate, couldn't see the child. They were only half through their term of servitude, but Gustaf was old enough to carry the good news to them.

She frowned, wondering for the hundredth time where the lad was. It was so unlike him to fail

25

her that she feared for his safety. Only her greater obligation to her sister and the child kept her from going to search for her father's tenant.

Gustaf. He had lived twelve full-cycles to her twenty, but he was the only lad in the area not pledged to mate. Her father had approached her more than once to consider a betrothal, but she couldn't bring herself to agree. On Thurlow the laws were not like those of Old Earth, which had sent her people to colonize the planet nearly a millennium ago. Mating was a commitment that could be set aside only by death.

The birth of little Fane was more than a blessing to the family of her father, Bar Redmond. It relieved Calla of the guilt that came with being childless. She couldn't explain to her father, but she dreamed that someday a special male would come into her life.

She closed her eyes and let an image fill her mind. The man was tall and strong with a comely face and sable hair that hung to his shoulders. More important than his arresting appearance was the beauty in his soul. His blue eyes were bright reflections of his goodness, his love. By concentrating very hard, she could feel the touch of his hand and the sweet caress of his lips on hers.

Calla nodded off, her head slumping forward, finally giving in to exhaustion. Her sleep lasted only a short time. She awoke with a shiver, realizing that the fire had burnt down to glowing embers.

Impatient with her romantic dream, she rose to build up the fire, taking a moment first to check on mother and child. Both were peacefully slumbering.

The logs ignited easily, and she entertained herself by watching fire devils rise from the burning wood. She loved to imagine faces in the brilliant orange flames. Sitting beside the hearth and crossing her legs with feline grace, she hugged herself and indulged her imagination. The comforting crackle of the fire helped her forget her longings.

Calla's mating had not been a love match. She took pale, dark-haired Quinn because her father desperately wanted to see the beginning of a new generation of Redmonds. Sonless fathers could practice matrilineal succession. She knew her mate had been enticed into the marriage by the richness of her father's lands and the fame of their equests. He came to her bed without passion and did his duty stoically. She dreaded their joinings, the rhythmic thrust of his body so lacking in tenderness that she had to steel herself not to resist. Bitterly disappointed in their union, she suffered even more when her moon-cycle flows continued without interruption.

She didn't rejoice in Quinn's untimely death; the loss of any young person was a tragedy. She mourned, but it was the loss of her chance for love that caused her sorrow. How could she feel a woman's passion for a child like Gustaf?

Flames danced in front of her eyes, and she indulged in another favorite fantasy: the coming of the Earth vessel. She was counting the days until the eclipse of the three moons and the arrival of the spaceship filled with trade goods that would supply the people of Thurlow for another sixty-six years. In exchange, the Earth travelers would fill their cargo hold with precious hyronium

27

extracted from ore found only on Thurlow. It was for this, the wealth and lifeblood of their planet, that all men worked half of each full-cycle in the mines.

Not even her father was old enough to have seen an Earther, but Calla loved to speculate about them. Although they shared common ancestors, she was sure the men were taller, stronger, and more fascinating than any Thurlowian. She knew her school friends had dreamed of them too, each young girl longing to be carried aboard a mystical vessel by a space hero.

Calla shook her head impatiently. It was past time to give up her girlish fantasies. Her mate was gone. She could never subject herself to the pawing and sweating of a callow youth like Gustaf, so she was destined to be the spinster aunt, taking comfort in the care of a robust nephew and the training of her beloved equests. That was her fate. It was futile to yearn for a worthy mate.

Again she dozed, but her rest was brief. She awoke with a start and jumped to her feet, confused and groggy but aware that a great crashing noise had roused her. An icy blast came through the open door of the room, and she heard the sound of boots on the flagstone corridor.

Her first thought was one of great joy: her father or Tadd had managed to get leave from the mines. She ran to the doorway and thought she was still dreaming. A dark man in a wet cloak pushed roughly past her, and behind him was the man of her fantasies.

* * *

Logan was close behind Warmond, angrier than ever to see how the Master of Apprentices smashed the door out of the aging frame, wood splintering in a noisy explosion. For the first time in his life, Logan was embarrassed for the Order, humiliated by the outburst of protest from the female.

"Is the child a boy?" Warmond demanded harshly.

"No! No, you can't come in here like this!"

Logan stepped into the room, startled by the female tugging on Warmond's sleeve, trying to stop him from approaching the basket by the bed.

"Great Power, have mercy!" Logan's words were an oath, and he knew he deserved discipline for his outburst, but he'd never seen a sight such as this.

The female was young but in the fullness of her womanhood, her long golden hair in wild disarray over her shoulders. He knew she was beautiful, as fair as paintings of Earth's Madonna found in books that were allowed in the Zealotes' libraries, but he had never seen her like. The shapeless bundles he passed on the roads, the homely crones who served as midwives, the careless children of Outsiders, none of them had prepared him for this creature.

Years of training and discipline told him he must avert his eyes, but he was helpless, so riveted by the vision in front of him that it seemed his adolescent dreams had been given flesh. She was wearing a garment suitable only for a bedchamber, a flowing gown of thin muslin that clung to her breasts without concealing the dark, ripe buds of nipples.

"Don't touch the baby!" she cried in panic.

Warmond, angry at her interference, cuffed her with the back of his hand, knocking her to the floor.

Impulsively Logan reached out, touching her shoulder before he realized the enormity of what he was doing. Still, he couldn't stop himself. He offered his hand, pulling her to her feet but not before he saw one bare foot and the smooth, creamy expanse of her calf.

His senses responded to her closeness with an impact that made him dizzy. His nostrils inhaled a fragrance as alien as the farthest galaxy and as pleasing as the flowering plants in the Grand Elder's garden. He heard her desperate intake of air, and it seemed to draw breath from his own lungs. His eyes wouldn't focus, yet he lacked the will to avert them.

Most shattering of all was the touch of her flesh on his. Her hand was warm, the top of it as smooth as the finest silk but as soft as down. He quickly hid his own hand in the folds of his robe to conceal an unmanly trembling. His whole body burned with shame and something even more devastating.

"Please don't do this!" she begged.

Her words cut through him like forbidden thrusts of steel, and the enormity of his reaction paralyzed him. He was breaking his oath, lusting after a female Outsider. He looked beyond her at a shapeless form under a heavy blanket on the bed, but the devastating effect of his sin stayed with him. He had never seen a face like this woman's: violet eyes like the farthest range of mountain peaks and full pink lips. Her waist

30

was tiny, and the soft mounds of flesh above them were wondrously full, tormenting him even as he struggled to control his thoughts. His knowledge of a woman's body came from scientific texts. Nothing in them had prepared him for the rich, lush, three-dimensional reality of this creature.

If only he were a youth, not yet bound by the Oath! He could confess his lustful thoughts and be cleansed by the bite of the rope. As an adult and a leader in the Order, he couldn't find relief from his fearful lapse of control in external punishments. Even as she turned away from him, he let himself gaze at her golden mane and the night garment clinging to her shapely backside and thighs. He ached with more than physical pain, wondering if he were losing his grip on sanity. His humiliation went so deep he wanted to run from the room like a boy caught in a shameful act, yet his fascination with the woman didn't diminish.

"It is a boy!" Warmond said with harsh-voiced satisfaction, replacing the covers he'd ripped from the infant in the basket. "As fine a specimen as I've seen in a long time."

Both women were weeping, but Logan's guilt drowned out the pitiful sound. He'd betrayed the Order and disgraced himself, and yet he couldn't take his eyes from the female. Was he enchanted, beguiled by an unreal vision into this betrayal of all he held sacred? Was this the danger in love between genders, that a man's senses become so jumbled that nothing mattered but the will of the female?

He slumped against the door frame, barely able to stay on his feet. He didn't understand what was happening to him, but the rest of his life loomed ahead like a black hole.

Chapter Two

The intruders' entry into their dwelling was like a nightmare, but Calla knew the cause of her terror was real. The man from her dreams was there in the flesh, tall and menacing in high boots and black breeches, his heavy wet cloak draped over broad shoulders. He'd come, but not to fulfill her longings; he was going to destroy her family's future.

"You can't take the baby!" she screamed, throwing herself at the other man who was leaning over the infant's basket.

The baby's soft cry was echoed by his mother's hysterical shrieks, but the kidnapper wasn't deterred by the agonized wailing. He knocked Calla to the floor with an impatient shove and peeled back the child's blanket.

"Bind that woman," Warmond ordered. "We have what we came for."

Logan stepped closer, not willing to believe the child was male without seeing for himself. Something was wrong—terribly wrong. The anointing ceremony was supposed to be a time of joy and thankfulness. In summoning a newborn, the Order saved him from the drudgery of the mines and the pathetic life of the Outsiders. The child would be blessed with a life of brotherhood and spiritual enrichment.

Employing the full extent of his empathic power, Logan was assailed by the violent emotions in the room. The young female on the bed was easy to read: Her pain and fear were mingled with hopelessness.

"Calla," the mother gasped between sobs.

"Do it now!" Warmond ordered, kicking at the female reaching up from the floor to tug at his leg.

Logan sensed the anger and defiance in the woman called Calla and knew he must obey Warmond. She wouldn't surrender the baby without fighting to the last of her strength. To protect her, he had to restrain her.

He reached for the length of rope coiled by his side and loosened the clasp that held it to his leather belt, but he couldn't bring himself to bind her. The coarse strands would chafe her delicate, blue-veined wrists, making angry raw sores if she struggled to free herself.

His hesitation didn't escape Warmond. The Master of Apprentices turned on him, his face contorted with fury.

Logan was stunned, but not by Warmond's anger, which was warranted by his own failure to obey. For a brief moment, Warmond's agitated state made him forget to shield his emotions. Logan could detect a curious mix of rage, triumph, and cunning in the Master of Apprentices. The rage was directed at Logan and was understandable; in the best of times there was no love between them. The triumph was natural; their long, difficult quest was over. But what was this sly, conniving undertone, this hint of secret motives?

Warmond quickly realized his vulnerability and shut out Logan's probe, but not before sending a message: Not even the Grand Elder could save Logan if he didn't obey instantly.

The moment of revelation lasted only seconds, but Logan was more convinced than ever that Warmond was hiding something from his superiors in the Order.

A long-fringed shawl was draped across the back of a chair, and Logan seized it, knowing this wasn't the time to risk a total rift with Warmond. He knelt and removed the woman's hands from the leader's booted calf, feeling more awkward than he ever had in his life as his fingers locked around her slender wrists. He held her hands with one of his as he reached for the long purple and gold shawl, but he was strangely disturbed by contact with her skin. She seemed more threatening than Warmond's angry commands.

The shawl was slippery and hard to knot. She fought him, trying to crawl away before he could bind her wrists together. Clutching at her flimsy night garment to prevent her escape, he ripped the muslin the whole length of her back.

Warmond chuckled, a soft evil cluck that brought hot blood to Logan's cheeks.

"The Master of Defense bested by a mere female?" he asked. "Must I uncoil my rope and render assistance?"

Calla struggled to her feet, taking advantage of Logan's flash of resentment against the Master of Apprentices, and raced toward the door with swiftness born of sheer panic. Logan jumped to his feet with enough presence of mind to give chase with the shawl clutched in his left hand. He ran after her, driven by humiliation as much as by the need to stop her from alarming her neighbors. Warmond would ridicule him for this episode. Logan's dignity would suffer whenever the Master of Apprentices chose to retell the incident in the Council Chambers of the Order.

Calla nearly made it to the opening where Warmond had smashed out the door, but Logan caught her from behind, reaching out to secure her in his arms.

Her night garment, torn by his own hand, was hanging in shreds at her waist. He locked one arm around her, shocked by the contact of his hand on her full, warm breast. She fought, straining against his hold, almost breaking free when he realized his palm was pressed against the hard little bud of her nipple.

In the cult, adolescent boys speculated about women's bodies, and Logan knew intellectually that these female appendages were necessities in the reproductive cycle. Nothing, however, not even the dangerous, prohibited curiosity of a youth, had prepared him for the way he felt about the pounding beat of her heart, the throbbing of her blood flow, or the smooth, warm seductiveness of the flesh under his fingers.

"Stop this hopeless resistance," he ordered in a voice made husky by his own embarrassment and confusion.

He moved his hand, taking great care not to brush against her other breast, fighting the kernel of curiosity that made him wonder if his touch disturbed her as it much as it did him. He felt as though the hard tip of her nipple had burned his palm, leaving a brand that would torment him with memories as long as he lived.

Afraid of giving her another chance to run, he grasped the firm, naked flesh of her upper arm, dismayed that even this less intimate contact sent rivers of fire coursing though his veins. What penance could he do, what sacrifice must he make, to atone for these wild, unsought sensations caused by a creature whose like he'd never even imagined?

"Please hold still," he said through clenched teeth. "I must bind you for your own safety."

"I don't care about my safety! Do you know what you're doing to my family—to my father's hopes? You have no right—"

"Must I do that for you?" Warmond taunted from the chamber at the end of the corridor.

With difficulty Logan forced both of Calla's hands behind her back, but still she struggled, strands of golden hair swirling over her creamy shoulders and the flawless skin of her back.

Bile rose in Logan's throat, and he fought an

unmanly surge of fear when he thought of what Warmond would do if this unruly female continued to resist. Lashing an Outsider was considered beneath the dignity of members of the Order, but Warmond had demonstrated that he made his own rules when he left the jurisdiction of the Zealotes.

"What you're doing is evil!" she screamed at Warmond's back.

"Gag her!" he ordered, watching to see that his orders were carried out.

"Hold your tongue, or you'll be silenced painfully," Logan quickly whispered, his breath warm in her ear.

His face, his hair, even his voice were familiar because she had seen him so often in her dreams. She could conjure up his image more readily than that of her own dead husband, but she had never expected to meet him, never imagined he would materialize as a ruthless cult member and kidnapper.

Calla went limp, drained of further resistance for the moment. She was mesmerized by the powerful thrust of his jaw, the firm fullness of his lips, the patrician shape of his nose, and especially by his vibrant blue eyes, deeply set under heavy lids and thick lashes. She recognized him as her fantasy lover, yet she had never met him, never even seen a man who resembled him. What kind of monster invaded a landowner's home and stole a newborn child?

According to the ancient tradition of the Order, a boy-child was blessed when he was summoned by the Zealotes. Her people, the Outsiders, no longer believed that. In these troubled times when defective newborns were more common than normal ones, secretive bands of cult members roamed the countryside to kidnap precious babies. Her father said the scarcity of children was the fault of the government, which forced young boys into the mines to meet the unreasonable quotas set by Earth. In his grandfather's day, no man did service until he'd sired a large, healthy brood.

"Does this give you pain?" her captor asked as he checked the tightness of the shawl binding her wrists. His voice was soft and—she could almost believe—remorseful.

He took a square of white muslin, the kind most men carried on a journey as an emergency bandage, from an inner pocket of his cloak and gently tied it around her mouth.

"If you have the sense to keep quiet, this will suffice," he warned. "Don't make a sound. Warmond, Master of Apprentices, has his own way of gagging people who defy him."

He nudged her back toward the bedchamber. She went without fighting him, but he was afraid her docile compliance was only a sham. He prayed that Warmond would be ready to leave with the infant before the woman made more trouble. Logan was duty-bound to carry out his mission for the Grand Elder, and to do so he couldn't risk an open confrontation with Warmond.

So agitated his face was moist with perspiration, Logan was anxious and alert for more resistance, but the woman sat on the floor beside the bed, eyes downcast and shoulders slumped in defeat. He

39

didn't want to look in her direction, but he had to be alert for further signs of resistance. He caught a glimpse of tears moistening her cheeks and couldn't tear his eyes away from her slumped form. With her hands tied behind her, she couldn't hold the remnants of her ruined garment over her breasts, and they spilled out in the full bloom of womanhood. He wanted to give her a blanket to cover herself, wondering when the torment of this evening would end for both of them, but Warmond was beginning the sacred ceremony of the summoning. Any interruption on Logan's part would be an unforgivable sin. It didn't matter if Warmond made him look like a fool by reporting his struggle with the woman. Of course, even the lowly apprentices in the Citadral would snicker behind his back, but Logan could endure that for the sake of his mission. He couldn't hope to keep the Grand Elder's confidence if Warmond forced him to take a Truth Oath and admit to sacrilege during this sacred rite, the welcoming of a new soul into the Zealotes.

Calla was trembling, but she clenched her jaw and tensed her whole body to keep from revealing her weakness to the intruders. She watched in horror as the one called Warmond shed his cloak and the coarse black shirt of the Order, then roughly removed the sleeping sack and diaper from the baby. Holding little Fane in both hands, he lifted him high above his head and began a chant that sent cold chills down Calla's spine.

"Pater Heven Sanctifeer—" he intoned in a trance-like voice, summoning the infant into the Order of the Zealotes.

"No!" Ede screamed, anguish overcoming her weakness and exhaustion as she heard the words that would rob her forever of her son. "You can't have him! He's mine! I nearly died to give him life!"

Warmond continued chanting, either oblivious of Ede's tormented protests or so indifferent to her agony that he didn't pause for even an instant in his liturgy.

In earlier times families who lost sons to the cult had believed this cruel ritual was a great honor. Now parents hid their newborn sons until they were past the age of summoning. If only Ede's birthing hadn't been so difficult! The three of them might have made it to the secret retreat in the mountains that the men in the family had readied as their sanctuary for the first year of Fane's life.

Calla burned with anger and indignation, repeating in her mind a vow: Fane would be restored to his family, even at the cost of her own life. For the moment she had to be silent and not give the Zealotes reason to kill her. If she died now, all hope of restoring her nephew to his parents and grandfather would perish with her. As soon as these men left, secure in the belief that they'd accomplished their aim, she would have to act quickly. Any chance of rescuing him would be lost before her father and Ede's husband were released from servitude in the mines. No family had ever regained a summoned child from the Zealotes once they took him inside the Citadral. The cult's influence was too powerful everywhere on the planet. It had been many full-cycles since any parents had dared to plead their case in the corrupt courts of Thurlow. Her only hope of saving Fane was to pursue the band of kidnappers and find a way to spirit him away before they reached their far-off territory. Her chance of success was almost nonexistent. Her only advantage was knowledge of the rugged, inhospitable terrain of the region. The out-country was more familiar to her than to the kidnappers.

Biting her tongue to hold back angry protests, she heeded the warning of the sable-haired Zealote and kept silent; but her mind was in turmoil as she planned a rescue effort.

"Logan, in the name of the Sacred Order of Zealotes, I bid you anoint this child with the oil of purification and redemption," Warmond intoned, so entranced by his own words that he didn't seem to notice the infant's wet contribution to the ceremony trickling down one of his upraised arms.

Logan knew his part; he drew a cork from a tiny vial of oil Warmond had in readiness. According to the rules of the ritual, a second cult member had to anoint the chosen child. He poured the oil into his cupped palm, hesitating a moment when he remembered his hand had been defiled by contact with the woman's flesh. By rights he should purify himself before participating in a sacred ceremony, but Warmond was too impatient to tolerate delay. Silently praying for forgiveness, Logan dipped his finger into the oil and made the sign of the triple moons on the head, heart, and tiny hands of the babe.

The ceremony concluded, but there wasn't any joy in the room, only the weak wails of the mother and the babe.

"Just let me keep him until my milk comes," Ede pleaded brokenly. "If I could nurse him once—"

"He'll be fed the pure milk of mountain stoogs," Logan said softly, stepping close to the bed and taking Ede's hand in his to give what little comfort he could. "We came prepared to meet his every need. He couldn't be more precious to us if the Great Power had handed him down from a heavenly realm into our keeping. Your son is a fortunate child. His life will be blessed with joys you can't even imagine. Please don't grieve. Rejoice for him."

"Enough!" Warmond snapped. "It's not our responsibility to coddle a female Outsider. We'll leave now."

He bundled the child in garments brought for the purpose. Once a baby was summoned, he couldn't wear clothing contaminated by Outsiders.

The room was deathly silent; the young mother's sorrow was too deep for further tears, and Calla knew she still had to be cautious and not call attention to herself.

Logan tried to block his empathic gift, but the suffering that assailed him was overwhelming. How many Zealotes knew about the misery caused by the summoning? Like all cult members, Logan lived a life of contemplation, moderation, and, above all, isolation from the destructive passions of the Outsiders. After seeing the pain inflicted by the summoning, he didn't know if he would ever feel quite the same about his life within the Citadral.

"Is it always like this when we summon a child?" he asked Warmond.

"No, the women in these wilder regions are overly possessive of their offspring," the Master of Apprentices said, placing the infant in a sling across his chest and adjusting his cloak to shelter the child from the elements. "Think of the glorious future in store for this male. I'm going to suggest the Grand Elder rename him Plato after the greatest of Earth's philosophers."

"If he were older, he could choose—" Logan said, knowing he was dangerously close to blasphemy. The Grand Elder had sent him to learn all he could about Warmond's summoning trips, but he hadn't expected to witness a tragedy.

Warmond was too elated by success to debate with his lieutenant. His smile, a slight stretching of lips in a face that seemed to be chiseled of pale gray granite, held irony but no menace—for the moment. His short-cropped black hair had dried enough to show the flecks of gray, and his stiff goatee gave his chin the illusion of being sharply pointed. In his mid-forty full-cycle, the Master of Apprentices was a lean, square-shouldered man slightly shorter than Logan. Few people looked directly into his eyes more than once; the cloudy gray pupils seemed to drain the spirit of anyone who dared stare into them. During Warmond's youth his peers had teased him about his whirlpool eyes. No one made light of them after he reached full manhood.

Logan risked a probe and found a profound sense

of satisfaction emanating from his fellow Zealote. Warmond had deliberately lowered his guard to share this moment of elation. It was unlike him, and Logan was more disturbed than he wanted to admit.

Warmond left the bedchamber with a curt command to make haste, but before following, Logan looked down at Calla. Their eyes met, and he felt her gaze searing his conscience, willing him to help her, demanding his compassion.

Tearing himself away, he took leave of the dwelling, knowing if he glanced back one more time he would no longer be master of his own destiny.

"Logan!" She called after him, speaking his name for the first time through the cloth he'd tied too loosely to muffle her voice.

Why had he shown her this kindness? Why had he trusted her to keep silent? Did he think a humane gesture would compensate for the enormous crime of stealing a child? If he had a conscience, she hoped it would torment him until the day he died! There was no forgiveness for a man who robbed a family of its future existence.

Calla called out to her sister, but Ede didn't respond. She was lying wide-eyed with shock and grief, too lost in despair to be of any help in Calla's desperate plan.

Struggling only tightened the knot in the shawl that bound her hands, but the fabric was stretchy. Gritting her teeth against the discomfort, Calla slowly worked it down over her hands, trying to ignore the painful compression of the bones. Just when she thought it was hopeless, her left hand escaped the bond. Quickly freeing herself, she tore off the gag and bent over Ede, offering her a sip of water.

"Drink, Ede, please. I have to leave you for a while, but I'll find Doran to care for you."

"No, don't go," Ede protested, but her eyes were dull with despair.

"I'm going to bring Fane back. I promise you!"

Ede was silent, anguish etched in the unnatural droop of her mouth and the ugly black hollows under her eyes.

Calla tried to reassure Ede, explaining her plan to follow the kidnappers, but her sister was unresponsive, too lost in grief to protest the dangerous, perhaps even foolhardy, plan.

"I love you," Calla whispered, pressing a kiss on her sister's clammy forehead. "And I'll be back with Fane. Believe that and get well—please get well, Ede!"

Tears flooded her eyes, but Calla couldn't let anxiety for her sister paralyze her. She rushed to her own bedchamber, knowing that the preparations she made in the next few minutes could mean the difference between life and death in the wild terrain beyond the security of settled territory. Stripping off the remnants of her ruined night garment, she gathered clothes from the pegs on her walls and quickly dressed in finely woven drawers that hugged her hips and thighs like a second skin. Over this she pulled on sturdy leather breeches, protection against thorns and brambles, and thick hose that tucked under the edges of the breeches just below her knees. Her calf-length boots, dark brown with hard, square heels, were designed for riding.

The rain might last for days, bringing with it unseasonable cold, so she put on layers of upper garments: a light chemise, a soft, open-collared shirt spun from the fleece of woolies, and a dark mahogany-colored leather jacket that matched her breeches. Over it all she donned a heavy, hooded cloak of violet wool, a wedding gift from her father who said the color matched her eyes. She regretted having to wear it in the rugged terrain of the out-country, but nothing else she owned could protect her so well from the elements.

She might be gone for many moon-cycles; everything she took had to be of the utmost usefulness, but her head was spinning, too full of emotions to plan as she should. Her father kept a kit to use when he drove their beasts to market, and remembering it relieved her mind. She ran to his chamber and found it in the huge domed trunk where he stored his possessions. She also found two leather bags made to hang over an equest's back. Quickly she took inventory of the tools of survival: compass, medicines, flint, and dozens of small items her father found useful on the trail. All she needed now was food and water.

The larder was well stocked; she stuffed the leather bags with nonperishable foodstuffs, not forgetting tinned milk for the child, and filled two large bovine bladders with pure drinking water. Now she lacked only one thing: a weapon.

Her father's dirk slid easily into the top of her boot, and she found his whip coiled in the hidden compartment behind the case that held their most

precious possessions: books the family had carefully preserved for many generations. As solace on
her lonely trip, Calla took her favorite, *The Wisdom
of Erikandra*, wrapping it in waterproof oilcloth and
tucking it into one of the bags.

Weapons were forbidden to ordinary citizens, but
every landowner risked hiding a few for emergencies.
Her father kept the whip, believing he could justify its
existence because he kept dangerously unruly male
bovines to service his herd. Calla wouldn't have this
excuse if a government sentry found the whip or dirk
in her possession, but the out-country was too wild
and unpopulated to warrant many patrols.

Checking one last time on Ede, she found her the
same, eyes open and brimming with pain.

"I'll send Doran to you," she promised, holding her
sister's hand and hoping she really could find the midwife and enlist her aid.

With a pang of conscience, she remembered Gustaf.
He was too faithful to the family to fail them without
cause. The tragedy would be compounded if anything
had happened to him. She couldn't dwell on failure,
but if she returned without Fane, her fate was sealed.
She would have to bow to her father's wishes and
marry the callow youth in the hope of conceiving an
heir. She didn't wish the lad dead, but the thought of
bringing him into her bed for marital intimacies made
her feel ill.

Far from abating, the storm had grown in intensity. The wind howled with demonic force, and Calla trembled in the face of its fury, lingering for a
panic-stricken moment in the open doorway. Of all

the dangers on the turbulent planet, she most feared the wind, the invisible force that tore down dwellings and uprooted the sturdiest phage trees.

Remembering the innocent newborn who had been carried out into the storm, she pulled the hood low over her face and struggled toward the stable burdened with supplies—and her own churning fear.

The long, low shelter for animals was built of the same clay blocks as their dwelling, but it was a windowless building, all the ventilation coming through narrow vents near the roof except when the doors at either end were open. They were always closed after dark, making the building a veritable fortress against the lepines, vicious wild felines that preyed on young bovines and equests.

The wind was so strong Calla couldn't open the door closest to their dwelling. An iron rod couldn't have secured the entrance as well as the gale hitting it broadside. She fought her way to the far end, each step a battle, and gained the thick-walled sanctuary breathless and weary. Would the Zealotes take shelter for the night? She couldn't believe they'd expose an infant to the storm, but both of them were fanatics, intent only on achieving their aims. Thinking of little Fane made her cold with dread. He belonged safe in his mother's arms!

She fumbled for the lantern kept beside the door, glad that her father was wealthy enough to use power-pack illumination. Earth technology was the only beneficial exchange Thurlow received for its ore, and most people were too poor to afford it.

The bright glow of the lantern was comforting, but her relief was short-lived. One of the equests was loose in the broad center aisle that ran the length of the stable between the stalls. The beast was pacing restlessly, unable to reach water or fodder because all the stall doors were secured.

Calla approached cautiously, wise enough to know an equest might charge and trample her. More than hunger and thirst was alarming this animal. Gustaf was tied across its back by ropes that went under the beast's belly to secure the lad's hands and feet. He was gagged and limp, and Calla raced to him, heedless of danger from the equest, hoping Warmond hadn't strangled him in the process of silencing him.

She secured the equest, catching its reins and tying them to a post, then clambered onto the beast's high back, the only way she could reach Gustaf's head. Her fingers felt thick and clumsy in her haste to remove his gag, but finally she succeeded, relieved to hear a faint cough.

"The Zealotes did this to you!" she exclaimed, giving him a minute to catch his breath while she scrambled down to work on the knots securing his hands and feet.

"I tried . . . they made me . . . show the way," he gasped. "Forgive me—"

"I know—it wasn't your fault, Gustaf! They took Ede's baby—a healthy boy. Did you find Doran?"

"I did—but they trussed her up and left her," he said, regaining the use of his normal high-pitched adolescent voice.

"In her cottage?"

"Yes, my lady, and she would have suffocated if the big one hadn't come back to loosen the gag."

He coughed and cleared his throat. "He tied me, or I wouldn't be talking to you now. A scary lot—the others never said a word."

"Others?" Calla felt her heart sink. She'd never once considered that the two cult members had an escort.

"Four others. Creepy how they didn't make a peep."

"Gustaf, listen carefully," she said, talking to him as she would a frightened child. "I'm going to follow them, but Ede needs help."

"My lady—no!"

"Obey me now, Gustaf, or answer to my father for leading them here!" She had never spoken so sternly to a servant, but desperation made her lose all patience.

"I didn't mean—"

"It doesn't matter. Just do as I say! Go to Ede. Give her fresh water and moisten some bread in broth. Take care of her until Doran comes. You'll have to be a man now, Gustaf. If Doran isn't able to come, go to the village for help when daylight comes. Ede's life is in your hands. Don't fail her!"

"No, I won't," he whispered, but his terror made him seem younger than his age. "If they come back—"

"You know they won't!" She wanted to shake him. Fate was so cruel, forcing her to depend on this cowering boy. Her life meant nothing if she had to mate with a spineless, dull lad she scarcely liked. "There's no time for self-pity!" She was admonishing herself too. "You have your task, and I have mine. See that the equests are cared for.

51

There are coins in father's desk drawer, the top one in the middle, if any need arises. You must act as head of the freehold, Gustaf. The time for being a child is past."

"I'll try, my lady," he dubiously agreed, wiping at a bit of mucous under his nose with the back of his hand.

"Trying isn't enough! Pledge your life to the care of my sister and the equests!" She struggled with words, trying to give him spirit and courage although she had little enough herself for her impossible mission.

"I pledge," he agreed, backing away because her strange new harshness frightened him. "Might I eat from your larder?"

Calla bit her knuckles to keep from slapping the silly boy.

"As you see fit," she said angrily, "but I hold you to account for my sister's health and the equests' welfare. Now go, and the Great Power be with you!"

She added a silent prayer, asking that the lad be given enough sense to keep from destroying all that her family had built up for generations.

With tears streaming down her face, she said good-bye to all she loved: her family, the land, the equests. If she couldn't return with her father's heir, she made up her mind to die trying. Life was meaningless if she had to suffer a second loveless marriage to a bumbling youth.

The wind bombarded the stable, screaming through the vents and unnerving the massive equests in their stalls. Several banged their heads against the thick wooden doors, and the thunderous crash of hooves resounded through the building.

Calla knew the risks in approaching one of the restless beasts, but time was working against her. The farther the Zealotes went, the more difficult it would be to track them. In a few days they would veer away from the established trail, and her task would be doubly hard, especially with the torrential rain erasing all traces of their route.

Galaba was Calla's equest: a magnificent rust-red mare with the spirit and endurance of a stallion, and the speed more characteristic of lighter-boned females of the species. Equests, as a rule, held themselves aloof from human masters, performing their labors docilely enough if their feed bags were kept full, but never losing their ingrained enmity for humankind.

Galaba's mother had died at birth, and Calla had squeezed milk from a saturated cloth into the new foul's mouth until another mare had been coaxed into nursing the orphan. Galaba was poor at birthing, producing two stillborn foals before Calla's father decided against further matings. Perhaps because the beast's maternal instincts had been thwarted, she accepted Calla with better grace than was expected from any equest.

Yet Calla knew no equest was ever tame; Galaba could trample her in a storm-induced panic. She might not accept the bridle or the saddle. Standing more than twenty hands high, Galaba was always dangerous, never to be fully trusted.

After using the lantern to find what she needed in the tack room, Calla hurried to Galaba's stall and opened the upper door, not encouraged by the equest's restless swaying, the huge hindquarters knocking so hard against one partition that the hard-packed dirt floor vibrated.

"If only you understood how badly I need you," Calla murmured, soothing the equest with calm words even though her own heart was pounding in her throat. Slowly, expecting those great teeth to rip into her arm at any moment, Calla slipped the bridle over the huge head, pausing to run her fingers through the thick, shaggy hair nearly hiding the beast's eyes, a gesture that sometimes calmed Galaba.

Cautiously she led the equest from the stall, securing the reins before trying to throw a saddle blanket over its back. If Galaba trapped her against the wall, she could be crushed to death with no ill intent on the part of the animal.

Murmuring softly, crooning words known to soothe equests, Calla finally was ready to leave.

The driving rain had abated, but the wind was pushing massive gray clouds across the inky sky. The eerie howling of the planet's airstream unnerved the equest. Sniffing and snorting, the beast pawed the ground but refused to venture forward.

"Galaba, Galaba," Calla crooned, stroking the big head from her perch on the equest's back.

At last she coaxed her mount onto the cinder path leading to Luxley. The Zealotes' lead was already great, and going into the village would be another vexing delay. Each moment counted, but she had to see that Doran was safe and able to care for Ede.

Heedless of her own safety, she gave the equest

its head, racing toward the village with the wind beating at her hooded face.

A dim light shone in Doran's window. Calla dismounted, the long drop jarring her legs, forcing her to consider what would happen if she were injured in the wild out-country. She was leaving behind all the security she had ever known. A pang of loneliness, stronger even than her fear, assailed her, and she keenly felt the absence of companions in her life. What future was there for a planet where healthy children were rare gifts? There was an ache in her heart for the babe she would never have and for the lover who would never hold her in his arms.

The door was closed, but Doran's cottage didn't have locks. A midwife gave her life to her people; no one was ever barred from her home.

Calla hurried inside and found the elderly woman lying on the floor beside a cold hearth, her wrists and ankles bound by rope that seemed thicker than her bones. A strip of black cloth covered her mouth, but the sound she made assured Calla that the wicked Warmond hadn't suffocated her. Doran might owe her life to the one called Logan, but Calla would never forgive him for his part in abducting her sister's newborn infant.

"Your sister?" Doran asked as soon as Calla removed the cloth.

"Not well, but her baby finally came—a healthy boy."

"They took him?"

"Yes." Tears came now that Calla had someone to share her sorrow. She bowed her head and took out the dirk, knowing she would have to cut through the ropes. The Zealotes tied knots that not even the fisherfolk could unravel. "I'm going after them."

"Please, child, no! There's more evil in the one called Warmond than you can imagine. The Power of Darkness hovers around that one. You'll be throwing away your life!"

"I'm not an empath like you, but I'm not a child either. I know there's little chance of success, but I can't go on living if I don't try to steal back the babe."

"You'll be in grave danger." Doran sighed as Calla succeeded in freeing her wrists.

"The other Zealote—what did you sense from him?"

For several long moments Doran didn't respond.

"Tell me, please!"

"He's capable of great good," the midwife said with seeming reluctance.

"But he helped kidnap the child!"

"Any member of the Order would do the same."

"Are you making excuses for him?" Calla bit her lip in frustration, finding the rope around Doran's aged ankles exceedingly difficult to sever.

"There are passions you don't understand, Calla, desires that drive a man like a leaf in a tempest. Stay with your family. You don't know what deep currents will engulf you."

"You're not prophetic. You can't know I'll fail."

"No, but recovering the babe will most likely be beyond your powers. He'll be guarded every moment of the day and night."

"I have to try!" Tears were streaming from her eyes, making it difficult to cut through the rope without injury to the midwife.

"The sable-haired man is an empath."

"Logan. His name is Logan. I saw him in my dreams. Not once but many times."

"Was he evil in your dreams?"

"No." Calla blushed, embarrassed to tell her elderly friend about her erotic dreams.

"Such strong feelings can only mean you dreamed of him as a lover," Doran said without being judgmental.

"Yes, but my dreams were false. He's the worst kind of enemy. He stole the future of my family when he kidnapped baby Fane. I loathe him!"

The rope fell free, and Doran rubbed her ankles, coaxing the flow of blood back to her withered feet.

"Have you had other prophetic dreams?"

"Only a few that could be called that. But none of them concerned significant happenings. I dreamed of a black foal, and one was born. I dreamed my father would give me a gift, and he brought a trinket back from the market. But such trivial foretellings are only coincidences, aren't they?"

"You'll have to learn the power of your dreams for yourself."

"Are you all right?" Calla asked, helping the midwife to her feet.

"I would be better knowing you'll stay with those who love you."

"I can't. Will you care for Ede?"

"You only needed to ask."

"Gustaf is with her now." Calla didn't succeed in hiding her distaste for the lad.

"He's too young to be judged," Doran said, using

her empathic gift to detect Calla's negative feelings. "Mayhap he'll grow into a worthy man."

"I doubt it, but if he does, the mines will claim him."

"Calla, wait until daylight. Don't ride into the out-country on a night like this."

"Time is my enemy. Even as we speak, the babe is slipping farther from my grasp."

"If the Great Power wills—"

"No, Doran, no! Don't try to change my mind. Promise to care for Ede, and I'll be gone."

"You have my promise, but there's one other way I can help you."

She hobbled toward a dresser with ordinary shelves for earthenware dishes and drawers below with white ceramic knobs as handles. Opening one, she took out a small cloth bag.

"The evil one called Warmond can shield his emotions from empaths, but he doesn't have the gift himself. Logan does, and this makes him far more dangerous. It takes many full-cycles to learn the secrets of shielding your mind, but this powder contains herbs that will give you temporary protection. It's potent and may cause illusions, but you must swallow all of it at once. Use it only in the most desperate situation. It will give you an aura that will shield your emotions, but only for a brief period."

Calla took the small gray bag suspended on a leather string and placed it around her neck, hiding it under her layers of clothing.

Taking leave of Doran, Calla rode with the wind at her back, away from the sea and from all that was familiar and dear to her except Galaba. Of all

58

the midwife's dire warnings, only one stayed in her mind: Logan was the most dangerous. Logan could prevent her from rescuing Fane, but any of the Zealotes could do that. He could take her life, but she'd witnessed his great reluctance to cause pain. Her heart ached as she thought of the tall, sable-haired kidnapper. The man in her dreams could turn her loins to liquid fire and transport her on wings of ecstasy. How could she dream of a fantasy lover and find him in the person of a cold, heartless, sexless member of the Order? What did her dreams signify?

The thick violet cloak couldn't keep her warm. The chill that sent shivers down her spine and wrapped icy fingers around her heart came from within.

Chapter Three

The fog was so thick Logan couldn't see the sharply pointed ears of his own equest. The coming alignment of the three moons caused great banks of moist air to roll in from the sea, blanketing the trail with a dense covering.

The vaporous mist even muffled sound, and he could hardly hear the clip-clop of his mount's massive hooves. He felt an urgent need for haste, instinct telling him they might be followed. Even though the able-bodied men of the region were serving their terms in the mines, a rescue attempt couldn't be ruled out. Warmond had admitted that mere boys and doddering old men sometimes banded together to pursue a summoned child. Although none of the Zealotes feared a rescue effort, Logan didn't want to compound their offense against the Outsiders by injuring any of them. The Zealotes' ropes were more than a match against any makeshift weapons available to ordinary folk.

Twice the men of the Order had stopped so Warmond could see to the needs of the child. Although too young to swallow more than a few drops of tinned milk, the infant wailed at frequent intervals. Logan could almost believe the cries were protests at being torn from his mother's care.

The trip back to the Citadral, the Zealotes' religious and political center, was a long and arduous one. Logan knew it was contrary to the teachings of the Order to feel as impatient as he did, but he felt an urgent need to purify himself, to submit to the rigorous discipline of the cult and again be blessed with peace of mind.

No sane man welcomed the pain of purification: countless hours of sensory deprivation broken only by the humiliation of burning rope lashes administered at his own request, then rigorous interrogation by his spiritual counselor. Yet it was the price he would have to pay to free his mind from the images flashing through it: violet eyes brimming with tears, hair like fire-tongues of gold, creamy breasts with rosy nipples. Calla's voice echoed through his consciousness. Even though she accused him of a heinous crime, he wanted to press his lips to hers and know the sweetness of her tongue, a desire as foreign to his nature as a wish to grow wings and fly.

His anguish grew with each passing hour, the painful swelling at his groin a lesser torment than his guilt. He was the Grand Elder's confidant and helper, respected by his elders and his peers, a leader and an example to the Youngers of the Order. He had succumbed, not to a mature man's temptations—the sins of pride and self-love—but to lust, a weakness of adolescents and Outsiders.

Logan rode behind the others, Warmond leading the way with the Youngers strung out between them. He chaffed at bringing up the rear, but Warmond's reasoning was sound: Logan, as Master of Defense for the Order, was the most resourceful defender if they were attacked from behind. Leaning forward in the saddle, he saw no sign of the equest in front of him, a troubling circumstance even in heavy fog.

Not wanting to be separated from his fellow travelers, he called on his empathic power, trying to locate the man ahead of him by probing his emotions. He found nothing. Only Warmond could thoroughly shield his mind, and he would never relinquish the lead to a Younger.

Logan tried again, disturbed because the Grand Elder had expressly warned him to know Warmond's whereabouts at all times.

Heedless of the risks in charging blindly through the fog, he urged the equest into a lumbering gallop, but the beast snorted disapproval and tried to swerve from the trail.

Logan strained to bring the equest under control, then tried again to make mental contact with another member of his group.

His power was limited to the distance a man might walk while holding his breath. A fast-moving equest could easily move out of range in only moments, but not at the pace necessitated by the fog. Logan searched, concentrating on the desolate areas on either side of the almost-invisible trail. Nothing came to him, not easily detected emotions like anger and fear, nor more subtle emanations born of discontent or joy. He wanted to rush headlong down the trail, but injury to the equest would be a serious setback for his mission.

There was one possibility he'd overlooked: his fellow travelers stopping for reasons of safety or rest. He could have passed almost within reach in the heavy fog without seeing them.

Regretting the delay, he turned the equest and cautiously retraced their route, depending on the beast to keep to the trail. Just when the search seemed hopeless, he sensed a buzz of anguished thought. Either Warmond had fallen behind and was catching up again or they were being followed.

He dismounted and secured the equest to a strong, low-hanging branch a dozen paces from the trail, then returned to lie in wait.

Calla leaned forward on Galaba, ignoring the heavy, wet rain darkening the shoulders of her cloak. The sky resounded with a thunderous boom, the first herald of yet another frightening storm. At least the wind, gathering more force as the weather worsened, was beginning to break up the fog. The trail ahead was still curtained by oppressive mist, but she could see the gritty, silvery sand underfoot and the vague outline of thorny bushes beside the trail.

Leaning forward, consoling the beast by stroking her massive head, she tried to ignore a growing feeling of despair. The Zealotes had to use this trail for at least part of their way back to the Citadral. As long as they were in the out-country, she had a slight chance of overtaking them, but when they left the established trail, her pursuit was hopeless. In order to bypass the almost impassable Mountains of Maharis, they would descend into the mysterious Valley of Sunken Craters, a place where Outsiders never went. She couldn't let herself admit defeat, not as long as they were traveling in the out-country, but she was terrified of going farther. Her people were forbidden to venture outside the known territory. Those few who did, desperate criminals or defectives who survived in subhuman form, never returned.

She was bone-weary and afraid of the new storm. A bolt of lightning split the sky with an eerie flash, but all she could see in that instant of illumination was a mass of dense black clouds. She didn't want to be alone in this bleak place!

Numb with fatigue, she could hardly remember her last sleep period. She wanted nothing more than to find a sheltered cava and lose consciousness, but she didn't dare let the Zealotes get too far ahead. She fervently hoped caring for the baby would delay them.

She straightened her back, willing herself to stay alert, then suddenly she was screaming, pulled from her mount and knocked to the ground. Stunned by the punishing impact, she looked up in shock. Her assailant stood over her, visible only as a dark figure shrouded by mist. She tried to prepare for death or worse, but she was too angry to die passively like a woolie led to the slaughter. She kicked out, her hard heels battering her assailant's shins.

Scrambling to her knees, she groped for the dirk concealed in her boot, but her attacker was too quick. His weight flattened her, and he straddled her back, capturing her hands and pinning both arms to the ground.

Logan's prisoner squirmed and bucked, trying to throw him off even though there was no chance of breaking free. His hooded opponent was small but plucky, surely a lad, not a mature man, and Logan's main concern was that other Outsiders were nearby. He whipped out a short length of rope from an inner pocket of his cloak and roughly attempted to subdue his struggling opponent by binding his wrists.

The shriek that accompanied this outrage was piercingly loud and familiar. Silky hair cascaded out of the hood and was immediately plastered flat by the driving rain, but Logan recognized his adversary: the female called Calla.

"It's you!" he cried out, letting her scramble to her feet.

Lightning lit the sky, and Calla saw her attacker.

"You're the Zealote Logan! Where is the babe? What kind of monster takes a newborn out in a storm like this?"

"Foolhardy, reckless female! What possessed you to follow? Don't you know a summoned child is never returned? He's a member of the Order now."

"He was stolen! You have to give him up!"

"The penalty for any member, even an infant, who leaves the Order is death! You can't reclaim him alive!"

She threw the untied rope to the ground, pushing it into the soggy sand with her boot tip as a gesture of defiance.

"Where is he?" she demanded.

"That's not for you to know!"

"He's near here! Let me take him home or kill me now! I'll follow until I find him." Her words were brave, but she was trembling.

"Woman, have you no sense? Your pursuit is hopeless."

He was wasting time. While he argued with the female, Warmond could be slipping farther away. Logan wanted to blame the blinding fog, but the disappearance of the other Zealotes alarmed him. The Grand Elder had sent him to guarantee delivery of a summoned child to the Citadral. There had been too many unsuccessful missions led by Warmond and too many reports of infants dying on the trip.

"I must return him to my family!" Calla insisted, hot tears mingling with the rain beating against her face.

"Your sister is young. She'll have another child."

"Her husband was sent to the mines!"

Logan knew what that meant, but he didn't know how to offer comfort to the woman. He didn't even know why it seemed so important to do so.

"You're young enough to give birth to a child yourself," he said impulsively, a suggestion that disturbed him. He imagined this beautiful creature performing the mating ritual with some loutish Outsider, and the image infuriated him.

Would his transgressions never end? The emotion of jealousy was degrading even in a beardless youth!

"My husband died in the mines!"

Rain streamed down her face, drops cascading from the tip of her proud but delicate nose. He wanted to shelter her in the folds of his cloak, but he tensed his shoulders and tightened his buttocks at the thought of the lashing that rash act would merit.

"I'm sorry." He felt impotent. He wanted to help her, but the rules of the Order made it a transgression to even talk to her. "You must turn back."

She stared at him without answering, and suddenly the sky opened up. The wind screamed, tearing at their cloaks, and hail bounced on the ground around them. Pellets of ice stung his face before he could pull up his hood for protection, but the woman dashed to her equest, heedless of her own safety. Before he could stop her, she was leading the beast into the thick brush.

Logan ran after her, sure that the snorting, rearing equest would trample her.

Pam Rock

"Let the beast fend for itself!" he yelled, catching her and trying to pull her away.

She plunged forward, ignoring him and mouthing words he couldn't hear. When he understood what she was doing, he was more puzzled than ever by this strange female. She was talking to her equest, earnestly conversing as though the dumb beast understood her!

The worst thing he could do was leave the trail. His own beast was tethered on the opposite side of the path that meandered through the out-country like a ribbon of silver sand. If he lost his way, he would have to rely on Thurlow's moons and the position of the stars to guide him back to the Citadral, and he might never catch up with Warmond and the child.

Suddenly the woman and the equest disappeared. He blinked his eyes in disbelief, but his puzzlement changed to alarm when a hailstone the size of his fist bruised his shoulder. A man without book-learning might believe the sky itself was falling!

Calla knew there were thousands of cavas, wind-scoured depressions in the soft rock hills, in this part of the territory, and at last luck was with her. She led Galaba to safety within a roomy, sheltered cavern just as the air turned white with massive hailstones. Looking behind her, she saw the Zealote bent over trying to protect his head from the onslaught. He was still moving, but if one of the larger ice pellets rendered him unconscious, his life would be in jeopardy.

68

She screamed, but the wind muffled her voice. Acting on impulse, she raced out of the shelter, shielding her head with one arm as she grabbed his cloak and pulled him toward the cava.

"You shouldn't have—" he gasped.

"Where is your equest?"

"On the other side of the trail."

"Poor beast," she said, stopping perilously close to Galaba's rear hooves.

Logan watched as she expertly hobbled the equest, wondering at the calming effect she had on her mount.

"A fine beast," he said awkwardly, feeling a need for words between them but not knowing how to make conversation with a female.

"She's mine. I care for all the equests on my father's freehold."

"This one has respect for you."

"Sometimes."

Her voice was as pleasing as brook water rushing over a rocky streambed, and Logan regretted the murky gloom of the cavern that obscured her face.

"Your father will find another husband to give you a child," he said, not understanding his own compulsion to offer soothing words.

The rules of the Order made her an alien, a creature unfit to be seen by righteous Zealotes, yet he felt a great need to know what sort of life she would return to.

"He already has." She didn't try to hide her bitterness.

"He's chosen a man you dislike?"

"Not a man—the boy you tied on an equest and left in our stable."

He laughed, then felt ashamed for mocking her.

"You're as hardhearted as that terrible man, Warmond!"

"No, please, don't believe that of me!"

The wind shrieked like a soul damned to eternity in the dwelling place of the Power of Darkness, giving Calla cold shivers that made her teeth chatter and her shoulders shake. The storm was trying to invade their shelter, and they instinctively backed toward the deeper darkness at the rear of the cava.

"You're cold," he observed in a husky voice.

"I'm fine," she lied.

"Our cloaks are woven without removing the natural oils that repel water from the fleece. Remove your wet one and warm yourself in mine."

Her silence was a refusal. She squeezed water from her hair and tried not to sniff from the cold.

"Are all your kind so stubborn?" he asked.

"My kind! Don't you see a human being when you look at me? What is this Order of yours? You steal children and pretend women don't exist!"

"You must know the story of our origin."

"When the troubles came after the great migration, a group of men withdrew from society to save themselves."

"Not to save themselves! To preserve the best of the Earth culture that came with them: learning, worship, music, philosophy, and especially the quest for truth." He was deeply offended by her view of the Order's beginnings. Did all Outsiders look with scorn on the Zealotes' purposes?

"Now you steal our babies to continue your precious culture and destroy ours!"

She slumped against the wall of the cava, trying to retreat as far from him as possible.

"Calla." He had difficulty saying her name aloud, as though the innocent syllables were a mystic curse. "Calla," he forced himself to say again, "your judgment is too harsh."

"Don't tell me what a wonderful life you'll give poor Fane!"

"It's true."

"No, it's not! He'll never have a family to love him. He'll never know what it is to care for a woman. He'll never hold a child of his own in his arms. You're denying him everything that's truly important!"

"All the men in the Order will be his brothers, his companions in the quest for Truth."

"Ha!"

"You don't know enough about the Order to justify your scorn." Still standing, he folded his arms across his chest, aware for the first time that the tops of his hands had been bruised by the hail.

"How can you justify the actions of a man like Warmond? He didn't care if Doran suffocated."

Logan didn't want to defend Warmond, nor could he tell this Outsider about his mission. He sat on the ground as far as possible from

71

the female without getting too close to the
equest.

"You wouldn't understand." He realized how petu-
lant he sounded and was once again ashamed.

His eyes ached from sleeplessness, and his body
cried out for rest, but he was too aware of the
female to hope for the oblivion of sleep. Hail
crashed on their rocky shelter, and the wind
howled like mythical hellhounds, but he could
still hear her teeth chattering.

Quickly, rashly, he moved across the width of
the cava and removed his cloak, offering it to
the female.

"I don't want anything from you but what's
rightfully mine—my nephew!" she said, but her
refusal didn't carry conviction.

"Lay aside your cloak to dry," he ordered, "and
accept the warmth of mine."

She obeyed, with much assistance from him,
shivering even more without her wet garment.

"I won't be in your debt," she stubbornly insisted.
"I'll share a corner of it, but I won't leave you
without a cloak."

He agreed with severe misgivings and sat stiffly
beside her, allowing only their arms to touch. He
tried to fill his mind with philosophical arguments
about the nature of the universe, but when her
head slumped against his shoulder, he didn't risk
waking her to move it.

Her rain-soaked hair smelled faintly of the
essence of floral blooms, and he tormented
himself by remembering every moment in her
father's dwelling. When she shifted in sleep and

rested her hand on his thigh, he touched it with the tip of his thumb, marveling at the delicacy and smoothness of her fingers. He stroked cautiously, exploring her smoothly rounded nails and the slight looseness of the skin over her knuckles. Her hand was narrow compared to his, and her wrist seemed too fragile to control the powerful equest she called her own.

"Great Power above!" he whispered fervently.

The female had enchanted him! He was behaving in a way disgraceful to his Order and demeaning to his person, yet he felt a great tenderness, an emotion more potent than the stirring of his loins or the rapid coursing of his blood flow. If he stayed close to her, he might stray beyond the redemptive powers of any penance.

He felt like a hollow man, a mockery made of straw and dung. He had no right to stroke the female's hand or inhale the perfume of her hair. He removed his hand, but when she curled against his side, oblivious to what she was doing, he put his arm around her slender shoulders and offered the warmth of his body, regretting it was all he could give her.

Calla was deep in her familiar dream. Her fantasy lover had never seemed more real. His golden skin was thrilling to caress, and his flowing sable hair fell across her face when he bent to part her lips with his tongue. She wanted him to touch her, to fill her with the river of his love.

"Calla." Logan whispered her name when she murmured in her sleep, but he didn't probe her dreams. Dreams were sacred; he wouldn't use empathic power to intrude even though his curiosity was a torment.

The rain stopped, and the first murky hint of dawn showed beyond the opening of the cava. Calla's head was on his lap, tangled hair falling across her cheek. As wakeful as he had been through the waning night hours, he wasn't aware of fatigue. He knew what he had to do.

Calla awoke slowly, at first aware only of a deep contentment, a soothing warmth that made her reluctant to leave her dreamworld. Something wonderful had happened, but she was too sleepy to know what. She smiled, remembering only a small portion of her nighttime fantasy but pleased by the remnants of her dream. To her great delight, she felt a flutter deep in her secret place. Letting herself doze again, she floated on downy clouds, reaching out for the love that no longer evaded her.

Her second awakening was less pleasant.

The gray light filtering into the cava didn't reach the depths where Calla lay. She blinked away her sleepiness, taking a few moments to remember all that had happened. Was it only a dream that Logan had cradled her head on his lap?

She stirred and became aware of the stiffness in her legs. The hard dirt floor felt cold as soon as she shifted position, and her cloak fell away from her shoulders. Her head was resting on one of the bladders, the partially empty water bag making a comfortable pillow, although she couldn't remember getting it from the front of the cava for that purpose. Her hands were numb, as though she'd slept on them, but she didn't realize the awful truth until she tried to sit. Her hands were tied in front of her!

"Logan!" she called furiously, not expecting an answer. How could he do this to her!

She struggled to her feet and discovered more of his treachery. Galaba was gone. Rushing to the cava opening, she didn't see the equest anywhere. The other water bladder and the leathers bags so essential to her survival were gone too. The kidnapper was also a thief!

The rain had stopped, and she stepped out into dreary gray daylight with no way of knowing if it was dawn or later in the day. The ground was waterlogged and soggy underfoot, so she clearly saw the prints where Logan had led away the equest.

"Wretch! Robber! Lying lout!" She hated him and despised his thieving cult!

She kicked wet sand against a pink-tinged boulder until water filled the depression left by her tantrum. Angrier than she could ever remember being, she stomped toward the trail, awkwardly trying to push aside vegetation with her bound hands. Wet leaves splattered her face, and the branch of a sapling whipped across her cheek, the sting bringing tears to her eyes.

Emerging from the brush, she found exactly what she expected: heavy impressions in the trail.

Logan had found his own equest and left with both animals, deserting her in this barren place without a mount.

Thinking more calmly, she returned to the cava. Her hands were bound with a green vine, much easier to cut through than a length of rope. She found a sharp corner on the sand-splattered boulder and stooped beside it, rubbing the vine against it. Slowly the rock cut into the fibers until only a few strands were left. She broke free, rubbing her wrists and flexing her fingers to restore circulation.

He didn't mean to kill her; the water he'd left behind was proof off that. Instead he was trying to force her to give up pursuit. She could save her own life by walking back to her father's freehold; the supply of water was more than adequate to give her the strength to reach home. She was hungry already, and without food, it was only sensible to return to her own people.

She wanted to scream in frustration! She couldn't go on without an equest, but admitting defeat, marrying the only available male, was unthinkable. Doran was wrong about Gustaf. His character was flawed. He'd never be a worthy mate, not even if he outgrew his adolescent gawkiness and became a handsome man. He was servile to his betters without earning their respect, but he played the tyrant with smaller children, taunting them until tears flowed or they ran away from him.

Logan wasn't quit of her yet. There was only one trail for the equests to follow, but she'd explored the out-country since childhood, encouraged by her father to learn as much as possible about the territory that might someday give them refuge. She knew a footpath that would allow her to catch up.

Thurlow had been colonized with high hopes, but in these times fear ruled the planet. Her father was afraid that someday his family would have to escape into the wilderness to survive. When the third moon, Amoura, was aligned with the moons of Primus and Secondus, the eclipse would allow a ship from Earth to enter the atmosphere. The difficulty of filling the hold of one of these Earth monsters grew with each succeeding generation. The hyronium, an essential power source on Earth, gave off a poisonous gas in the mines, and it was this that caused defective newborns. The vapors became more potent as the tunnels were worked for many years, and the government claimed to be too poor to properly vent the mines. The officials lacked the engineering genius to solve the problem, and the autocratic politicians wouldn't slow down production to try new methods. Earth's minions to a man, they cared about nothing but the power and riches that came from providing hyronium for that distant, technologically superior planet.

The rain had ceased, but the day was damp and dreary, mist still swirling over the soggy ground. Calla knew the unusual weather would last until the eclipse. Heavy precipitation worked in her favor. The trail would be a quagmire in the low spots, but the footpath followed a rocky ridge. If Logan had to make any detours, she might catch sight of him before dark.

Without the companionship of Galaba, Calla felt intimidated by the eerie, damp out-country. The footpath led through dark forest, the trunks of the trees rough with scaly bark. The drooping branches were heavy with sharp green needles, and patches of slimy blue moss clung to trunks and limbs. Even on a sunny day, little light penetrated the heavy blanket of trees. The silence was almost complete; even when she stopped and listened intently, Calla couldn't hear the chirp of an avian twittering in the air or the rustle of small creatures in the thick underbrush.

She tried to hurry, but often she had to climb over rocky obstacles or squeeze through almost solid walls of vegetation. Her boots squished, her cloak was weighed down by moisture that dripped continually from overhead branches, and the air was heavy with exotic fragrances that made breathing difficult.

Drinking frequently, she knew water was the most important source of her strength, but her stomach began to clamor for sustenance. Her father had taught her to live off the land, but food-gathering was a slow, laborious process. She didn't dare wander far from the footpath, not if she hoped to overtake Logan. He wouldn't stop for rest or food until he rejoined the others.

She couldn't think of him without a red mist of anger building behind her eyes. Her heart pounded and threatened to explode with fury when she thought of all he had done to ruin her life. She should be with Ede, helping her learn to nurse her precious babe, joyfully caring for the child until their family could rejoice together over his birth.

Her arms ached to hold her nephew again; her life seemed empty without this child to love.

Her stomach rumbled from hunger, and she took it as a favorable sign when she saw a fruit-laden bush of verdeberries beside the path. The tiny, smooth-skinned green morsels were juicy and tart, a small handful taking the edge off her ravenous appetite. Her luck held when she found a cache of rainwater, a fresh clear trickle falling down the side of a cliff. She drank until her stomach gurgled, then she refilled the water bladder.

She longed for the dry stockings in her saddlebags, keeping her mind on the creature comforts Logan had stolen from her because it was too painful to think about the man. Her dream was so puzzling, she couldn't begin to think of an explanation. What evil spell possessed her, making her dream over and over again of a Zealote, a member of a cult that held themselves aloof from all women?

She was following the base of a steep, rocky hill, watching every step because the ground was pitted and crumbling. Several times she had to climb over or skirt around small landslides, evidence that torrential rains and hail were taking a toll on the out-country.

The sky was darkening, but she didn't know whether night was near or another storm was building. The footpath was becoming more treacherous, and she fell several times when crumbling rock gave way underfoot. In spite of her caution, she nearly missed her footing when the path narrowed along a ledge, then suddenly dropped off into nothingness. She grabbed for a stunted bush pushing its way between two boulders on the side of the cliff and managed to hang on while her feet fumbled for a firm footing.

Breathing hard, her legs shaky from the close brush with death, she rested with her back against the cliff and tried to decide where to go. The path had broken up into a landslide. She couldn't go on. She knew how to get back to the main trail, but now there was no chance of catching up with Logan before dark.

To reach the trail, she had to climb; the easy path had disappeared, so she retraced her route until she came to a steep but accessible hill. Scrambling on hands and knees, she searched for footholds and laboriously pulled herself upward.

By the time she reached the main trail, the sky was a dark violet-gray above the treetops. It was raining again, a steady drizzle that collected in the depressions left in the soft sand by two equests. Because of the rock slide, her shortcut probably hadn't brought her as close to Logan as she'd hoped.

She followed the track, sometimes sinking ankle-deep in the silvery grit, other times taking to the brush for short distances to avoid quagmires. Unanswerable questions were preying on her mind. Why was Logan was still alone? Why hadn't the other Zealotes waited for him? Where was baby Fane?

The trail narrowed and grew steeper, too rugged underfoot to follow in total darkness. She couldn't hope for any of the moons to penetrate the thick cloud cover, so Calla wearily started looking for a secure place to stop and rest.

She found it when she rounded a sharp curve and came upon the glowing embers of a fire. A pile of sticks lay beside a shallow pit, as though someone expected her to come along and build up the flames again. Cautiously checking on both sides of the clearing, she saw no one. The prudent thing to do was move on and find a safe cava to spend the dark hours, but she saw something in the dying embers that called her back to the clearing. Half a plump bunnus, a choice but scarce land-running creature, was dressed and cooked on a green stick stuck into the ground beside the fire pit. Her first thought was that someone had set a trap for her and baited it with succulent game.

She tossed a few sticks onto the embers, sitting back on her heels as they burst into flames. Only a skillful trekker could find dry fuel after a deluge.

Her stomach grumbled, and she dislodged the green stick, sniffing the crackly brown skin of the bunnus.

The carcass could be poisoned. She tore off a tiny bit of skin and sniffed, her mouth watering at the tempting aroma, but she tossed it into the fire, reducing it to a bit of blackened ash. The few sticks blazed invitingly, making her realize how cold and wet she was.

If this was a trap, she was already caught. Running would be futile if Logan or his Zealotes were observing all she did. Succumbing to the comfort being offered, she threw the rest of the kindling on the fire and sat down to tear with fingers and teeth at the roasted creature. If she was meant to die this night, it wouldn't be from starvation.

The meat was tender and mild-flavored with a natural salty goodness made even more satisfying when she drank from the bladder of water between bites.

The rain was only a light mist, and she found shelter under an overhanging branch that still let her bask in the heat of the little fire. Pulling off her boots and laying them on the other side of the fire to dry, she thrust her damp stockings toward the flame, wanting nothing more for the moment than to have warm, dry feet. How unkind of Logan to deprive her of Galaba! Didn't he know she would follow on foot—or crawling on her belly if that was the best she could do?

Sleeping in the open was too dangerous, but she would allow herself the luxury of drying her feet until the fire burned down. She didn't intend to doze, but the flames danced in front of her eyes, lulling her into slumber.

Chapter Four

Calla awoke suddenly, jarred out of sleep by a crunching sound. She held her breath and listened, identifying the rustle of twigs being trampled underfoot. Another stick snapped, and she got to her feet in a crouching position. The fire was low, but a few small flames rose above the charred sticks, just enough to make her more visible than the stalker in the brush.

Before she could move, she saw five dim shapes emerging from the forest at widely spaced intervals. She first thought the Zealotes had come for her, but the misshapen figures hanging back in the shadows didn't have the look of normal men.

"Defectives!" she said under her breath, watching in horror as the shapes inched toward her.

She'd heard rumors of the marauding bands, but like most people she dismissed them as scare-tales, spooky stories in the realm of folk-lore. Most defective children died shortly after birth, and the few who survived with their greatly elongated heads and abnormal brains were vulnerable to a host of painful and disfiguring diseases that made their lifespans very short.

"I'm a friend," she called out, trying to keep fear from her voice. "I mean you no harm."

There was a rhythm to their approach: shuffle, pause, shuffle, shuffle, pause. She couldn't pick out the leader, and it wasn't even possible to know if they were male or female. Some heads were twice the length of a normal human's, and as they drew close, she saw the patchy stubble on their domes. Their noses were broad and flat, and their lower lips hung slack, exposing gums with crooked little teeth.

They formed a semicircle on the opposite side of the fire, staring at her with bulging, browless eyes. Their clothing was so ragged it resembled litter gathered for recycling, but their feral odor was worse than the fumes of human or animal waste. It stung her nostrils and made her want to gag.

Their stillness was even more ominous than their shuffling approach. She felt pity for the pathetic outcasts, but common sense warned they were dangerous. Her dirk was hidden in her boot, but, to her dismay, it was on the other side of the fire too far away to reach.

Five pairs of strange, subhuman eyes stared without blinking, their expressions sly and appraising.

The smallest of the five, probably a female, made a soft keening sound, rubbing her bony crown and pointing at Calla's mane of unruly hair. A big, humpbacked defective cuffed her mouth, knocking her into the dirt where she lay whimpering like a lost child.

Calla felt sorry for the creature, but she saw something that made her blood run cold: a glint of metal in the big one's hand. They were armed!

"I'll give you whatever you want," she promised urgently, not knowing if they understood her.

They whistled among themselves, and she felt sure they meant to kill her.

A leafy branch blown down by the storm lay near the fire, and she pushed it into the hot embers with her foot. At first she was sure it was too damp to burn, but the fired dried the leaves enough to ignite them. She grabbed her makeshift torch and waved it at the defectives, making an arc that sent sparks scattering among them.

The branch burned brightly for a few moments, and the defectives backed away. She checked the ground for other branches and saw none; already the foliage was consumed and the torch was dying. Worse, more defectives staggered out of the brush behind her, bringing their numbers close to a dozen.

"Stay away!" she cried, brandishing the extinguished torch.

She'd imagined a dozen ways to die alone in the wild out-country, but death at the hands of these poor, wretched creatures was more frightening than any natural end.

A big one in the rear made an eerie whistling sound through his nose, and the rest crept closer. Sick with fear, Calla edged away.

"Stay back! My friends are coming!" she bluffed, waving the branch even though the charred end didn't make them cower.

The big one who had cuffed the female charged toward her in his shuffling gait, lunging at her with the metal object in his hand, a vicious-looking fork meant for carving meat. She struck at it with her branch, fending him off until the charred wood broke off. She tried to back away, but he stabbed her upper arm. The long, sharp tines went through her thick cloak and penetrated her flesh with searing pain.

The others smelled blood, pressing closer at this evidence of her weakness. She tried to run, but they formed a tight circle that cut off escape.

A foul-smelling creature grabbed at her, and she screamed, lunging around the fire in a desperate bid to get her dirk. Better to end her own life than be tormented by the savage defectives.

She expected them to fall on her all at once, but a whirring sound cut through the air. The nearest defective fell headlong to the ground, clutching at his face where a rope had lashed it.

Another screamed, and then another, although the rope fell faster than her eye could follow. She saw a knife fall and looked up to see a one-eyed monster clutching his hand and grunting in fear and anger. She armed herself with the dirk, but before she could join the battle, all of the defectives were shuffling back into the brush.

"Give me your dirk," a familiar voice insisted. "I can't allow you to use metal against a human, not even a defective."

"It's my only weapon!"

"The dirk didn't help you in this encounter."

She stared at the tall cloaked man, knowing she should be grateful but resenting his high-handed demand.

"Please," Logan said, "don't make me take it from you."

"Haven't you taken enough from me?"

She threw it as hard as she could into the brush behind her, defying him in the only way she could.

"You've just given them another weapon," he said angrily.

"They'll never find it." Her arm hurt so much she couldn't hold back her tears. She opened her cloak, sticky with blood, and clutched her wounded arm.

"They're born scavengers. They'll find it if they have to search for a moon-cycle."

They heard the eerie whistle of a defective, the shrill cry too close to ignore.

"Come with me," he ordered, taking a moment to kick sand over the last embers of the fire.

"Will they attack again?" she whispered.

"It depends on how many are in the band— and how brave they are."

She shivered and followed him into the brush, remembering that defectives had emerged from both sides of the trail.

They entered a black world made treacherous by

uneven ground and thick vegetation. She tripped on an exposed root and fell on her hands and knees, crying out when the jolt sent fiery pain through her wounded arm.

"Quiet," he whispered, taking her hand in his and leading the way.

To her great relief, their trek was short. Even before he led her into a small clearing, she heard the restless snort of a barrel-chested equest.

Not a flicker of light from the sky above Thurlow penetrated the thick, black cloud covering, but Logan seemed to move by instinct.

"Are you well enough to ride your own mount?" he asked.

"Oh, yes!" Her nostrils detected the odor of damp fur and rancid breath, sweeter to her at this moment than the aroma of freshly baked fruit cakes. "Galaba," she murmured, feeling her way through the dark to the beast.

"Your equest is tied to mine," he whispered urgently, boosting her onto the saddle. "Just follow. Don't make a sound until I give the word we're safe."

Bone-chilling whistles could be heard from every direction, all the proof Calla needed that the defectives had regained their courage and were stalking them. She felt for the bovine whip looped and fastened to one of the saddle bags, relieved to touch the wooden handle bound with strips of rawhide. She'd never used a whip, believing as her father did that patience and kindness could sway most beasts, but she uncoiled it now. Could she use it against a poor pathetic creature like the female who admired her hair? The cruelty of striking out at living flesh made her feel ill, but she had to survive. If she died, there was no one else to restore Fane to his family.

She held the leather coiled lightly in her fingers, gripping the handle in her moist palm. Galaba docilely followed the other mare, a blessing Calla fully appreciated. When two equests were antagonistic, they were known to fight until one was dead. A skillful trainer's most important job was to group compatible beasts and weed out those fit only for the yoke of agri-labor.

They passed out of the brush, the equests' hooves no longer muffled by rotting vegetation underfoot. The slightly luminous quality of the silver sand showed they were on the trail again, and Logan's mount increased its pace, falling into a deceptively clumsy gallop. Healthy, mature equests could outrun any animal but an adult lepine, and their endurance was unmatched on the planet. Their only handicap, besides their temperament, was awkwardness. They couldn't change course or maneuver with any agility, so evading heavy rope nets or pits in the ground was almost impossible. Calla prayed the defectives hadn't set traps in the trail ahead of them.

They rode through the night, stopping several times to listen for the haunting whistles of their pursuers. Calla's arm burned as though the red-hot tines of a fork were stabbing her flesh again and again, but she gritted her teeth to keep from whimpering.

*   *   *

At last the woods around them were silent except for the faint buzzing of insects feeding in the undergrowth. The band of defectives was far behind them, but Logan was extremely wary, slowing the equests and scanning with his empathic power. Although the defectives' emotions were muddled and incoherent, they retained enough human characteristics for Logan to detect them at close range.

The gray light of dawn brought their surroundings into focus. The vegetation was changing, and they had to avoid vicious spines on overhead branches and thorny tendrils growing across the trail. The underbrush was less hospitable for all forms of warm-blooded life.

Logan was exhausted, his body screaming for rest, but it was his dilemma, which grew more serious with each passing hour, that gave him the most distress. He was burdened with a female at a time when his mission for the Order was crucial. It was one thing to abandon her when she was strong and healthy. Now Calla was limp with fatigue, and her injury was terribly worrisome. A stab wound was subject to severe infection. Metal corroded rapidly on Thurlow, and when the impurities entered the blood flow, the victim suffered raging fever and dangerous complications.

"Where is the babe?" she asked, the weakness in her voice masked by urgency.

"With the others. We'll speak of it later."

"No! Why aren't you with your Zealote brothers? Why did you come back for me?"

"There are no simple answers. We have to find

a secure shelter and see to your wound."

"There are gorous bushes here. That means we'll find ancient pere trees. My father always uses a rotted trunk for shelter. Some have hollows larger than a cavern."

"Can you lead the way to one?" He was surprised by her knowledge and too weary to understand why Warmond hadn't shared this information with him on their way to Luxley. There was little the Master of Apprentices didn't know about the terrain of Thurlow. Why had he chosen to be secretive about a fact that could be vital to survival?

Logan was obsessed with learning the answer to this question and many others concerning Warmond and his mission, but he couldn't leave Calla. She would almost certainly die if he abandoned her.

She led the way, leaving the trail at a place where the spiny vegetation was less dense. She followed signs her father had taught her: ropy yellow vines clinging to tree trunks, then clumps of blue spore-filled sponge plants hanging from low branches. In a short time she located an ancient pere tree so huge the village of Luxley covered less ground. The smell of rotting wood was strong but fruity like a fermentation cask, and she found an opening by following the base of the trunk.

The great hollow was all she'd predicted: a woody cavern large enough to shelter the equests and give the riders space safely removed from the beasts.

"Let me see what I can do for your wound,"

Logan said when the equests were hobbled.

"First tell me where my nephew is!"

"With Warmond and the Youngers. I lost them in the fog, but nothing has changed. The babe is being taken to the Citadral. You must accept that he's a member of the Order now."

"He's a child kidnapped from his family!"

"Summoned for great honor."

"If honor is so important to you, how could you steal a child, steal an equest, abandon me to be eaten by cannibal defectives?"

She was so furious she forgot her pain, and the self-righteous look in his steely blue eyes only fired her anger. His face was as bland and expressionless as an image carved from stone, but his eyes flashed denial of all her accusations.

"You interfered with an ancient ritual, then recklessly followed brothers of the Order."

"You left me without an equest, without food or an effective weapon!"

"You had water enough to return home. Did you really think you could walk to the Citadral?"

"I only followed the footpath because it was a shortcut—until a landslide blocked the way. I could have overtaken you and gotten my equest back."

She walked to her beast, stroking its hairy throat and murmuring in the strange way the animal seemed to understand. When she turned to face him again, her eyes filled with tears.

"You're in great pain."

"My heart aches for the babe."

He unfastened her cloak, a bit confounded by

the layers of clothing under it, but she didn't resist
him in any way. She followed him a safe distance
from the equests and removed her leather jacket,
shivering a little as she laid the ruined garment
aside. After many sunless days the forest seemed
as cold as the surface of the farthest moon. She
removed her shirt, then stood shivering in her
thin chemise.

Logan stepped forward quickly and ripped the
torn and bloody sleeve from her shirt, then helped
her don it again. The chemise revealed the full
swell of her breasts, and he couldn't endure the
sight. Not if his life depended on it could he let
his eyes glimpse their perfect shape and texture,
the ivory flesh and rosy ripe nipples.

He threw aside his own cloak, welcoming the
icy bite of the air as perspiration moistened his
forehead, trickled under his arms, and ran in
rivulets down his spine.

Females were a torment! Calla clouded his mind
when he should have been unraveling the puzzle
of Warmond's behavior. In her presence he felt
challenged and anxious, like a youth before a
contest of strength and agility. In his apprentice
years Logan had been a champion among his
peers, running faster, jumping higher, and climbing more rapidly than all the others. Yet always
before he had to prove himself, he suffered the
same stress symptoms he felt when he was near
her: his stomach knotted in agony and his body
took on a sheen of perspiration.

Not trusting himself to speak, he cleansed her
wound with drinking water and applied a soothing

unguent known to fight infections. Already there was some sign of festering, and he bandaged it carefully in the way all Zealotes were taught.

"Did you leave the fire and the portion of meat for me?" she asked unexpectedly.

"Yes."

"Why?"

"I wanted to delay you so I could get back before you caught up with the defectives. I didn't expect to them to be that far back on the trail." He took a deep breath, then decided she had to hear the truth. "The ones who attacked you are probably only a small part of the band. I found a net trap, spore, and broken animal bones. There could be a hundred or more."

"No one has ever heard of so many living together!" She winced when he secured the bandage, splitting the ends to tie them.

"They must be breeding."

"That can't be!"

"It's the only explanation," he said, taking a small vial from his saddle pack. "Their numbers are increasing, so they're forced to hunt nearer to civilization. The fork shows they've been scavenging near a settlement."

"They're dangerous!"

"Here, swallow this," he said, "then drink a lot of water."

"You'll drug me and desert me," she said suspiciously.

"I wish I could leave you!" he said fervently. "I'm afraid you've become my responsibility."

"I don't understand. You abandoned me in the

cavern and took everything I had."

"Don't make too much of my help," he said ruefully. "The rules of the Order forbid me to jeopardize a human life. After I left you in the cavern, I hid in the brush and watched to be sure you returned to your own kind. Instead, you took an alternative path."

"You didn't follow me on the footpath. It's too narrow for equests."

"No, but I was sure you'd never overtake me on foot. I thought your only option was to turn back and go home."

"Then how—"

"I caught a glimpse of a defective shadowing me at midday, so I watched for overhead nets and pits in the trail. When I found a trap, I knew there was a large band. I didn't know how many had migrated to this part of the out-country, but I did know you were in grave danger. The wild ones will kill you whether you have anything they want or not."

"You came back to protect me." She felt woozy but blamed it on his potion.

He wrapped her blood-stained cloak around her shoulders and led her to a dark corner of the hollow.

"My conscience forced me to try." He sounded bitter.

"How did you know I'd come back to the trail."

"I had to credit you with enough sense not to get caught in the brush after dark. I tried to estimate how far you could travel and where you would return to the trail. That's where I left the meat and the fire."

What he said was the truth, but only a small part of it. He'd searched for her frantically, driven by guilt and fear for her safety. Whatever lay ahead for him, he couldn't continue his mission until she was safe.

"Poor creatures," she said in a drowsy voice.

"Poor creatures?"

"The defectives. No living being should suffer the way they do."

"They were going to kill you!"

"I know they're savages, but they only attacked me because they don't see themselves as human. One of them, probably a female, wanted to touch my hair, I think. The leader cuffed her to the ground, but she was only curious because I'm so different—"

"Because you're so beautiful," he said, speaking from his heart but immediately regretting it.

She stared at him, for a brief instant believing he was the man of her dreams. His face softened with tenderness, and she very much wanted to touch his cheek, bristly now with the beginning of a rich, brown beard.

"Get some sleep," he said curtly, turning his back because he was afraid his eyes would betray the forbidden emotion he felt for her. Thank the Great Power she wasn't an empath!

He wanted to probe her mind, to learn why a mere female had the largeness of heart to feel compassion for creatures who would have killed her. A few of the noble minds of the universe, spiritually blessed and intellectually powerful, had taught forgiveness such as she demonstrated, but he'd never imagined finding it in an Outsider, a female Outsider! He wanted to know more about her, but he didn't invade her mind with his empathic power. It seemed a sacrilege to use his gift to violate her privacy.

She wanted to stay awake, to hear his voice and watch his face, but her eyelids were heavy, her mind clouded by fatigue. She curled up, cradling her head on her uninjured arm, and slept while he stood watching.

Logan studied her, no longer feeling a need for sleep. There was a childlike purity in the softness of her cheek and her pink, slightly pouty lips. Her hair was tangled, and he tried to imagine separating the locks and combing them with his fingers.

Better at reading other people's emotions than his own, he didn't understand his reaction to Calla. Certainly he respected her; she had courage, determination, and loyalty to her family, traits the Order allowed him to admire. He didn't understand her sentimental attachment to the newborn, but he could understand what the loss of a boy-child meant to her father, who was himself without a son. One moment Logan felt something more like awe than simple admiration; the next the woman maddened him. She was stubborn and short-sighted, so careless of her own welfare that she was dooming his mission.

He paced, but his eyes were continually drawn to the woman sleeping under his cloak. He wasn't cold, in spite of the icy chill that permeated the hollow. Instead his blood was fiery in his veins, and he needed some demanding physical activity to burn off his excess energy.

He gave water and grain to the equests and curried their tangled coats, readying them for the long trip still ahead. When all was done that could be done, he sat on the ground, mesmerized by her rhythmic breathing and innocent beauty.

Duty called him! His mission was like the weight of a mountain strapped on his back. He couldn't move forward, but the urgency of taking action preyed on his mind constantly. Warmond had yet to send one of the Youngers back to find him, even though it was the duty of the leader to account for all his men. For reasons Logan didn't understand, Warmond wanted to complete the quest without his lieutenant.

The day was well advanced when Calla stirred again. Logan held a bladder of water to her lips, holding her head so she could drink. Her cheek felt hot when he touched it with the backs of his fingers, and he was frightened for her sake.

He desperately needed to pursue Warmond, but anxiety about Calla kept him by her side. She was still in great danger. He'd never known so many defectives to hunt together. Their numbers had made them braver than any known band. He'd only heard of one verified incident where they attacked a normal adult, and it had happened deep in the wilderness. They robbed and killed an outcast, a criminal wanted for many crimes including the murder of a member of the Order.

A government patrol found a shattered human skull and the convict's prison bracelet in a barren place over a half moon-cycle's ride from the nearest settlement.

Was it the coming eclipse that gave the defectives courage and befuddled his own thought processes? He couldn't see a solution to his dilemma. Every moment he delayed, he was failing in his mission and disobeying the Grand Elder. He could be charged with treason to the Order, and his only defense would be his concern for a female Outsider. The Grand Elder would strip him of his honors, his status, perhaps even his life. Yet if he left her now, the defectives would find her. They traveled slowly, lacking the endurance to go long distances in a short time, but as soon as it was dark they would be on the move again. If their numbers were as great as he suspected, they would fan out on both sides of the trail and advance as slowly and steadily as an incoming tide. Not even her equest could save her if she tried to get past their traps and return to her father's freehold.

She couldn't return to her people alone, and he had to go forward, skirting the Mountains of Maharis into the Valley of Sunken Craters.

He trembled at his audacity in making himself her guardian, but he couldn't sacrifice her for the sake of his mission. He had to take her with him.

Sitting just outside the sheltered hollow, he lapsed into an alpha state. He didn't dare sleep, but a short period of total relaxation would refresh and restore him. Colored light, yellow then blue, first in spots and then in waves, moved behind his closed lids, and for a short time his mind was blessedly blank.

His senses functioned while his mind was on another plane, so the first distant whistle brought him to full alertness. The sky was still a murky gray. The defectives must be starving if they were scavenging before full darkness.

He didn't need to wake Calla. Her defenses were as keen as his, and the eerie signal made her stagger to her feet. Light-headed and parched, she was still more frightened than ill. Logan removed the hobbles from both equests, but she mounted without aid and was ready before he finished tying her mount to his.

"For your protection," he said. "You're weak from the infection in your wound."

Before she could protest, he looped a rope around her waist, then under the beast's belly and across its shoulders, a primitive but effective way of securing her seat.

"If we can outdistance them to the Valley of Sunken Craters, we'll be safe. They won't follow there."

"You're taking me to Fane?" she asked in disbelief.

"I won't abandon you," he said, knowing any promise he could make would fail to satisfy her.

They rode through the night, leaving behind the plaintive wails of the defectives. Fear kept Calla awake, but she'd never had to struggle so hard to stay erect on an equest's back. Her raw, burning wound throbbed relentlessly, and she continually fought dizziness and blurred vision.

The wind was gusting without letup, and the higher they climbed, the colder it became. She huddled inside her cloak, shielding her face with the hood, satisfied that Galaba would follow the black equest.

Shortly after dawn Logan stopped to rest the animals, walking over to remove the rope that secured her. She impatiently waved him aside when he offered to help her dismount. She felt strange, not exactly dizzy but light-headed. When her feet hit the ground, the whole planet seemed to spin, and her legs collapsed like columns of loose sand.

Logan saw her drop to the ground and acted without thinking, scooping her into his arms and carrying her away from the equest's massive hooves.

"I'm fine," she gasped, not wanting to admit being feverish and weak.

The terrain had changed again, with massive living pere trees spreading their branches over the trail and blocking out all but patchy bits of sky. The trail had forked just before dawn, and Logan took the unfamiliar branch, not the one her father followed to market his beasts in the coastal town of Mogog.

Her mood was as bleak as the sunless, frigid day, and the man who held her seemed as alien as the purple-gray foliage crowding the trail on either side. She wanted to cling to his neck and press her lips to the warm column of his throat, but his scowl frightened her. He looked like a man at war with himself, consumed by some

Pam Rock

inner turmoil and immune to any comfort she
could offer.

She was light in his arms but a weight on his
heart. He lowered her to a dry patch of ground,
knowing he had to tend her wound but dreading
what he'd find. She was feverish; her flushed cheeks
and listless eyes told him that, but he didn't know
how serious her condition was.

The water bags were low, but he remembered
a small waterfall a half-day's journey up the trail.
He had little else to treat her wound; Warmond
carried the medical kit along with supplies for
the child. Logan had found a few medicines in
Calla's saddlebags, but none that were effective in
fighting an infection caused by corroding metal.

"I don't like being a burden," she said, mis-
reading the reason for his frown.

He didn't respond. It served no purpose to
blame her for his situation. She followed the
babe because she loved her family. He admired
her devotion, even though he deplored her fool-
ishness in trying to pursue members of the Order.
Her only possible success would be staying alive
long enough to return to her home.

He tried not to think what her death would mean
to him. The Grand Elder had informed him when
his parents died, first his mother and a few years
later his father. Since he'd never known them, their
passing affected him very little. His apprenticeship
was over by then; his vows had been taken. He was
allowed a brief period of respectful contemplation
for the Outsiders who gave him life, but their loss
didn't touch his heart.

102

He mourned when Tomos, his elderly monitor, died; he was the brother who had supervised Logan's course of instruction between his tenth and thirteenth years. Unlike some monitors, Tomos had been patient, fair, and slow to discipline, and Logan honored his memory with tender sadness.

The thought of losing Calla was different, devastating even though he had no right to feel a connection to her. He'd invaded her home and stolen a child of her blood. The boy would have a better life; Logan didn't doubt that. He did deplore the violence of the summoning and the grief it caused.

Steeling himself for the worst, he helped bare her arm, trying to shield her from icy blasts of wind as he unwrapped the stained bandage.

"It could be worse," he said, trying to hide his anxiety.

"I broke my ankle when I was twelve. This isn't nearly as bad," she said, trying to make light of her pain.

"How did you do that?" He cleansed the inflamed skin with a moistened cloth, then carefully washed the wound itself.

"I fell off an equest. Not Galaba, a stallion my father told me not to ride."

"Did you disobey your father often?" He applied the unguent, concerned because the small jar was nearly empty. But the wound would heal; it was the poison spreading through her system that worried him.

103

"No, but when I did, I always seemed to engineer my own punishment. Six weeks on crutches meant I had to stay indoors and help my sister in the kitchen."

"Isn't that what little girls are trained to do?" He used his last clean cloth to make a fresh bandage.

"What do you know about little girls?" she teased, wanting to see him smile.

"Nothing at all."

He didn't lose his solemn expression, and she wondered if her weakness had something to do with his gloomy mood.

"I'm a burden to you," she admitted.

"One I deserve."

Her arm ached from shoulder to wrist, and she blinked back tears. Even if they caught up with the other Zealotes, she was too weak to steal back the baby.

They shared a hasty meal of tinned finney and dry biscuits, but she was too weak to swallow more than a few bites of the oily seafood. She did drink, consuming water as though it could quench the fire in her blood.

"Lean on me," he said when it was time to leave.

"That isn't nec—" Pinpoints of light exploded behind her eyes, and the world went black.

He caught her as she collapsed, her hair brushing his lips and tickling his nose. Breathless with anxiety, he held her against his chest, indecisive for one of the very few times in his life.

He could turn back and take her to Mogog, but

this detour would cost him many days of travel. He knew nothing of the healers there, and, worst of all, the inhabitants hated the Order. It was the one village where Zealotes were forbidden to go. He couldn't rely on them to care for Calla if she wasn't able to ride into the village alone.

Taking her home would guarantee good care for her, but he would have to contend with the defectives. How could he watch for traps and pitfalls, control two equests, carry the woman, and still be prepared to fight off the emboldened scavengers?

The third alternative was a terrible gamble, but it would allow him to press forward on his mission. He could carry her with him through the Valley of Sunken Craters, but he had never made that journey on his own.

The Valley of Sunken Craters was the most desolate place on Thurlow. Massive, impassable craters were scattered through a waterless, treeless expanse so barren not even the lowest form of life could survive there. It was a natural maze, with sheer blood-red walls that formed natural canyons, many of them death traps that formed natural canyons, many of them death traps with sudden drop-offs. A traveler could wander indefinitely without finding a passage through the dead-end canyons.

Warmond had led them through the maze. Logan had to rely on his memory, on the landmarks he had carefully noted, and on his own sense of direction. If his recall served him well, if he didn't make a single mistake, if he didn't have to retrace his route, he could pass through the valley in two days. Then it was an easy ride to a village friendly to the Order where Calla would receive the best of care.

Legend had it that a party of Zealotes had lost their way in the Valley of Sunken Craters many years ago. They tried for nearly a moon-cycle to find the passage, dying one by one when their water ran out. The last man expired within sight of the pass to civilization. Most of the bodies were never found. From then on all parties sent out by the Order were required to travel with a map. Warmond, as the leader, carried theirs. He left Logan behind knowing he would have to pass through the valley without one.

Was he putting his mission or Calla's welfare first? Logan didn't know, but he held her limp form, cradling her head on his chest, and knew he'd give up his own life for her.

He revived her by holding a twig from a tispah bush under her nose, but she was confused, believing the defectives had stolen her baby.

She couldn't ride alone, not even anchored in the saddle. He shifted his gear to her equest and managed to seat her in front of him on his mount.

He'd never ridden double, never held a woman so close, and it was sweet agony. Sheltered by his arm, her head was tucked under his chin, her soft, golden hair falling forward over her forehead and cheeks beneath her hood. He sat like a statue at first, thankful for the heavy cloak that covered the supple curves of her body but longing to touch the breasts that haunted his memory.

They rode all day well into the night, but he knew she needed deep, restorative sleep. Her restless, fitful napping in the saddle wasn't enough to turn the tide of her illness.

He stopped at last because it was what she needed. There was no shelter, but he coaxed the equests into lying down on the trail, knowing they were too lazy and awkward to rise again without firm prodding from him. He made a nest between the two, not risking a fire in case defectives were scavenging in this part of the forest too.

Calla refused food but drank deeply from a water bladder. He spread both saddle blankets on the ground but knew there was only one way to keep her warm through the night: his own body heat.

Removing both their cloaks to use as blankets, he stretched out beside her, not sure how to arrange his length beside her slender form. She seemed frail, although he knew her flesh was firm and her arms strong enough to handle a massive equest.

She curled on her side, knees drawn up and cloak pulled high over her ear. Her back was toward him, and he stretched out on his, leaving space between them. The sandy ground was soft, the storm had blown over, and the equests were effective barriers against the chill breeze. He was as comfortable as a traveler could be in the open, but he lay rigid and uncomfortable, as far from sleep as he could be.

The night was still except for the occasional

rustle of creatures too small to be a threat. He needed rest, longed for sleep, but he couldn't force himself to relax, not by doing his alpha, not by exerting his will.

"I'm cold."

Her voice was a faint whisper, but it shocked him. His temples throbbed, and his body was as stiff as a log. Then, torn between the repressive indoctrination he'd received as a youth and his natural compassion, he slowly rolled on his side.

His heart was pounding, but he pressed the length of his body against hers. Both were fully clothed, but he felt her heat and absorbed her warmth as he gave his.

Her shoulders were slender and her back tapered down to a small, neat waist, but her lips were seductively round, nestling against him like a pillow on his lap. He didn't know where to rest his hands, and an inner voice warned him to move far away from this damning temptation. Instead he touched the back of her knees with his and let their stockinged feet rub together.

She mumbled and snuggled closer, tormenting him but too ill to realize it.

No penance was severe enough to wipe this night from his mind! He lusted, trembling in his effort to exert control. Nothing in the Order's biological textbooks explained how a male went about penetrating a female, but he yearned for release from the tension in his body. Like most youths, he had suffered through a period of nocturnal emissions, but his pleasure had been minimal and his guilt monumental.

Perhaps he was being tested. His whole life had been an exercise in obedience and self-control, but he had excelled without the need to overcome many temptations. He had always wanted success within the Order more than anything else.

He had to remember that Calla was no temptress. She wasn't offering herself to him. She was desperately ill, her body violated by a filthy metal weapon. The poison was spreading; all day he had watched her grow weaker, at times so delirious she didn't know where she was.

She shivered, her shoulders trembled, and she pressed against him, oblivious to his labored breathing.

He put his arm around her waist, careful not to disturb her wound, and laid his hand over hers, alarmed by the dry heat under his palm.

"So cold," she whispered, her teeth chattering.

He pulled her closer and lay his leg across hers, giving her warmth in every way he could. He held her, murmured to her, brushed her cheek with his lips.

Long after she stopped shivering, he still trembled with need.

Chapter Five

Her dream was tranquil. She lay with her head cradled on Logan's chest, his heart beating under her ear and his arm around her shoulders. She remembered pain and chills, but he'd banished them, giving her warmth and a sense of security.

Still dreaming, she slid her hand between the fastenings on his shirt front and burrowed her fingers into silky hair that tickled like the whiskers of her pet, Kitkat. Exploring with the tip of her middle finger, she found his nipple, a minuscule knob that seemed too delicate for his powerful chest. She stroked until the friction made her finger hot, then leaned over and opened his shirt.

He was wide awake as soon as she cradled her head on his shoulder in her sleep. Her eyes were closed and her breathing was so quiet and measured she seemed to be in a trance. He watched in fascination when she slid her hand under his shirt, but he wasn't prepared for the breathtaking sensations caused by her gentle caress. He'd never been touched on his nipple, not even a cold, impersonal examination by a healer, but this useless little appendage seemed to be connected to his groin by a sizzling hot wire. He couldn't let her continue, but she seemed to be acting in the thrall of a dream. Was this the kind of fantasy that filled female heads? He found it hard to believe her dreams were this erotic, but he groaned and did nothing to stop her.

Her fingers were nimble and quick; she opened his shirt before he realized her intent. Hating himself for not restraining her, he watched as she lowered her head and caressed his nipple with her tongue.

"Calla, no," he managed to gasp, light-headed with excitement when she nipped at him with her teeth.

Was this what Outsiders taught their women? He knew she'd been married, and jealousy overwhelmed his better instincts. Struggling with irrational envy, he remembered her husband was dead, but the thought of any man holding Calla in his arms was unbearable. He tried to discipline his mind, but delight clouded his senses and made him lose control over his thoughts and reactions. He tried to summon up images from his life within the Citadral, those things which gave him great pleasure: the melodic singing of the apprentices' choir, the Grand Elder reading aloud from inspired teachings, the meeting of minds found only between brother Zealotes.

He reached out to pull her away, but her hood fell off, revealing the golden tangle of her hair. Just then she took his nipple between her teeth and suckled it. He expected his heart to fail from the shock! He forgot the Order, his vows, even his mission, as he buried his fingers in her locks and pulled her mouth to his.

He kissed her, discovering there was more to learn about a woman's mouth than a whole library of books could reveal. Her lips were full and soft. They moved under his, inviting and teasing until blood roared in his ears. With feverish eagerness, he explored her teeth with his tongue until she made a strange little sound and let him slide into the welcoming cavity of her mouth.

He was swinging on a rope over a bottomless chasm, but he let go, plunging into the unknown, not caring about consequences. Without knowing his own intent, he eased her onto the blanket and bared her breasts.

Her eyes were wide open, and she pushed at his shoulders, making a small incoherent sound.

He had learned from her. Leaning over, he gently caressed one breast with the tip of his finger, beginning far from her nipple and drawing invisible circles until he touched that precious bud. He was amazed when he felt it swell and harden, more amazed when she pulled his head down. He'd never suckled as a babe; never thought to do so as a man. But the honey-sweet taste of her breast made him dizzy with longing and so weak he thought his spine had dissolved.

He heard the snort of an equest and a soft voice repeating his name, but they were meaningless sounds intruding on his sensual delirium. He wanted to hold her naked body in his arms; he yearned for an intimacy so complete they would cease being separate individuals, but he wondered if a greater measure of pleasure than this would burst his heart.

Calla emerged from her dreamworld, and, at last, she wasn't alone. Logan's beard was deliciously scratchy on her bare skin, and he nipped at her breast just hard enough to assure her this was reality. She pressed her hands against his shoulders, but not to push him away. She was desperately weak, but his strength seemed to flow through her palms when she touched him.

He made her ache, the joyous ache that only came to her in dreams. She didn't know how to make love; her ignorant young husband had relished doing his duty, performing frequently and forcefully, but all he required of her was compliance, that she slide down her breeches to accommodate his battering. Sometimes he hurt her, but he never made her ache with longing.

Happiness made her head swim; she wanted to hug Logan close but lacked the strength. The sky above was gloomy gray, but she couldn't seem to focus on it. Again she saw pinpricks of light exploding behind her lids.

Her sudden stillness alarmed him, and he realized she had lost consciousness. He sat up and felt for the pulse in her throat, terrified for a moment that she was dead. Her blood flow was

113

strong, and her breath was even, but he wasn't comforted by the look of serene contentment on her face. She was ill, desperately ill! And he was a Zealote, governed by a set of rules so strict that even a flicker of curiosity about a female called for painful penance.

He covered her with both cloaks and stalked into the brush, so disgusted with himself he threw aside his shirt, broke off a handful of whip-like shoots from the base of a pere tree, and took a trial swing at the trunk. It landed squarely with a loud crack, but when he tried to reach over his shoulder and lash his own back, most of the shoots fell out of his fist onto the ground. The few sharp stings made him feel more silly than chastised.

He laughed bitterly and gave it up. He was beyond the curative powers of penance. Calla was desperately ill. Not in control of her actions! He'd done a rash, foolish thing, and somehow he'd have to live with it. When she was safe and his mission was complete, he'd renounce his leadership position in the Order and retire to one of the rural retreats. Not all Zealotes were worthy of life in the Citadral; those who failed were sent or went by choice to one of the agri-centers that supplied food for the Order. He would face a lifetime of hard labor—but he might find peace of mind.

Slowly, dejectedly, he went back.

It rained again while they traveled through the fringe of the forest, a cold driving deluge mixed with sleet and hail. The only shelter Logan could

114

find was under a low-hanging branch where he kept Calla dry in the folds of his cloak. She hadn't regained consciousness when he lifted her from the equest's back. Huddled on his lap, she seemed frail and vulnerable.

While the storm raged, he tried to recall the intricate route through the Valley of Sunken Craters. If he didn't get lost, they could reach the friendly village of Ennora in two days. Calla would get the care she needed, and he could leave her there until he arranged for an escort back to her home.

If he made even one mistake in the maze of canyons, her death would be quicker and easier than his. That much he could promise her. He stared bleakly at the sheet of rain soaking the brush and felt more inadequate than he ever had in his life.

The next day they left the rain behind. Calla still rode with Logan, but her fever broke on the morning they left the forest. She was weak and light-headed, barely able to stagger the length of an equest, but she was better. It was her secret.

When she found Fane, she would have to return with him through the Valley of Sunken Craters. If they made it safely, she knew another route through the forest to Mogog, and from there she could find a fishing craft to carry them home. Riding Galaba and traveling only by day, she felt sure she could avoid the defectives. The greatest danger on the return trip was the chance of getting lost in the valley. She had to memorize the safe route through the treacherous canyons and drop-offs without letting Logan know. He had to think she'd given up on getting possession of her nephew.

She was certain he was going to leave her behind when he went to the Citadral. Unless he believed she was too sick to follow him, he would find a way to restrain her.

Feigning more distress than she felt wasn't difficult; deceiving Logan was. She remembered waking in his arms, emerging from an erotic dream to find him fondling her breasts. He'd touched her tenderly, making her feel desirable. She still had difficulty separating her dream from reality, but Logan was in her thoughts by day and her fantasies by night.

By the time they descended to the floor of the valley, a white-hot sun was almost directly overhead. The Valley of Sunken Craters was the driest place in the explored part of the planet, and even during the cool season, the equests had to wear bags to protect the pads of their hooves.

Logan folded their cloaks and tied them on Galaba's back, then improvised a head covering from her chemise because nothing in her saddlebags was suitable. For himself he deftly fashioned a burnoose from a strip of muslin carried for the purpose.

Calla knew it wasn't a kindness to crowd against him in the heat, but she couldn't let him know she was well enough to ride alone. Her thighs rubbed against his; her bottom slid between his legs no matter how hard she tried to inch forward. She wasn't insensitive; she knew he was tormented by her closeness. Although he'd participated in the kidnapping, it wasn't part of her plan to make him suffer. She knew he wasn't evil, but she couldn't let anything or anyone deter her from finding Fane and returning him to his family.

"We won't get lost, will we?' she asked, pretending sleepy confusion although she'd carefully studied every step of the way through narrowed eyes.

"I know the way," he said gruffly, using as few words as possible whenever he spoke to her. He didn't blame her for his unpardonable lapse, but she was a constant reminder of his sinful lust.

"It wasn't a bad thing—touching me." She didn't need to be an empath to know he was filled with self-loathing, hating himself because he'd shown a moment of weakness.

"You're used to immoral ways."

"Immoral!" She forgot to sound sick and weak. "When a man and a woman touch, it's a good thing. They share feelings. Members of your twisted cult are afraid of giving any part of themselves away."

"Is that what your husband did—give you part of himself?" His voice was harsh and accusatory.

"We didn't have a good marriage," she admitted. "It was only an arrangement—"

"You didn't touch him with your tongue?" he asked bitterly.

"Never! I don't know why you ask!"

"For no reason," he lied.

Pretending that their brief exchange had exhausted her—and this wasn't entirely untrue—she closed her eyes, peeking out from under her lashes every few minutes.

They couldn't ride at night; without a map he might miss one of the landmarks that meant the difference between life and death for both of them. Exhausted by the heat, conserving water because none was available in the valley, they shared a light meal of tinned meat from her supplies and flat bread with dried fruit baked in the kitchens of the Citadral.

For the first time in many nights they could see the triple moons of Thurlow in a cloudless sky. Primus and Secondus were small and yellow with faint white halos; Amoura dominated the sky, her great craters showing as faint shadows on the pale blue surface. The meteorites trapped in her orbit looked like a bride's transparent veil, but it was this luminous field of hurling missiles that kept Earth vessels from more frequent visits.

They fell asleep, wrapped in their cloaks because the valley was as cold by night as it was hot by day. Logan made sure the space of a man's height was between them; there would be no dream-inspired touching this night.

The sun was remorselessly hot, and high canyon walls like giant sticks of red chalk boxed them in. Calla despaired of remembering the way back by herself, and Logan's frown deepened with each passing hour, a visible sign of his deep anxiety.

The next night the equests snorted restlessly, not satisfied with the small measures of water that were

118

all Logan could spare for them. Calla suspected he was shorting himself to give her extra, but for Fane's sake she drank all he offered.

Late in the night, when she was sure he was sleeping, she walked in circles around their campsite, exercising to bring strength back to her shaky limbs.

Logan awoke at dawn too parched to feel well-rested. Calla was wrapped in her cloak, with only her dusty red boots showing. His scowl deepened, pulling his brows closer to his troubled eyes.

He searched the ground and found the trail she'd made in the loose dust, circling round and round until the path was as plain as a cinder road.

"Did you sleep well?' he asked, squatting beside her and watching her face as she awoke.

"Yes, I believe so." She rubbed her eyes and tasted the fine grit that adhered to her lips.

"You must have slept facing the wind," he said, testing her. They both had expressed gratitude for the absence of wind in the valley.

"Oh, so I did." She brushed at her face and hair, then read disbelief on his face.

Her tracks were clearly visible from where she sat.

"I got cold and walked to warm myself," she lied self-consciously.

Instead of sharing my warmth, he thought, feeling as bleak as the landscape around them.

"You're well enough to ride your own equest," he said, his tone telling her the decision was his.

Following on Galaba made it easier to watch for vital landmarks, but Logan treated her as a healthy person. Her water ration was the same as his, and he didn't stop for rest that morning, even though the sun drained her strength and made her senses swim.

By midday she knew their relentless pace was more than just a way of testing her. Her deception seemed petty compared to the enormity of the valley and the difficulty of finding a way through it. They traveled until darkness closed in.

"We can't go farther tonight," he said tensely, speaking to her for the first time in many hours.

It was the end of their second day in the valley, the time when he'd hoped to be through the maze.

"Are we lost?" Her mind was a confused jumble of directions: turn right at the triple towers; choose the low path between the peaks that looked like a fairy castle; skirt the half-moon crater on the left side. . . .

"No—I hope not."

He was hobbling his equest, double-checking the rope between its dusty rear legs. The beasts were thirsty. They would wander off in search of water if he gave them a chance, and then animals and humans would be doomed.

"We've traveled two days—"

"I know." He walked over to help her dismount, and she fell down into his outstretched arms, collapsing like a doll stuffed with rag-puff blooms.

"Today was too much for you," he said, his voice bitter with self-anger.

120

"No, I deserved it! I wanted you to think I'm sicker than I am." She was too tired for deceit.

"You still believe you can follow me to the Citadral and steal your nephew, don't you?"

"I don't call it stealing! He's my sister's babe."

He eased her to the ground with her back to a canyon wall and went back to the equests to get a drastically depleted water bladder and one of his saddlebags.

While they shared their meager meal of dried fruit and biscuits, Logan urged her to drink her fill of water.

"I shouldn't have shorted you during the day," he said.

"I drank as much as you did."

"If we are lost, Calla," he said, "a few swallows of water won't make any difference."

"We're both going to die, aren't we?"

"If we don't find the way out of the maze tomorrow."

Hearing him speak the truth gave her an unexpected measure of peace, as though facing the worst took away some of the terror of the unknown.

"I can only promise you one thing," he said speaking softly. "To make your passing quick and easy."

"No!"

"Don't reject my offer too quickly. You don't understand how long and painful death can be. This infernal red dust will burn off your boots and make cinders of your feet. Your tongue will swell and blacken. The equests will die and sustain us for awhile—but only to prolong our suffering."

"No! I love Galaba—I never could—"

"I'm sorry," he said, not understanding his outburst, only knowing that the thought of her suffering was the worst thing he'd ever had to face.

"We'll be rescued! The Zealotes will send someone to find you."

"Warmond doesn't want me found."

"Why not?"

"I wish I knew. His obligation as leader was to send a brother back to find me. He didn't."

"Someone else in the Order might miss you."

"Possibly, but no one will try to find us. The Grand Elder won't send men out to die for nothing, and the search would be hopeless."

"The Earth ship will come. They'll want to explore the Valley of Lost Craters for new hyronium deposits, and they'll find us instead."

He smiled ruefully, amused by her fanciful imagination even though their situation was desperate.

"I don't think we'll see an Earth man here. What made you think of that?"

"All schoolgirls dream of meeting one of the space travelers."

"Did you—when you were a schoolgirl?"

"I've had dreams," she said, glad it was too dark for him to see her blush, "but I think I'd be afraid of an Earth man."

He laughed with genuine amusement, amazed that she could cheer him even in the face of death.

"You're the most fearless person I know," he said, meaning it.

122

"I am afraid," she said softly.

"And it's my fault. I thought it would reassure you to know I'd never let you suffer. We're traveling slower than I thought, but our situation isn't hopeless. If we see a solid rock wall broken by a natural gate any time tomorrow, we'll be all right."

"And if we don't?"

"If it isn't visible in a very short distance, we'll backtrack to the black crater and try to discover where I went wrong."

"Logan, will you do one thing for me if we're going to die?"

"Anything I can."

"Hold me in your arms. Don't let me die alone."

"I swear to do so on my honor as an elder in the Order of the Zealotes," he said solemnly, aware of the irony of giving his oath to break a sacred rule.

"No, just promise as a man."

"I promise," he said, his throat so tight he was barely able to make himself heard.

He didn't take her in his arms that night. If he had, she would have prepared herself to die.

In the morning they drank sparingly and gave the equests only enough water to calm them for another day's travel. They had one full water bladder left between them, enough to sustain two humans for several days, but the beasts would go mad with thirst if they didn't get a full ration in a very short time.

Calla was beginning to despair of remembering the route through the valley, especially since they came to a dead end and were forced to backtrack. To distract her mind, she took out her precious book, *The Wisdom of Erikandra*, when they stopped to rest their mounts for a few moments. She had never needed the warm, amusing sayings of her favorite seer more than she did now, and reading a few as she rode would be a solace.

They started off again, and she opened the first page just as her equest reared and snorted nervously, thirst making it increasingly hard to handle. She didn't fall, but the book did, crushed under one of Galaba's great hooves.

Calla dismounted and retrieved the book, greatly saddened by its battered condition. The creamy leather covers were badly stained by red dust. When she tried to brush them with a corner of her shirt, the gritty sand streaked as though a malicious child had scribbled on the bindings.

So excited she was afraid Logan would notice, Calla quickly searched for and found a pebble-sized bit of grit, tucking it into the waist of her breeches so she wouldn't lose it.

Later, riding out of Logan's sight behind his equest, she used the red grit to write the directions she remembered on the endpapers. The gait of the equest made her hand unsteady, and her writing instrument was anything but satisfactory. But in a short time, she had a crude map with enough markings to jar her memory at a later date. Now if Logan could find the natural opening that led to safety, she could follow his route through the

Valley of Sunken Craters to return to her family with baby Fane. She tried not to worry about all the obstacles that faced her before that was possible, if it ever was.

Later, when Logan dropped back to ride beside her, the book was hidden away in her saddlebag.

"I recognize this place from the journey with Warmond," he said, the ghost of a smile softening his sun-bronzed features.

Many hours later they passed through the natural opening in a towering, bloodred wall and saw in the distance the gentle swell of a dark green hill. To celebrate, they drank deeply from their remaining store of water and divided the rest into the shallow metal basins each of them carried in a saddlebag to water equests.

They weren't going to die, and Calla wondered if that meant Logan would never again hold her in his arms.

The distance to the green hills was longer than Logan remembered, but he didn't seethe with impatience or urge his equest into a faster pace. He was greatly disturbed, but it was an inner turmoil unrelated to his need for a speedy return to the Citadral.

He'd never been a coward, never turned away from a challenge, never feared the end that came to all men. But when there had been a chance they would both die in the maze of canyons, he'd been truly afraid for the first time. He could have accepted his own end philosophically; he couldn't

stand the thought of Calla dying a slow, excruciating death.

She had taught him a new kind of courage:
refusing to give up as long as a spark of life
remained. Her courage was his greatest concern.
She would never give up her search for the babe,
not as long as she lived. But if she didn't return
to the safety of her home, she was in mortal
danger. There was no way to secure the release
of a summoned one—not the child Fane and not
himself.

He tried to think of a foolproof plan to protect
her, but he couldn't think of a way that wouldn't
harm her. Nothing short of imprisonment in a
government dungeon would keep her from rashly
rushing into danger, but he couldn't hand her
over to the authorities on a trumped-up charge.
He railed at himself for not coming up with a
clever solution, not realizing that his emotions
were clouding his brain. Nor would he admit to
himself how reluctant he was to part from her.

Calla was saddle-weary and still weak from her
infection, but her arm was healing well, thanks to
Logan's care. At the first opportunity, she had to
plan her search for Fane. Logan had forced her to
drink the tinned milk while she was desperately ill,
but he hadn't touched the coins secreted in both
of her saddlebags. She had more than enough to
buy supplies for a return trip.

She thought of Ede and longed to see her sister's bashful smile again. She imagined the sad
homecoming when her father and Fane's father
returned from the mines. Only she could bring

joy and hope back into their lives, but if she failed to retrieve the babe, she would never see her family again.

In one full-cycle Gustaf would be on the threshold of manhood, still too young for the mines but old enough to plant his seed. Her father would insist on a marriage between them; Calla wouldn't be able to look into his careworn face with its deeply etched sorrow lines and defy him. She would be bound for life to a craven bully. If she again failed to conceive, she wouldn't even have the consolation of a child.

A life with Gustaf seemed more repulsive than ever, but one thing had changed: She didn't see death as an alternative. As long as she was alive, she could hope that someday she would find her soul mate.

Big wet tears ran down her cheeks. She fell behind the huge black equest and blotted them with a corner of her makeshift headgear. The pain of losing Fane paled in comparison to the prospect of never seeing Logan again. She hated the cult that had made him what he was!

He'd put aside his headgear now that they'd left the burning red sands behind them, and his long, wild mane held a glint of burnished copper. The sun was playing tag with scattered clouds and was no longer a great danger to their skin. He'd stripped off his heavy black shirt, the uniform of the Order, letting the light breeze cool his naked torso.

Did he suspect how much she wanted to run her hands over the golden sheen of his muscular shoulders and trail her fingers down his perfectly sculpted back? Could he guess that her eyes were riveted on his lean waist and undulating hips? The rhythmic gait of the equest made him sway gently in the saddle, his thighs and buttocks encased in black leather breeches that fit like a second skin. She wanted to ride in his arms again more than she wanted to breathe, but to him she was only a temptation he had thrust aside as soon as she could cling to the back of her own equest.

Her wool shirt felt scratchy in a dozen places from her shoulder blades to her navel, but she ignored these minor itches. Her thoughts were causing her the most distress, and she hugged her breasts protectively with her free arm. Her nipples were hard knobs that ached incessantly; she flexed and unflexed her thighs until she was afraid the motion would become a nervous twitch like her Great-aunt Bertella's constantly flickering eyelid.

In the Valley of Sunken Craters Logan had offered to end her life if their situation became hopeless. Yet he'd risked his own life and his status in the Order to save her from the defectives. At first the thought of dying at his hands had shocked her; now his offer haunted her. If she asked it of him, he was willing to break one of the most sacred rules of the Zealotes: to never take a human life. He was willing to sacrifice his beliefs and his honor to spare her the torment of a brutal, inevitable death.

As long as there was hope, it was easy to say no to his offer. Would she have had the courage to refuse him if Galaba died, if the sun scalded her body and boiled her brains, if breathing was torture and living meant unbearable pain and anguish?

Hold me now, Logan, her heart cried out.

Leaving the scorched valley behind them, they climbed into a range of mossy green hills, pausing to rest beside a rushing brook. The water was as transparent as glass and as sweet as the springwater on her father's freehold. They filled the bladders with water and let the equests drink their fill, then secured them for the night. The sun was still visible on the horizon, and Calla was surprised that Logan was willing to stop so early.

"Would you like to bathe?" he asked.

"I'd love to."

"I'll stand guard on the knoll," he said, pointing to a hilltop, "although I think the inhabitants of this region are gentle and friendly."

She watched him take his post some distance away, his back toward her as she eagerly stripped off her grubby clothing and stepped into the swift-moving water. It was shallow and cold, but she sat on the stony bottom, letting wavelets rush around her shoulders. Leaning back on her hands, she let the water swirl through her hair and sprinkle her face, reveling in the sensation of cleanliness until her teeth started chattering.

Logan knew his intentions weren't honorable, but he had already broken his vows, disobeyed the rules of the Order, and put himself beyond the redemptive powers of penance. When he solved the riddle of Warmond's strange behavior, he would retreat from life in the Citadral. There was no going back when he took this step. If he lived to be ancient and doddering, his life would hold nothing but hard labor and lonely contemplation. He wanted to take with him an image that would sustain him in his darkest hours: the sight of Calla bathing in the stream.

He circled around to a vantage point he'd noticed when they approached the stream. Concealed behind a boulder cushioned with the velvety green moss that covered everything in sight, he could see her standing on the bank, screwing up her nerve to brave the cold water. She was proportioned like a classical Venus, the arch of her back so graceful it made his throat ache. Her waist seemed tiny, hardly more than the span of his hands, but she had a woman's hips, her full round bottom wiggling in a delightful way when she walked into the stream.

She lifted her heavy locks of hair from her back, and he held his breath, hoping she would turn in his direction. Instead she eased her way into a sitting position, her movements so expressive he could almost feel the icy water lapping at her belly, flowing over her breasts, and swirling around her shoulders. He could only imagine the little chill-bumps on her comely arms and thighs.

He stared, hardly daring to inhale air, knowing that he would lock this picture in his mind and hold it close to his heart until the day he died. When she leaned back and let the water flow through her hair, fanning it out on the surface of the stream, he expected to die from sheer joy.

Still he watched, knowing he should hurry back to the knoll before she noticed his absence. His patience was rewarded when she stood and faced in his direction. Her hair was clinging to her head, and even the shape of her skull pleased him beyond belief. She raised her arms to wring the water from her mane, and he was mesmerized by the fullness of her breasts, the taut swell of her stomach, and the water-darkened thatch between her legs.

Just when he thought nothing in life was as beautiful as Calla standing in the stream, she ran toward the shore, leaping and twirling as though she were suddenly possessed. She waved her arms and danced on the bank, making his heart pound like that of a massive, overheated equest.

She was drying herself, letting the mild breeze caress her body and blow hair around her face.

Logan returned to the hilltop, keeping his back averted until she ran partway up the slope and called to him. To his surprise, he didn't feel guilt for invading her privacy or breaking yet another rule of the Order. Without knowing it, she'd given him a gift to help him face his bleak, cheerless future. He'd never forget the texture and shading of her skin, the way her hair fanned out on the water, the grace of her movements, or the joyful innocence of her dance.

She'd given him the perfect gift: a vision of matchless beauty. He didn't even consider spoiling the moment with his carnal needs.

131

Pam Rock

Calla had dressed slowly, not feeling at all good about what she'd done. She saw Logan leave the knoll, and she felt his eyes on her as surely as if his lashes had flickered against her skin. She danced to tempt him, every movement crying out for the release only their coupling could bring. She was ashamed for acting like a harlot, and humiliated because she'd longed so fervently for an encounter that could cost him his soul.

Silent and depressed, she wearily waited on the knoll while he bathed in the stream below her. She didn't feel she deserved to cast her eyes in his direction.

Late the next morning they descended into a valley so lush and green it belonged in a picture book to tempt new colonists to settle on Thurlow. They followed a path of ground shells past prosperous farms and generous-sized dwellings made of smooth pink and purple stones cemented together. Calla couldn't identify the crops, but she knew that nothing like them grew in the settled parts of the out-country.

A herd of woolies slowly meandered across their path, delaying them until Calla was ready to let Galaba stomp and snort to scare them on their way. To her surprise, Logan waited patiently, smiling at a youth in a flowing smock and raggedy muslin breeches who was dawdling as much as the beasts in his care. The boy waved, touching his hand to his forehead in a gesture of respect, and Logan responded with a friendly salute.

She was even more surprised when a rotund, balding man hurried from one of the stone cots and waylaid them, lowering his head in respect until Logan greeted him.

"Blessed sir, can I offer you refreshments, fruity cake and fresh sweet curds?"

"You're very kind," Logan said. "Only an urgent mission keeps me from accepting."

The man bowed respectfully, but Calla looked back to see him staring, wide-eyed with amazement.

When they were out of sight, Logan turned and spoke urgently.

"Put on your cloak and pull up your hood!"

"It's too warm."

"Calla," he said patiently. "Do you know what a strange sight it is in this valley for a Zealote to be traveling with a female?" A beautiful female, he added to himself.

"People have already seen me."

"A few country folk. It will be several mooncycles before they take their produce to market and gossip about seeing us. By then it won't matter."

"Why won't it?"

His behavior was more puzzling than ever, but he refused to explain. She reluctantly hid in the folds of her violet cloak, but Logan still fretted, knowing the vibrant color was almost as odd to the people they passed as the sight of a Zealote with a female.

Near dusk they entered the village of Ennora, where families were congregating in the cobbled street to enjoy the fresh breezes and sweetly scented air before the hour of sleep. Calla watched in astonishment as the women fled into the stone houses crowding the road and the men bowed, touching their foreheads in respect. They called out friendly greetings when Logan acknowledged their gestures.

"They . . . adore you!" she whispered in amazement.

"They revere the Order," he said matter-of-factly.

"Then you don't steal their babies?" she asked with some of her previous bitterness.

"A babe was summoned from this village less than a full-cycle ago. The villagers consider it a great honor that the boy was welcomed into a life of piety and grace."

"And wealth?" she asked, comparing the fine sturdy homes and well-dressed villagers to the poor cottages and ragged people of Luxley. "Does the Order pay for taking children here?"

"Of course not." He was offended. "They recognize what an honor it is."

"Do the men work in the mines?" She couldn't understand the great disparity between the prosperity of this village and that of out-country settlements. There were great resources and good land around Luxley, but the men were given little freedom from mining to develop their own holdings.

"Certainly they do—but they meet their quotas willingly."

"Do you mean the young boys aren't forced into the mines before they can father large families?"

"I don't know. The Order doesn't meddle in the affairs of the government," he said stiffly.

"They pay to keep their own members from service!" she said, repeating the belief of her own people.

"There is more than one way to render service to Thurlow."

"You sound—you sound like Warmond!"

This barb stung more than she could know, but Logan only squared his shoulders and lapsed into a deep silence. He didn't understand the hostility of the Outsiders, but he had a more pressing problem: how to keep Calla out of grave trouble. If she followed him to the Citadral, he wouldn't be able to save her life.

Chapter Six

Passing through the village, they followed the path
of crushed shells to a large stone cot with orderly
beds of herbs and flowers in full bloom in front.
Calla followed Logan's lead, tying her equest to
an iron rail provided for that purpose.

"Where are we?" she asked, taking in the exotic
blooms that lined a narrow cobbled path to the
door of the cot. The air was heavy with a strange
scent, much like the fragrance of spiced fruit but
with a compelling quality that made her nose
tingle.

"The midwife lives here. She's famous as a healer
and a friend of all the people in the village."

"Is she the Order's friend too?" Calla didn't try
to hide her antagonism. How could the people
here welcome Zealotes who deprived them of
their children?

"I believe she is, although I know her only by reputation," he said stiffly, dreading what he had to do this night.

A sleek black felina darted out from behind a brilliant orange plant with tiny yellow blossoms, startling Calla so much she cried out. This beast was no playful pet like her Kitkat; it was longer by half, with sapphire eyes that regarded the visitors with hostility.

"Vooron, bad Hexacon!" a high-pitched voice called from an open window.

The felina dashed away, and in an instant the door was flung open.

"Blessed sirs, welcome to my humble cot!"

The woman who bowed, then bounded toward them, was almost as wide as she was tall, a plump little person whose head hardly reached to Calla's waist. Thick gray braids were coiled over her ears, and she wore a full yellow smock and a dark green skirt that showed only the tips of pointed pink slippers.

"We're weary with travel, Midwife Grunhild, and the Order holds you in high esteem. May we intrude and beg your hospitality?" Logan asked.

"Oh, what an honor—you give me great . . . Oh, I forget myself! Please come inside—oh, I'm so thrilled to . . . forgive my humble dwelling—"

Calla expected the rotund little woman to roll around on the ground in the throes of a seizure, so great was her excitement in receiving a Zealote into her home. Calla caught Logan's eye, wanting him to know how scornful she was of all this adulation.

He smiled sheepishly, a bit embarrassed to have Calla witness the midwife's excessive enthusiasm. Although it was true that some of her prosperity was due to her reputation as a friend of the Order, the woman was a rarity, a natural healer. She wouldn't lack patrons, even without the Zealotes' goodwill.

They stepped into a large kitchen, the beams hung with drying herbs, bulbs, and edibles. The air was heavy with an intoxicating aroma, and Calla wondered if the midwife's exuberance was induced by inhaling her own remedies.

Shelves built against the whitewashed walls were loaded with bottles, baskets, and bundles, a healer's stock of medications, and the huge stone fireplace glowed warmly, making the room cozy and inviting.

"Sit here, sirs, please—put yourselves at ease," Grunhild said, dancing around them like a cork bobbing on the sea.

"You can remove your hood," Logan said solemnly to Calla.

She did, letting her hair stream out.

"By the three moons!" the midwife said, forgetting to close her tiny round mouth as she stared at Calla.

"I'm on an extraordinary mission," Logan quickly said. "At the Grand Elder's request."

Grunhild looked as startled as if the stones of her hearth had suddenly started dancing a jigaway.

"You're female," was all their hostess could say.

Calla almost laughed, but she saw something in Grunhild's face that made her glad she hadn't. The midwife was terrified!

"It's not what you think," Logan quickly said, realizing how frightened she was. "I'm not a renegade. The Order won't punish you for your kindness to us. I'll take a truth-oath; what I tell you here is not a lie."

The little woman's face was as white as it was round, her pale blue eyes darting furtively from window to window as though she expected an invasion at any moment.

"What about the Master of Apprentices?" she asked apprehensively.

"He'll never learn we were here, nor would he care if he did discover it," Logan assured her.

"You swear so on a truth-oath?"

"I so swear," Logan said, using the Order's most sacred vow to reassure her.

She beamed, her relief so obvious that Calla sighed aloud, glad that the tense moment had passed.

"Can I trouble you to let the female refresh herself?" Logan asked courteously.

Calla found herself being whisked down a corridor with two doors on either side and ushered into a cozy little bedchamber. There was a basin with water piped in, a narrow bed with a colorful scrap-work covering, and, miracle of miracles, a long polished metal mirror on the wall. She was so surprised to see her own image after such a grueling trip that she didn't notice when the little midwife left, locking the door on the outside.

Logan conferred with the midwife for quite some time, then let her go to do his bidding. His plan wasn't perfect, but with the help of the Great Power, it might succeed.

Calla wasn't vain, but she was curious about the changes she saw in the mirror. At twenty full-cycles, she was full-breasted and attractive to the eye, but the arduous trip had refined her beauty. Her cheeks had lost the last trace of youthful pudginess; her hips and thighs were slimmer and firmer. But more important than these superficial changes, she had a melancholy look that softened her mouth and made her eyes dreamy. Her illness had left faint smudges under her eyes, but they only highlighted the deep violet of her pupils. Her heart told her that Logan, more than the rigors of their journey, was responsible for transforming her, but she resolved to fight her feelings for him and try to forget her fantasies. There was no future with a Zealote; she had tempted him and been rejected.

She sprinkled cool water on her face and brushed her hair vigorously with a brush she found on a small shelf over the basin. Not until she'd made herself more presentable did she try to open the door.

"Logan!" She pounded angrily on the solid wooden door. "Let me out!"

She couldn't hear a sound beyond the confines of the room, and the only window was a narrow slit above the bed, an opening so small she couldn't slip one leg through it.

"He's left me!" she cried out in pain. Tears of anger streamed down her cheeks. She'd prepared herself to part from him, but how could he desert her without a word of farewell?

The door flew inward, and Grunhild's bulk filled the lower part of the doorway. Calla opened her mouth to protest her treatment, then saw Logan standing behind the midwife.

"I thought you'd left me," she said, trembling with anger and relief.

"No," he said. "We'll sup with Grunhild."

The midwife bustled into the bedchamber, all smiles now that she understood the role she was to play.

"You'll want to put aside your travel-worn garments," she said, lifting the top of a big chest at the foot of the bed. "It's laughable to think you could wear anything of mine, but my late, sainted mother was tall and slender like yourself. I've kept her things all these full-cycles, just on the chance they might be useful. The penzel wood in the trunk keeps them as sweet-smelling as laundry fresh from drying in the sun."

Calla saw Logan leave the doorway, but in spite of her anxiety, she was pleased by the prospect of clean garments. Grunhild pulled out a blue muslin dress with tiny white flowers woven into the cloth. It was faded, whether from years of storage or countless washings Calla couldn't tell, but the long skirt was full and smooth, wrinkled only on the fold lines. Her breeches were filthy, and the scratchy shirt had bedeviled her since she'd sacrificed her chemise for a head covering; the gown was a blessing.

"How wonderful of you to let me borrow it!" she said gratefully.

"If it pleases you, then it's a gift. Alas, I favor my father's people, and I've no use for it." She laughed merrily, as though her abundant flesh were a great joke. "Now do hurry and join us at table."

Her little steps were deceptively quick, and she was gone before Calla could thank her. This time the door wasn't locked; she checked to be sure.

Calla quickly scrubbed herself from head to toe, using the strongly scented green soap left in a dish by the basin. She rinsed out her underdrawers and draped them on a towel rack to dry, but only folded her breeches and shirt in a neat pile. If Logan decided to ride that night, she didn't want her traveling clothes to be wet.

She hadn't wanted to ask to borrow undergarments, but the soft muslin felt wonderful on her bare skin. The bodice was a little tight, flattening her breasts and pinching slightly at the waist, but it was a small price to pay for feeling totally clean. As an afterthought, she slipped the little bag Doran had given her around her neck, concealing it as best she could between her breasts.

*   *   *

Logan watched indifferently while Grunhild hastily laid out a hearty meal. Her larder was full, and she was generous, setting out mealcakes baked that morning and fruity preserves to spread on them. Her curds were the freshest available in the village; her tuber stew was well-seasoned and rich with bits of meat. Most importantly, her ale had aged to a potent tang; Logan took a small sip, then poured a huge mug for Calla. He filled his own mug with the golden juice of sweeteve fruit.

Calla seemed to linger forever in the bedchamber, and he tormented himself by imagining what she was doing. Was she brushing her hair, the bristles crackling through those golden strands? Was she standing naked, working foamy lather over the gentle swells of her body? What did a female do that took such an agonizingly long time?

She hadn't left the chamber unseen. Whether he was sitting, staring dolefully at Grunhild's busy preparations, or morosely pacing the flagstone floor, he kept watch on the door.

When Calla did come out, she was even more beautiful than she had been naked by the stream. Her hair glistened, falling over her shoulders like spun gold. Her face glowed, her cheeks were pink from scrubbing and her lips naturally rosy. The dress fit snugly on top, the thin blue muslin taut over her hard little nipples, hugging her slim waist in a way that made him want to circle it with his hands. The skirt billowed out over her hips, swaying suggestively as she walked barefoot down the corridor to the kitchen. Her feet and

143

ankles were shapely and white under the hem of the dress, and Logan had to resist an impulse to fall on his knees and kiss her pale toes one by one until the tickling of his whiskers made her giggle.

They sat across from each other, tentatively nibbling at crunchy purple shoots Grunhild had piled high on a wooden platter along with tiny pickled avian eggs and flatbread spread with a dark, strong-smelling paste. Nothing here was quite the same as it was in the out-country; even the food tasted strange to Calla.

"Try my flatbread with turot spread," the midwife urged, placing several of the dark green rectangles on Calla's plate. "Ennora has the best streams for crustaceans on the planet."

Calla wasn't an adventurous eater, but she sampled the delicacy to please her hostess. The first bite made her eyes water, but under Grunhild's beaming scrutiny, she finished the portion on her plate. The green paste was so hotly seasoned her tongue felt scalded. She reached for the mug sitting by her place, cooling her mouth with a foamy beverage that reminded her of the brew her father made every full-cycle when he finished his term in the mines.

Even at her wedding, Calla had only been allowed a tiny cup of her father's potent brew, but the mug filled to the brim was large enough to water an equest.

"My feet are cold," she said, smiling apologetically at her hostess. "Will you forgive me if I get my boots?"

144

Without waiting for an answer, she ran down the corridor to the room where she'd left her things. Shutting the door behind her, she rushed to the basin and held her mouth under the flow of tepid water, drinking until she felt bloated to cool her burning tongue.

She understood what Logan was planning. He was going to slip away in the night. The huge mug of ale must have been his idea. He wanted to befuddle her senses so she wouldn't have the presence of mind to follow him.

Pulling on her boots with desperate haste, she decided to play his game. Let him think she was too confused to notice his leave-taking! That would make it easier for her. She had to follow when he left; only he could lead her to the Citadral. The people in this village were too friendly to the Order; they would never give a female directions to the Zealote stronghold.

She reached for the door handle, then remembered the gift that gave Logan his great advantage: He was an empath. If she tried to deceive him by pretending to drink, he only had to probe her mind to know she was faking.

Had he probed her mind on the journey? She didn't think so. He seemed to respect the privacy of thoughts—even though he'd gazed on her from a distance while she was naked in the stream. But if he intended to leave her, he wouldn't hesitate to violate her mind.

She lifted Doran's little bag over her head, tangling hair in the leather cord in her haste. Doran's herbs would only protect her for a short time. How would she know when to take them? She tucked the bag in the top of her boot and wondered if this were the only way to win the risky contest with Logan.

As she left the room, she did one more thing to give her an advantage. The key was in the keyhole on the outside of the door. She slipped it into her boot.

"Where is Grunhild?" she asked, returning to the kitchen to find Logan alone.

"She had to go into the village to minister to a young woman about to give birth. Grunhild is afraid she'll have a difficult time." He was leaning forward, his elbows on the well-scrubbed plank table where a feast was spread for the two of them.

"Will she sell the babe to the Order if it's a healthy boy?"

He didn't answer, but his eyes grew stormy.

By the Great Power, he thought angrily, sometimes this female provokes me beyond what mortal men should have to endure!

He forced himself to smile for the sake of his plan, but his thoughts remained glum.

They ate with gusto, saying little as they tried to compensate for their hunger on the trail. Calla was still thirsty from the hot turot paste. She lifted the heavy mug at frequent intervals, pretending to drink deeply, but only enough ale went into her mouth to leave a trace of foam on her upper lip. Logan couldn't see the contents of the mug as long as he was seated, but she had to dispose of the ale before he stood up.

"I'm so thirsty," she said, giggling for effect. "I wonder if Grunhild has more of this delicious beverage."

"I saw her carry a pitcher back to the larder," Logan said, sounding pleased. "Let me refill your mug."

"Oh, no! That wouldn't be proper! Men don't wait on women at the table. It would be demeaning to you." She jumped to her feet and hurried to the larder before he could see how full her mug still was.

A door at the back of the long, narrow storage room led to a garden plot, and Calla hurriedly dumped the ale on a row of herbs. In case Logan checked the pitcher, she threw the rest of the contents out the door, then carried her empty mug back to the table as carefully as if it were full.

Throughout the rest of the meal, she laughed for no reason and sucked the rim of the mug as though it gave her the greatest possible pleasure.

When they had eaten their fill, Logan stood and stretched, looking down on Calla—and her empty mug. She heard him sigh and knew he would soon try to desert her.

When he walked to the front door and looked out, making an idle comment about what a pleasant evening it was for sleep, she quickly retrieved Doran's herbs from her boot and emptied the contents of the bag into her mouth. They were dry and bitter, but she forced herself to swallow, reaching across the table to wash down the residue with the dregs of Logan's sweet fruit beverage.

147

"I'm so sleepy," she mumbled, propping her chin in her hands and hoping she looked like a foolish female who'd overindulged in potent ale.

"Before we sleep, I need to talk to you," he said, sitting on the floor beside her bench, wishing her toes were still bare so he could rest her delicate feet on his lap and store up one more memory of her for his bleak future.

"By now Warmond has taken the babe to the Citadral for his renaming—"

"Renaming?" She forgot to act intoxicated. "His mother gave him a fine name!"

"It's the custom," he said patiently. "When the ceremony has been completed, as it probably has by now, he's taken to a training center, a place where children can grow up receiving the special care and education a Zealote must have."

"How . . . how . . . how terrible!" She sniffed, hoping she sounded befuddled.

"No, he'll love his early years. I remember my first training center with great appreciation." He didn't tell her that all boys were sent back to the Citadral when they attained ten full-cycles. The training there was harsh and rigid, designed to pick the Order's future leaders and discover those fit only for hard labor in the rural retreats.

"You must understand. Your nephew won't be in the Citadral. Under no circumstances are you to try to enter the grounds, even though the gates are open by day."

She nodded, then pretended to doze off, hiccupping to reinforce his belief that she was intoxicated.

He shook her shoulder until she opened her eyes.

"Calla, listen to me. I'll arrange for an escort to take you home. Please trust me. Please understand that this is what must be. Now we both need to go to our beds." He doubted that she would remember all he said, but Grunhild had been coached to repeat his urgent message about not going to the Citadral.

He looked into her eyes, and Calla felt a little tingle on her forehead, a teasing sensation not unlike a feather passing over her skin.

Logan probed with the full force of his power, not letting his guilt and unhappiness interfere with the urgent need to know what plans were in her head. Did she believe he meant to stay the night in Grunhild's cot? Would she accept the hopelessness of trying to find the babe? Did she understand how dangerous it was for her to go anywhere near the Citadral?

Her mind was blank; the strong drink had left her as compliant and unsuspecting as an innocent babe. She would sleep through the night, perhaps well into the morning hours. By the time she realized he was gone, it would be too late to follow.

No one in the village would dare reveal the way to the Citadral. Only a few trustworthy elders knew the complicated route, and a woman who asked about it would send any one of them into a dither.

Calla slumped, cushioning her head on her arms as they rested on the table. She feigned sleep, wondering if he would desert her now.

With a sigh so deep it sounded like a moan of pain, Logan lifted her in his arms. She cradled her head on his shoulder, as she had during her illness, and he carried her toward the little bedchamber.

Leaving her was the hardest thing he'd ever had to do. He lowered her gently to the bed, then reached down to pull off her heavy riding boots. She turned on her side and stirred. When he grasped the boot again, it stuck. For a moment she seemed to be awake, mumbling incoherently and rolling onto her back. He decided not to risk waking her by removing her boots, but he couldn't force himself to hurry away.

Her lashes were feathery little spikes; her skin was smooth and flawless. He touched her cheekbone with the back of his fingers, then became bolder when she didn't react. Slowly, painfully aware of the gravity of what he was about to do, he lowered his lips to hers.

Calla's heart thudded erratically, and her arms trembled with the need to encircle his neck. At first his kiss was like the flutter of velvety merryfly wings, so gentle it made her eyes swim behind closed lids. His breath was warm and caressing on the bow of her lip. When he tasted the sweetness of her mouth with the tip of his tongue, she was sure no other moment in her life would compare to this one.

He kissed her then, the hard pressure of his lips making her feigned sleep a torment. Was he testing the depth of her unconsciousness? She wanted to match his passion and return his kiss with all the passion she'd experienced only in her dreams. She wanted to call out his name and beg him to hold her in his arms.

Logan felt an answering quiver when he obeyed the dictates of his heart and kissed her with abandon. During all the adult days of his thirty-two full-cycles, he'd accepted celibacy as an inconvenience, a lifestyle compensated by his honors and success within the Order. Now it felt like a great length of iron chain crushing his chest, squeezing out his life forces.

He caressed her face with his lips, bolder now because she'd shown no signs of waking.

Probing her mind had seemed dishonorable; a person's soul was her own. Touching her body didn't; he was a captive of her beauty, robbed of his future because she'd enchanted him.

To save her life, he had to leave her, but she would always be with him in spirit. He touched her eyelids, the lobes of her ears, the soft skin of her throat. He wanted to know her totally, but time was his enemy. If Calla woke up . . . if the midwife returned and found him with her. . . .

He could face his own bleak future, but he couldn't endanger Calla's precious life.

He straightened to leave, then dropped to his knees to kiss her one last time. Her breasts rose and fell in rhythm with her rapid breathing, and he laid his head on her torso, not knowing if he had the strength to desert her. Without conscious intent, he slid his hand under the hem of the soft old dress, finding the satiny expanse of her thigh, then the secret place for which he had no ready name. He stroked her downy thatch, then touched her as he would a fragile piece of priceless glass.

She cried out, and he felt a tremor more astonishing than if the planet had rocked on its axis. Terrified for her sake, remembering the terrible danger to any female who challenged the Order, he stood and retreated to the door.

He wanted to tell her things for which he had no words. Calla had changed his life; his brothers in the Order would say she'd ruined it. He was standing on the edge of a great chasm, and his next step might send him plunging headlong into destruction. Yet he was sure he would never regret their days together.

Walking out to the corridor, he felt as though a giant had tried to rip him into two halves from the middle of his skull to his aching groin.

He shut the door as silently as possible, then remembered to turn the key in the lock. It was gone! He wanted to bounce the midwife like an oversized ball for making off with the instrument so crucial to his plan, but the rotund female was still away.

There wasn't time to search for a duplicate key. If he could reach River Rondel before Calla woke up and followed, there was no chance she would ever find the ford by herself. The way the ale had affected her, the key was probably unnecessary.

Calla felt as though she'd turned to stone. Her legs were as heavy as concrete pillars, and she didn't know where she'd find the strength to move them. How could a living, breathing man be such a fool? How could Logan turn away from her for the sake of an evil cult that perverted the natural way of life?

How could he leave her?

Hot tears welled up, and she sobbed brokenly, loving the man and hating that he was a Zealote with every molecule in her body.

How could he go back to the Order and leave her here alone?

His promise of an escort home meant nothing to her. Did he really think she'd return and accept Gustaf as her husband? She shuddered at the thought of his grimy hands on her body, his black and broken nails leaving scratches on her shoulders, her back and thighs.

There wasn't time for regret. She forced herself to stand, then hurried to the chair where she'd left her shirt and breeches.

They were gone! The sky showing through the narrow window was dark now, but the three moons gave enough illumination to let her see the pale wood of the chair seat and the slats of the back. Was this part of Logan's plan, to steal her riding clothes just as he'd stolen her equest the last time he deserted her? Never mind that Grunhild had done the dirty deed for him! Calla clenched her fists, so angry she wanted to scream.

Thank the Great Power she'd made it impossible for him to remove her boots! She tested her underdrawers hanging near the basin to see if they were dry, but the cloth was cold and clammy.

153

Never mind! She could ride as she was!

One thing she didn't want to leave behind was her violet cloak. Grunhild had hung it on a peg by the door before Logan conspired with her. Perhaps neither of them had thought to hide it.

She eased the door open, fearing Logan had left the little midwife there to guard her. She sighed with relief to find herself alone. The corridor was dark and empty, and Calla crept toward the kitchen, putting each foot down as carefully as possible so her soles wouldn't scrape on the flagstones.

The fire on the hearth had burned down to faint embers, and Grunhild hadn't returned to light a wax-stick. Less afraid of discovery, Calla rushed to the wall pegs and felt for the heavy wool of a cloak. There was only one hanging there, and she snatched it eagerly, carrying it over her arm as she ran out of the cot.

She didn't expect to find Galaba still tied to the iron rail. Logan had done all he could to delay her; he wouldn't forget her mount.

How would he explain returning to the Citadral with an extra equest? Calla didn't believe he would even try. That meant Galaba had to be near, hidden from sight but not stolen this time.

At the rear of the cot, a cluster of outbuildings sat at the far end of the garden. She ran toward them, watching her footing on the uneven stones of the path. The first structure was only a shed for the implements Grunhild used in her herb beds. It was too small to conceal a beast the size of Galaba.

The next was locked, but Calla pounded on the rough wooden door without hearing an answering snort from an equest. The third had only a half-door, and Calla whistled softly into the depths, rewarded by the massive head that emerged through the opening.

"Galaba," she whispered, crooning to the beast.

No doubt the midwife had been too short to do more than lead Galaba to the shelter. The saddle and blanket were still on her back, and her saddlebags were in place. The water bladders were deflated, holding only meager remainders, but she didn't expect to ride through parched land. The Order controlled the richest agrarian territory on Thurlow, and that meant a plentiful supply of water.

Wasting no time, Calla freed Galaba and set off in pursuit, but when she reached the end of Grunhild's lane, the road forked. She had only the vaguest idea of where the Citadral was, and she couldn't risk asking any villager to enlighten her.

While she tried to decide between the left and right forks, Galaba set off on her own, walking into the woods that lay beyond the road.

Calla nearly halted the mare, but then she remembered the many days her equest had followed Logan's great black beast. She didn't have a clue about the direction he had gone, but Galaba seemed to know exactly where to go.

Knowing what a risk she was taking, Calla leaned forward in the saddle, desperately searching for some sign of Logan.

Galaba ambled through the woods, following a narrow sandy path Calla could barely see. She held the reins so tightly her hand began to ache, and her eyes felt gritty from the effort of trying to see in the dark. Tiny creatures scurried in the underbrush, and the call of a treetwit startled her.

None of these senses, neither sight, hearing, nor touch, told her what she desperately needed to know: whether she was going in the right direction. Her nose confirmed it just as she was beginning to despair. She detected the pungent, earthy odor of an equest's droppings and put her faith fully in Galaba's tracking ability. If she ever returned to her father's freehold, she had to convince him to try breeding her mare another time. Galaba had skills rare in an equest; it would be a shame to let her bloodline end.

As my father's will, Calla thought sadly, wondering how on earth she would find Fane. She hadn't the slightest idea what to expect at the Citadral. In her imagination, it loomed like a dark fortress, evil and impenetrable, but Logan had let slip that the gates were open during the day.

Would Fane be gone, whisked away to an even more elusive location, or did Logan mention training centers in the country only to discourage her? She couldn't trust anything he said, not after he'd so blatantly tried to cloud her mind with potent ale.

As much as she resented his deceit, she wasn't angry about the most outrageous thing he'd done: touching her while he believed she was in a drunken stupor.

What a fool he was, to think he had to steal what she was so willing to give! Now that she could trust Galaba to follow him, she closed her eyes and let scalding tears squeeze out from under the lids.

If his warning proved to be true, if entering the Citadral meant death, she could at least die knowing the one thing she wanted for herself in life was unattainable: his love.

Logan found the shallow ford on the River Rondel at dawn and stopped to rest his equest among the trees on the far bank. His anguish in leaving Calla had grown into a dull, numbing ache that colored his world dreary gray. He tried to focus on the puzzle he still had to solve: Warmond's strange behavior. The Master of Apprentices flagrantly disregarded the rules of the Order when he was in the out-country, but his motives were a mystery—one the Grand Elder wanted solved.

In the interest of stripping Warmond of his honors if this could be done, Logan decided not to confess his transgressions to the Grand Elder until his mission was completed. He wouldn't be doing his elderly mentor a favor by going to a retreat when his services were badly needed. But if he told the Grand Elder what was in his heart, the old man would have no choice but to banish him. He wasn't deceitful by nature; his decision to delay admitting his change of heart caused him pain.

While the equest grazed, Logan badly needed to snatch a brief nap, if only to clear his head and better apply himself to the problem of Warmond's conduct. He opened his saddlebag, empty of food supplies now that his journey was nearly over, but bulging from the cloak he'd hastily stuffed into it when he left Grunhild's. The night had been mild; he hadn't needed his outer garment for warmth. But the ground by the river was damp, and he wanted to wrap himself in it to keep dry.

He reached for his dusty black garment and was stunned to pull out Calla's vivid violet cloak.

Holding the thick wool between his fingers, he was assailed by memories of her: laughter and ready compassion, greatness of heart and spirited courage.

He realized, of course, that he'd grabbed the wrong cloak in the dark, rushing as he was to quit the cot before his resolve failed him. Hugging it to his chest, he remembered how it felt to hold her in his arms and inhale the fragrance of her hair. He touched the thick wool to his cheek, brushing it against the short beard that had sprouted since he'd first met Calla.

He shuddered, and a convulsive tremor shot across his shoulders and down his arms as though all the energy in his body was flowing out through his hands. He clutched the cloak so hard his knuckles went white, and for the first time in his life, huge tears of anguish burned a path down his face. Now that he knew what a woman could mean to a man, he would never again know contentment or happiness.

Chapter Seven

Logan rode through a lush, tree-studded valley and up the slope to the gates of the Citadral. For the first time in his life, he was indifferent to the magnificent spires that soared toward the sky. The labyrinth of walls, laboriously constructed from highly polished blocks of gleaming white stone, didn't excite his admiration or remind him of the glories of the Order. Day after day, from full-cycle to full-cycle, the Zealote masons added on to the splendid complex of buildings and towers, but Logan didn't feel any of his usual pride in their accomplishments. Generation after generation of stoneworkers toiled on the elaborate master plan of the original architects, the workmen living and dying for the sake of the Citadral, but their skill and sacrifices no longer awed him.

159

If the child, Fane, was selected to be trained as a mason, he would begin working in the dusty workshops of the builders as soon as he was strong enough to fetch and carry a master's tools. The grit would coat his skin and irritate his eyes, eventually working its way into his lungs until his nights were tormented by hacking coughs. Was this the wonderful future Logan had promised Calla her nephew would enjoy?

He rode slowly through the open gateway, the massive wooden doors open during daylight hours because no outsider would dare intrude without authorization. Each night, at exactly the moment when the sun disappeared over the horizon, a team of six Youngers would ceremoniously push the heavy double doors shut and secure them until dawn. Logan painfully admitted to himself that the Order had no enemies to keep out; the barricade kept rebellious apprentices and discontented Zealotes from slipping away under cover of darkness. He'd always accepted the rigors of training and the harshness of the discipline as a framework to accomplish great things. Now that his feelings for Calla colored his every thought, he wondered how many brother Zealotes led lives of quiet misery.

He dismounted and led his equest on a path through elaborately planned gardens and vast expanses of emerald grass. Every pleasing shade in the universe was present in the lovingly tended plots of flowers and shrubs, but not even the heady fragrance gave him any pleasure. The blooming glory of a pale yellow rosbiscus tinged

160

with lavender on the tips of the petals called to mind Calla's flowing golden hair and luminous violet eyes. The delicate pink of a yissy blossom was a pale imitation of her soft flesh; the dark rosy buds on a fever bush made him tremble with longing for her ripe breasts.

A pair of apprentices nervously saluted him, but he impatiently gestured them out of his way, too preoccupied to give the customary response. In the stable he left his equest in the care of an elderly brother, but Logan was too wrapped up in his thoughts to acknowledge the existence of the puzzled Zealote.

Shaking off his lethargy, Logan made his way to his own quarters on the upper floor of the council members' wing. He had to make his report as soon as possible, but appearing before the Grand Elder in his filthy, travel-stained clothing was unthinkable. His saddlebags felt heavy on his shoulder, but he couldn't leave them behind for an apprentice to fetch, not with the damning violet cloak still stuffed into one bulging bag. His common sense urged him to destroy it, to take it to the incinerator immediately, but he couldn't bring himself to sever this last link with Calla.

What excuse had Warmond given for returning to the Citadral without his lieutenant? How much of the truth could Logan present to the Grand Elder without playing into Warmond's hands? No matter how much his feelings toward the Order had changed, Logan still revered the Grand Elder. He couldn't desert him or allow himself to be banished until Warmond was no longer a threat.

With grim determination, Logan knew he had to prepare mentally for a confrontation with the Master of Apprentices. As much as it would gall Logan to be in the man's presence again, he couldn't let Warmond go unchallenged.

Several Youngers sat on one of the massive stone benches lining the garden walk to Logan's quarters. They were deep in meditation, hoods pulled forward to mask their faces. Without probing, Logan could sense their innocence and naiveté. He envied them their youthful purity, a mindset lost to him forever. Calla had changed his life, robbed him of zeal and dedication to the Order, but he wouldn't willingly give up one precious memory of her. His bittersweet longings gave him great pain, but deserting her was the only way to keep her from harm.

He shuddered, trying not to imagine what would have happened if she'd been able to follow him to the Citadral. During his apprenticeship, he'd heard the story of a drunken female who wandered into the sacred precincts many generations earlier. She died for her foolish error, bound from ankles to neck in coils of rope and thrown from the Tower of Penance. Even if he discounted the adolescent embellishments of the older lads who told the tale, he didn't doubt the cruelty of Calla's fate if she tried to search for her nephew within the confines of the Citadral's stone walls.

His room was at the end of a long flagstone corridor, the white plastered walls of the hallway hung on both sides with paintings by Zealote artists. Usually Logan found joy in the vivid landscapes and surreal renderings of Thurlow's three moons, but he hurried toward his quarters without paying attention to them. The passageway vibrated with the chords of an ancient symphony, but the recorded orchestration didn't stir Logan's emotions or evoke his admiration. He was glad to shut his thick, soundproof door and collect his thoughts in the solitude of his chamber.

As a council member, he could call upon the riches of the Order to furnish his private rooms, but Logan had never taken advantage of his position to enrich his surroundings. His chamber was spacious with a crystal chandelier hanging from the lofty ceiling and heavy forest-green drapes on the long, narrow windows, but these luxuries has been installed by one of the room's former occupants. Logan continued to use the simple furnishings that had been allotted to him as a Younger: a long, narrow four-poster bed, a large but battered desk of some dark wood too heavily varnished to be identified, a wardrobe and dresser in the same nondescript style, and a straight-backed chair. He'd never allowed himself the comfort of a cushion for the seat or a pillow for the back, believing that slight discomfort improved his concentration. The dark gray stone floor was polished to a high gloss by industrious apprentices, and Logan covered part of it with a round braided rug, faded and frayed, his only legacy from a mother he'd never seen.

The only pride he took in his possessions was reserved for the well-read tomes on his overflowing bookshelves. No money changed hands between the brothers in the Order, but for years Logan had invested all his work credits to acquire a library. The Zealotes combed the universe for writings on religion, philosophy, astronomy, science, humanities, and the arts; and Logan was among the most avid readers. His status allowed him to own any book without permission from the censors, and he used the privilege of his position to obtain volumes overlooked or scorned by the Master of Libraries.

In the solitude of his own room, he felt giddy with fatigue. His ears were ringing, and he understood for the first time how it might feel to lose the elasticity of his muscles, to be saddled with an old body. He ached from the constant pummeling of his backside on the back of an equest. His shoulders and back were stiff with tension, and his calves were painfully knotted. He longed to visit the baths, to soak in steamy aromatic water and pamper himself with a deep massage. The Order's body conditioners had magic in their fingers; they could draw fatigue from over-stressed muscles and knead a man's flesh until it tingled with renewed vigor.

Shaking his head impatiently, he stripped off his soiled clothing and hurried into his small water closet. In spite of the gold faucets his predecessor had installed, the room was basically utilitarian. The walls, floors, and fixtures were stark white, the tiles kept immaculately clean by apprentices.

Logan turned a knob and stepped under a spray of warm water, quickly lathering his body with harsh yellow soap. He washed away the grit from his travels, purifying himself for his interview with the Grand Elder, but his spirit was too troubled to take pleasure in being clean again.

The last time he'd bathed, he'd been tortured by the vision of Calla running naked from the stream. This memory came back, exciting and tormenting him until he stood under a blast of icy water, not to punish his flesh but to relieve himself of pressures he could no longer control. He tried to concentrate on his report to the Grand Elder, but Calla's glistening flesh seemed more real to him than the withered old man waiting for news from him.

Confession, punishment, banishment, all the carefully ordered safeguards against a man's base passions, seemed ineffectual against the storm of emotions Calla had aroused in him. All he had left was his honor, but he clung to it tenaciously, resolved he wouldn't fail in his duty.·

He quickly shaved, then donned a white robe, the official garb worn only by Zealotes with master status when they appeared before the Grand Elder. Naked under the ultra-soft woven fabric, Logan felt unmanned by the silky caress of the luxurious cloth. He tied a golden sash around his waist, pulling it tight, then thrust his feet into sandals with thick rope soles.

As the last step in his preparations, he brushed his damp sable hair into a tight tail, securing it at the nape of his neck with a black elastic band. Long hair was a privilege of high rank; once a Zealote was elected to the council, his hair could only be cut in a ritualistic trimming once every full-cycle. In spite of this, it would be unseemly if Logan let his thick, heavy locks curl naturally and fall loose around his face in the presence of the Grand Elder.

Although he was properly groomed and garbed for his interview, Logan felt far from ready to face the Grand Elder. He had an uncomfortable awareness of self: The network of nerves in his body were electrified by his uneasy spirit; his extremities tingled; he could hear the beating of his heart. His breath came in great gulps, and his scalp ached where his hair was pulled tight.

He tried to meditate in the extreme position: legs spread, arms outstretched at his sides, head bowed. Even this exercise failed him. His concentration was as poor as a fledgling apprentice's; he would have to face his superior without the inspiration of his inner voice.

To reach the Grand Elder's sanctum, Logan followed a complicated maze of corridors, finally reaching the hub of the Citadral, a commons area where even apprentices were allowed to speak aloud. He absentmindedly returned greetings from several of his peers, but reacted with irritation when two Youngers blocked his way into the executive wing.

"Move aside," he said impatiently. "I have to request an audience with the Grand Elder."

"A moment, please, master," the taller of the two young men said, standing his ground so Logan couldn't pass him.

"Garth and Ignasus." Logan recognized the pair as two of the Youngers who had accompanied Warmond on the summoning expedition. "I thought one of you would turn back to see if I needed assistance."

Garth's face turned an unsightly red under his fine flaxen hair, and his companion studied a bit of lint on the sleeve of his black robe, picking at it to keep his eyes averted.

"We were never so ordered," Garth said in a barely audible whisper.

Logan took a deep breath to hold back his anger. The Youngers didn't deserve his condemnation. Warmond was a ruthless autocrat; only a very foolish brother would oppose his orders.

"Are you acting on Master Warmond's instructions now?" he asked.

"Yes, sir. The Master of Apprentices requests that you come to his chamber immediately."

"He must know I have to report to the Grand Elder."

"Oh, he does, sir," Ignasus said, the fear in his voice reminding Logan of a particularly harsh lashing the young man had endured at Warmond's hand. "But it's urgent he see you first."

"We must bring you to him," Garth said with mock severity. "We have orders—"

"To drag me there by force if necessary?" Logan stared at the coil of rope hanging from Garth's sash. Usually only the monitors carried them within the confines of the Citadral. He smiled to reassure them. "You won't need to bind me. I'm agreeable to a conference with the Master of Apprentices."

Garth grinned in relief, and a bit of color returned

to Ignasus' sallow face. Neither of them had any illusions. Logan was Master of Defense, and the two of them were no match for his expertise, even if they had the will to oppose him.

Trying to hide his anger at Warmond's high-handed tactics, Logan followed the two Youngers. He wasn't ready to confront the Master of Apprentices, but he couldn't allow Warmond to vent his anger on innocent brothers.

Logan entered Warmond's sanctum alone, seeing it for the first time. A Zealote's chamber was an extension of his inner life; the members of the Order were discouraged from using their private rooms for business or social purposes. Logan would have preferred to meet in one of the many conference rooms available for the purpose, feeling vaguely contaminated by the room's opulent furnishings. The chamber seemed dark, even though the heavy bloodred drapes were partially open allowing a feeble ray to sun to illuminate the intricate black, red, and gold pattern of the carpet, a rare hand-loomed antiquity of a type seldom seen on Thurlow.

The furniture was as oppressive as it was ornate. The bedstead had a massive headboard of carved black wood with mythical creatures cavorting among fanciful flora. A carved chest and dresser were companion pieces, and the desk dwarfed that of the Grand Elder. The coverlet on the bed was blatantly luxurious, black with thin silver stripes that glistened with a satiny sheen, but the paintings overwhelmed all the other furnishings. Every wall was covered all the way to the ceiling with huge, ornate gesso frames, each one containing an allegorical scene painted in thick oils in a style reminiscent of Earth's Italian Renaissance art.

His senses were so assailed by massive, fleshy figures, some double the height of a man, that Logan didn't see Warmond standing in a shadowy corner.

"I believe you share my love of fine art," Warmond said, startling Logan by stepping forward to reveal himself.

"I admit I've never seen this style before."

"Surely you recognize the scenes from Earth mythology. Here's Ulysses, confronting the Cyclops—"

"You must have an urgent reason for waylaying me on my way to report to the Grand Elder," Logan interrupted, averting his eyes from a particularly gruesome painting of a dragon standing over a mutilated human form.

"Perhaps you should sit." Warmond gestured at a high-backed chair upholstered in black leather. "The news I have isn't pleasant."

Logan's lower back and shoulders ached with tension, but he shook his head, more uncomfortable in this private chamber than he'd ever been in any other place. There was no sight of female flesh in Warmond's paintings, no acts of debauchery forbidden by the Order, but the pseudo-classical scenes all had an overt cruelty that made Logan's blood run cold.

"I have questions," Logan said. "Why didn't you send a Younger back to learn my whereabouts?"

"There were extenuating circumstances." The

Master of Apprentices bowed his head and pursed his thin, bloodless lips. His hair was combed back severely from his face, making his features look more hawkish, and the deprivations of his last journey had left him gaunt, as fleshless as a mock figure made of sticks.

"Explain them to me," Logan demanded, beyond the point where he could force himself to use the respectful form of address.

"Most regrettably, I have to tell you the child died."

"That can't be!"

"There's always a risk taking a newborn from its mother's breast. The Outsiders are poor birthers, at best. I doubt the babe would have lived in any situation."

"He was healthy!"

"He wasn't a defective, I agree. But you know nothing of the ailments that can end a new life. I've had much experience—"

"You've lost other babies!"

The accusation hung between them like a challenge. Logan probed Warmond's mind but found it totally guarded.

"Spare yourself the effort." Warmond ran his hand over his forehead, as though brushing away the slight pressure caused by Logan's probe. "As my lieutenant on the mission, you have a duty to perform."

"What duty?" The taste of failure was bitter on Logan's tongue.

"You must inform the Grand Elder that the child did not survive the trip."

170

"You haven't reported to him?"

"I sent word that I was ill—critically ill, in fact. That infernal rain brought on an old illness—fever and chills. I had to send the Youngers ahead without me after the child passed on."

"They brought the child's body here for burial?"

"You know that's not permitted unless a babe has been officially renamed and received into the brotherhood."

"Where is he?"

"I buried him myself at great cost to my health. Since my return, I've been confined to this chamber by my weak condition."

Logan didn't waste words wishing him a swift return to health. He quickly left the chamber, too shocked by loss to even see the two Youngers anxiously hovering in the corridor.

The baby had been healthy; Logan remembered signs of his vigor: a demanding cry and sturdy limbs. Riding in a sling against Warmond's chest, he had been protected from the elements, sheltered from cold. Fane should not have died!

Sick at heart, Logan ached for Calla, knowing how great her grief would be. She'd risked great danger to follow her nephew, and now she had tragic news to carry back to her family.

Logan's eyes burned, and his heart mourned.

Thank the Great Power Calla hadn't been able to follow him to the Citadral! She wouldn't have accepted Fane's death without confronting Warmond himself. Her grief would have sealed her doom.

Heavyhearted with concern for her, he slowly made his way toward the executive wing. There was nothing he could do to ease Calla's burden of loss, but he could ensure her safety. Not even his duty to the Grand Elder was more important.

Instead of going toward the audience chamber, he went outside and hurried across a vast expanse of flower-studded lawn to the Hall of Learning. The apprentices were still confined in their study cubicles, but the day's lesson-giving had ended. Logan quickly located his friend Perrin in his office where he was preparing a lecture for the next day's period of contemplation.

"What wisdom are you distilling for your young scholars?" Logan asked in the teasing tone men use with close companions.

"By all that's sacred!" The fiery-haired giant grabbed Logan in his arms and lifted his feet from the floor.

"Enough, you lout!" Logan smiled in spite of his low spirits. Perrin was his peer, and since childhood they'd shared a friendship akin to a blood tie. A fierce warrior and powerful leader, Perrin had surprised himself and all who knew him when he elected to follow the path of a teacher. His brutish appearance and abrupt speech struck terror in new apprentices, but all his scholars learned to respect—even revere—his patient, gentle instruction. He never uncoiled a rope, yet his lads worked diligently and obeyed with goodwill.

"Rumor had you dead!" Perrin said, wiping away the tears of happiness flooding his cheeks.

"Perhaps I was meant to be—"

"Not here," the teacher whispered. "I trust my lads—but I swear the walls have ears." He led Logan toward a deserted courtyard where only the instructors were allowed to relax and refresh themselves.

As quickly as possible, Logan told Perrin what had happened on his trip, but he couldn't burden his friend with his secret feelings for Calla.

"The woman," he said, concluding his story, "is still at the midwife's. She has to be told her nephew is dead. Then she needs an escort back to her family's freehold."

"I can arrange it," Perrin said, proving his loyalty by asking no questions. "Some of my scholars have achieved the status of Younger. I'll dispatch two of the most reliable—"

"Four would be better. I don't like the way the defectives are massing."

"Odd they've become so brave."

"Or so desperate. I have many things to tell you about the Outsiders, Brother, but I can't delay my report to the Grand Elder another moment."

Relieved for Calla's sake, Logan hurried to request an audience, but his double failure weighed heavily on his heart. He had neither child nor explanation for the Grand Elder. In his own mind he was convinced Warmond's intentions were sinister, but he didn't have a shred of evidence to back up his suspicions.

Waiting in the anteroom, seated on a long, gilded bench with white brocade cushions, Logan tried to formulate an explanation for the failure of his mission. In his heart he knew he'd betrayed the Zealote way, but it was too soon to ease his conscience by confessing to the Grand Elder. Before he brought

173

about his own banishment, he had to protect the Order from Warmond's manipulations.

The Grand Elder's counselor was Brother Niall, a stooped, emaciated man who had been a peer of the leader in the days of their apprenticeship. Although Niall was feeble and sometimes confused in his thinking, he still managed to summon Logan into the audience chamber with haughty dignity. When he remembered it, he was the only member of the Order who was allowed to call the Grand Elder by his given name: Brother Zachary.

The first time Logan had stood in the Grand Elder's presence, he'd been a terrified young apprentice, sure that he'd committed some unforgivable offense. Although the Grand Elder had embraced him like a son and followed his career from that day forward, often giving him more honors than he deserved, Logan never completely lost his awe of the ancient Zealote, a man who personified all that was noble and good in the Order. Now, when he had so much to report and even more to hide, Logan's stomach was once again churning with tension.

"Logan, I have eagerly awaited your return."

The vast chamber was so dark Logan could scarcely see his superior, but he approached the gilded armchair that sat on a dais at the far end of the room. He got down on his knees and touched his forehead to the cold tiles.

"Stand up, stand up! The moments of my life are numbered, and I haven't time for protocol."

Logan was surprised by the Grand Elder's impatience with formality, but he quickly stood, gradually getting used to the dimness. A single oil-burning lamp sat behind a translucent screen in a far corner, all the light the Grand Elder's diseased eyes could endure. The magnificent glass chandeliers and the mirror panels on the walls were covered with black gauze to guard against reflections. The frescoes on the ceiling were only dark shadows, and no one had seen the sumptuous carved and gilded furniture in many full moons. But never, to Logan's knowledge, had the Grand Elder allowed his affliction to interfere with the gestures of respect demanded by his high office.

"Come close. Sit here by my feet so I can touch your face."

Logan obeyed, scarcely breathing as his superior's paper-dry fingertips explored the ridge of his forehead, the planes of his cheeks, the set of his jaw.

"You're disturbed," he said. "There's much tension in your countenance. As I feared, your long absence was a bad sign."

"The news is very bad, Master." Logan suppressed a shiver when the gnarled fingers brushed across his lips. He tried to picture the Grand Elder as he had been: straight-backed with flowing white hair and a proud head, his blue eyes gentle with understanding even when his craggy face was rigid with authority.

"Tell me the worst."

"We summoned a child but it died."

"What was the cause?" The sorrow in the old leader's voice came from the depth of his soul.

"I can't say. I wasn't present."

175

"Explain."

"I became separated from the others in a heavy fog. Only when I returned a short while ago did Warmond tell me."

"I don't like the sound of this." Now he sounded like a weary old man. "How many Youngers were with Warmond?"

"All of them, Master."

"None backtracked to find you?"

"None, Master."

"Something is terribly amiss." The Grand Elder stood and descended from his chair, his dark robe brushing against Logan. "Continue with your mission, my brother. We must know more about Warmond's activities before we confront him in the council. My inner voice is warning me of a great calamity, and the Master of Apprentices is a threat to all of us."

Logan's breath, bottled in his lungs as he waited for the Grand Elder to question him in his usual penetrating way, escaped in a great sigh as the ancient leader slowly made his way to his inner chamber. Sorrow and anxiety had dulled the man's perception; Logan had expected searching questions about his own role in losing the child. He'd never lied to the Grand Elder, but he was prepared to conceal his feelings for Calla at any cost. Eventually the Grand Elder would have no choice but to banish him from the Citadral, but first Logan had to learn the truth about Warmond.

Cold with repulsion, Logan let himself think the unthinkable: that the Master of Apprentices of the

Zealotes was responsible for the death of a summoned child.

Returning to his chamber, Logan knew he had to resume his accustomed routine as soon as possible. That meant changing into his black robe and appearing at the evening meal, even though his anxieties pushed away all interest in food.

Minutes later he was folding his white robe, preparing to go to the dining hall, when a heavy hand pulled the lever that rang a bell in his chamber. Although there were no locks within the Citadral, no brother entered the private chamber of another without warning.

"Perrin!"

His friend filled the open doorway, his face a brilliant red under his fiery hair.

"I've come to borrow that book," he said, stepping into the room and pushing the heavy door shut behind him.

"What book?"

"No book, Brother. It isn't safe to be open about your activities in these bad days. A messenger came to the gate looking for you. Thank the Great Power, one of my lads was nearby and brought him to me, believing you were still away."

"What messenger—"

"From the midwife, Grunhild. I destroyed the letter and rewarded the messenger for his silence."

"Tell me the message!"

"When the midwife returned to her cot, the female was gone, and so was her equest."

"I told Grunhild to hide it!"

"So she did. You underestimated the female."

"I'm in your debt," Logan said, struggling to hide the full extent of his anxiety.

"There are no debts between us," Perrin said, "but don't look so grim. There's no way an Outsider—a female at that, can find the way to the Citadral."

"I pray you're right."

Logan's cloak was too long, so she'd wasted precious time in the woods hacking off the bottom, afraid she'd trip at a crucial moment. If Fane was still in the Citadral, he might be spirited away at any time. If, as Logan believed, he was gone, she faced another dangerous trip best completed before her nerve failed her. Thank the Great Power that Doran's herbs had caused no side effects.

The sun was low by the time she reached the massive walls of the Citadral, but she was gratified to see the heavy wooden gates open and unguarded. She pulled the dark hood forward until her feminine features were totally submerged in its depths and walked onto the forbidden grounds with long— and she hoped masculine—steps. The beauty of the imposing spires and the vivid colors in the gardens momentarily dazzled her, but fear overwhelmed any impulse for sightseeing. She moved as briskly as possible without breaking into a run, terrified when a tall, black-robed Zealote walked toward her. Her heart stopped, and she tried to think of a plan in case he questioned her. She worried for nothing; the somber-faced brother passed with a mere nod, which she acknowledged by bowing her head in a gesture of humility.

Why hadn't she questioned Logan more closely

about the workings of the Citadral? Not that he was ever willing to discuss his life within the Order! Across the width of a garden plot vivid with purple and red blossoms, she saw three Zealotes rushing toward a huge building with no spires. They were too small to be full-fledged members of the Order, so she assumed they were apprentices who were, perhaps, hurrying toward an evening meal. Unlike the black-robed man who'd passed her, they were wearing cowled robes of a dull slate color. She realized Logan's heavy cloak might make her conspicuous inside a building where outerwear was too warm. In a community of men, her height would attract attention too, but the young Zealotes had given her a solution. Her best disguise was to dress as a lad in one of their coarsely woven gray robes.

The Order was a commune, and she hoped that meant common use of clothing, at least for boys who were still growing.

Every complex of buildings, whether it was a lowly freehold like her father's or this magnificent cult center, had to have a work area. Calla located some utilitarian wooden sheds behind the gleaming white stone buildings and found what she needed without attracting any attention: the laundry.

The long, low-ceilinged building reeked of strong soap and musty air, but it was blessedly deserted. She ran between a long row of metal tubs on legs, out a rear door left open for ventilation. There, pinned to a maze of laundry lines, were black robes and gray robes in lengths to fit everyone from small boys to tall men. She found one of the slate-colored apprentices' robes nearly dry and ducked behind a row of hanging bed sheets to strip off Logan's cloak and Grunhild's dangerously inappropriate dress. Her other things were safely stowed in saddlebags on Galaba's back, and her precious equest was hobbled near a stream and fresh grass in the woods bordering the Citadral.

The robe was scratchy, and she pitied the boys who wore them every day, but she was more concerned with safety than comfort. She disposed of the cloak by hanging it beside several others on the line, but she didn't dare leave the dress where its discovery would alert the Zealotes to a female presence. Wadding it into the smallest possible bundle, she dug a hole under a bush with the toe of her boot and kicked dirt to conceal it.

Peeking around a corner of the laundry shed, she saw a group of apprentices hurrying down a path. Nothing suited her purpose better than to have all the Zealotes occupied by their supper. She could search for a nursery, a place where an infant could receive care, without too many dangerous encounters.

"Soiled your robe and had to steal a clean one, did you?" A chubby-faced, dimpled brother with only a few wisps of faded brown hair on his dome chuckled at her startled jump. "Well, Brother Burton isn't one to see a lad punished for what he can't help. Come along with me to the dining hall. If any of the monitors are perturbed by your tardiness, I'll say you were doing me a good turn."

"Thank you, sir," Calla mumbled, trying to lower her voice, hoping the helpful Zealote wouldn't become suspicious. "I'm not hungry."

"Nonsense! No lad should sit through evening contemplation without a full belly. Come along now, before I change my mind about your raid on my laundry."

Given no choice, Calla reluctantly hurried along at his side, too afraid of attracting attention to think of running away. At least Brother Burton pulled his black cowl over his balding head, all but covering his face, so she felt safe hiding in the scratchy folds of her pilfered cowl.

After hard days of travel, illness, and emotional upheaval, she was finally inside the fabled Citadral. Calla was terrified but fascinated too, seeing the forbidden world that claimed Logan's loyalty. She'd never dreamed the Order had such huge buildings, and the multitude of cult members in the dining hall took her breath away. Seemingly endless rows of wooden tables filled the long, high-ceilinged room, each one occupied by silent Zealotes, their bowed heads faceless in the depths of their cowls.

The gray-garbed apprentices sat at tables closest to the four large entryways, while at the far end a long table sat on a raised platform. She prayed she could blend in at one of the nearby tables, but a heavyset brother in black challenged her.

"You're late, apprentice!"

"My fault," her self-appointed guardian said. "Find your place quickly, lad."

She had no idea where it was safe to sit, but she scampered over to a table of older boys who seemed to be about her size and slid onto a place on the end of their bench, hoping the apprentice who usually sat there wouldn't challenge her. Crossing her fingers inside the long sleeves of the robe, she hoped she could slip away before someone forced her to talk.

From one of the entryways Logan surveyed the massive communal dining area, scarcely noticing the legions of servers who glided mutely down the rows. He could see that Warmond was occupying his place at the head table, but the place of honor was empty. It had been many full-cycles since the Grand Elder's eyes had permitted him to dine in the well-lit room.

"The Master of Apprentices has rejoined us, I see," Perrin said.

"His illness is conveniently over. We must talk further," Logan whispered. "And the female must be found. I need to know where she is before she blunders into serious difficulties."

"Surely she won't come this way." The big man lowered his usually booming voice. "There's no chance she can find the Citadral. Most likely she's on her way back to her people."

"I wish I could believe that."

Logan was at war with his conscience, wondering how much he could tell his friend. He urgently needed Perrin's help in searching for Calla, but he didn't want to alarm him. He was chafing to go himself, to ride the fastest equest in the stable and track her down, but he had to go through the motions of resuming his normal routine. That meant sitting through a meal and being seen at the evening contemplation.

The two men started toward the head table, among the last to take their places. Logan would never know why he turned his head, why he noticed an apprentice at the end of a bench three tables away, but before he could recover from his shock, it was too late.

He caught only a glimpse of the profile hidden in the depths of a cowl, but he'd memorized every feature of that face, thought of it by day and dreamed of it at night. He started toward Calla, desperately trying to think of a ruse to pluck her from the room, but not even his quick reflexes were enough to save her.

A server carrying a heavy tray of soup tureens stumbled, regaining his balance but jarring the bench where Calla was sitting. She was thrown forward, but the apprentice beside her reached out to prevent her collision with the dishes on the table. The lad's well-meant reaction was her undoing. He knocked off her cowl, exposing her long golden hair and undeniably feminine face.

"By all that's sacred!" the apprentice cried out, breaking the supper silence at the sight of the creature beside him.

A dozen monitors converged on the table, ropes unfurled ready to put down an unruly group of apprentices or single out a troublemaker. Even the most ruthless and single-minded of these Zealotes was momentarily halted by the shock of seeing a female in their midst.

Logan rushed forward, ready to do what could be done, but before he could reach Calla, a voice boomed out from the front of the room.

"I accuse this female of invading our sacred Citadral!" Warmond shouted over the confused babble in the room. "And I accuse Brother Logan of conspiring against the rules of the Order!"

Chapter Eight

Calla watched in horror as a dozen coils of rope snared Logan and pulled him to his knees. Black-robed Zealotes surrounded him like vultures closing in on a doomed creature.

"He didn't bring me here!" she screamed, trying to push her way toward him.

The brothers, apprentices and full-fledged members alike, scurried out of her way, as though physical contact with a female would contaminate them. She nearly reached the circle guarding Logan when one of the monitors recovered his wits and grabbed the sleeve of her robe.

"Restrain this creature!" he bellowed, whether in fear or rage Calla wasn't sure.

A score of eager apprentices pounced on her, gleefully eager to see and touch the female who'd invaded their sacred Citadral. They took advantage of the confusion to satisfy their curiosity. One ripped the robe from her shoulder and squeezed her breast under the pretext of restraining her. Another fell at her feet and took possession of one leg, while a bigger, more daring lad pressed himself against her backside and tried to slide his knee between her legs while his peers shielded him from sight. Gray-robed apprentices shoved close on all sides, and her struggles did nothing but encourage them.

One of the boys shrieked and another whistled shrilly, apparently warning his friends of danger. Calla was knocked to the floor, but her attackers fled, driven away by the ropes of their monitors.

Her robe was in shreds; she'd been prodded, pinched, and bruised on all sides, but she was more frightened now that only a pair of black-robed Zealotes stood over her, their faces contorted into masks of fury and outrage.

"I came here on my own," she tried to explain. "No one helped me."

"Your words defile our ears, female. Do not speak."

"What have women done to make you hate them so much?" she pleaded.

A rope whistled through the air and bit into her exposed shoulder, searing her flesh and making her scream in pain.

"She hasn't been judged! It's unseemly to chastise her!" A fiery-haired giant stepped forward, putting himself between Calla and the Zealote who'd raised his rope to lash her again.

"She's defiled our sanctuary. She deserves to die."

186

"Only the Grand Elder can make that decision!"

Logan watched helplessly as Calla was mobbed and then lashed. He strained against the ropes binding his arms to his sides, but he was fighting too hard for breath to regain his feet. When Perrin stepped in to save Calla from being beaten, perhaps to death, he had an instant of relief, but fear for his friend was added to his burden of fear for Calla. Would Perrin side with him and suffer his fate? To Logan's great relief, the big man hastily organized a handful of monitors to escort the two of them to the Grand Elder's chamber, then disappeared in the crowd.

Jerked to his feet, Logan was shoved forward to follow Calla and her captors through the commons area into the executive wing. He knew Perrin had only bought them a little time. The rules of the Order were inflexible, and the Grand Elder wouldn't try to circumvent them, not even for the sake of the affection he had for Logan.

There was no waiting, no time to think of what to say to his revered mentor. Logan knew he was innocent of bringing Calla into the Citadral, but his tender feelings for her had provided the opportunity to follow him. It was the only way she could have found the Citadral so quickly. He remembered the missing key and knew she had outwitted him. His emotions had blinded him, and his poor judgment was their undoing.

She didn't know Fane was dead. Her sacrifice was for nothing.

The audience chamber was filled to capacity with black-robed Zealotes. The apprentices had been ordered to their quarters to contemplate the penances due them for allowing their eyes to be defiled by the sight of a female. Logan felt like weeping for each and every lad, not because of the fleeting punishment they would endure but because none of them would ever know what it was to love a woman. At least their ignorance would protect them from the aching sense of loss that colored everything he did.

The chamber was shrouded in darkness; the faint light behind the screen was absorbed by hundreds of midnight-black robes, every cowl drawn forward as though grieving for the brother who had betrayed their Order.

A few elderly Zealotes keened in the old way, mourning the blow to their brotherhood, but when the Grand Elder appeared, the room became as silent as a cavern of the dead.

"Who accuses our brother, Master of Defense Logan, of treachery to the Order?" the Grand Elder asked in his voice of authority.

"I accuse him of violating the trust bestowed on him and allowing a female to defile our sacred Citadral," Warmond said, moving like a shadow to the front of the chamber and prostrating himself in front of his superior.

"Did you see him in the company of the female?" the Grand Elder demanded to know.

Logan could hear the tremor in his mentor's voice and knew how desperately he wanted proof of his innocence. The elderly leader's sorrow was

188

one more burden on Logan's conscience, but all he wanted for himself was to see Calla leave the Citadral free and unharmed. Rationally he knew it was impossible, but part of him couldn't accept her death.

"Better than that, Master." Warmond rose snake-like to his feet, his dark form seeming to undulate in the faint gray shadow in front of the Grand Elder's chair. "I have physical proof of Brother Logan's treason."

In a silence so deep the assembled brothers seemed to be holding their breaths in anticipation, Warmond reached out for a bulky object held by a Younger standing behind him.

"This is a cloak, Master, a garment of a deep violet shade unknown within the Order. Its length is appropriate for the female apprehended in the dining hall."

"You're saying the woman wore it when she entered the grounds?" the Grand Elder asked.

"No, Master. She wore a Zealote cloak. Brother Burton found her at the laundry but mistook her for an apprentice. When he realized she wasn't one of us, he ran there and found a cloak cut off to accommodate her height hanging on a drying line."

"All this talk of cloaks is beside the point," Perrin called out from the midst of the crowd. "Brother Logan is a trusted member of the council. This accusation is an outrage."

"Then perhaps he'll explain why this violet robe was found in his chamber!" Warmond shouted, waving the damning garment above his head.

"Bring the woman close," the Grand Elder softly ordered, his voice betraying his suffering.

Calla was pushed into the clear space in front of the elevated chair. She stood without bowing, too frightened to think of anything but holding the remnants of the gray robe across her breasts.

"Does this violet garment belong to you?" the Grand Elder asked softly.

"I don't know, sir—Master. It's too dark to see it."

"Bring another light and drape the cloak on the female," the Zealote leader ordered, pulling out a pair of thick black-lensed spectacles from the folds of his cloak.

Calla flinched when the soft wool was laid on her lacerated shoulder.

"It fits as though made for her," Warmond was quick to point out.

"This is contrary to everything the Order stands for," Logan protested. "The Master of Apprentices has his own reasons for—"

"Silence! Let the female speak." The Grand Elder sounded like a testy old man, but his voice still commanded the respect of every man present. The room became silent.

"I came here on my own to find my nephew, the infant Fane," Calla said. "I'm not one of you, so your laws shouldn't be used to judge me. If I've committed a crime, let the courts of Thurlow judge me."

"Everyone on this planet knows the Citadral is sacred to the Zealotes and forbidden to females," the Grand Elder said. "But very few Outsiders know its location. You could not find your way here without assistance. Name the person who revealed the secret route."

"No one! I followed—" She broke off, afraid to connect Logan in any way with her ruse. "I followed a robed figure, hoping he was a Zealote who would lead me here. He never saw me. It was only blind chance that I ended up using him to find this place."

"In any case," the old leader said wearily, "coming here was as futile as it was foolish. The babe is dead."

"No! I don't believe it! He was a healthy babe—a strong, beautiful boy. He must be alive! You've hidden him somewhere!"

Logan watched in agony as Calla defied the Grand Elder and broke into tears of rage. Freed of his bindings before entering the audience chamber, he moved toward her on impulse, overwhelmed by a compulsion to offer comfort. Heedless of the consequences, he reached out and let her collapse against him sobbing and trembling with anger and denial.

"Set her free!" Logan cried out to his old mentor. "She's ignorant of our ways. Blame me for showing her the path to Citadral—although, by all that we hold sacred, it was never my intention to do so."

"How did you get her cloak?" Warmond shouted over the startled buzz of voices.

"Perhaps the brother who violated my chamber can answer that! Are we like the Outsiders, that every brother now needs a lock to keep out his peers?"

"Uncovering treason to the Order justifies a thousand small offenses!" Warmond shouted.

Fighting for Calla's life, Logan pulled her closer to the Grand Elder's chair. "Please, Master, remove your dark lenses for just an instant and see this women for what she is. She's not a Jezebel, but our own apprentices have treated her like a harlot, mauling her and tearing away her robe. She didn't come here to corrupt our brotherhood. She's maddened by grief over the loss of the child who's the last of her father's line. It's not the Zealote way to pass judgment on—"

"Don't claim that she's insane!" Warmond vehemently interrupted. "She came here to steal back a summoned child."

"I have heard enough!" Brother Zachary, Grand Elder of the Zealotes, spoke with the fire that had made him their leader. "Imprison the female. She has sealed her own fate. The law calls for a two-day period of confinement for contemplation of her crime, after which she must hear the judgment of the Council for Sacred Matters."

"No! You must give me back my nephew! I know he's not dead!" Calla was pulled from Logan's grasp and dragged, struggling, into the midst of the stunned brothers.

"Master of Defense Logan, you have betrayed yourself by touching the female and by speaking on her behalf. Because of your high status, your punishment shall be decided by your peers. Until the Council for Sacred Matters convenes to give its ruling, you will be confined in the Tower of Penance. Use the time to contemplate the enormity of your transgressions. This is my last word on the matter."

Logan found it hard to believe what he was hearing: The Grand Elder accepted Warmond's charges. It was the Grand Elder himself who suspected Warmond of treachery, and it was at the elderly leader's request that Logan accompanied Warmond on the summoning journey. Logan knew the Council for Sacred Matters had never been called during his lifetime. Only the Grand Elder could activate it, and it was well-known that only weak leaders foisted their responsibilities on the ancient men who were elected for life to this council. Brother Niall, counselor to the Grand Elder but an elderly man who lived in the past, was its head.

More dazed than docile, Logan allowed four nervous monitors to escort him without resistance across a brick courtyard into the Tower of Penance. The senior among them lit a single black wax stick at the entryway, the only light permitted in the area of the confinement cells.

"Put him in the harness," the leader ordered.

Logan heard the collective sigh of relief, but it didn't give him any pleasure to know his burly guards still feared him. One, the largest of the four, took a cage-like contraption from a hook on the wall and slipped it over Logan's head. Made of stiff strips of leather, it fit over his torso from shoulder to thighs, allowing him to walk but pinning his arms to his sides. Logan knew the secret of collapsing the contraption by bending one critical strip, but he wasn't ready to become an outlaw, not while Calla was imprisoned and in mortal danger.

Feeling safer now, the monitors partially led and partially shoved him down a dark corridor into the depths of the huge tower, then down a curving flight of steps hewn in solid rock. Logan was familiar with the layout of the tower: the confinement cells, the interrogation and discipline chambers, and the huge circular room on the uppermost level where penitent brothers were welcomed back into the good graces of the Order. He had never seen the dungeon level, a place where only the most serious adult offenders were confined, not to do penance or restore inner peace, but to await punishment.

The air below ground was cold and musty, smelling faintly of disinfectant because the Order placed a high value on cleanliness, even in this dismal place.

"Calla!" Logan yelled as loud as he could, repeating his call before one of the monitors pressed a hand over his mouth and nose.

"Don't punish our ears in this close space," the senior monitor warned. "She's not so close that you can betray the Order again by having words with her."

Gasping for breath, Logan probed the monitor's mind and believed him. Very few Zealotes had mastered the art of lying, and, to his sorrow, these men weren't among them. Whatever the

194

Council for Sacred Matters decided, Logan knew what his worst punishment would be: his fear and concern for Calla.

His place of confinement was so small he could scarcely take three paces in any direction, but, unlike the black corridor that led to it, his cell had a source of illumination: a tiny opening high in the wall. Thurlow's giant sun was already sinking on the horizon, so only the faintest possible light reached the depths of his prison. When his eyes became accustomed to the dimness, he could make out the whitewashed stone walls and the minimal creature comforts: a covered pit for sanitary purposes and a wooden platform the length of one wall that had to serve as a bed. Because his guards hadn't removed the harness, he could only stand or lie; he couldn't bend his torso to sit.

At first he paced as best he could in the tiny space, so frantic with worry for Calla that he was ready to explode. Added to his fears for her life was his deep puzzlement about Warmond. Why was he so eager to get rid of both of them? Was Calla right? Was the babe still alive? Warmond might resent, even hate, Logan, but it was unheard of for one brother to search another's chamber for damaging evidence. Was Calla right? Was the babe still alive? Was there more than personal enmity behind Warmond's accusation?

Needing to focus all his mental powers on this mystery, he stood motionless, his forehead pressed against a cold stone wall to cool his feverish agitation.

His thinking went in circles. If Warmond had murdered the child, what was his motive? If the babe was alive, why had the Master of Apprentices lied? And where was Fane now?

No amount of contemplation could give him an answer, Logan realized. Gradually, as the cell was deprived of the last hazy light of dusk, his thoughts focused on his fate—and Calla's.

He knew what to expect for himself. The most lenient sentence possible was banishment, and he'd already resigned himself to a life of hard labor in a rural center. The worst punishment, more cruel than torture or death, was to be ostracized. If this was his sentence, he would be forced to remain within the confines of the Citadral, but no living soul would speak to him ever again. No one would acknowledge his presence, nor would he ever again be allowed to speak to anyone without incurring severe punishment. The few Zealotes sentenced to this terrible fate were guilty of the most heinous crimes against the Order. Watched by all the brothers, they were even denied the means to commit suicide. The only respite was insanity. A few poor mindless creatures who were not dangerous to others wandered the corridors of the Citadral, wearing robes patched with bright remnants of cloth to warn away apprentices, who were forbidden to bedevil them.

If this was Logan's fate, he would never be permitted to touch a book again. The only thing he would read was the duty roster, which assigned the outcasts to the most menial and unpleasant tasks. Instead of eating with the other brothers, he would be forced to eat from a feeding trough outside the kitchen where table scraps were dumped after each meal.

Although Logan preferred death to this life of unending humiliation and solitude, he was too consumed by anxiety for Calla to dwell long on his own future. Somehow he had to find her, free her, and ensure her safe return to her family. Unfortunately this course of action had one great obstacle: Calla herself. Would she give up her quest for the babe, believing as she did that he was still alive?

He laid at last on the hard plank bed, enduring the worst agony of his life: his inability to save the woman he loved.

When Logan was led away, Calla's spirit went with him. She could face her own death, knowing that only a miserable life with Gustaf awaited her at home, but she hated herself for putting Logan in jeopardy.

"What will happen to him?" she begged the monitors who flanked her on either side.

Instead of answering, one of her captors made a noose of his rope and slipped it around her neck.

"Follow," he said curtly.

The rope chafed, but it wasn't tight enough to choke her. She understood the purpose: to lead her without having to contaminate themselves by touching her. Tempted to take the easy course and make them strangle her, sure that some horrible death awaited her, she called on all her inner resources and forced herself to follow docilely. If she could do anything to clear Logan of the unfair charge against him, she had to live long enough to make the effort.

They took her outside, across grounds that had seemed beautiful in the sunlight. In the dusk, many of the plants drooped, spilling over the paths in sinister tangles, sinuous tendrils tripping her more than once. Each time she stumbled her captor yanked the rope, burning the flesh of her throat.

She expected to be confined in some monstrous underground dungeon, but they took her back to a complex of wooden outbuildings of the same type as the laundry. At the far end of a long row of similar structures they stopped in front of a heavy plank door held shut by a crude wooden bar. One monitor opened it while the other loosened his noose and slipped it over her head. They didn't give her a chance to walk into the dark, windowless hovel. One of her captors kicked her backside with his sandaled foot, plunging her forward to land on her hands and knees on a dirt floor.

The door slammed shut with unnecessary force, and she fell forward on her arms, weeping from sheer frustration.

The Zealotes were beasts! She hated each and every detestable brother: the nasty apprentices who treated her like an inanimate object; the horrible monitors who lashed and kicked her; the hypocritical Grand Elder who looked like someone's kindly grandfather but condemned her for her gender. And most of all, she hated Warmond! Why wasn't he satisfied with persecuting her? Why did he accuse Logan of the worst crime a Zealote could commit?

She cried until her head ached, but not because of the injuries to her pride and person. There was one Zealote she could never hate, and because of her he was in terrible trouble. She tortured herself, trying to think of what she could have done differently. Coming to the Citadral had been a reckless gamble, and she'd lost. Could she have done less? Fane wasn't dead! The Zealotes wanted her to believe he was, but she would never accept their lie!

Had she come to this dreadful place only for the sake of her nephew? She cried harder, tormented by guilt because, in the secret recesses of her heart, she'd never given up hope that somehow Logan would become her lover. He could never be hers for life; his bond with the Order was too strong. But if he gave her a child, she would always have a little part of him in her life.

Too exhausted for more tears, she lay motionless on the ground, slowly becoming aware of a familiar odor. She rose, stiff and weak-kneed, rubbed her sore bottom, and pulled her cloak away from her lacerated shoulder. She ached in a dozen other places from the pinches and prods of her youthful attackers, but all her pains were minor compared to her anguished spirit. What horrible thing would the Zealotes do to Logan? She was terrified for his sake, but the pleasant scent in her makeshift prison was acting as a balm on her emotional wounds.

She was in a storage shed, a place where fodder for the equests was stored. Groping in the dark, she found bales of sweetgruss stacked higher than her head in some places. She pulled one to the ground and expertly untied the bindings, letting the aromatic stalks make a natural bed. As a child she'd loved to play in the fodder room, and the familiar smell slowly released her from consciousness and let her fall into a sleep haunted by vivid nightmares.

Her first day passed in solitude broken only by hasty feedings. The door opened twice just enough for a hand to push a tray of food and water into the shed. She left the trays on a bale of sweetgruss far from the door, wondering if a monitor would come inside to fetch them. They only piled up, the contents half-eaten because it seemed to be the Zealote's intention to fatten her for the kill.

On the second day she had a visitor—if a man who talked through a door could be classified as such.

"Woman," a vaguely familiar voice called out.

"I'm still here," she said, answering just to hear the sound of her own voice.

"I have a clean garment for you. I'll open the door a crack so you can pass the apprentice's robe to me."

"Bring it to me yourself," she challenged, sick to death of the Zealotes' peculiar ways.

"Please, I did you a good turn."

"You're Brother Burton. You did me a very ill turn by finding the robe I cut off to fit me."

"I had no choice. If the Master of Apprentices found out—"

"I understand," she said, sympathetic in spite of her feelings about the Order. "Come in. I'll change behind a bale of sweetgruss."

"No, please! Pass out the soiled garment."

She heard something in Brother Burton's voice that penetrated her despair: fear. The Master of the Laundry was scared to death—of her!

"I won't hurt you," she assured him.

"Please!" He sounded ready to cry. "I'm too old to do penance."

"Just for looking at me? What about the apprentices who attacked me?"

"Many felt a need to go to the Tower of Penance, but I'm not so thick-skinned as when I was young."

How could she understand this strange cult that claimed Logan's allegiance? She only knew that, if Fane were still alive, she couldn't abandon him to the care and teachings of the Zealotes.

"Here," she said, quickly stripping off what were only torn remnants of a robe.

Brother Burton passed a neatly folded bundle through the door, but all she saw of him was a work-roughened hand and part of his sleeve.

The clean garment was more sack than robe, sleeveless and long enough to reach to the toes of her boots. The dark brown color was one she hadn't seen on a Zealote, but it was old and frayed in spots. The worst of her anxieties returned when she realized it might be penance garb.

She tore it off her body, shredding the old cloth until there wasn't a scrap large enough to make a cleaning rag. Let them do what they would, she would go before their accursed High Council in her beautiful purple cloak without a demeaning Zealote garment under it.

"Logan, I need you so badly," she whispered, wondering how much longer she could stand the pain of being apart from him.

On the third day Calla nibbled on a bit of bread left from the previous day and finished the contents of her water jug. Air slots high in the walls of the shed let streaks of morning sun climb down the bundles of fodder, so she was sure the time for her morning rations had come and gone. The Zealotes weren't wasting food on a female who was sure to be condemned to death that day by the High Council for Sacred Matters.

By midday angry storm clouds blocked the sun, releasing a torrent of rain that made her prison dank and cold. Hungry, thirsty, and shivering in the folds of her cloak, she could only think of one horrible truth: Logan was in mortal danger because of her.

When the monitors came for her, they made her hide her face in the depths of her violet hood. Again they dropped a noose around her throat to avoid touching her, but at least the thick wool of her cloak saved her from further chafing.

She'd never been in a government court, but she knew they convened in public buildings where anyone could be a spectator. The High Council was meeting unobserved in a remote, windowless structure at the far edge of the Citadral complex. The monitors removed the rope that circled her neck, then opened a narrow black door and roughly shoved her into a dark chamber.

When her eyes adjusted enough to see the interior of the chamber, she had a hard time believing she wasn't trapped in a nightmare. The walls, floor, and ceiling were black, and the only light came from a circular platform in the exact center of the square room. There, almost at the level of her head, a group of Zealotes stood with their backs toward her, holding thick black wax sticks.

She didn't know where to go. There were no chairs, no benches or witness boxes; no monitors were present to tell her whether to stand or sit. In fact, not one of the council members, for that was what she supposed them to be, turned to look in her direction. She circled the platform, guided by the light each Zealote held. Finally she found a slight opening between two of the stooped, hooded, ancient brothers. Logan was in the center, on his knees in a cruel contraption that held his arms to his sides.

No one stood there with him; he was facing judgment without anyone to speak on his behalf.

"He had nothing to do with me! I found my own way here! It was my decision!" she shouted, but not one of the judges gave any sign of hearing.

She frantically circled the ring of High Council members, but not one of them acknowledged her presence. They were going to condemn her without even glancing in her direction!

One of them spoke to Logan, then he was given an opportunity to speak, but to her consternation, she didn't understand a word. The Zealotes had a secret language, the existence of which no Outsider even suspected.

They didn't care if she learned this or any other secret of the Order. She was going to die anyway!

Desperately needing to see Logan, to receive some sign of recognition from him, she crowded against the high platform and reached up to push aside the robes of two council members. One of them paid no more attention to her than he would to a bit of dust landing on the hem of his garment; the other kicked his sandaled foot at her, missed, and nearly toppled over. They were feeble old men, the most ancient she'd ever seen. The fat black wax sticks, held without holders and with complete indifference to hot drops burning their hands, illuminated sunken eyes, deeply lined faces patterned by spidery purple veins, and grotesquely protruding chins and noses. The ravages of time and their bizarre ritual made them seem more frightening than the defectives.

"Logan," she whimpered softly, wanting to be heard only by him. "Say what you must to save yourself. There's no hope for me, but I don't want you to die. Please forgive me!"

He gave no sign of having heard her, and a skeletal old Zealote droned on without pause.

She refused to die without speaking what was in her heart. "Logan, I love you! Please give me some sign that you forgive me."

Hardly daring to breathe, she watched his stoic expression melt. His lids flickered, and his lips parted, silently mouthing what she had to believe was, "I do."

Suddenly, ominously, she could understand what was being said. The Zealotes were taking turns, reciting a list of Logan's crimes in the language of Thurlow.

" . . . permitting an accursed female to enter our sacred grounds—"

" . . . possession of a garment that touched the flesh of—"

" . . . betrayal of your sworn—"

They were all calling out his transgressions at once, as though each was judging a different facet of his crime.

"Now our decision," one Zealote said, cutting off all the others.

They didn't confer; there was no vote. Calla realized the verdict had been decided before Logan was brought before them. This was only a ritual— a farce played out to heighten their own feelings of importance.

"As Master of Defense you have served the Order with great honor. For this reason, leniency is possible."

Logan heard the word "leniency," but it didn't lesson his agony. He strained to see Calla, but her pale, frightened face was nearly submerged in the violet hood.

"You are to be held in the depths of the tower and ostracized until the eclipse of the moons, at which time you will put yourself under the guidance of the Master of Penance until he deems you fit to take your rightful place once again within the Order."

Logan shifted his weight from one aching knee to the other, unable to believe the High Council for Sacred Matters had shown so much mercy. He would suffer—no doubt his penance would be severe and last the maximum time, one moon cycle—but in an unbelievably short time he would be fully reinstated without loss of rank or position.

The Grand Elder hadn't forsaken him. Logan could see his mentor's influence in the council's decision. The wily old leader had used this ancient council to make it seem he wasn't showing favor to the Master of Defense.

He needs me, Logan thought. He must fear Warmond more than I thought possible if he's willing to compromise his principles to save me. But the Grand Elder couldn't possibly suspect the depth of his feelings for the female. Logan knew the worst of his punishment would come when sentence was pronounced on Calla.

"What is the fate of the woman?" he asked. "She deserves to share in your leniency."

"Death." The sentence was hissed by every ancient in the circle.

"She didn't know what she was doing!" Logan cried out.

"Defend her at your peril," the skeletal Zealote warned.

"When?" He could hardly choke out his question.

"In the darkest hour of this night, she'll be wrapped in coils of rope, each end secured to an equest, the beasts to be driven in opposite directions until the spirit of life departs from the craven creature."

Calla backed against the wall and sank down, too shaken to support her own weight. She'd tried to prepare herself for the worst, but this was beyond imagining. They were going to squeeze her to death!

At first she thought she was hallucinating, but her illusion was a reality: The circular platform with the Zealotes on it was slowly sinking into the floor. Too stunned by her sentence to move, she watched as the circle of black-robed cult members descended to her level, then started to sink out of sight, the candles flickering as they went down.

With a desperate burst of energy, Calla crawled on her hands and knees to the edge of the hole, looking down at the pinpricks of light for one last sight of Logan. He looked up, his face a tormented mask in the feeble light.

"Tonight!" he mouthed. "Tonight."

Then every candle was extinguished, and Calla was left sobbing in total darkness. At least Logan would return to the life he knew and loved.

The door opened, the light momentarily blinding her, and she had only an instant to wonder what Logan had tried to tell her.

Tonight. Tonight she was going to die. She hugged herself, pressing her legs together and shivering in fear.

Pam Rock

When the monitors came for her, she refused to stand and be led by a rope. They gave feeble jerks on the noose, but neither had the will to be responsible for her premature death in the end, so they supported her between them, half-dragging and half-carrying her back to the shed with its sweet, heavy scent.

Chapter Nine

Logan couldn't tear his eyes away from Calla as the circle of judgment descended away from her. Her hood fell off and the golden hair spilled forward, hanging down in the black hole that was swallowing him. Soon all he could see was the pale oval of her face, then that too disappeared.

He'd lost all track of time as the High Council for Sacred Matters theatrically badgered him, keeping him on his knees for endless hours while they pretended to consider his testimony and render their judgment. It was clear the Grand Elder had ordered them to decide in favor of leniency, but Logan was heartsick that the leader hadn't been merciful to Calla.

The platform stopped and a small door slid open. The council members passed through it in order of rank, the taller ones stooping to avoid hitting their heads. When the last ancient brother exited, the door closed leaving Logan alone in total darkness.

He was sorely tempted to escape from the leather cage, but it was too soon to betray his intentions. He had to be content with lying on his side, stretching his legs to restore flexibility in them while he tried to plan a way to save Calla.

He desperately needed to know how much time remained before her execution, but no Zealote would speak to him until after the eclipse of the three moons. Moments passed with the slowness of hours as he lay on the circular platform waiting for something to happen. Had they forgotten him? Was this to be part of his punishment, to lie at the bottom of a pit while Calla's life force was wrung from her body? Bitter tears flooded his eyes, and he tried to gauge his chance of climbing up the steep stone wall.

Just when he'd decided to throw off the cage and try to ascend the wall, poor as his chance of succeeding was, the platform creaked into motion again, descending to depths Logan had never known to exist within the Citadral.

Was this how the ancient Zealotes had dealt with their enemies? He knew the Order's history well, but until he'd been pushed through the small door where the council exited, he'd never suspected the existence of the circular judgment platform.

At last the platform came to rest and an even smaller door opened, a murky hole hardly wide enough to accommodate Logan's shoulders. A head appeared in the opening, and a pair of massive hands grabbed Logan's feet and hauled him into a narrow, frigid corridor lit by a smoky torch in a wall holder.

He had urgent questions, but fortunately he remembered not to utter a word. He was ostracized, and the penalty for trying to communicate with a brother was a severe lashing. If there were any way to help Calla, he couldn't squander his time or strength.

His best guess was that this level was far below the dungeon of the Tower of Penance. The four monitors sent to transfer him to a cell were burly brothers who seemed too large for the narrow corridor. Even without the infernal contraption to hamper him, Logan didn't have space to break free and overcome them. In only moments he was flung facedown into an even smaller containment chamber than his previous cell, and there wasn't an opening to let him see the sky. At least the torch in the corridor wasn't extinguished; the guards probably assumed it would burn out on its own after they made their way safely to the surface. Logan could make out the empty hollow of a cell too cramped to allow him to stretch out full length.

The last sound he heard for what seemed like an eternity was the laughter of his guards as they left him alone in the bowels of the planet.

As Master of Defense—responsible for teaching many different techniques—he knew every trick and device for escaping from an enemy's stronghold. Marshaling all his strength, he bent the strap that was the key to removing the cage and felt the punishing bands loosen around his shoulders. By inching the loose strap downward through his stiff fingers, he started a chain reaction. Agonizing cramps shot through his arms as he strained for freedom, but at last the cage slid to the floor and he stepped free.

The door of the cell was much more challenging. Still tortured by arm cramps, Logan knelt to study the heavy iron bars, the first he'd seen in the Citadral. Even in the dungeon, the Zealotes used a minimum amount of metal, relying on thick wood to imprison wrongdoers. The existence of this iron cage far below the other confinement cells was one more puzzle, one Logan didn't have time to analyze.

Great Power, he pleaded, let me escape before it's too late for Calla. Cold perspiration soaked the back of his brown penance garment, and his fingers felt raw as he ran them over the bars trying to find a weakness. Using one of the leather straps from the cage, he tested the soundness of the frame, pitting all his strength against rivets pounded into solid stone walls.

"You won't get far that way."

Logan's heart pounded erratically, reacting to the shock of being surprised by a visitor, an ancient brother whose tall frame was draped in a robe with bright yellow and green patches, the dress of a mad Zealote.

Afraid he was being tested, Logan didn't answer. An insane brother wouldn't be subject to the severe rules against communicating with the ostracized, but speaking, even to a madman, would subject Logan to discipline.

"They gave me a key, fools that they are. They believe you're too honorable to take advantage of a crazy man." The ancient brother opened the door. "Of course, they're all afraid to bring your tray themselves, and the Grand Elder ordered you have food and water twice each day."

Did prisoners eat an evening meal at the same time other brothers did? Logan was still reluctant to speak.

"No reason you should trust me. Mad as a pointy-headed defective, that's what they think I am."

The old man set the tray on the floor, and Logan knew it would be ridiculously easy to overpower him. Yet something—instinct or curiosity—made him probe his visitor's mind instead of attacking him. He found no deception.

"Brother Perrin sent me to borrow a book. If that's not enough to make you trust me, the young female is going to have the juice squeezed out of her like an overripe kangoo fruit."

"Perrin sent you?"

"I volunteered."

"Who are you?"

"Brother Turnaby. You've seen me a hundred times." He dropped his hood, revealing a long, weathered face that drooped on one side, his mouth hanging slack on the side he no longer controlled.

"When were you declared mad?"

"Just before you left on your mission with that black-hearted cur. Warmond suspected I knew something, so he had the Master of the Psyche certify me crazy. Thought no one would listen to me—but there are more of us than he knows."

"I have to stop the execution!"

"You'll have your chance, if that's what you decide to do when you've heard me out." The old man drew a bundle from an inner carrying pouch of his robe. "Breeches and a shirt. Put them on."

"Why are you doing this?"

"Warmond has to be stopped. All the babies who allegedly died—I've heard echoes of infants wailing where no crying should be. He's keeping them."

Logan stood stark naked, too stunned to continue dressing.

"Imagine what a wicked man could do with an army of young men wholly dependent on him, raised by him in some secret place," Brother Turnaby speculated.

"Does Perrin believe this too?"

"He wants proof. Only you can get it."

"How could Warmond get away with stealing babes? The Youngers—"

"They're helpless. We believe those who aren't too terrified to serve his purposes are rendered susceptible to suggestions by a hypnotic drug. They repeat his lies and think they're telling the truth."

"Brother Turnaby, do you have any idea where he keeps these children?" Logan hastily pulled on

214

the shirt, ready to leave the instant he heard the old brother's whole theory.

"A place that's close but difficult to find. I've seen him return with black crud on his boots, foul petrolia that's too unstable to use for fuel."

"The Marsh of Misery? Tell me quickly."

"No one could live there. Too many volcanic spews, too many fissures, ground too unstable. But beyond the Flaming Sea, the ground is solid and fertile—ideal for a secret retreat. I haven't ventured that far, but I believe he takes the babes there. The distant cries I heard could have been babes Warmond was smuggling out."

"How can Warmond return to the Citadral so quickly if he spirits them across that treacherous sea?"

"He must use a secret route, but he's too quick for the likes of me to follow."

"Why tell me now?"

"I told Perrin first. I'm an old man shuffling along like a defective. I had to speak to someone before it's too late—before Warmond's plan is the undoing of the Order. Brother Perrin said you were our best hope."

"What do you know about the female's nephew?"

"He arrived here alive. I don't sleep well—and when a man is condemned to wear this accursed madman's robe, he becomes all-but-invisible to most of our brothers. I see and hear things, and no one notes my comings and goings. Without intending to, Warmond helped in my quest to discover the truth when he had me pronounced insane."

Acutely aware of each passing moment, Logan had to ask one more question.

"Where are they keeping the woman?"

"She was in the shed where sweetgruss is stored. I don't know if she's still there, but you have several hours before they prepare her for execution."

"Thank you, Brother Turnaby." Logan started to leave, but the old man's trembling hand restrained him.

"The Grand Elder himself has the only key to the Circle of Judgment, so you can't go up that way. Monitors are stationed on every level of the stairs between here and the surface."

"I have no choice. We'll see if my training is enough to overcome them."

"With six or even ten, you might have a chance but there's an army of monitors between you and the female. For the sake of the Order, leave the Citadral without her."

"My honor doesn't allow it."

The old Zealote sighed in resignation. "Perrin warned me you'd be stubborn on this point, but our brotherhood desperately needs you. Take my robe. Speak to no one and shuffle like an old cripple. Maybe you can reach the female and leave the Citadral before anyone penetrates your disguise."

"I can't leave you here in my place."

"It is my decision."

"You'll be ostracized—or worse. I can't accept your sacrifice."

"I'm an ancient, Brother Logan. Pain is my constant companion and infirmity is my master.

Let me vindicate my continued existence by giving the tattered remnants of my body for the sake of the Order. Don't deprive me of this opportunity to enrich my spirit."

"You leave me no choice."

"Save me the struggle of trying to remove my robe with this dead arm. Take it from me."

"Let it appear I overcame you."

"No, my brother."

"I'm sorry I probed your mind."

"I allowed it. Warmond isn't the only Zealote to master the mind shield. No one will learn your plans from me."

Logan put on the worn robe with its bizarre patches, thankful it concealed his riding garb. When Brother Turnaby insisted he use his sandals too, Logan did so without wasting time to argue. The monitors had taken everything but the penance garb from him, and bare feet, even on a madman, might attract attention.

"Thank you, Brother Turnaby." Logan embraced the ancient brother, who was already trembling from the cold in a ragged old under-robe, and tenderly slipped the penance garment over his head, conscience-stricken because he knew it wouldn't alleviate the old man's suffering.

"I haven't been so pleased with myself in more full-cycles than I care to remember. Only swear to me you won't give up your quest until you find where Warmond hides those missing summoned lads."

"I so swear."

"Take the tray."

"You'll need food."

"Only leave the pitcher of water. I've little appetite for prisoner's fare."

Pulling the hood low over his face, Logan shuffled away, trying to perfect his gait before a monitor saw him. He found the narrow, winding staircase carved in solid rock and tried not to think of Brother Turnaby's fate.

He passed the first monitor without attracting even a flicker of interest. With every step he took, he had to remind himself to shuffle slowly, not to dash from level to level as he so desperately wanted to. If Brother Turnaby was wrong about the time . . . If Warmond found a way to advance the hour of Calla's death . . .

The monitor on the next level stopped him, but only long enough to snatch a wedge of uneaten protein-solid from the tray to appease his own hunger.

"I see the Master of Defense has no appetite," he mocked.

There was a torch burning on every level, but the stairways were like dark wells, the walls damp and cold. Logan couldn't believe how deep the confinement chamber was. After each flight, he expected to regain the surface, and each time he was disappointed. After he reached a more heavily guarded corridor four-times-four levels from the cell where he'd left Brother Turnaby, he finally saw a square opening in the wall. The sky was a vile gray, so close to full darkness that Logan had to exert his fullest measure of self-control not to hurl the tray at a pair of monitors leaning idly

218

against the wall and absorbed in conversation by the exit.

He shuffled past them and thanked the Great Power that not even the door of the Tower of Penance had a lock.

The Citadral grounds were teeming with restless brothers, but no apprentices could be seen. No doubt they'd been ordered to their quarters and were frantically trying to find hidey-holes with windows to catch a glimpse of the execution. Logan felt sick at the thought of such a brutal death for Calla, but at least Brother Turnaby had been right about a madman's invisibility. Zealotes wandering among the gardens paid no attention to him.

Every spire was illuminated as though it were a night for sacred rituals. The needle-like edifices rose toward the sky with a golden glow, and Logan's throat ached with regret because he no longer felt part of the Order's high calling. He was a fugitive from punishment, dishonoring himself and the Grand Elder who had arranged the most lenient possible punishment for his crime.

He didn't have time for regrets or self-pity. Still remembering to shuffle, although the slow gait was maddening, he went to the storage shed Brother Turnaby had mentioned.

He approached cautiously, but there were no monitors on guard. The door swung open when he touched it, and he groaned aloud in disappointment. Calla wasn't there.

She had to be in a place where members of the Order couldn't be contaminated by her female essence. He checked several outbuildings, too pressured by time to walk at Brother Turnaby's pace. There was no sign of the woman.

The laundry was deserted, and so were the structures where meat was smoked and bread was baked. The three moons taunted him as he continued his search, but dark clouds were moving across the sky, threatening to block their light. The Master of Monitors would give the signal to begin the execution. Would he begin earlier if clouds blackened the sky?

Running now, his breathing labored from anxiety, he saw a lone figure walking along a path among the deserted outbuildings. He followed, recognizing the solitary walker as one of the Youngers in training to be a monitor. Logan's blood ran cold when he saw what the Zealote was carrying: a huge coil of rope, the heavy kind used to secure large animals.

The Younger was delivering the death rope.

Logan followed, trying not to direct his anger at the young man who was only doing his duty.

Falling back into the shadows, Logan saw him speak to a pair of monitors posted by the door to the outbuilding where animals were brought for slaughter. Sickened by the grim irony of confining Calla in such a place, Logan watched until the Younger left.

One of the monitors picked up the rope and went into the slaughter shed, whether to taunt Calla with the instrument of her death or to begin binding her, Logan didn't know.

Still carrying the tray, he hurried toward the remaining monitor.

Calla was numb, as though a mind-dulling drug had taken possession of her, but all she had to do was allow a single thought of Logan to penetrate that protective fog, and she would start crying again. Her life meant nothing without him, and now they would never know the sweet ecstasy of belonging to each other. She regretted this more than the loss of her life force, but at least Logan would retain his place in the Order. In time, perhaps a full-cycle or maybe only a few moon-cycles, he would forget her. That was her cruelest punishment.

The shed reeked of old blood, a nauseous scent of death that not even zealous cleaning could completely eradicate. The detestable Zealotes were denying her even the clean, homey perfume of sweetgruss in her last moments.

The door opened, and she dully noted the arrival of a dark figure. When he lit a lantern, she saw a short, muscular Zealote, his hood thrown back to reveal a bland face distinguished only by thick, meaty lips. She saw the rope coiled over his arm and hoped she wouldn't vomit in fear.

"Thought you'd like a look at this." He lifted the heavy coil off his arm and unwound enough to send one end dancing in her direction.

The rope slapped against the hem of her cloak, and she shivered at the threat in his gesture.

"Won't be long now. I'm the one who strips you naked and holds one end while Brother Darius coils

221

the other around you. We were chosen by lot."

"Congratulations." She hated this swaggering Zealote, but she wouldn't allow herself to be bullied by him. "Won't you be contaminated?"

"Well worth a bit of penance," he said. "I could help you, you know."

"Help me escape from your crazy cult?"

"Cheeky female." He dropped the rope and stepped close, touching her face with a calloused finger. "You won't be so free with words when you're wrapped in number six rope."

"Why are Zealotes afraid of women?"

"No fear about it," he said angrily. "Just no use for you. You shouldn't make me angry. I meant it about helping you. You'll have an easier death if I strangle you before we put on the rope. Of course, it's a risk for me. I'd have to be rewarded."

"How?" She loathed this tormentor, but his offer was tempting: a quick death without the humiliation.

"There's only one thing I want . . . the thing women do with men. My only chance ever."

She looked into his face and knew she couldn't buy an easy death that way.

"Touch me and every Zealote in the Citadral will hear me screaming!"

The door banged inward; she opened her mouth to scream, but nothing came out.

There was no struggle. The Zealote in the peculiar robe moved so quickly her tormentor didn't have a chance to react. In an instant he was sprawled out on the bloodstained ground, and she was in Logan's arms.

*   *   *

He reached for her instinctively, a gesture of reassurance that instantly became much more. Part of him had been dead, and now he was wholly alive again. If he hadn't found her . . .

"I thought I'd never see you again," she whispered, putting her arms around his shoulders, hardly able to believe he was solid flesh, not an apparition conjured by her terror.

"I've immobilized your guards, but they'll regain consciousness in about the time it takes an equest to circle the Citadral four times." He stepped away and stripped off the monitor's robe. "Wear this over your cloak. There are brothers everywhere on the grounds. The dullest of them will give the alarm if he sees violet fabric."

"They gave you leniency—you can't be caught with me."

"Hush," he gently warned. "First we need mounts. Without the fastest equests in the Citadral, we're doomed."

"The gate—"

"Closed, and no two pairs of arms can open it. But an equest and enough strong rope can. I'll take this."

He picked up the loathsome coil of rope and slung it over his shoulder.

"Follow at least two—no, four—paces behind me. No one walks with a madman."

"Madman?"

"Later!"

He stepped out, grateful now for the roiling clouds that plunged the night sky into total darkness. He walked as fast as Brother Turnaby possibly could, wishing he dared look over his shoulder to be sure Calla was a safe distance away. Not daring to take a shortcut across the spacious gardens for fear of encountering curious brothers, he followed a well-trampled dirt path to the stables, pausing to hide the coil of rope where he could quickly locate it again.

Two magnificent beasts were hobbled in the paddock beside the largest of the stables, and Logan knew they'd been chosen for their exceptional strength to carry out Calla's sentence of death. Zealotes were everywhere, as agitated as cuttlebees when their nest was raided. Logan changed course, using the distraction of the equests to shuffle behind the structure that housed them. Hoping he was safely out of sight, he cautiously turned to see if Calla was still following.

She was gone.

Frantic, he backtracked, forced to limp past clusters of Zealotes all around the paddock and the broad open entrance to the stable. A few of the hooded figures carried torches, but there wasn't enough light to spot Calla in the crowd.

He slowly made his way into the stable, grateful that no one paid any attention to a madman with patches on his robe.

The Citadral had the largest stable of equests on the planet housed in a long row of similar outbuildings. Tonight only two of the beasts interested the onlookers. The restless animals still confined in their stalls were unattended except for one dark figure leading a black mount toward Logan as he entered the building.

"The beasts are in a frenzy—they sense something's afoot. I've managed to calm this one. Speak gently and you can saddle it."

"Calla!" Logan was so astonished he said her name aloud, then quickly recovered his wits and looked around to be sure they were alone.

"I'll get another mount."

He remembered her gift with equests and didn't delay her with warnings to be careful. He recognized her cleverness in walking openly into the stable, but leaving it was another matter. No Zealote left the Citadral at night, so there was no legitimate reason to requisition an equest unless . . .

"This time follow close!" he ordered, stripping off his robe and turning it wrong-side-out to hide the patches. When he was ready, he rode boldly to the exit.

"Equests for the Master of Apprentices and the Master of Monitors to view the execution!" He shouted to be sure as many Zealotes as possible heard his excuse for taking the animals.

The beasts were required by law to follow the pathway along the wall. Logan forced his mount to move at a slow, measured pace, chafing because they were so far from the gate. When would Calla's guards regain consciousness? Had Brother Turnaby's switch been discovered?

He stopped once to retrieve the hidden rope, but no one challenged him.

The murky darkness swallowed them up after they left the confusion in the stable area, and

225

Logan was beginning to believe they could escape. His relief was cut short by a sudden confused babble coming from behind them.

"There they are!"

Warmond's voice rang out, and thundering hooves made the earth tremble.

Logan raced his equest toward the gate knowing Calla could keep pace, but in his heart he lost all hope. Time was against them. Not even an equest could pull open the gate before Warmond and his band of followers overtook them.

Just then the turbulent wind swept one moon free of clouds, and Logan saw the gate moving as though by giant invisible hands.

His elation lasted only an instant; then he saw his benefactors: Perrin and a host of gray-clad lads.

Before Logan reached the opening, the lads had scattered, racing for safety in their own quarters, but Perrin stood, urging him on with frantically waving arms.

"Come with me!" Logan shouted, slowing the equest so Perrin could mount behind him.

"It's not my destiny!"

"Perrin—"

"No! Just go!"

The hoodless giant lashed out with his rope, striking the hindquarters of Logan's equest, making it plunge wildly into the night beyond the Citadral walls. Logan heard Calla's beast pounding behind him, then the one sound that could win their freedom: the gate clanging shut.

He looked back over his shoulder but the thick wooden barrier blocked out the waving torches and the big man who had single-handedly pushed shut the massive portal and delayed their pursuers.

They were free, but at a terrible price. Perrin, his peer-brother, his companion since boyhood, would be ostracized for life for this deed. There wouldn't be any leniency for the Zealote who thwarted Warmond's pursuit of the fugitives.

Calla heard a piercing sound and recognized it as the mournful keening of a grief-stricken soul. Logan was expressing his pain in the Zealote way, crying out in agony because his friend had sacrificed himself.

The spires of the Citadral, illuminated by a power generator so precious it was used only to provide ritualistic glory, allowed Calla to find Galaba. Without the tallest spire to guide her onto the right path, she would have had to abandon her equest. No matter what happened to her, she didn't want the Zealotes to gain possession of the finest mare her father's freehold had ever seen.

While Calla transferred her saddlebags and stroked the beast's long, silky hair to calm it, Logan prodded her mount from the Zealote stables into running on a trail toward the village of Ennora. Their pursuers wouldn't be misled for long, but for the moment the ruse worked. They heard a large band of pursuers chase after the riderless equest. Moving with utmost stealth, they followed a little-used trail in the opposite direction.

She didn't ask questions or make suggestions. Logan took her silence for what it was: her way of letting him mourn for the friend and the life he was abandoning.

They rode all night without leaving the broad, fertile valley the Zealotes called their own. At dawn they rested the equests in a sheltered glen, taking advantage of a narrow, crystal-clear stream to fill the one water bladder left with Calla's saddlebag on Galaba's back.

"I want to see you safely returned to your own people," Logan said, at last breaking his long silence.

"No. I can't go back and tell them Fane is dead."

"You may not have to. Brother Turnaby, the ancient who gave me this robe," he plucked at it sorrowfully, "believes all the lost children are alive, not dead, stolen by Warmond for some purpose of his own."

"I knew Fane couldn't be dead!"

"He could be. Brother Turnaby might have imagined hearing a babe's cry—he was declared insane by the Master of the Psyche. That's why he wore this atrocious robe."

"Do you believe him?"

"Enough to go myself to confirm his story for the sake of the Order."

"Even now you're thinking of the Order?"

"The Zealotes are my brothers. There are many who would never turn against me."

"Where is Brother Turnaby? What else did he say?"

"He suggested a place where the babes might be. I accept that he believed what he told me; he took my place in a vile cell deep below ground so I could be free to learn the truth."

"Tell me where this place is."

"No." He smiled ruefully. "I won't have another ruined life on my conscience. I'll find a place where you can hide until I return with your nephew or news of his fate."

"No! I'm coming with you."

"I'm still a Zealote, Calla. I can't travel with a female."

"I'll hide whenever people are near. I'll do just what you say!"

"How can I believe your word? You pretended to be intoxicated at Grunhild's cot so you could follow me."

"You gave me no other choice."

"What of your promise not to enter the Citadral?"

"I only promised not to enter with you. It was never my intention to endanger you in my search. Why didn't you let them kill me?"

"The law of the Order forbids taking a human life. Most Zealotes believe females are exempted. I don't."

"That's a cold, unfeeling answer."

"It's the only one I can give," he said, miserably aware he understood very little of the workings of a female mind. Instead of expressing gratitude, she seemed angry at him for saving her life. "Not too far from here, there's a wild region where early colonists from Earth once lived. There are many caves, much larger than cavas, for shelter. You can wait for me there. I'll bring the babe to you if I find him. You have my sacred vow."

"How will you know him?"

"Why—he's a babe." He shrugged and started to mount the huge black equest Calla had chosen as his mount.

"Are you sure he's the only infant Warmond stole on his last mission? There could be many babes about his age and size."

"Unlikely."

"Not impossible."

"You yourself would be sure of his identity, even though you saw him only as a red and squealing newborn?" he asked, annoyed that she was able to provoke him to sarcasm.

"Yes, I saw a small mark when I helped in his birthing."

"Tell me what it is."

She got onto Galaba's back. "You gave your sacred word to return Fane to me if he's still alive. You can't do that unless I go with you. You need me."

"Need you?" A fleeting smile made him look less haggard. "Need a female?"

"You've saved my life twice. I might be destined to repay my obligation to you."

"I don't understand the ways of females," he said, trying not to admit the truth to himself: her presence would make the distance seem short and the hazards inconsequential.

They traveled through the day, so exhausted they rode abreast to help each other stay awake.

"No one is following," Calla said when dusk overtook them in the high arid land of ancient cave dwellings. "The equests need rest. So do we."

"We have a safe lead on Warmond's band, but he won't give up. The Grand Elder will feel obligated to mount a search for us too. Be sure, they won't give up."

Logan knew that by now Brother Turnaby's trick had been discovered. If Warmond had returned to the Citadral to mount a full-scale search, he would know the ancient brother wasn't insane. He'd never accept his rantings and ravings as genuine. Logan shuddered, agonized by the suffering Brother Turnaby would have to endure to keep the search for stolen babes a secret.

"We'll rest," he agreed, "as soon as we see a suitable place."

Dusk fell, but they rode on over a flat, high plateau with scrubby growth and dull, gray rock outcroppings. In the distance jagged mountains were beginning to blend with the purple-black sky, and Logan knew it wasn't safe to travel unfamiliar territory in the dark.

A sudden burst of lightning split the sky, frightening the equests but also revealing an opening in a cliff just ahead. Logan led the way, but the distance was deceptive. Before they reached it, rain fell in icy torrents in this place where precipitation was usually scanty. Logan's inner voice warned that worse was yet to come before the long-awaited eclipse of Thurlow's moons.

Chapter Ten

Calla and Logan worked without words, securing the equests under a ledge because the tiny
doorway of the ruin wouldn't allow the beasts
to enter. Logan uprooted an armload of soggy
bushes known to be safe as animal feed, while
Calla found water streaming down a rock wall
and collected some.

A prickly, thick-branched bush was sheltered
from the rain beside the entrance, and Calla
carefully broke off enough partially dry fuel to
start a small fire with the flint she carried in
her saddlebag. Logan crawled in ahead of her,
wary of drop-offs or other hazards. The small
chamber seemed dry and sound.

"Let me light your sticks," he said, his hand
groping for hers in the dark to take the flint
from her.

She gasped aloud when his hard fingers explored her hand, then waited in anticipation until tiny sparks finally ignited the brush, bringing light and the promise of warmth.

Their shelter was more than a cave. Some ancient human had made it a home, and now it was a ruin with vague lines and symbols scratched into the soot-blackened walls. The fire smoked, but a circular opening in the rock ceiling provided ventilation in the confined space without loss of precious warmth.

"I've never heard of a place like this," Calla said, stretching out her hands to warm them over the flames.

"The first colonists used them for shelter while they worked the mines here. When the mines were depleted, the settlements were abandoned."

"What a hard life," Calla mused, her eyes searching the corners of the dwelling.

"Primitive, without any of the benefits of civilized society."

"Were there Zealotes then?" She was searching in her saddlebag.

"No." He stripped off the madman's sodden robe and laid it to dry at the back of the shelter.

"When I asked the guard—the one you found with me—why Zealotes hate women, he got angry."

"The question was improper." He took a small tin she handed him, but ate only a few of the salted seeds it contained before returning it to her.

"That's all we have left. Eat your share," she urged.

233

"No."

"My question wasn't as improper as the guard's offer. He was willing to strangle me, to give me an easy death. In exchange I had to . . . I had to do the thing women do with men."

"Did you agree?" He felt anger and, even more puzzling, a searing pain.

"I did not!"

"He told you a falsehood," Logan said, more to himself than her. "No Zealote would dare take a life, but it's rare when any member of the Order deliberately lies."

"He was only trying to use me?"

"I fear so."

First Warmond's treachery, and now a lecherous trick by a monitor. Logan clenched his jaws in fury, heartsick at the corruption seeping into the brotherhood.

"I still would like to know," Calla said, inching as close to the fire as possible without singeing the Zealote robe she still wore over her cloak. "Why do Zealotes hate women?"

Logan was quiet for a long moment, but at last he reluctantly answered. "Perhaps you've earned the right to know. You nearly lost your life because of the alienation between Zealotes and females."

He removed the black band still holding his hair in place and let wet, rain-darkened strands fall forward over his face. Calla understood his hesitation; he was searching for the right words.

"As you can see, life was hard for the first colonists. Earth sent them to mine the ore, but they brought very little machinery with them. The cost was prohibitive. The work was punishingly hard—but at least the mines here didn't have the poisonous gas that plagues the newer, richer tunnels. The first generation of settlers was dedicated to the mission of supplying Earth with a new power source in order to save that crowded, depleted planet. But the original colonists died off, and their offspring lost their sense of purpose. Sixty-six full-cycles is a long time to wait for the meager goods Earth sends in exchange for ore."

"They continued to live in places like this?" Calla glanced around the dark-walled cave, wrinkling her nose in distaste. It was so cramped Logan could stand upright only in the very center.

"Yes. The men spent much of their time underground while the women raised crops and managed as best they could to care for children and provide food. There was no culture as we know it: no schools, no villages, no centers of worship. The people turned away from the Great Power and from Earth's moral codes. They became a generation of savages, with some even worshiping the Power of Darkness and practicing human sacrifice of children."

"Why blame women?"

"Look at these walls." He took an unlit branch and made a torch of it, holding it close to some scratches in the soot.

Calla leaned forward, then quickly turned her eyes back to the fire. She'd never seen such things. The torch had illuminated crude line drawings of men with fantastically enlarged sex organs pleasuring themselves with female figures in bizarre positions.

"They called it free love," Logan said, too uncomfortable to look into her face. He dropped the torch into the fire and sat on his heels, staring moodily at the opening. "It was a time of anarchy. Men refused to work and abandoned their families in quest of sexual gratification. Women lured their mates' friends and brothers into their arms. The whole society was maddened by lust, insatiable for gratification. All stable systems collapsed; our race was threatened with extinction on this planet."

"And women were to blame?"

"No more than men, but at the time separation of the sexes seemed the only salvation. Our first Grand Elder found a few zealous men who wanted to save human life on Thurlow, but only those totally committed to high principles were accepted as members of the Order."

"But why hate women?" She yawned, so fatigued she was ready to drop but still driven to know the reason for the Order's hostility to her gender.

"Women were shunned to make it easier for the brothers to live uncorrupted lives devoted to high ethics. Hatred is a corruption of this."

He wanted to sing the praises of the Zealotes, to tell her how the brothers had labored to restore order and establish a workable system, relinquishing most of their political power when their goals were realized. He wanted her to understand, but he was too disillusioned, too weary, to go on. He didn't have pat answers for all the questions she was sure to ask.

He also didn't know where this thing called love fitted into the philosophies he had studied so diligently at the Citadral.

"You're soaking wet," he said. "Why not dry your robe beside mine?"

Her body was chafed wherever her cloak had rubbed against tender flesh, and she longed to change into the breeches and shirt still stuffed into her saddlebags. As for the Zealote robe she still wore over her cloak, she loathed the smell of it, the feel of it, the way it reminded her of its owner.

"I won't wear this robe anymore. I'll consign it to the fire."

"No—at least keep it in case you need to pose as a Zealote again."

She was so weary his voice seemed to come from a great distance. Sinking down, she pillowed her head on the saddlebag, too exhausted to do anything about her clothing.

"Calla, take off the wet robe before you sleep."

She moaned but made no move to comply.

"At least dry the Zealote robe," he urged.

He crawled over to her, afraid she'd become ill again if she slept in sodden garments. Awkwardly, over her sleepy protests, he lifted the black robe over her head and unfastened the catches on the violet cloak that had incriminated him.

Stunned as though by a blow to the head, he dropped his hands to his sides. He'd never imagined Calla was naked under the cloak. Her creamy flesh was incandescent in the glow from the fire, more beautiful than any work of art the Zealotes had created. Her eyes flickered, then stayed open, but she seemed more confused than embarrassed.

"I wouldn't wear the horrible brown sack they gave me—"

"No." He was saying no to himself, trying to deny himself the incomparable pleasure of feasting his eyes on feminine perfection.

She groped for the edge of her cloak, but her fingers were stiff. Fumbling for a fastener, she succeeded only in covering one breast with her hand.

His rational mind knew her gesture was innocent, but the sight of that slender hand fondling her luscious, ripe breast was the first truly erotic sight his eyes had ever seen. Dizzy, faint with longing, he felt desire at a level so deep, so primitive and compelling, that he expected to die if he couldn't satisfy the demands of his flesh.

"Calla—" His voice came from somewhere deep inside himself.

"I—" She couldn't find words to express the way love erupted within her at the sight of his face softened by passion.

He extended his hand, four fingers and a thumb that didn't seem to belong to him, and gently, tentatively touched the curve of her hip. He'd never patted a woman's soft bottom, never even rested his chin on the fuzzy head of a newborn, but now he realized how great his sensory deprivation had been.

Slowly, so the great joy of caressing her wouldn't annihilate him, he moved his hand to the delicate depression of her navel, over her slender waist until he held the weight of one breast in his hand. She cupped the other, lifting it and offering a rosy-brown nipple like a goddess making a sacrifice.

He was on the edge of a precipice, torn between the safety he'd always known and a reckless plunge into the unknown. Once over the edge, he could never go back to familiar, solid ground.

The flames were burning low; their fuel would soon be exhausted, but Logan felt a fire like the sun itself burning within him. Calla's face was the moon Amoura, glowing, enticing, eternal. Her breasts were Primus and Secondus, mysterious surfaces to be worshiped by the credulous and explored by the brave.

"Logan," she gasped, "it's not wrong."

Light flickered on the low ceiling of the cave; then all Calla could see was Logan's face hovering over hers, moving closer until the strong, hard planes were blurred by tears of joy in her eyes. When his lips met hers, she fought to contain her happiness, overwhelmed by his slow, shattering kisses. He nibbled her lower lip, drawing it between his teeth and sucking until she thought she'd explode with pleasure.

Both of his hands were on her breasts, his fingertips lightly pinching her nipples into stone-hard nubs. Unresisting, sinking deeper and deeper into a well of pure passion, Calla reached up from the folds of the cloak that cushioned her body from the hard dirt floor and touched the face that had first come to her in dreams. She loved the lean hollows of his cheeks, the power in the sweep of his jaw, the soft flicker of his lashes on her fingertips, even the scratchy bristles of his beard. Pulling his head to her breast, she lost her fingers in his soft locks.

Abandoning her mouth was cruel separation; tasting her breast was so arousing it stabbed his groin like iron pincers.

He felt her fingers sliding down the length of his back, tickling the end of his spine, digging into buttocks encased in leather breeches.

He didn't think—couldn't think—but he rose to his feet and stripped off his clothing, almost tossing one boot into the burning embers in his haste to return to her.

She was mesmerized by the sight of his body: powerful shoulders so graceful her eyes teared, a broad chest with male nipples like enchanting dark buttons, lean waist and hips—and when he turned to discard his breeches—tight, round buttocks endearing in contrast to the rest of his hard, strong, masculine form.

He knelt over her, and she tentatively touched the swollen organ she was too shy to look at directly.

His fire was being stoked by a lightning bolt; she caressed him and the intensity of his need became unbearable. He wanted everything her touch promised, but he doubted his ability to endure another moment of such burning ecstasy.

Their makeshift kindling had burned so low he saw her only as a pale outline, but the beauty of her form was engraved on his brain. He sought, then found, her downy soft mound and moist, secretive slit.

Calla wanted to lose herself in Logan's passion, become one with him, but too many brutal matings with an unwanted husband had left their mark. She sighed, willing and hopeful, but tense, and tried not to stiffen when he explored her with his finger.

Suddenly, without warning, he rolled her over as though she weighed no more than a bundle of sticks and lifted her hips.

"No!" she screamed, then sobbed, crying out again and again, "No, no, no!"

Logan stopped, more shocked than if her flesh had turned to white-hot metal. Had he misread her willingness? He felt like an unschooled fool, humiliated by lack of understanding.

"I just meant . . . I mean, not like that," Calla said more calmly, rolling onto her back and realizing she'd hurt him.

"I don't understand." He sat back on his heels, appalled by what he'd tried—and failed—to do.

"Not like an animal."

He couldn't have been more surprised. "What other way is there?"

"Logan!" She knew he was innocent, inexperienced. She would have given anything she possessed—even Galaba—to be virginal again for him, but she'd never imagined he didn't know how to . . .

He hung his head, still burning to penetrate her moist feminine stronghold, but caring much more that Calla think well of him.

"I'm sorry—"

"No, don't be. I didn't scream because of anything you did."

"Why, then?" He felt like a man sinking in a bog: desperate to save himself without the knowledge or means to do so.

"My husband—"

"You told me he's dead!"

"He is—but when he lived, there wasn't love between us. He wasn't—gentle."

"He hurt you, and you're afraid I'll do the same?"

Her eyes were swimming with tears. "I'm sorry—" She bit the back of her hand to smother her sobs.

"I'll sleep with the equests." He stood, glad that the fire was nearly dead so she couldn't see how devastated he was.

"No, I won't let you!" She jumped to her feet, putting herself between him and the opening.

"Calla—" The female mind confounded him! Did she think she could stop him with her slight female body?

Before he could lean down to grope for his clothing, she pressed her full length against him, locking her arms around his waist with more strength than he'd believed possible. Her breasts flattened against him, and her chin dug into his chest. She locked one leg around his limbs as though to trip him. Then her hand started to move.

Logan hardened against her, a warrior's club in search of a sheath, sliding between her thighs as she dug her fingers into the firm pads of flesh on his backside.

"Like this, as we stand?" His voice was hoarse with rekindled passion.

How could she teach him when she'd never experienced tender lovemaking? She tilted her head and parted her lips, knowing that only the feelings they had for each other could help them.

Kiss was the word for what they did, but Logan didn't need experience to know it was much, much more. He sampled her lips like a delicacy, nibbling, savoring, then demanding more. His tongue filled her mouth, and the rippling sensations that raced through him were as exciting as they were novel. The more he delighted in this sweet, slippery cavity, the more he wanted to be deep inside her secret cavern.

Something strange and wonderful was happening to her. She was blossoming, opening herself without doubt or hesitation. Her legs collapsed, more like the gentle folding of a fan than a fall, and she brought him with her to the welcoming spread of her cloak. Her hand taught him what words had failed to explain: the gentle way of mating.

His lips were everywhere: on the hollow of her throat, the crease of her elbow, the lobe of her ear. His tongue moistened her lids and bedeviled her navel, his teeth teased her nipples and clamped down on her knuckle. Her lips were jealous, wanting his mouth, possessively grasping his lips when he gave her the opportunity.

He didn't need to probe her mind to sense her intense pleasure—pleasure she delighted in giving and receiving. His thighs trembled and his groin throbbed; he was desperate for sweet release but still afraid his lack of expertise would turn her away.

How could he be so hard, and yet as soft as velvet? So forceful and still gentle? She couldn't circle his swollen member with her thumb and forefinger, but she served as his pilot, guiding him into her channel.

Did she surrender control or did he seize it? She wrapped her legs around his heaving buttocks, riding and being ridden. Her senses reeled and stars exploded against the low ceiling of the cave.

Faster now, carrying her with him, he released his lightning bolts, shuddering convulsively until the last of his strength drained away.

At first her tremors frightened her; then she felt him explode inside her, trembling in her arms until he collapsed beside her like a man who'd lost his life force.

He was lying on the cold floor of the cave, drenched in perspiration and so weak he couldn't lift his arm to brush a strand of hair from his eyes. He was drained, his passion a frenzied memory except for the trembling in his thighs. This was nothing like releasing his seed in a nocturnal emission, and he wasn't sure he was meant to survive the intensity of mating with such a wondrous creature.

"You'll freeze," her soft voice murmured near his ear.

Calla, sweet Calla. He found the strength to cradle her against him, then he slept.

She put her leg across his and her head in the crook of his arm, then pulled her cloak over both of them. Before she could close her own eyes, she realized he was asleep.

Earlier she'd been ready to drop from exhaustion; now she was wide awake, too conscious of Logan to surrender to sleep. Her mouth was swollen, but she'd never known such deep contentment.

What a crime duty was, when it meant mating with a shallow, unfeeling youth. Her exuberance faded, and she imagined what her future would hold if she went back to her father's freehold. How could she face the rest of her life without Logan? Not even in the afterglow of their lovemaking could she deceive herself. Logan had wanted—no, needed—to possess her, to know what it meant to be a male with a female, but in his heart he was committed to the Order. Even if they ostracized or killed him, he would be true to his oath. The Zealotes had made him one of them; all she could do was hope to save her father's grandson from such a tragic fate.

She wept inwardly, suppressing the burning tears that might disturb Logan's sleep. He was hers for a few more days. She would have to love him enough to last the rest of their lives.

The dreary gray light of dawn woke Logan and urged him to hurry on with his mission, but Calla's head was cradled on his chest, her cheek warm and soft against his skin.

He felt . . . he felt wonderful: stronger, younger, more determined than the weary shell of a man who had ridden to this place. He'd experienced euphoria before, but only after hours of ritualistic baths and body conditioning. Never as a spontaneous reaction to joy!

He smiled at the golden cascade of hair fanned out across his chest and moved closer to Calla, at this moment regretting every moment of his life not spent with her.

Then his euphoria faded. While he was exploring paradise with Calla, Perrin was in the hands of the angry Grand Elder—or even worse, Warmond. The fiery-haired giant would never betray Logan's mission, not until there was proof of Warmond's treason, but his interrogation would be horrendous. And what of Brother Turnaby? If he fell into Warmond's hands, he didn't have the strength to survive torture.

Calla stirred and pressed her knee against his groin, stirring memories and making him yearn to possess her again even before the day began.

"Love," he whispered, sensing that a black cloud was obscuring his newfound happiness.

Guilt, sharper than any he'd ever experienced, made him gently remove himself and crawl naked into the cold morning air outside the cave. He could now accept the mating of a man and a woman as natural, even good, but how could he let his mind be clouded by desire when his friends, the Order itself, cried out for his loyalty?

246

The view outside the cave was as grim as anything he'd ever seen: gray rocks, barren cliffs, depleted patches that had once been garden plots, and abandoned cave-homes. It was like his life: devoid of joy and promise.

He'd renounced penance, the cement that bound the brothers of the Order to its tenets. How ironical that he was facing a greater punishment than any devised by the Zealotes: numbering his days with Calla, constantly desiring her, knowing he would have to give her up to satisfy the demands of his honor.

Chapter Eleven

When Logan left her, Calla snuggled under her cloak, hoping for his quick return. Time dragged, and her impatience grew until she couldn't wait any longer. Shivering as the chill air assailed her bare hide, she crawled to the opening.

Was this a Zealote way of greeting dawn? Logan stood naked with his back to her, head slumped, arms outstretched, legs far apart and shadowed at the cleft by the badge of his gender. She wanted to run to him, meld her form to his, and create warmth between them where none existed apart.

His stillness made her hesitate. Was he communing with the Great Power or listening to his own inner voice? Either way, she couldn't intrude on his meditation, but she felt no shame in watching. The sight of him brought back the wonder of the night. Her nipples ached and hardened as she remembered his caresses; her groin pulsated and grew moist. When he finally turned toward her, she saw he was ready to resume their lovemaking.

"Get dressed quickly," he surprised her by calling out. "Then see to your equest. We have to be on our way."

"Do you think Warmond is close behind us?"

"Just hurry."

How like a man to give orders and expect her to obey without question! She fumed, but she was honest enough to admit it was disappointment, not resentment, that fueled her annoyance. She couldn't fault him for wanting to put distance between them and pursuit.

She dressed quickly in her crumpled shirt and breeches, stuffing the hateful Zealote robe into her saddlebag. When she left the cave, Logan was still standing as she'd first seen him.

"I thought you were in a rush," she said, not hiding her irritation.

"Yes," he agreed lamely, wishing he didn't have to pass her with his swollen organ betraying his weakness. "I'll dress now." He walked into the cave, relieved when she didn't follow him.

He'd forgotten his hunger for food until he started to dress. His stomach was concave, so empty it rumbled as he fastened the front of his shirt, and stuffing himself into tight leather breeches caused more discomfort. Was this also part of his punishment, to have his body constantly warring with the demands of his honor?

249

*   *   *

They rode without talking for many hours, finally stopping to take advantage of a water hole marked by a crumbling well wall. Calla was impatient with his long silence, needing as she did to talk about their coupling and the consequences. Did he think nothing had changed, that she could blindly follow him as she had before he tried to desert her at the midwife's cot? Was she afraid she'd make demands or try to come between him and his devotion to the Order? Finally she couldn't stand his silence any more.

"At least tell me where we're going," she said after he filled the water bladder.

"Yes, you should know. Brother Turnaby thinks Warmond has the stolen children at a retreat by the Flaming Sea."

"But we aren't going in that direction." She'd always enjoyed the study of geography and had a good grasp of the immense planet's surface, at least as much of it as humans had explored.

"We're detouring around the Marsh of Misery. Brother Turnaby thinks Warmond has a secret route to the Flaming Sea, but we can't risk traveling through that pestilent quagmire."

"Is there anything edible in this barren area?" Hunger was making her weak, and she hated feeling light-headed.

"A few small land creatures, but most wouldn't give us a bite apiece. Not worth the time to trap them. Drink your fill of water, and by nightfall we should reach Bordertown."

"What will we find there? I've heard places like that are dangerous."

In Luxley there were always rumors about outposts in barren areas, little villages where outlaws and even defectives could come and go without interference because it was too costly to keep government patrols in such desolate places.

"We'll be able to barter for supplies, I hope, and maybe get a little rest." His eyes were troubled, but he smiled reassurance. "You won't be in any danger with me."

Measuring their progress by the range of mountains they would have to cross, Calla thought their journey would go on for a moon-cycle, but Logan assured her this wasn't so. He always seemed to know the way, although he didn't have a map or a directional guide, so she set aside her fears for the moment. In any case, she preferred facing danger with Logan to being separated from him, but it wasn't courage that made her willing to stay by his side in any circumstances. Every moment with him was precious.

The sun remained hidden behind a thick cloud cover, but they didn't have to contend with rain or lightning. The wind plagued them, becoming tempestuous, whipping up dust that swirled on the ground like fog, sometimes forming small whirlwinds that blinded the equests and battered the riders. Logan pulled the cowl of the madman's robe, still reversed to hide the patches, over his head, and Calla tried to protect her face in the folds of her hood. They were able to continue riding, but the dust storms made it impossible to talk about the things Calla had on her mind.

Logan had never gone this way, but he'd heard of it from a monitor, a peer and friend from apprentice days, who had tracked—but not found—a runaway apprentice. To ease Calla's mind, he told her this but not in the words of his friend. The mountain pass Logan sought was marked by two peaks shaped like a woman's breasts. At the time Logan had thought the monitor's description was improper, but now he could see no other comparison would be as accurate. He described the peaks to Calla as cone-shaped; riding beside her, he was uncomfortable with anything that betrayed his constant thoughts of her seductive form; her sweet, giving body; her warm, sensual flesh.

He knew his lust would subside; his preoccupation with mating would disappear when he was busy with demanding tasks. It was his feeling for Calla that would torment him as long as he lived. Even now, forced to make another hazardous journey, she was serene and uncomplaining, ready to face whatever lay ahead without wavering in her quest to rescue her nephew. If she would sacrifice so much for a babe who wasn't even the fruit of her womb, what would she do for her own child? Or for a man she loved with all her heart?

They rationed water and suffered from thirst. The sand seeped under their clothing and into their hair, until finally even their mouths felt

252

gritty. Knowing there wouldn't be any moonlight to guide them after dark, Logan pushed the equests to the limit of their great stamina, not wanting Calla to spend a night in this sandblasted area without shelter.

The sky darkened, and Logan almost decided to settle for a makeshift shelter rather than risk overlooking the trail to Bordertown. He knew there was no other place to obtain supplies, and he wanted a coil of rope almost as much as he craved food. Even if he hadn't lost the death-rope at the gate, it would have been too heavy for Zealote defensive tactics. More than anything else, he had to find rations for Calla. It was also his secret hope to find a safe temporary haven for her while he hunted for Warmond's hideaway. He didn't have any fears for his own safety, but the prospect of taking Calla into Warmond's secret retreat, if it existed, terrified him.

The wind lessened in ferocity, and he could see a faint light not too far distant. They rode down a steep incline, then followed a dirt trail into a settlement that did nothing to ease Logan's fears on Calla's behalf. His journey with Warmond had taken him to many remote, shabby villages but never to a place as desolate and unsavory as Bordertown.

The roadway was only a wide, trampled trail; the buildings were hovels not fit to shelter beasts. No skilled laborer had touched these huts. Most resembled packing crates reinforced by odd bits of planking nailed every which way. They had one thing in common: instead of showing the silvery sheen of aged wood, they were bleached nearly white. The sandstorms that plagued the area scoured every stick of wood in sight and plastered the whole settlement with grit.

Only one structure was more than a story high, a blocky, three-level building with a faded sign: ALE HOUSE.

"Bring your saddlebag," Logan said. "I'm afraid we'll have to do some trading."

She dismounted and secured Galaba to a sagging rail, then tried to shake the grit from her person. How did sand get to the creases between her thighs and torso? Would she ever be able to wash all of it from her scalp? At the height of the sand flurries, her cloak had protected her no better than an umbrella in a tidal wave.

The street was deserted, so nothing prepared her for the noisy, milling crowd in the large common room of the Ale House.

"The dregs of society," Logan whispered. "Let me do the talking."

A filthy, bearded creature brushed against her, and she watched with horror—and pity—as he limped away on one leg and a crude peg made from an equest's thighbone. She took him for a maimed miner and saw many of his ilk in the room, some guzzling ale and others trying to cadge drinks from the fortunate few who had money to spare. She saw, too, a trio of fisher-captains with faces weathered to the texture of red leather. They were known to be too crotchety for human society on land when failing strength and health forced them quit the sea.

She'd seen rough men when she went to market with her father, but one occupant of the room frightened her more than all the rest: a defective sitting with its back against a wall, picking apart a heel of bread and sticking bits between its needle-sharp little teeth.

"Have you any coins?" Logan asked, hating to admit how ill-prepared he was for this mission. Zealotes didn't use money within the Citadral, and when they ventured out, only the leader of each band was issued government currency. Brother Turnaby didn't have access to Thurlow's money—he might not be aware of its existence.

Calla dug into her saddlebag and pulled out the few coins she hadn't left for Gustaf to use in looking after her sister.

"Two ale," Logan called out to a short man with yellow-green eyes and no brows who stood behind the bar, filling mugs from a spigot inserted in an ale barrel.

Elbowing a space for two, Logan put Calla in front of him to better spare her the jostling of filthy, drunken outlaws and derelicts.

"I don't want this," she hissed when Logan put a wooden mug in her hand.

"It's better to look like thirsty travelers," he whispered close to her ear.

"Should I have worn the Zealote robe?"

"No one here cares. Only a renegade Zealote would come here. They'll think I ran away to be with a female."

He picked up the mug and took a huge swig, downing it as she saw the men around her doing.

255

The dark liquid was cloudy and vile-smelling with none of the foamy bubbles she associated with ale. Cautiously she took a sip—and nearly gagged swallowing it.

"It's horrible!"

"But wet. I thought you had a taste for strong spirits."

"You know I threw out Grunhild's!"

"Then your penance is to drink this foul concoction," he ordered in mock seriousness.

"You think I can't?"

"Can you?" He took a long swig.

Stung by his teasing—but rather enjoying it too—she took another sip and felt slightly nauseous.

"The trick is to throw it down your throat too fast to taste it," he said.

She looked over her shoulder to gauge his sincerity and loved the wicked little smile on his face. Closing her eyes and trying not to smell it, she gulped down half the contents of the mug—and discovered he was right. The moistness of it eased her parched throat and did wonders for her thirst.

"Who's the head man, and where will I find him?" Logan asked the barman.

"That'd be Fatjack. Table in the corner."

"How will I know him?"

"He's got no meat on him. Weighed more than three men once, but the govs gave him twenty years for selling little girls. Guards made a game of sweating off his meat. Now food doesn't do right by him. Have a care with him, brother."

"You were a Zealote," Logan said.

256

"Yes, and I'd rather do twenty like Fatjack than go back."

"I'm not here to bring you back."

"Thought not." He leered at Calla.

Logan pushed his way through the crowd, making sure Calla followed close behind. The crowd thinned out away from the bar, and he could hear tinny music from some unseen source, perhaps an ancient device for rendering recorded tunes.

"How did you know he was a Zealote?" Calla whispered.

"I probed his mind."

He surveyed the long, dim room and nearly collided with a female giant. She was taller even than Logan and flaunted enormous breasts that jutted out of a low-cut black garment that fit like the skin of a meatstick.

Calla could smell rancid perfume and the sour musk of countless bodies clinging to the woman.

Apparently Calla's trips to market with her father had made her more worldly in some ways than Logan. He didn't seen to know how to get past the creature.

"I love Zealotes," the giantess purred, flicking a hank of coarse raven hair over her back, causing her breasts to jiggle in an incredible way. "You're all so pure, so moral—so horny!" She cackled at her own cleverness. "So come with me. Let me do for you."

"He's mine!" Calla said, putting herself between Logan and the servicer before he could respond to her lewd proposition.

"A shame." The whore ambled away, scratching her backside which was every bit as stupendous as her bosom.

"You've saved me this time," Logan said, turning his head to hide an amused smile.

He steered her toward the far end of the room where an assortment of derelict tables and benches were randomly scattered on the sticky, gritty floor.

"A feisty one ya got there, Zealote. Being as ya got no proper use fer a bitch, I'll take 'er off yer hands and give ya a good-nuf equest—a young'n with plenty a spirit left."

A man in scruffy miner's garb with a bushy gray beard and an empty eye socket seeping green pus eyed Calla with his one good eye.

"I think not," Logan said politely. "I have an equest and only this one female to tend it."

"Hahaha. A waste that is, but I heard ya Zealotes fancy beasts. Maybe ya'd consider a yotee, fur like silk and a donger like—"

"No, thank you," Logan said, putting his arm around Calla's shoulder and emphatically leading her away from her would-be buyer.

"I don't believe that!" She was more shaken than she wanted to admit.

"We won't be here long." He wasn't smiling now.

Logan didn't doubt his ability to protect Calla from a bestial slaver, but could he control his own rage? The thought of that vile creature getting his hands on her nearly stripped him of all restraint. She wasn't his possession, yet any threat to her welfare terrified him. How could he risk her life by taking her to Warmond's retreat, if it did in fact exist? Yet it was unthinkable to leave her in Bordertown among slavers and worse.

Logan saw an emaciated skeleton of a man sitting alone at a round corner table, piling what looked like picks for teeth into neat mounds.

"Don't go near that table, Zealote." The man who blocked his way looked like the twin of the servicer: huge, beefy, raven-haired, and wicked.

"May I speak to the proprietor?"

"Not now. He's doing his sums. Got to see if this place makes a profit. Very bad to disturb him now."

"When then?"

"Sit yourself at a table. Have a bit of grub. He'll send for you when he's ready."

Logan chose the only empty table against a wall, feeling more and more vulnerable without a coil of rope.

A lad wearing a filthy apron that may have once been white came to their table carrying a tray made of woven stalks.

"You sit there, Zealote, and you've got to buy." He snickered as though he couldn't imagine a member of the Order with coins to spend.

Logan had three left from Calla's small hoard, not nearly enough to supply them for the rest of their trek. Laying them on the table, he asked what they would buy.

"A loaf of bread, a bit of sauce to slop it in, and—if the cook's in a good mood—a few fingers of bungee juice."

Logan nodded assent, apologizing with his eyes for using her coins.

"Money is useless to me. All I want is to find Fane," she said to spare his pride but regretting she wouldn't have fare to hire a boat to take the babe home. Now that she saw what things cost away from her own people, she realized her coins were practically valueless.

Their meal came and both were relieved to find it edible. The bread was dark and heavy but served hot, and the sauce was thick and creamy with bits of meat. The bungee juice was fermented but still sweet and spicy.

"I think Fatjack can supply whatever we need," Logan said thoughtfully between bites. "But we're short of trade goods. I may have to offer my equest."

"No! I have other things to trade!" She opened her saddlebag and started piling the contents on the pitted tabletop. She didn't need to be told there was little in it to interest a convict alehouse proprietor.

Logan picked up the one small volume she'd brought along.

"The Wisdom of Erikandra."

"I would hate to part with that."

He remembered his own library of precious books and felt a sharp pang of loss. No matter what he found beyond the Flaming Sea, he couldn't see a way to return to his old life. He might never see a single one of his books again.

"Put it in the inner pocket of your cloak. It won't interest Fatjack."

"No, I'll give up anything I have if it will help find Fane."

As she spoke, a defective shuffled up to their table and looked at their food with doleful eyes. Calla shrank from him, then sternly took herself in hand. He was only a lad, and a hungry one if his hollow cheeks and protruding eyes were any indication. Trying not to wrinkle her nose at his strong odor, she broke off a generous piece of her bread and started to hand it to him, then dunked it in the sauce first.

"It's so much nicer with a bit of flavoring," she said kindly.

"Thank . . . you . . . for . . . kindness."

A burly man in a filthy apron barked at the defective and cuffed the side of his cone-shaped head, but he shuffled away biting on the moist bread.

"He spoke to me!" Calla could hardly believe it.

"Defectives have some intelligence, but he's the brightest I've come across. Maybe his parents brought him here rather than let him run off with a wild band and be reduced to savagery. He may have some skill that helps him survive."

"If he can talk, it means he can learn. He could be taught useful things. He could have a worthwhile life!"

"Yes." Logan shared her compassion for the lad, and he was stunned to realize that male and female minds could bond just as their bodies did. Each day with Calla brought new revelations, and he wondered what else he would learn from her.

The servicer's burly twin ambled over to their table and interrupted Logan's thoughts. "Fatjack said come over now."

Logan probed the man's mind and was disturbed by currents of malicious glee. Unlike the Zealotes in the Citadral, the outcasts here seemed unaware of being probed. Alone with Calla in this hostile place, Logan had no scruples about using his rare gift. He needed an edge to ensure their survival.

Fatjack watched with cold, reptilian eyes as Logan seated Calla and drew a chair close to her for himself. An emaciated skeleton of a man with an enormous head, he watched them with the wariness of the hunted.

"What do you want from me?" He ran his fingers through lank strands of iron-gray hair combed across his nearly bald pate in a futile attempt to conceal his gleaming skull. His shirt and breeches were rich, brown leather, new and well-sewn, but they hung slack on his body like the skin of a starving bovine.

Logan didn't underestimate him. "I need food to last at least a quarter-moon-cycle, a coil of new rope, blankets, three water bladders—"

"Things are costly here, Zealote." He spoke to Logan but watched Calla. "What do you have to trade?"

"This." Calla pushed her saddlebag across the table, the flap open to show him her father's trail gear and the wadded Zealote robe.

"Your woman speaks for you?"

Logan probed his mind and saw a filthy image of what Fatjack would do to Calla if she fell into his hands. A vein throbbed in Logan's forehead, and he wanted to throttle the man.

"Can we make a deal?" He dug his nails into his palms, knowing it would mean death for both of them if Fatjack gave the signal.

"The woman, what price for her?"

"She's priceless. She can't be bought."

"A Zealote with a hard dong. I never thought I'd see it." His laugh was oily, like rancid fat sizzling in a pan. "You don't bring much to the table."

"I'm not asking for much. The saddlebags are thick and heavy—worth more than a few supplies."

"Not to me. I don't care much for traveling." He laughed again, exposing scummy yellow teeth. "I'll take the ruddy equest."

"No!" Calla cried out, then hated her weakness in doing it.

Traveling with one equest would slow them, but Logan weighed this against setting off without food, adequate water—and especially a rope. "Take the black, and you have a deal."

"No, friend Zealote. I don't make blind deals. My man saw the Order's mark burned into that beast's haunch. If I try to sell it, I'll buy myself more trouble than I need. The ruddy beast or nothing."

"Out of the question. It's not my beast to trade."

"It's mine," Calla said, sorrowfully weighing Galaba's welfare against Fane's fate in the hands of Warmond. "The deal is done, but only if you give us a chamber for the night with a door that locks, a tub of hot steaming water, and soap that won't burn off a layer of skin."

"When you tire of her, Zealote, I'll give you a price that will make you the richest renegade who's ever left the Order. We don't see spirit like hers in the females who come this way. But for now, I accept the deal."

He snapped his fingers and a gaunt, stoop-shouldered woman hurried to the table. "My mate, Oldgirl. Tell her what you require." He pushed the saddlebags back to Logan with obvious contempt. "You'll find she does what I say—exactly what I say." He cracked his knuckles with a loud, disgusting sound.

So furious he was breathing hard, Logan followed Calla and the scrawny woman down a dark corridor to a staircase so narrow he had to turn his shoulders to climb the steps. He heard Calla reciting a list of their needs, the woman agreeing in a listless voice.

They passed the second-floor landing and continued upward to the topmost floor, then down a dark hall to a door at the far end.

Oldgirl entered first, striking a spark to light a wax stick. "Wait here," she said woodenly, leaving them alone.

The room was small with rough beams in the low ceiling, but not as dirty as the common room. There was a real bed with a faded covering. Dust on the table was undisturbed, suggesting that overnight lodgers were rare.

"At least there's a window," Logan mumbled, not understanding why he felt so piqued. Was it because Calla had taken control of the bartering? He knew it wasn't worthy of him to belittle her sacrifice, but something more than her equest was involved here. She had deflated his ego; he'd never felt let down in quite this way. How would he ever puzzle out all the complications of dealing with a woman?

"Yes." Calla stared at the square opening even though the heavily oiled paper that served in place of glass made it impossible to see anything in the dark of night. She didn't want Logan to see her tears and know how much she hated losing Galaba.

"We can leave now," he said. "Forget this infamous deal—it's nothing but a swindle. I won't have you sacrificing Galaba."

"No." Her voice was anguished but calm. "Your equest can carry both of us. Nothing matters except finding Fane."

"If Warmond really has a secret retreat."

"I can't go back without knowing."

Logan knew he couldn't either, but it galled him that he had to agree to her sacrifice.

"If you guess how many fingers I'm holding up," she said with forced gaiety, "you can have the first bath."

"No—" He almost said, "My love."

"I hate sand in my hair."

"While you bathe, I'll see about getting the supplies we've been promised. We should leave at earliest dawn."

Oldgirl returned in reasonable time, bringing with her the burly twin and two lads in soiled

265

aprons. Between them they half-filled the tub with
steaming water, leaving behind half a kettle more
of hot and a pitcher of cold.

"I want to get the supplies now," Logan said.

"As you wish," oldgirl said.

"Tinned food only. I'll choose it myself from
your stores."

He couldn't imagine this faded, spiritless woman
giving him any trouble, but he wouldn't breathe easily until Calla was safely away from Bordertown.

He started to follow Oldgirl but came back to
caution Calla.

"Lock the door. Open only if I rap twice, pause,
then rap once more."

She bolted the door, wishing he'd asked her to
go with him but sensing she'd done too much
already.

Sand! It was embedded in her scalp and sand-
wiched between her toes. She scrubbed with the
square cake of soap Oldgirl had left and rinsed
again and again until the bottom of the tub was
scratchy with grit.

She was just climbing out when Logan knocked,
urgently repeating his sequence of raps as she
wrapped a none-too-generous towel around her
torso.

"No one tried to bother you?" He stepped into
the room, rope coiled over his shoulder, full water
bladders around his neck, and a heavy woven sack
of foodstuffs in hand.

"No—and it feels wonderful to be free of sand."
She took the bag while he bolted the door. "I'm

sorry the water in the tub is sandy. Maybe Oldgirl will change it for you."

The light of a single wax stick glistened on her moist shoulders, and he grew even more uneasy as he worried about their precarious position.

"No, let them think we're sleeping. I don't trust Fatjack or any of his crowd. I made a point of saying we'll leave at dawn—but we'll be gone long before then."

He averted his eyes and laid his burden on the bed, recoiling the rope to carry it in the Zealote way.

"I feel guilty squandering the water, but there is enough warm left to rinse your hair."

"Calla, I haven't time."

"You're as uncomfortable as I was. Does the Order have some rule that says you can't bathe?"

"No." He laughed softly, entertained by her powers of persuasion.

"Then do me a kindness and scrub yourself, since we'll be sharing a mount."

"Put that way, how can I refuse?"

He went to the far side of the bed and stripped off his robe and boots, not at all sure how to go about taking a bath in Calla's presence.

"I can look away if you like, but it's so dark you could have two heads and I wouldn't notice."

Not quite that dark, he knew, well aware that the towel hugging her body ended where her legs began.

She pretended indifference and started packing foodstuffs in the saddlebag, but noisy splashes made him hard to ignore.

"Sand is glued to my scalp," he grumbled, trying to pretend he didn't see Calla bending over the bed to load their supplies.

"You aren't using enough soap."

She walked over and took the bar from his hand, working up a handful of suds and massaging them into his scalp with her fingertips.

Her fingers caressed the contours of his head, making lazy circles in and around his ears, loosening the tension in the back of his neck and sliding down to knead his shoulders. He sighed with pleasure, but her touch was nothing like that of the body conditioners he knew. She was untying all the knots in his back and doing it with a feathery touch that sent shivers down his spine.

"Lean forward and cover your eyes," she ordered. "I'll rinse you."

Using her fingers to search for stray grains of sand, she slowly trickled water over his head, rubbing and pouring until the last cool drop was gone. How strange to bathe a man—to minister to his needs as though he were hers to nurture and cherish. She squeezed as much water as she could from the thick sable mane that clung to his wet back, then used the edge of her hand to scrape drops from his forehead.

How much could one man stand? he wondered, capturing her busy little hand as she tangled her finger in his chest hairs.

"A towel—"

"A problem, master," she teased. "Oldgirl left us only one."

"Then you'll have to share."

He stood and climbed from the tub, stepping so close her towel absorbed some of the water dripping from his torso.

"The air will dry you." Her voice was a husky whisper, and he didn't need experience to hear the invitation in it.

"If I have to shiver, so must you." He reached behind her and pulled the damp towel away from her skin, letting it fall in a heap between their feet.

"Fatjack's helpers made lewd remarks while I was getting supplies."

"About a Zealote with a woman?" She trailed her fingers over his chest, making little whorls in the damp hair.

"Yes, but I don't feel the way they suggested."

"You don't want me?" She idly fiddled with the little hollow of his navel.

"I don't want to violate you. They spoke as though women exist only to pleasure men."

"To scrub their backs—" She flattened both palms on his torso, letting the tips of her fingers toy with his curly bush.

"She-devil," he whispered hoarsely, crushing her against him and squeezing her bottom hard enough to make her squirm. "You cloud my mind." He kissed her soundly, lifting her against him.

"Oh, Logan," she whispered so softly he could barely hear her. "In a kinder world we would be—"

"My mind is exploding with things I want to say to you, but I don't know the right words."

He crushed her mouth with his, probing deeply with his tongue, sucking the sweetness from the depths.

"Explode," she gasped, wrapping her arms his neck, locking her legs around his, opening herself in a way she'd never dreamed was possible.

Mindless with exertion, Logan surrendered to the rhythm of passion, swelling, thrusting, seeking deeper and deeper into mysteries he'd never even imagined. He'd never felt stronger, never used his powers more fully, never wanted anything as much as he wanted to carry Calla to unexplored heights.

Her arms slipped, her legs slid down, she was breathless from his mind-searing kisses. She wanted to laugh or cry or scream, and rippling sounds escaped from her soul in an inhuman torrent. She was out of control, plunging into a new world of sensation, riding a tidal wave that shook her very being. She was riding a lightning bolt, and when it struck, she went into convulsions of ecstasy.

Before she could go limp in his arms, he came with the force of a volcano, spurting, bubbling, boiling over in a mad rush, the release so draining and so exhilarating he trembled like a leaf in a tempest.

For a long time they stood, locked in each other's arms, wanting the moment never to end.

At last he carried her to the bed and gently folded the covering over her.

"Sleep a little while," he murmured.

"Lie beside me." She sounded like a sleepy little girl.

"I can't risk falling asleep. I don't think Fatjack intends to let us go in the morning."

He dressed, slowly and reluctantly, so drawn to the slender shape on the bed that separation from her seemed like a form of death. Standing over her because he was afraid the comfort of sitting would lull him to sleep, he watched her like a man enchanted by a celestial spirit.

A soft knock on the door made him instantly alert. He waited, in no hurry to open it for anyone, but the raps became more insistent.

"Who is it?" he asked, his mouth close to the door crack.

"Do . . . man."

The name was strange but he recognized the hesitant speech pattern of the young defective who had begged at their table. Logan opened the door and motioned the lad inside.

"Man . . . and . . . man, wear—" He pantomimed pulling a hood over his misshapen head. "Man . . . and . . . man. Ask—" He pointed urgently at Calla, who was awake but still lying flat.

"Two men in hoods asked about the woman?"

The defective nodded his head vigorously and pointed from Calla to Logan, from Logan to Calla.

"Doman, is that your name?"

More vigorous nodding.

"Are the men Zealotes like me?"

"Bad . . . Zea . . . lotes."

"You've paid for your bread a thousand times over, lad. Here, take what you want." Logan held out the full saddlebag, but the defective shook

271

his head. Calla sat, clutching the bedcovering over her nakedness, and watched without fear as the defective rubbed his nearly bald dome and pointed to her long, damp tangle of hair.

"Defectives must love hair," she said. "Quick, the knife I took from Grunhild is in my boot. Give it to me."

"You don't need a weapon against this lad."

"No, I only want to reward him."

She grabbed the knife from Logan and cut a long lock from the back of her head, handing it to the lad.

Doman parted his lips and whistled softly, then hid the hair under the rags he wore. "Fire . . . stick."

"Give it to him," Calla said, but Logan didn't need urging.

"Fat . . . jack . . . house . . . burn . . . fast."

"They'll catch you. It's too dangerous." Logan reached to take the wax stick from him.

"Think . . . Do . . . man . . . no-think . . . hide . . cave . . . bread . . . thank."

"Here, take these," Logan ordered, pressing a handful of tinned foods into the defective's free hand. "Thank you, and good fate."

Calla started pulling on her clothes before the door closed on the defective. "He'll get caught," she said, terrified for the lad's sake.

"I don't think so. He's right. They don't know about his intelligence."

They divided their supplies without talking, and Calla started to rush toward the door.

"Not that way. We could walk into Warmond's hands."

"Doman's going to start a fire. We can't wait."

"This way."

Logan smashed out the oiled paper covering the window and let down his coil of rope, securing it on a leg of the bed with a knot only Zealotes had mastered.

"I'll go first. Start down the instant I touch ground. You'll feel the rope go slack. Keep your feet against the wall for leverage."

Heart pounding, afraid she wouldn't be able to make herself follow, she watched in dread as his dark figure shimmied down the rope and became invisible in the darkness below.

Expecting to die, but preferring to do it in Logan's arms, she hung the saddlebag around her neck and crawled through the window opening.

Logan watched, his heart swelling with admiration as he saw her inching her way down the rope. Zealotes were trained from boyhood to climb and descend ropes; she overcame beginner's fear and managed to come down three stories in a time that was respectable for any apprentice.

The instant she touched ground, he whipped the rope hard against the building, hating to make noise but rewarded when the end of the rope tumbled to the ground. He'd traded Calla's equest for this weapon; he wasn't leaving it behind.

Neither mount was where they'd left them, but he hadn't expected Fatjack to make it easy for them to leave. Logan hoped to find the Zealotes' mounts in their place, but they'd been too cautious to leave them in sight in this town of outlaws and outcasts.

Motioning Calla to stay hidden at the rear of the building, Logan raced to a tiny outbuilding, the only one on the property. It was secured by a padlock the size of his fist, but Fatjack hadn't dared put both beasts in such a confined space. The black Zealote equest was hobbled behind the shed, and Logan wasted no time preparing it for flight.

He swept Calla up behind him and urged the beast forward. She looked behind, expecting the Zealote trackers to be on their trail.

"He did it!" she cried out. "The Ale House is on fire!"

Logan looked back to see a square of fiery orange at a main-floor window. Doman had ignited Fatjack's supply room. He prayed the defective had made his escape, then turned his full attention to the unfamiliar path ahead of them. They'd lost their pursuers once before; the Great Power willing, they'd do it again.

Chapter Twelve

The massive equest pounded through the night, driven to a frenzy by the crackling fire and the acrid smell of burning wood. Logan gave the beast its head, knowing blame for the arson would fall on him. When Fatjack recovered from the shock of seeing his alehouse go up in flames, he would look for the culprit, never suspecting a defective was capable of deliberately setting a blaze.

Fatjack's men might become a nuisance, but the two Zealotes worried Logan much more. Alone, he was a match for any four members of the Order, but the need to protect Calla made him more vulnerable.

By the time the equest slowed of its own accord, the fire was far behind them. A smoky orange haze tinged the sky, making Logan wonder if wind had spread the conflagration through the settlement. He shivered, imagining all the inhabitants of Bordertown swarming after them like a pack of rabid canines.

Calla relaxed her legs, tightly wrapped around him during their frenzied retreat, and loosened her grip on his waist. Both of them had clung for their lives, desperately trying to stay on their mount's back because an equest in full flight moved like a rock slide: violent and unstoppable.

Logan dropped to the ground, not surprised his legs were shaking and his backside felt whipped. The equest was lathered with foam that fell in great strings to the ground, and its sides heaved from the exertion. The frantic dash had accomplished one thing: They'd put enough distance between them and pursuit to risk a short rest.

As a precaution, Logan knelt and put his ear to the ground, but he didn't detect the earth-rumble that meant equests galloping in the vicinity.

He reached up so Calla could slide down through his arms, but when her feet touched ground, he didn't release her. He pressed his forehead to hers, their blood flows racing through throbbing veins, and felt as though danger had made them one. He experienced a new kind of desire, a need so deep and compelling he wanted to absorb her into his own being.

"I never want to ride an equest again," she murmured against his chest.

He laughed softly and gently caressed the saucy swell of her buttocks, playing mind games with himself to decide what part of her most delighted him.

"Ooooh." She moaned and cuddled closer, almost making him forget the danger behind them.

The equest snorted nervously, and Logan hurried to restrain it, knowing the beast might make another headlong dash—and leave them stranded in dire trouble.

"Mount!" he ordered.

Calla hurried to obey, not knowing his struggle to control the equest was a small battle compared to mastering his own desires. Urges that had been dormant throughout his manhood threatened to consume him. The danger, the escape, and the flight had made his blood quicken and his adrenaline flow, but having Calla in his arms for only a moment lit a raging fire that made the burning of the alehouse seem like a minor bonfire.

They continued their flight at a slower pace, anxious to let the equest recover its strength. They seemed to be creeping through black fog, seeing neither the trail ahead nor the dual peaks marking the pass to the Flaming Sea.

Logan knew Fatjack would expect him to head back toward civilization. The Flaming Sea was a nightmarish place even hardened criminals avoided, but Warmond and his followers probably suspected his destination. If poor Brother Turnaby had been forced to talk . . .

Logan's mood became grim as he worried about the brothers he'd left behind. His only chance of clearing Perrin was to prove Warmond was conspiring against the Order. That meant going

277

back to the Citadral, no matter what the cost to himself.

It meant leaving Calla.

Their way grew steeper as they followed a rough, narrow path around huge boulders and past rock walls. Logan stopped one more time to rest the equest and tie a rope loosely around Calla's waist so she could doze without fear of falling. He was bone-weary himself, but he put aside thoughts of sleep. All that mattered was putting distance between them and the Zealotes.

Finally the route became too steep to risk traveling in the dark, and Logan reluctantly reined in. He secured the equest and spread one of their thin blankets, really no more than a ground cloth, that Oldgirl had included in their bartered supplies. Tenderly, not wanting to wake her from an exhausted sleep, Logan lifted Calla from the mount and laid her on the blanket.

He stretched his arms and legs, then tried to meditate, but anxiety made it difficult to summon serene thoughts. When, in a short while, the first glimmer of dawn showed beyond the mountain, he sat to watch the sky lighten.

This was no normal dawn. A green-tinged haze broke through the murky darkness, and he knew it was a sign of the coming eclipse. Most men lived to see only one coming of the Earth vessel, and Logan was edgy about the arrival of space travelers. Earth was the Thurlowians' ancient home, but that planet's insatiable demand for hyronium was a cause of evil.

It was unlikely Logan or anyone he knew would see an Earther. The government used a great deal of stealth in offering hospitality to the few representatives from the ship who set foot on Thurlow. The story released by the Ministry for Earth Relations was that space travelers arrived in an exhausted condition and needed to recoup in absolute privacy. The Zealotes, who were skeptical about all the government conniving, generally believed the travelers were heavily guarded to keep their technology from falling into the hands of malcontents on Thurlow. A small army of determined men could take over the planet if they had the weapons and technology carried in a single spaceship.

Only the Zealotes had an organization strong enough to threaten the government, but their policy was coexistence: not challenging established procedures unless there was a conflict with their own interests.

Logan stood and paced, feeling as if he were on the verge of a startling revelation. Did Warmond's intentions extend far beyond the confines of the Order? If the Master of Apprentices did have a secret retreat, what would Logan find there? Was his evil plan connected in some way to Thurlow's rare triple lunar eclipse and the coming of the Earth vessel?

Calla cried out, caught in a netherworld between dreams and reality, wanting to awake but unable to break the chains of slumber.

"Calla, love," Logan whispered, rushing to her side and comforting her with his arms.

She whimpered in fear, and he gently kissed her cheeks, her eyelids, the corner of her mouth.

Night terrors dissipated, and Calla started returning his kisses, warm with gratitude at finding him so close when she needed him.

Slowly, to spare her the pain of separation, he disentangled himself, making meaningless sounds he'd never before uttered; coos and endearments as alien to him as the snorts of the equests. He wondered if a universal language existed to be used only in expressing feelings between male and female.

Knowing he'd never unravel the puzzle of Warmond's intentions while his thoughts were centered on Calla, he resolutely stood and insisted they quickly eat their fill and be on their way.

Oldgirl had begrudged him every tin he took, but he didn't trust any other food she brought from Fatjack's kitchen. The seeds, hardbread, and dried bovine sticks were uniformly salty, but by showing restraint, they made a decent meal and didn't short themselves on water.

They continued, able now to see the twin peaks overlooking the pass to their destination. As the elevation rose, the path became narrow and steep. Tall, thin-trunked trees with sharp, almost black needles cut off most of the green-tinged light that penetrated the cloud cover.

As the day wore on, they moved above the tree line and were forced to hug rock walls so the equest could maintain its footing on the narrow switchback trail. The way twisted and turned, sometimes doubling back almost parallel to the route they'd already covered.

Calla had chosen well when she picked the black equest from among the many fine animals in the Zealote stable, Logan thought with admiration, but even this powerful beast was tiring under the strain of carrying two riders uphill.

Suddenly the path narrowed even more, and the equest put one hoof forward into nothingness. Calla screamed, and Logan vaulted over the beast's head, using every ounce of strength he possessed to exercise control over their mount.

The beast was down on one knee, agitated but apparently unhurt. Logan guided it over the pitfall, trembling from the exertion until the equest and Calla were safe on a wider section of the trail.

Calla's heart was pounding in fear, but she was awed by Logan's quick reflexes and agility. She looked down, terrified by the sheer drop. He'd saved her from plummeting down a rock wall.

"I'll lead the beast for now," he said.

"I'll walk too."

"No, ride while you can. There's rougher terrain above us."

The going was treacherous. Every time the trail curved or narrowed, Logan was alert for drop-offs, and more than once rocks and other debris nearly blocked their way.

Their pace was excruciatingly slow, but Calla didn't tire of watching Logan, his shoulders broad and tense as he led upward.

"Have you ever wondered about your real family?" she asked, wishing she could know everything locked in his heart and mind.

"The Zealotes are my family."

"But your birth parents—"

"The Grand Elder has been like a father to me."

"I can't believe you've never been curious." She spoke with compassion, not reproach.

"When my birth mother died, she left instructions to her kin. They traveled a great distance and bribed a villager in Ennora to bring me a carpet made by her own hands. I value her gift, but she's only a shadow on my heart." He wanted to tell Calla how completely she filled the empty place that had always existed in his heart, but words again failed him.

"What will happen now that you've opposed the Grand Elder? Will the Order accept you back? What about your sentence of leniency?"

"Those decisions rest with the Grand Elder."

"Oh, Logan!" She slid from the equest's back, wanting to be closer to him. "There are other ways to live. The Zealotes could father their own young instead of breaking the hearts of young parents by robbing them of their healthy offspring. I worry my sister may never recover from the sorrow if I can't return Fane to her care."

"Calla—"

An inhuman scream pierced the air, and the equest bolted with a snort of terror, jerking away from the lead line and throwing Logan against the solid rock wall. Slow to maneuver at any time, the beast charged past the human, mindlessly hurling its great bulk forward. Dust billowed from the charging hooves, but this time there was no broad, flat trail to accommodate the animal's frenzy. The path narrowed sharply at the next curve, but the beast was unstoppable. Before its brain could register the hazard and slow the mad stampede, the equest plunged over a sheer drop-off, carried by its great weight to a plateau far below.

A dark shape dropped down from the cliff above them before Logan could focus on the danger. Their attacker was a midnight-black lepine, a sleek and powerful wild feline, able to take down and tear apart an equest four times its size. It moved toward Calla and swiped at her with one dagger-sharp claw, missing only because she recognized the enemy for what it was and automatically backed away.

Logan saw the vicious claw narrowly miss Calla's face and instinctively became the Master of Defense, sizing up his opponent and leaping forward. He threw himself at the back of the lepine, locking his arms around the creature's thick throat.

The path was wider here than it was below or above them, but Calla screamed in terror, sure the thrashing beast would throw Logan over the edge. Dazed and horrified, she saw the feline arch its back and try to throw off its attacker, slashing and biting as it strained to kill the man.

Her instincts served her well too; she found the knife secreted in her boot but didn't dare call out to get Logan's attention. If she distracted him, the crazed lepine might succeed in throwing him. Even if he didn't plunge to instant death, the contest would be over; Logan would be ripped to shreds by those vicious talons.

Too dizzy from shock to stand erect, she crawled on hands and knees toward Logan and the frenzied creature locked in mortal combat.

The lepine tore up dirt and unearthed rocks, sending a shower of debris sliding down the cliff. Logan willed his arms to exert even more pressure. His only hope was to break the beast's neck, but the lepine's loose hide was like shifting sand, thwarting his effort to apply a deathlock.

The beast rolled and grappled, straining to use its teeth for a deathblow, and Logan felt his own strength ebbing away. He could see Calla move closer, but a warning died in his throat when he saw a glint of metal in her hand.

"Throw it!" he shouted.

Calla used her last measure of resolve and sent the small weapon soaring through the air, willing it to land within reach of Logan's outstretched hand.

He reached for the knife, but in doing so he loosened his armhold. The lepine took instant advantage, throwing Logan to the ground, raking its claws down his shoulder.

The warm fluid of life ran down Logan's arm, but his hand connected with the handle of the knife. Drawing on his great reserve of strength, he plunged the weapon into the belly of the attacking beast.

The maddened lepine howled in pain and fury and made a death lunge at its enemy, mindlessly unhinging its lethal jaws for a killing stroke.

Logan rolled to the edge of the precipice, clawing at the ground with his nails, knowing if those vicious teeth raked his body, he would surrender his life force.

Logan was going to die! Calla saw the wounded lepine marshaling its remaining strength. She acted without thinking, grabbing a rock the size of her fist and throwing it toward the beast, not with any hope of killing it but expecting it to turn on her and spare Logan.

The lepine screamed like a man under torture, but it didn't turn on Calla. With a final unearthly screech, the beast leaped at its prey.

It was the moment Logan was waiting for. He rolled away from the edge. The lepine was too weak to stop its momentum. It went soaring down the sheer rock drop-off, its passage marked by dark blood on the dull gray ledge.

Calla stumbled toward Logan, collapsing in his outstretched arms. She heard sobs and didn't know they were hers. Their bodies entwined, their hearts beating wildly as one from fear and exertion.

"You saved me," she gasped.

"No, it's you who saved me."

"My stone didn't distract the lepine."

"Be sure that you did save me!" Pinpricks of light exploded behind his closed lids, but in his last thought before losing consciousness, he knew the prospect of losing Calla was more terrifying than death itself.

She was on the edge of panic, so afraid for Logan's sake she couldn't stop trembling. He was limp in her arms, his robe and shirt hanging in rags and wet with blood. Ripping the remnants away from his shoulder as best she could, she wadded the fragments of cloth into a crude pad and pressed it against the bloody wound. The bleeding gradually subsided, but there was nothing else she could do for him. Their water and supplies were at the bottom of the mountain, tangled up in the battered remains of the ill-fated equest. She couldn't help but believe Galaba would have stood courageously and fought the feline.

The sky was darkening, not normally as it did with the sinking of the sun, but ominously, the green tinge nightmarish on the steep precipice. The rain began slowly, cold drops dampening her bent head and trickling down her face. She pulled off her cloak to shelter Logan, but not before a sudden deluge pelted his face.

The cold rain restored his consciousness but made him wish he could stay lost in dark dreams. His head cleared, but the deep slash-marks on his shoulder were a burning agony. He turned his face to the rain and let the icy drops wash over his parched lips.

"Calla."

She tucked her cloak around his head, shivering herself but crooning words of comfort.

"Too much blood spilled. We have to move," he said.

She knew he was right. Lepines in the Out-country were known to run in packs. They couldn't risk staying so near the smell of fresh human blood. The rain might buy them time and wash away the smell by morning, but there could be other beasts close by already aroused by the carnage.

Logan struggled to his feet, revived by the cold rain and fearful for Calla's sake. They haggled over the use of her cloak, but not for long. After a few words, they huddled together under rain-stained fabric and wearily started on the upward trek.

The rain was short-lived, but it made the path more treacherous, the loose grit and rocks giving way under foot with alarming frequency. At last, when the night did overcome them, they found an illusion of shelter under an overhanging ledge.

They were both weary in a way that defied sleep. "I've never known a lone man to kill a wild feline," she said as they huddled under her cloak, greedy for the bit of heat their closeness gave them.

"Fear of losing you gave me strength greater than one man's," he softly admitted, gently patting her cold hand.

He was hiding some secret anguish from her, and she wished for the gift of probing minds to learn what it was.

"Your spirit is troubled," she said.

"I only hope the lepine was hunting alone."

"One attack a day is more than enough, but I don't think you're afraid of any wild creature."

"Perhaps not." He moved slightly and winced at the daggers of fire rippling through his torn flesh.

"We've shared so much danger—but you don't trust me to share your thoughts."

"It's not distrust of you!" He deeply regretted unintentionally hurting her. "I don't know how

I feel about many things, Calla—love. Today I took life with a metal knife."

"The feline died from its fall!"

"Without the wound, it would have killed me instead."

"You're disturbed because you killed it?"

"No—of course not. While your life was threatened—" He was too full of strange emotions to continue.

"I forced you to use a weapon you disapprove of." Her tone was reproachful.

"You saved both our lives by giving it to me."

He was tormented, not by his necessary use of her weapon, but by his own inadequacy in telling her all that was in his heart. The Citadral loomed large in his thoughts. There his friends were in jeopardy and his own fate would be decided. It was the one place Calla could never go—and he was compelled by honor, duty and friendship to return to it. The burden on his spirit was more painful than the wound in his flesh.

Calla rose up on her knees and gently pressed her parted lips against his. He held his head motionless, feeling a touch as light as the flicker of an eyelash rove from one corner of his mouth to the other. He sighed and cupped her chin in his hand, his soul reaching out to hers even though he couldn't offer her promises.

She imagined kissing a statue carved of cold stone; for a long while Logan was no more responsive than such a creation. She despaired of ever possessing any part of his heart, but their close brush with death made her cherish each precious moment with him even more than before. Softly sighing, she slumped away from him, startled when he clasped her with his strong arm and claimed her mouth with a force that robbed her of breath.

Her kiss was more refreshing than clear springwater, more energizing than the foodstuffs the equest had carried to the base of the precipice. Even through his pain and anxiety, he was stirred by her closeness, aroused by her sweet, seductive kisses.

"What will happen to us?" she whispered, finding the courage to ask when he held her close.

"I'd hoped to reach the twin peaks tomorrow. Without food– water—an equest—"

He didn't need to spell out the hopelessness of their quest. If they didn't find water in the morning . . .

At first Logan thought a stone had fallen over the precipice below them; then it sounded more like a small rock slide disturbing their dark solitude.

"I heard something!" Calla sat upright, alert and wary.

Logan fumbled with the rope still secured to his waist. Calla's peril hadn't given him time to uncoil it for use against the lepine. This time he would be prepared, although it was agony to use his left arm in any way.

"It's coming closer." She looked in all directions for a place to hide, her survival instinct sharpened by the perils she'd faced, but she knew the cliff behind them was solid rock. There were no hidden cavas or protective crevices on this high mountain trail.

Logan pressed his ear to the ground, steeling himself against throbbing pain.

"Only an equest can make the ground vibrate with such force, but I don't understand what I hear." He rose to his feet and positioned himself between Calla and the approaching menace.

"Are the Zealotes coming?"

"Someone is—but I only detect the rumble of a single mount."

"Could they be riding double?"

He silenced her with a gesture and probed the trail below with his mind, desperate for some clue about their pursuer.

"Nothing!" he whispered. "I can't pick up a single thought or image."

"Maybe the mountain interferes."

"It shouldn't—not as close as this rider is. There's only one person who can completely shield his mind."

"Warmond." She thought of her knife, lost in the bowels of the lepine, and bent to find a rock that could offer some defense.

"If I die, know that I love you," Logan urgently whispered, drawing her close for a precious instant.

"If you do, I'll throw myself from the cliff. I won't go back for the Order's grisly execution."

He hugged her close, horrified by the thought of her mangled body lying on the rocks below.

Then the time for thinking was past. Massive hooves rumbled up the trail, and Logan could hear the wheezing breath of a hard-pressed equest. He held his rope ready, knowing he would have only one chance to capture the rider.

The beast slowed, and Logan cursed the ill fate that made the rider so cautious. He could imagine a stealthy Zealote dismounting and using the equest as a shield against his rope.

All he could see was a dark, shaggy shape, but before he could stop her, Calla ran past him toward the beast.

He followed, heart pounding, sure she was doomed by a wild impulse to save him.

"Galaba! Logan, it's Galaba!"

She buried her face in the beast's shaggy side, stroking the great throat and murmuring the soothing words she'd learned as a child. The equest's muzzle was lathered, and its sides heaved from the exertion of galloping up the steep trail, but the animal calmed under her touch.

"I don't believe it." Logan let his rope hang slack.

"She followed us!"

"Fatjack must have been tracking us. It's our good fortune the beast got away from him so close to us."

"No! Galaba can track. I would never have found the Citadral if I hadn't given her free rein. She followed the scent of your equest then, and she's done it again."

"If what you say is true—"

"How can you doubt it? Look, here are water bladders, a saddlebag. Fatjack must have readied her for travel, and she escaped."

"It's too good to be true." Weary and weak from loss of blood, he stroked the beast's muzzle, surprised by a snort of approval.

"This means we can find Fane!" Calla said, revived by the excitement of recovering her equest.

They drank deeply from one of the water bladders, then Calla cleansed his wound. When she'd done all she could for Logan, they slept side by side on Fatjack's thick blanket.

She awoke at dawn and used the green-tinged light to examine Logan's wound. Fatjack had provided for emergencies, including a medical kit in his gear. She spread healing unguent on the slash marks and bound his shoulder in strips torn from the alehouse owner's spare shirt.

They broke their fast on better food than Oldgirl had provided for them.

"Fatjack must have had a secret store somewhere in the settlement," she mused, enjoying a handful of dried fruit more than anything she'd ever tasted.

"He was a slaver. He was planning to kill me and sell you—when he was through amusing himself."

She went pale, and he was sorry for telling her.

"You probed his mind?"

"Yes, and it was like descending into a filthy sewer. Put him out of your mind. He's done us a good turn after all by letting Galaba escape loaded with supplies."

She fed the rest of her sweet treat to Galaba. "We will find Fane now."

"Soon," he promised, hoping against hope the child was still alive.

Chapter Thirteen

When they left the narrow pass between the twin peaks, Logan and Calla were glad to see the Flaming Sea spread out below them, its dark green surface mirroring the peculiar hue of the sky. Their relief at escaping the treacherous mountains was short-lived, however. As they stood on the heavily forested crest, they saw a fiery burst erupt in the sea and shoot into the air, throwing off sparks like miniature stars. The fiery display was quickly extinguished, but the awesome sight left them both speechless.

Both were riding now, and Logan felt Calla's arms tighten around his waist.

"Can't we follow the shoreline?" she asked, awed by the prospect of crossing the explosive body of water.

"I'm afraid not. The Marsh of Misery will block our way on either side. The only way to reach firm ground on the far shore is to sail directly across."

"Galaba is surefooted."

"Not on ground that sucks up all life-forms. We'll have to build a raft. On the water, we at least have a chance of missing the firebursts. The petrolic activity on the seabed is erratic. Little volcanoes erupt whenever the pressure builds up, but we might be lucky enough to cross without coming close to one."

"The marsh won't shoot tongues of fire at us."

"No, but there are fissures everywhere. The ground oozes oily black goo. Not even Galaba can get through it."

They made good time on their descent. The trail was broader and easier, gradually sloping downward, but darkness came with unnatural suddenness, another sign of the coming eclipse.

"We'll rest easier tonight," Logan promised. "Felines hate the odor of petrolia. They won't come down this far, and the Zealotes won't risk missing us by traveling in the dark."

He secured Galaba by an enip tree, taking great care to avoid the sharp needles on massive branches drooping down to the ground in some places. The prickly vegetation was a natural defense against wild predators, but Galaba's thick coat protected her hide.

With the beast's needs met as best they could

be, Logan led Calla to the base of a great tree where a dead branch hung loose and bare, a natural shelter from the wind.

His hands were stiff from cold. He badly wanted to build a fire for Calla's sake, but the risk of providing a beacon for the Zealotes to follow was too great.

"At least we have Fatjack's trail rations," she said, spreading a blanket over the bed of dead needles that cushioned the ground and laying out a few containers.

They ate slowly, making a game of guessing what they were eating, since it was too dark to be sure. From a far distance they heard the thin wail of a lepine, and Logan sensed Calla's tension.

"The beast is angry because we've evaded him," he assured her. "Sound carries in the mountains. That feline could be a day's journey behind us."

"How can you be sure the smell will keep them away?" She wrinkled her nose, not liking the sulfurous odor but finding it too faint to be reassuring.

"Everything the Zealotes discovered over the ages has been recorded," he said to reassure her. "Reading tomes of knowledge used to be my greatest pleasure."

"And now?" she whispered, instinctively huddling close to ward off the cold in the warm circle of his arms.

He laid back on Fatjack's soft blanket, pulling her on top of him. "I still hunger to learn—from you."

"I don't know how to teach." Her cheek was

pressed against his chest, her torso stretched out the length of his. When he spread his legs, hers were trapped between them.

"You've taught me what it means to love a female," he murmured into her hair, sorrowful because his life was inexpressibly sweet at this moment and the joy would be stolen from him when they left their safe bower. "No matter what happens tomorrow, this is the happiest I've ever been."

She rose above him, straddled his hips and leaned forward to tease his lips with feathery kisses. Her tongue bedeviled his nostrils, making him feel like sneezing, then tormented the tip of his nose. When her lips touched first one eyelid and then the other, he thanked his Zealote training for the self-control to savor her arousing attentions.

Her wandering tongue explored the whorls of his ear, sending little shivers down his spine, and he willed himself to remain motionless, tense with desire but consumed by curiosity.

Darkness was complete, but he saw her with his mind's eye, her golden hair dangling over his face, her lush lips parted just enough for the pink tip of her tongue to tickle his throat.

He remembered the cave where the colonists' descendants had scratched wanton figures on the sooty walls and pitied them for their ignorance. What he felt for Calla was so much more than lust, so much deeper than an urge to penetrate her.

His fingers ached with the need to touch her, but he kept them still, so enchanted by her unhurried exploration that he preferred suffering to breaking the spell.

Calla was more afraid than she'd ever been. The intended execution and the attack of the lepine had threatened her life; losing Logan forever would destroy her soul. She silently cursed the darkness for hiding his beloved form from her gaze, but she was determined to memorize every inch of his body, to know his contours better than she knew her own, to store up memories for the dismal days of separation ahead.

She'd never undressed a man, and his passive acceptance of her caresses promised no assistance. Slowly, because her hands were unsteady, she slipped the bone buttons on his shirt through the woven loops that held them, parting the coarse fabric until his chest was bare.

"Will you let me shiver in the night air," he murmured, "when only your flesh can warm me?"

She quickly stripped off her clothing and boots, then knelt at his feet and tugged until his tight-fitting leather boots slid off. Leaning over him again, she stroked the silky down on his chest.

"Don't be a coward," he challenged, capturing her hands and bringing them to the close-fitting waist of his breeches.

"Some things a man should do for himself!"

"No, you're the instructor. I'm in your hands."

"I'm only a learner!"

"Then learn by doing . . . my darling." Words of endearment were foreign to him, but they seemed to spring up without conscious intent when his mind was full of love for Calla.

She giggled, a self-conscious trill that was beautiful to him.

Hesitantly beginning, she found his breeches were much like hers, held fast by lacing in the front, but even when he arched his back and lifted his hips, she felt daunted. Biting her lip, she gave the task her best effort.

She didn't disappoint him. Slowly, her agile hands pulled down the wear-softened leather, freeing his swollen member, exposing his thighs and calves until the garment tangled around his feet and he impatiently kicked it away.

"Roll over," she teasingly commanded.

He obeyed, even though it was torture not to take her in his arms and form a lover's knot.

Straddling his hips, she tickled her own cheek with his thick mane of hair fanned out over his back, then massaged his arms and shoulders, taking care not to disturb his wound although he had pronounced himself nearly healed. She loved the texture of his skin, the hardness of his muscles, and the furriness hidden under his arms. Stroking his back, she squeezed her knees against his side, then trailed her lips down his spine, rewarded by his deep moans of pleasure.

She wished they could melt into one being, joined forever in one body with one spirit. Touching wasn't enough to satisfy her deepest needs, yet her hands moved over him with a will born of desire.

He forced himself to relax under her hands, even when a questing finger sent shocking ripples coursing through him. Her innocent curiosity was a torment and a delight, and he knew a single coupling wouldn't satisfy the demands of their passion—or their love.

She loved his legs—strong, hard limbs—long and firm and sprinkled with silky hairs. Even his toes pleased her, but when she separated them one by one, he lost his stoic endurance and begged for mercy.

Filled with a longing so intense it hurt, she wanted to offer her soul and body to this man she loved beyond reason. Nothing between them was forbidden; nothing he wanted could cause her pain except for the one unbearable act: leaving her. As a symbol of her total acceptance, she knelt by his side and leaned forward on her elbows, offering herself the way he had first tried to take her, giving him the gift of full and complete trust.

"I'm not as ignorant as I was," he murmured, pulling her on top of him and spearing her with the ease of a practiced lover, although love was his only guide and mentor.

She'd never been so ready for love, and when he reached up to cup her breasts in gentle hands, she lost control, surrendering to explosion after explosion with mindless joy.

He knew, in the most primitive depths of his being, that something extraordinary was happening. His own response was instantaneous and mind-shattering. He gave himself wholly to the moment, rocked to the core by the impact.

The world beyond their secluded bower ceased to exist. He kissed her, at first with gentle gratitude, then more forcefully. She'd sensed the latent strength in his powerful limbs and muscular torso; now she experienced it, reveling in his sensual demands, as tender and loving as they were insatiable.

When they came together again, their joining was as natural as the tide washing over the shoreline, as cosmic as the explosion of a star.

The sky was tinged with eerie green streaks before their passion wore itself out, and even then separation seemed like a taste of death.

When he stood and moved away from her, Calla moaned, bringing him back to kneel by her side.

"Forgive me, precious love!" He kissed her brow and nuzzled the soft spot behind her earlobe. "Not even your mare should be ridden so hard."

"No mare was ever ridden so well." She pulled his head down and parted her swollen lips.

He gently kissed her, but his throat ached with sorrow at the prospect of parting from her. In the cold light of dawn, he couldn't push aside his fears for the safety of his friends and the welfare of the Order, but leaving her would strike a deathblow to his spirit.

They dressed and broke their fast in silence. Calla tried to blame her gloomy mood on fatigue, but lying in Logan's arms had been more restorative than a long, deep sleep. Not even finding Fane could compensate for the bitterness of a life without Logan. She hid her tears from him, but in her heart she wept.

Their journey was all downhill now, and the prickly enip trees of the mountains were soon replaced by tiki trees with feathery leaves that reminded Calla of giant fans. They were both walking, guiding Galaba down the steep end of the trail.

"How can we cross the Flaming Sea without a sizable boat built by nautical craftsmen?" she asked, unnerved by the spectacle of a fiery eruption closer to shore than the one the night before.

"These tiki trees have shallow roots. I can see a number of fallen trunks near the shoreline. They're the lightest wood on the planet—highly valued for small craft when they're accessible to safer seas."

"We can't float across the sea on a log!"

"No, but I'll tie several together with vines and use Fatjack's blanket as a sail."

They were uncomfortably close to the shoreline now, and the stench from the marsh was nauseating. Still, the thought of being burned alive by one of the unpredictable firebursts was much more daunting than travel along the shoreline. She shuddered and asked Logan if they could stay in shallow water along the bank instead of sailing on deep waters.

"The safest way is right across the middle; the shallows are as unstable as the marsh. We could disappear forever in one of the whirlpools."

"Then let's go quickly before I lose my nerve."

"We can't attempt it until evening. Once it's dark, we can watch for sudden ripples of light. They signal pyrotechnic activity."

"No fisher captain would risk sailing on this sea."

"No sane man would," he agreed, "but only the greater depths are really dangerous. The phenomenon usually occurs a long distance from the marshy bottom along the shore. Don't be too anxious. I'd rather risk a burning boat than a rematch with a lepine when we cross the mountains again."

In her heart she didn't believe they would ever retrace the route back to civilization together, but she didn't add to his worries by saying more.

He knew, as the possibility of finding Warmond's secret retreat grew more real, there was no place on the planet more dangerous for Calla. He had to keep her away from the Master of Apprentices.

Making the log raft proved to be an easy chore, thanks to Logan's skill and her quick grasp of nautical principles. When the fallen trunks were securely lashed together with tough, rubbery vines, they were both satisfied their craft would float.

They shared a bittersweet meal before the end of daylight, but Logan was very quiet, trying to find words to convince her to stay behind. Failing in this, he meditated by the shoreline for a short time until he clearly saw what had to be done. He thanked the Great Power for the uncanny talents of Calla's equest. Galaba was as fast as any Zealote mount, and, unlike the usual cantankerous equest, the mare was loyal, even seeking out its mistress from a great distance. He was convinced Calla would be safer on this shore with Galaba than in a retreat ruled by Warmond. She could easily hide in the thickets of tiki trees if the two Zealotes pursuing them crossed through the pass. From the vantage point by the Flaming Sea, she could spot them long before they became a threat. He was sure the brothers wanted him much more than a fugitive female, and they wouldn't waste time hunting for her alone.

Still, he couldn't find words to convince her to stay behind.

Logan's silence was a torment. Calla wasn't an empath, but a bad feeling she'd had while they toiled together building the raft grew stronger and stronger. Of course, he was anxious about the dangers ahead, and his love made him afraid for her sake. But she was sure he was hiding something from her.

Restlessly wandering along the strip of solid shoreline where they'd built the raft, she wished there were words to convince him she preferred death to separation from him. She scanned the mountain peaks they'd left behind, remembering all the places they'd journeyed since their odyssey began. Her eyes were swimming with tears, and at first she thought they were playing tricks on her. Blinking hard to sharpen her vision, she cried out to Logan.

"The Zealotes just came through the pass!"

He ran to her side, uncoiling his rope and planning his strategy as he watched the two dark riders in the distance. The two pursuers had solved his dilemma. He didn't doubt he could overcome them. Bound and gagged, they would have to go with him as hostages. This left no room for Calla on the small raft. He would convince her to stay behind with Galaba until he returned from scouting Warmond's retreat.

She saw his small smile of satisfaction, but before she could question him about the reason, something dreadful happened on the distant trail. Both equests bolted, throwing their riders and leaving them to the mercy of attackers: three, possibly four famished felines.

The Zealotes were down, and she could only imagine the details of the gruesome carnage. Recoiling in horror, she let herself be enfolded in Logan's strong arms, not wishing such a grisly fate on any living being.

Logan could feel her trembling in his arms and murmured comfort as best he could. "They won't come this way," he promised. "The stink of the marsh repels them, or we would have been their victims last night."

The sun was setting, and a faint twinkling of light marked the line where black ooze from the Marsh of Misery was feeding into the sea. They both knew without talking about it that the time had come to launch the raft of logs with its crude blanket-sail anchored to a slender sapling.

Logan dressed in the madman's robe with the patches concealed, carrying only his rope and a long piece of driftwood to use as a paddle. Hating himself for the deception but knowing Calla would never remain behind willingly, he asked her to tote a few of their meager possessions farther inland and hide them in the hollow of a tree to supply them on their return trip. The water was calm, lapping gently at his feet, and he watched her walk past Galaba, who had been given her freedom but showed no inclination to desert. Assured that the shaggy beast would be there for her, he gave the raft a powerful push and boarded it in one sweeping motion, using the paddle to propel it away from the shore.

Calla whirled around in a panic when she heard the oar slapping on the water. Her instincts had been right! The traitor was deserting her again!

She ran to the water's edge, shouting frantically. "Damnation to you, Logan! Master of Defense and deserter! You can't leave me here alone!"

"Wait here for me!" he cried out. "I left all the food, and Galaba will take care of you."

"Come back!"

"It's too dangerous to take you, love!"

"Come back!" She was blinded by tears, and she'd never been so angry in her life. He had no right to decide her fate by himself. She'd come this far, and she couldn't be left behind.

"I'll bring Fane to you if it's in my power to do so." He was shouting now, feeling bereft even though she was still within sight.

She wouldn't be left behind! Driven by outrage and the stronger emotion of love, she plunged without thinking into the cold dark sea.

Logan watched, stunned and horrified as she tried to swim in pursuit. Her strokes were strong and sure at first, but her boots and heavy cloak weighed her down. The harder she struggled, the heavier the wet cloak became, threatening to pull her under if she didn't manage to unfasten it soon.

Logan made his decision the instant she plunged into the sea. Praying he wouldn't be too late, he frantically fought to paddle toward her. After all they'd been through, he couldn't risk losing her in the depths of the night-black sea.

"How could you be so foolish!" he railed, pulling her sodden form onto the raft, his heart pounding with fear at her recklessness.

He held her close, torn between needing to smother her in kisses and wanting to chastise her backside. Nothing the Order had taught him applied to what he felt now: murderous rage, quaking terror, blinding love.

"I could have lost you!" he said, holding her close, trying to warm her trembling form. "Why did you take such an idiotic risk? I was going to come back for you!"

"I couldn't risk never seeing you again," she said, her teeth chattering from the cold dunking.

He held her hard against him, punishing her mouth with hard, angry kisses. Cold seawater dampened his robe and shirt, but he was hot with passionate fury, frightened to the core of his being by the risk she'd taken to be with him.

"Forgive me," she pleaded. "I don't want to live without you."

He groaned, a deep mournful sound that came from his soul, then helped free her from the soggy weight of her cloak. This time her lips sought his, chasing away the watery chill as they joined their mouths.

The sail was makeshift and far from reliable; the raft was rudderless and had to be paddled to stay on course. Reluctantly he had to let her shiver alone while he tested his navigational skills on their clumsy raft.

Overhead there was a small break in the clouds, showing the three moons were nearly aligned. Then the thick atmospheric cover blocked out all celestial light, and they were alone on a treacherous black sea.

The farther they sailed, the choppier the sea became.

"The lunar activity is making the water rough," Logan explained, wanting to say many things to her but still shaken by her plunge into the dark waters. "Why don't you rest awhile?"

"No, I'll help you watch for the twinklings that mean a fireburst is coming."

Now that she was actually on the surface of the Flaming Sea, she had more confidence in Logan's ability to steer the raft around sudden bursts of shooting flames. He was as adept a sailor as he was a rider, a fighter—a lover. Even though they were in serious jeopardy, she was constantly aware of his masculinity—and his tenderness.

They both saw the first warning ripple, but the fireburst that followed was relatively tame, just a small spray of fire in the distance, extinguished soon after popping to the surface. Logan heard her deep sigh and smiled in the darkness. How could he ever hope to understand a female who dove into unknown waters but quaked at a distant eruption? He felt like weeping, knowing he'd never have a chance to begin this most fascinating of all studies. When he returned to the Citadral— and there was no way he could not return—his life would be out of his control. The Grand Elder wasn't a vindictive man, but Logan would have to suffer as an example to the others. He could still save himself, but only by sacrificing Perrin and the welfare of all the Zealotes. Whatever Warmond was planning, the Master of Apprentices could destroy all that was good in the Order: centuries of devoted service. Even though Logan clearly saw all the imperfections in the brotherhood, he was still one of them. His honor wouldn't allow him to abandon his brothers.

The wind was with them, and Logan only had to use the paddle to keep the raft on a straight course across the sea. Even the three moons seemed to smile on their voyage, making an appearance when they were well past midpoint and needed to see the lie of the far shore.

"Look," he cried out to Calla, who was still shivering in damp clothing at the opposite end of the raft. "There's a cove."

She stared ahead just as a sudden rippling light appeared on the surface of the sea. It was the biggest she'd seen, and she shouted a frantic warning.

Logan was headed toward the inlet, but the trail of light was coming directly toward them. Before he could take evasive action, a giant arc of flame exploded so close both of them were momentarily blinded. Logan paddled furiously, but the tongues of fire overtook them, lapping greedily at the logs.

"Jump," he screamed, blocked from her by a wall of fire that divided their raft.

He learned what panic was in that instant as he frantically fought the drag of his robe, trying to swim to her end of the flaming raft. When he saw golden locks emerging from the water, he was too relieved to worry about the daunting distance to shore.

"I'm beginning to miss the Valley of Sunken Craters," she sputtered, fighting to keep her head above water.

They struggled, swimming side by side, abandoning the sodden violet cloak and helping each other remove their boots and tie them around their waists with the two ends of Logan's rope. He was a powerful swimmer, but she matched his even, steady strokes for as long as she could. Behind them the raft was only a smoking cinder, devoured by the hungry fireburst.

"If we hadn't seen the warning ripple—"

"Don't think of it," he counseled. "We've enough trouble ahead of us without looking back."

When they finally reached shore, they lay, panting, wet and exhausted, watching skittish clouds flirt with, then obscure, the triple moons.

"Logan." She whispered his name, awed by the miracle of their survival but afraid they might not be alone on the sandy shore.

"My love, you must be freezing. Two dunkings on a night as cold as this."

He reached for her but soon realized he was too cold to warm her.

Standing, he sank to his calves in loose, dry sand that still held some of the sun's warmth.

"Lie still and trust me," he said.

After a few moments she realized he was digging, hollowing out a space large enough for both of them to lie. After she slid into the depression, he pushed a layer of sand over her shivering length, then joined her and covered himself as best he could. With her cheek cradled against his, she fell asleep feeling as warm and secure as she would in her own bed at her father's freehold.

When she awoke, there was enough eerie, green light to see the terrain around them. The water looked darkly menacing, but it wasn't the Flaming Sea that made her heart pound in fear. Their snug bed in the sand was within sight of a dark gray wall towering over the landscape in a clearing among the enip trees.

"Logan!" she whispered urgently.

"I see it. We won't have far to travel today."

"Is it Warmond's stronghold?"

"Most likely. There are no known settlements on this side of the sea."

"Can they see us?"

"The wall is solid, but there could be a walkway on top of it. So far, I haven't seen any sign of movement."

"There's no way we can build another raft to take Fane away without being seen."

His sandy hand reached for hers, causing their shallow mound to break apart.

"Warmond must make frequent trips, but he's never gone for very long. There must be a secret route back to the Citadral, one that takes much less time."

"Through the Marsh of Misery?"

311

"Through it, around it, under it, over it!" He didn't try to conceal his deep frustration. Escaping from Warmond's retreat might be much more difficult then finding it, and he could imagine what would happen to Calla if he failed.

"I can't leave Fane in a place like this!" Much as she abhorred the idea of having him raised by the Zealotes, she was sure a much worse fate awaited him behind the somber gray wall of Warmond's fortress.

Worst of all, she and Logan might put him in even greater danger by trying to take him away.

Chapter Fourteen

They warily surveyed the fortress, using the enip forest as cover, but no one appeared to challenge them.

"Wait here, and I'll go closer," Logan said without any real hope she would willingly stay behind.

"I'm going wherever you go." She wasn't being brave; the suspense of not knowing what was behind the wall was more than she cared to handle alone.

"I could tie you to a tree," he said, only half teasing.

"You wouldn't—would you?"

He shook his head, afraid for her sake even if she hid among the trees. There was no safety for either of them in this place.

"This isn't a primitive ruin left by the ancients." He frowned at the smooth gray walls, not made of blocks and mortar as he'd first believed but smooth like poured concrete. "The workmen who built the wall used a sophisticated technique, one not in common usage on Thurlow."

"It's high enough to hold off an army."

"Yes, and without a grappling hook, I can't scale it."

They couldn't learn more without leaving the forest, but Logan knew the trees offered only an illusion of safety. They were trapped on a large peninsula with no craft to escape by sea, and any attempt to penetrate the territory beyond the fortress would surely be thwarted by great tracts of marshland.

Their hands linked together, they cautiously approached the wall and followed the perimeter, amazed at how large it was.

"Except for the dark color, it's a replica of the Citadral wall," Logan said, chilled by the realization that Warmond had used those dimensions for his stronghold.

The green glow filtering through the cloud cover heightened their uneasiness, and it began to seem they would never find their way into the fortress. When they finally came to a heavy iron gate, their anxiety only increased. Their view of the interior was blocked by a freestanding section of wall inside the fortress that seemed to exist only for that purpose. Or was it designed to keep the occupants from looking out? Logan pushed on an iron bar and found exactly what he expected: a locked gate.

He was barred from entering, but he called upon the full power of his mind probe, trying to learn something about the inhabitants. The evil and unhappiness emanating from the enclosure made him feel physically ill, but he continued his probe, detecting an undercurrent of hatred and also a disturbing sense of purpose. He deeply regretted bringing Calla to this place, but she was safer at his side than alone in this contaminated place.

Calla watched his face pale and his eyes become unfocused. She didn't possess Logan's special gift, but she could sense the malevolence in the air, a cloying suggestion of evil that chilled her to the bone.

With silent agreement, they backed away from the gate and stood in the shadow of the wall to plan their next move. Logan was studying the gate, confident he could climb over it with the help of his rope. The real problem was unlocking it for Calla once he was inside.

"Listen!" She gripped his arm, knowing what the oily creak breaking the early morning silence meant.

The heavy gate swung open, and a hooded figure emerged from the arched opening in the wall. The gatekeeper was a small person, and at first Logan thought a youth had been assigned the task of opening the entrance. Then the hooded figure stepped out to urge a small flock of woolies out to graze, and Logan was astonished by what he deduced: Warmond was harboring females!

The girl approached them, head bowed, a care-worn creature whose elfish face was pinched and haggard from something other than aging. She was less than a stone's throw from them when she froze, startled by the pair of bedraggled figures in Zealote robes not unlike her own.

Logan quickly probed her mind and found fear and weariness, along with dull resignation and a mind-set that believed the unexpected was always bad.

"I've heard this is a place of refuge for those who are sick of the Order's tyranny," he quickly said, pushing himself in front of Calla.

Indecision clouded the girl's face for a moment, but she was easily swayed by Logan's handsome countenance and soothing manner, Calla noted.

"A shame you brought that one with you," the girl said, appraising Logan with a hunger that made Calla seethe. "Well, there's always a need for help with the brats. The Great Power knows I'd rather see her than me in the nursee."

"Walk behind me. Know your place," Logan ordered Calla, stunning her with his harsh command.

She opened her mouth to protest, but his warning glare made her obey in silence. Reminding herself that he must sense something she wasn't capable of detecting, she grimly followed, angry at herself for feeling a stab of jealousy when the haggard girl possessively tucked her hand in the crook of Logan's arm.

Inside the compound people were emerging from a maze of low buildings constructed of the same dark gray material as the walls. Some of the inhabitants of the fortress yawned or stretched, the gestures of humans roused from sleep. A black cinder path led to a massive building, flat-roofed like the others but decorated with obscure symbols and painted maps of constellations. The size was the only resemblance to the Citadral. This structure was as large as the important buildings of the Citadral, but there were no graceful spires or gleaming white walls.. The grounds were bare dirt except for a few scraggly patches of edible plants; there were no spacious gardens with multicolored blooms.

A few women wore cloaks like their guide's, but most were dressed in shapeless smocks belted with segments of rope and drab gray or brown skirts that brushed their bare ankles. The males frightened Calla, even though they all seemed indifferent to her existence. Except for a few young boys, they wore the familiar garb of the Order, but the austere robes didn't conceal their unkempt state. Unlike the Zealotes, most were bearded, some with tangled masses of facial hair that gave them a wild, undisciplined appearance. Before they'd gone very far, Calla noticed another difference from the brothers at the Citadral. There were no old men, no ancients spending their last years in honor and comfort. She desperately wished Logan could tell her what he sensed about this strange, isolated community.

The girl led them toward the large building.

"Go," she ordered, pointing to the only visible opening in the otherwise solid wall of the structure.

The girl turned to leave, but Logan followed her. Calla watched them share a brief exchange, then he walked back toward her, words spilling out of him.

"It's worse than I thought," he said, taking care no one but Calla could hear him. "The men are mostly malcontents—runaway Zealotes—none of them strong-minded enough to shield their thoughts, but they're much more dangerous than those who obey the Grand Elder. You have to search for Fane in the nursee. Don't leave there on your own. I'll find you. And darling, please forgive me!"

To her complete astonishment, he cuffed her with the flat of his hand, a blow that stung her cheek but, she quickly realized, did no real harm. On instinct, she fell to her knees and covered her face, pretending much greater injury than she felt.

Through slitted fingers, she watched him walk back to the scrawny girl, who laughed aloud and seemed delighted by his unwarranted blow. Beyond them a husky, black-bearded man shouted at a woman who followed him. The thin, stoop-shouldered creature ran to obey his command, and Calla realized the awful truth: the renegade Zealotes might keep women in their fortress, but they were nothing but slaves. She didn't need to be an empath to realize the females existed to do men's bidding. Their guide respected Logan because he abused his woman!

Logan returned, yanked Calla to her feet, and slapped her backside, establishing his dominance over her for the benefit of numerous men who were watching his display of power.

She followed him, head bowed, trying to look cowed and to control her impulse to plant the toe of her boot in a strategic place.

No one spoke to her, but Logan was surrounded by renegade Zealotes who seemed to be enjoying a colossal joke at her expense. On market trips with her father, she'd observed how men fell into instant camaraderie based on nothing more binding than their gender, and she resented being a nonperson even though Logan had to mistreat her to save their lives.

At last Logan went away with the others, apparently to break his fast in a communal dining hall.

"This way for you, girlie," ordered a tall, mannish-looking woman with sharp features and sparse gray hair. "Nothing for your belly until you've earned your keep."

Hoping the woman would take her to the nursee, she followed docilely, trying to ignore rumbles of hunger and anger at her treatment.

"In here first," the woman ordered, wrinkling her nose in disgust at Calla's still-damp clothing sprinkled with sand. "Strip off those foul garments."

Calla cringed at being made to stand naked while the woman poured a kettle of cold water over her head and shoulders. She shivered and dried herself on a square of coarse cloth, then accepted a white smock and long brown skirt like those the woman was wearing.

"Dress and be quick about if you don't want a few licks with a strap," the woman said. "Then get your hiney through that door."

Calla ground her teeth together but kept silent, hurrying to dress but not because she feared the nasty female who gave the orders. This was her chance to find Fane, and her hands trembled with excitement as she pulled on the shapeless garments. Thankfully, she was allowed to wear her own boots, not forced to go barefoot as most of the women did. If they had to carry Fane into the marsh to rescue him, she would be thankful for footgear.

Stepping through the door to the nursee, she was astounded by row after row of criblets woven of marsh reeds, almost all of them occupied by young babes. Losing confidence in her ability to recognize her nephew, she stood dumbfounded while the supervisor gave her work orders.

"Begin feeding gruel in that row. Give them as much as they want—we raise healthy babes in this nursee."

But not healthy nursemaids, Calla thought, observing a number of other women performing the myriad tasks necessary to care for children. Without exception, the other workers had the same haggard, undernourished look as the girl who'd opened the gate. None of them took any notice of her, nor did they speak to each other. These children didn't bring any joy to their caretakers, and Calla wanted to weep at their plight. A babe was a great joy to the Outsiders; neighbors would come by just for the chance to hold an infant. These women were too miserable to enjoy the smiles and coos of a precious new life.

In the Citadral the Zealotes' treatment of her

had been barbaric, but maybe death—even a horrible one—was preferable to these women's enslaved existence. They seemed to be trapped in private worlds of misery, incapable of reaching out to each other for comfort. Was this what it was like to be ostracized? How could Logan willingly return to a life that would cut him off from companionship, compassion—love?

"Check the nappies now," the head mistress of the nursee ordered.

Still hungry, with no hope of a meal in the near future, Calla began her search for the significant birthmark, the task made easier by her assignment. Fane's distinctive mark was a large oval on the back of his left thigh, and she couldn't miss it if she changed him.

Logan ate well on hot cakes and fried meat sticks, seemingly accepted by all the renegades around him. They were more interested in knowing how he'd come to possess Calla than in his escape from the Citadral. He wasn't surprised that her golden hair and lush body excited their lust, but he did wonder how long her beauty would last under the kind of treatment these men meted out to their women. Destructive abuse for no reason was beyond his comprehension. He couldn't even understand why an Outsider would misuse an equest; ill-treatment of beasts was unknown in the Order's stables. It was even more demented to abuse a female, robbing her of the attributes that made her desirable. He could only pray Calla would understand why he had to play a role with her; hurting her was the last thing he ever wanted to do.

He probed the minds of those around him, surprised because they were too insensitive to detect his invasion of their consciousness. Their thoughts were as disturbing as Fatjack's and the other slaver's, and Logan's intestines knotted with fear for Calla's sake if anything should happen to him. Even if they accepted him into their ranks, would he be strong enough and clever enough to protect her from so many unprincipled renegades?

He knew the men who surrounded him were willing to believe his fanciful story of abducting Calla, but the only authority any of them had was over the enslaved women, many of whom they'd stolen from remote villages. They answered to an all-powerful leader. As Logan probed, he especially tried to get a mental picture of the route they used on excursions to the outside world. Visions of an underground waterway came to him, but he couldn't pinpoint its location through the disjointed thoughts of the men around him.

"Come this way, newcomer," a lad said with none of the respect apprentices showed their elder brothers in the Citadral.

Logan bit back a rebuke and followed a pimple-faced youth to a small building with a plain exterior, a structure much like all the others within the fortress walls.

The lad closed the door, leaving him alone in a chamber more opulent than the Grand Elder's. His senses were assailed by a riot of color: gilt furnishings with scarlet brocade, rich purples and blues the shades of which he'd never seen. There was more than he could take in at a glance, but the paintings on the wall sent a chill up his spine despite the overheated atmosphere of the stuffy room. Their intent was the same as the crude sketches on the ancients' cave walls, but these painted images were lush and fleshy, a virtual sea of overripe bosoms, swollen buttocks, and peachy-pink limbs contorted in the most seductive positions. Logan had seem figures painted by the same hand in less obscene poses. This artist had decorated Warmond's room in the Citadral.

He braced himself, loosening the rope to be prepared for the long-overdue confrontation with the Master of Apprentices.

"Welcome, renegade. I am Xanthe," a woman purred, entering the room in a sweep of glittery colors and musky scent.

Tensed to face his adversary, Logan was speechless in front of the creature who greeted him.

"You're admiring the paintings. They're gifts from my master, and be assured, I gave a full measure of pleasure for each and every one," she hissed seductively.

She was exotic, but Logan found himself repelled by her carefully orchestrated opulence. The black kohl rimming her dark green eyes didn't disguise a network of deep lines, and not even her shimmering robe made of many layers of scarlet gauze could conceal the slight sagging and puffiness of a body that had once been full and luscious.

Logan sensed a dangerous mixture of hostility, anger, and passion radiating from the woman and chose to remain silent.

"So you're another refugee from the Order. I suppose my master can use you—when I'm finished with you—although he's harvesting a superior crop of his own for the future leadership of the Fellowship."

His silence seemed to unnerve her. She continued to fill the void with strident chatter, all the time circling him like a scavenger in search of carrion and running a blue-tipped finger up and down his hard chest. Her molestation sickened him, making him feel soiled, but he didn't flinch. She couldn't control her own tongue, let alone her wandering hands, and he nourished hope that this bitter female would reveal Warmond's secret plans.

"He has quite a contingent under his control," she said, stepping close enough to press her fleshy knee against the inside of his. "A private army amassed over the years. All the babes the stiff-necked Zealotes thought were dead—for years he's brought them here along with those pathetic women he's enslaved to run and fetch— and produce more brats. Of course, he brought me here for other reasons." Her laugh was chilling, and he had to steel himself not to push her away when she pressed her ponderous breasts against his chest.

"I won't be exiled in this foul outpost much longer." She cackled her satisfaction, dropping her hand to fondle him more outrageously.

Suppressing the urge to shove her away, he broke his silence to goad her into revealing more.

"I can't believe your master would dare have anything to do with the Earth vessel that's due."

Her laugh was a cackle. "When he has the technology on that ship, he'll be ruling Thurlow—from the Citadral. No doubt he'll find some petty use for a renegade like you." She squeezed him so hard he had to bite back a cry of protest.

"I don't believe anyone can get past the government defenses."

"Believe, you fool! He's more powerful than you can imagine!" Her eyes shone with madness, and she started pacing in front of him like a performer on a stage of old.

"You'll thank the stars you abandoned that impotent brotherhood of fools to be part of the army of the Power of Darkness. When my master rules the planet, the Zealotes will be sent to the mines. He'll decide how much ore reaches Earth—and what the price will be."

Although she didn't mention her master's name, Logan knew it: Warmond. He had to return to the Citadral and warn them. Once again, after so many centuries, the Zealotes were the only ones who could ensure the future of the planet. Warmond had to be stopped, but he couldn't abandon Calla and Fane.

He'd lost all track of time during his imprisonment and travels, but soon the moons would eclipse, creating the conditions that made travel through the asteroids possible. Warmond's devious plan would be set in motion, and nothing the corrupt government could do would stop him.

"Enough of this!" Xanthe said, growing bored with the talk that left Logan's thoughts spinning. "I can think of much better ways to pass our time. You can service me now."

Logan swallowed his revulsion as the bizarre crone wrapped serpentine arms around his waist, digging her claws into his backside. In one fluid motion, he pinned her arms to her sides, pressing his face threateningly close to her garishly made-up countenance.

"Where is he?" he demanded.

As if really seeing Logan for the first time, Xanthe's expression crumpled.

"You!" she said, her hatred a tangible force in the cloying atmosphere of her chamber.

So many babes and so little time, Calla thought, as she hurriedly performed her duty with each child in the row assigned to her. No matter how hard she tried to hurry, she couldn't be careless with the precious little beings assigned to her care. Each tiny bottom had to be soothed with lotion; each nappie pin had to be securely closed. One of the other workers reprimanded her for holding a crying child too long.

"Waste time coddling a female," she warned, "and you're the one who'll be bawling."

Calla knew the Zealotes only "summoned" male infants, but not even the powerful Warmond could control the sex of the children born to the females in the retreat. She felt sure that the girl babes who survived faced a life of enslavement.

The babe on her shoulder burped loudly and stopped crying, but Calla seethed with anger at the thought of females left to suffer because of their gender. At least the male babies were properly nurtured, but that didn't help her locate Fane in the crowded nursee.

She continued her duties, growing less and less optimistic about her chance of locating and saving Fane. How could she face her sister again if she failed to return her beloved son after coming this close?

A lusty wail from a babe two rows over broke into her gloomy reverie. None of the smock-clad workers, some of them with bulging bellies, went to comfort the distressed child, and the wail grew more insistent.

Calla stopped what she was doing, a sudden joy bubbling up in her heart. She recognized that cry! Even at the moment of birth, Fane had roared at a full-throated pitch with powerful lungs. It must be her nephew complaining so loudly!

Abandoning her assigned duties, she rushed toward the cry. Before she reached the babe, a man's voice barked a question.

"Where are you going? Only Hezibah touches that one!"

Calla's blood ran cold, and she stopped dead in her tracks. She would recognize that voice anywhere: Warmond!

"Out of the way, fool!" The head mistress shoved her aside and scurried to her master, dropping to her knees and pressing her lips to the hem of his raven-black robe.

Calla bowed her head, shaking her hair forward to conceal as much of her face as possible. Hezibah's whining, fawning words disgusted her, but she concentrated on looking humble, slumping and averting her eyes to be as inconspicuous as possible:

All activity in the room ceased, and Calla realized the others must share her dread of the man who ruled the fortress. Warmond controlled his people with fear and cruelty; none of them wanted to attract his attention.

"Ah, I see your time is near, Delia." He put his hand on a young girl with huge, dark eyes, reaching under her smock to stroke her huge belly. "Give this one a daily ration of milk from a bovine heifer. I don't want a son of mine to come into the world weak and puny."

Calla willed herself to remain immobile, hoping against hope Warmond was too busy inspecting his breeding stock to notice her. With his attention distracted by Hezibah's jabbering and the distress of the young mother-to-be, she took tiny, silent steps toward a cluster of women a short way from her. She didn't even exhale as she tried to blend into a group of white-smocked workers.

Warmond was giving orders to Hezibah, at the same time warning the others of dire consequences if any dared disobey her. The words Calla heard stunned her.

" . . . how important this child is. I went a great distance to find an Outsider who would serve the purpose. The Power of Darkness demands a sacrifice to ensure the success of our master plan. This babe must remain untouched by unclean hands. You cannot imagine the punishment in store for any of you who disobey this order!"

His words brought a silence to the nursee that even the babes respected; not a word or a whimper could be heard. Even Hezibah seemed cowed by his mad plan and his threats.

Calla was trembling, so angry she wanted to attack Warmond with her bare hands. The Master of Apprentices was going to sacrifice her nephew to the forces of evil to ensure the success of his insane plan!

Her only chance of spiriting Fane away was to remain undetected. She slumped even more, edging her way behind a taller woman with faded red hair drawn into a bun. When Warmond left . . .

"One of you nearly ruined my sacrifice!" he said in a hard, angry voice. "If any of these creatures approaches the chosen child again, I hold you responsible, Hezibah."

"The foolish one was just brought to us. I haven't had time to teach her all she needs to know." The head mistress seemed to physically shrink under Warmond's disapproving gaze.

"See that she is suitably punished," Warmond said, his cold reptilian eyes searching for the culprit.

The other women were subtly distancing themselves from her, moving away just enough to show they didn't deserve to share in her punishment. Calla found herself alone and exposed, and she still didn't have proof that it was Fane who would be the victim of Warmond's hideous sacrifice.

"In case anyone thinks of substituting another babe for the special child, foisting off a sickly or imperfect specimen to save him," the Master of Apprentices said to his terrified slaves, "I can identify him by this mark." He walked over, picked up Fane, and held him up, exposing the unmistakable birthmark on the back of his thigh.

He was her sister's babe! Even though she trembled for his safety, Calla had confirmation. Somehow she had to prevent the grisly sacrifice.

Before she could begin to formulate a plan, Warmond had returned the babe to its criblet and singled her out as the guilty worker.

He walked over and grabbed her wrist in a viselike grip, sending raw shocks of pain through her hand and arm. She steeled herself against the agony and stared at the flagstone floor, hoping against hope Warmond wouldn't recognize her. Whatever the punishment she might have to endure for being a careless nursee slave, it was nothing compared to what the Master of Apprentices would do if he recognized her.

"Understand," he said, making a show of her distress to further terrify the other women, "that females exist to obey and please males. You do not make decisions. You do not act without permission. The only alternative to following the rules is pain."

He buried his hands in Calla's hair, letting the locks caress his fingers as though he planned to pleasure himself at her expense. Then, without warning, he yanked so hard she screeched in agony, unable to avoid looking directly into his diabolical eyes.

"You!" His face registered surprise, instantly replaced by an expression of pure malice. "I can't believe you're here alone. At last I'll be able to remove the final obstacle to my plans. Where is Logan?"

"I don't know!" She couldn't hold back a scream when he tortured her scalp again.

"I'll pull out every hair on your head if you don't tell me where that self-righteous meddler is!"

"Here I am."

Logan stepped into the nursee, dragging Xanthe's bulk, putting her in front of him despite her struggling and cursing.

"I didn't trust him," she sputtered, looking at Warmond with beseeching eyes. "I tried to use my guile to learn the truth." There was fear in her voice, and she went limp under her master's cold gaze.

"A trade," Logan said. "Your mistress for Calla." Xanthe's slack form was even harder to manage than her resisting bulk. He wrapped his arm around her neck to hold her upright.

"An even exchange?" The Master of Apprentices laughed, but there wasn't any mirth in the sound. "I think not. You'll do me a favor if you dispatch that aging hag. She hasn't produced a single son, and what she does do, any of these can do as well." He gestured with contempt at the horrified workers, a few of whom had edged their way to their own offspring, making maternal gestures in the presence of unspeakable evil, as though their love could ward off harm.

"Master!" Xanthe's wail of anguish stirred Logan's compassion, but he still felt contaminated by her lewd behavior.

"In fact, I'll personally see to the training—and the discipline of this one," Warmond sneered, releasing Calla's hair but pulling her against him as a shield.

"Calla . . . love," Logan gasped, releasing the wailing Xanthe, realizing too late that he'd revealed how important Calla was to him through the folly of his words.

Chapter Fifteen

Fane wailed as though he wanted a voice in his own fate, but not even his appointed keeper dared go to him.

Logan released Xanthe, not caring that she stumbled away, whining for mercy from the master who had rejected her.

"Out of my sight, you craven slut!" Warmond ordered in a deadly soft voice.

While Xanthe staggered out, Warmond gave a shrill whistle.

"To think the saintly Logan has sacrificed everything for a female," he said with leering satisfaction. "Was bedding her worth the price?" He tightened his hold on Calla, locking his arm around her throat.

"Let her go. I'm your enemy, not her."

Calla winced as Warmond made a show of his power over her.

Logan took single step toward her, but Warmond stopped him by cutting off Calla's breath long enough to make Logan fear for her life.

"Don't kill her!"

"It serves my purpose to let her live—for now." He released his chokehold but held her secure with both arms.

Warmond's whistle had brought help from his followers; from the corner of his eye Logan saw four burly robed men edging toward him on his right. One person stood between him and Warmond's bodyguard: a dark-haired girl with huge eyes and the swollen belly of a woman near the time of birth.

"This girl is carrying Warmond's child!" Calla shouted. "Use her as—"

Warmond's hand cut off her words but not her hopes as she anxiously watched the four men stalking Logan, trying to find an opening in his defenses.

With his rope in hand, Logan didn't quake at the prospect of battle with four trained Zealotes, but he'd never seen a worse place for combat. A scuffle could overturn criblets, and the precious babes might be trampled underfoot. He doubted all the women could dash to safety in time, and fear for their lives and the children's kept him from becoming the aggressor.

The dark-eyed girl seemed paralyzed by fear. Logan instinctively probed her mind, confirming what Calla said, but he found a depth of terror unlike any he'd ever encountered. She was little more than a child, yet she'd been ravished and abused by Warmond until all that remained was raw fright.

If he used her as a shield, she might die of fear.

Calla watched in horror as Logan stood motionless, letting the four men get close without grabbing the pregnant girl as hostage. Their lives were hanging in the balance, and the man who'd attacked a wild feline with his bare hands didn't seize the female slave.

Logan recognized two of his attackers as Youngers from the Citadral, the same who rode with Warmond on summoning missions. The other two were older, rougher-looking ex-Zealotes with unkempt beards and dirty matted hair, signs they were renegades who'd rejected everything the Order taught.

One of the rough men lifted the pregnant girl out of the way, and Logan heard a muffled sound of protest from Calla. He was ready to give his life for her, but would she understand why he couldn't add to a slave's burden of terror?

"Are you as good as they say?" one of the older men sneered. "Or do you need the Order behind you to be a big man?"

Logan watched while they formed a half-circle in front of him, giving him the advantage of a wall behind him but cutting off all escape routes. The layout of the nursery was simple: row after row of criblets with a work and storage area at the back of the room. There were four doors, but two were open revealing a kitchen and a storage room. Xanthe had crept out the exit to the courtyard where older children were playing. The entrance Logan had used was crowded with nursee women watching the confrontation from a vantage point where they could quickly back away from trouble. A few, braver or more motivated than the others, were gathering babes to carry them to safety, but their task was hopeless. Any scuffle was sure to injure or kill some of them.

So quickly no one saw him move, Logan flicked his rope toward the largest of his attackers, locking it around the frantic man's throat. Anyone trained by Zealotes could escape from a neck coil, but the unkempt man was clumsy. The noose would keep him out of the fight while he tried to work himself free and catch his breath.

With one man temporarily disabled, Logan faced odds he was sure to overcome—with a rope and suitable battleground. Now he had neither, and Warmond whistled again, signaling for reinforcements. Logan had only bought a few moments by taking out his most aggressive opponent, and he had to immobilize the others without upsetting criblets.

Calla struggled against the hand gagging her and the arm restraining her, but Warmond seemed to enjoy the fight, using her resistance as an excuse to inflict pain.

Logan threw himself at one of the robed attackers, circling his throat with his hands until the man slumped to the floor, sure to be unconscious for some time. Only the two Youngers remained, and he knew his reputation was his strongest weapon against them. They hesitated, too inexperienced to function as a team, and Logan selected the sturdier of the two as his next target.

Just when Calla thought Logan would succeed, the room filled with Warmond's men, their hard-soled boots sounding like an army's march on the stone floor.

Logan went down, literally buried in a sea of angry, swarming renegade Zealotes.

"Don't kill him yet!" Warmond ordered. "I've waited for a long time for this. The Master of Defense is going to die very, very slowly."

Logan was dragged to his feet, his face bruised and his nose bleeding. Four men held him, and the others formed an unbreakable knot around him.

"Bring his rope here," Warmond ordered.

The men obeyed him as quickly as the enslaved women in the nursee had, and Calla was nauseous with loathing. Tears of anger flooded her eyes. Why hadn't Logan seized the only hostage who mattered to Warmond, his unborn child?

The young man who brought the rope was short of breath and rank with perspiration, as though he'd just fought a great battle instead of acting as part of a mob. At his master's direction, he fumbled with the rope until his awkward fingers managed to tie a noose at the end.

Calla was so sure they meant to hang Logan, she was relieved when Warmond slipped it over her head.

"Don't fight it," he warned. "It isn't quite time for your ultimate experience, but I promise you many little deaths before then."

Calla looked at Logan, his head bowed and his hands bound behind him, and her eyes filled with tears. How could a love like theirs be snuffed out by evil?

"You'll find another lover," Warmond purred in mock sympathy, tormenting her cheek with the scratchy end of the rope he was holding in his hand.

"Release her, Warmond!" Logan roared, his spirit revived by the threat to Calla.

"Regrettably," he said, ignoring Logan, "I don't have time to take my pleasure with you now, but once you've been bedded by the Master of Apprentices, you'll forget the Master of Defense."

"Never!" She lashed out without thinking, so blinded by disgust she slapped his hollow cheek, the blow sounding as loud as thunder in the room full of his stunned followers and slaves.

His blow sent her crashing to the floor, her head reeling from the impact, but all she could think of was Logan's cuff when he was trying to win acceptance from the males. Her father had never raised his hand in anger, and she was too outraged to weep. What kind of beasts were these people, that they mistreated humans with no remorse or pity? She could understand the savagery of a lepine that killed to survive, but Warmond and his followers were like a cancerous growth on the planet. If they succeeded, life on Thurlow would lose all value and meaning.

"Get up, you stupid slut!" Warmond ordered, kicking her with the toe of his boot. "You'll learn respect before I'm through with you. Now, just so you won't entertain any hope of rescue, I'm going to let you see what happens to those who oppose me."

Yanking on the rope tied to her neck, he led her past Logan, giving her a moment to take in his battered face and stricken expression.

"Calla—" Logan started to say something, but one of his captors cuffed him in the face before he could get the words out.

While Logan watched helplessly, Warmond led Calla away like a pet on a rope, tugging more than necessary to keep her fearful and off balance. Logan strained against the ropes binding his hands and feet, but even with his skills, it would take hours to work free.

They formed a procession, Warmond leading with his captive, followed by two Youngers straining to carry Logan, whose bound ankles didn't allow him to walk. He knew Warmond wanted to humiliate him, displaying the Zealote's Master of Defense trussed up like a beast to be slaughtered. One Younger supported the weight of his shoulders; the other carried his feet, and from what Logan could see and hear, the procession grew longer and noisier with each step they took.

A group of children ran beside him, daring each other to dart forward and touch the captured Zealote. Encouraged by laughter from some of the men, they found sticks and branches and made a game of whipping the prisoner.

Calla couldn't stop herself from looking back, even though her pity could only add to Logan's suffering. Hot tears ran down her cheeks at the sight of the indignities heaped upon him, but she didn't understand why he hadn't acted to save himself—and her. Taking the mother of Warmond's child as a hostage had been their only chance.

The fortress walls enclosed a great deal of barren land, beaten to a gray, stone-like hardness by natural forces and the trampling of humans and equests. At first Calla thought they were taking Logan to an empty field to execute him, but Warmond stopped in the shadow of the high wall and looked down with satisfaction at a round grate set into concrete.

He ordered Logan's feet untied, motioning a dozen or more of his best men to surround him.

"Let me explain to those of you who are unacquainted with creeches," he said, smiling at the effect his words would produce on the fainthearted. "While this fortress was being built by slaves we brought from the Outside—"

"What happened to them?" Logan interrupted.

"We ran them into the marsh when their tasks were done. We even gave them food and water for the trip."

"No one can survive in the Marsh of Misery."

"So the musty old tomes relate. I wanted proof of my own. My most trusted followers searched the perimeters for many moon-cycles, but not a single good fellow emerged from the marsh."

"You're inhuman!" Calla said.

"Is being human a virtue?" Warmond bent down and pulled away the iron bar that bolted down the grate. "If you like other life-forms, you'll love the creeches. You two, let down a rope and hold it so Dobner can go find a creech for us."

"Please, master, no! What have I done to deserve a trip to the pit?"

"Nothing yet, but if you don't find one of my pets—and fast—you'll share the fate of the Master of Defense."

"Fit punishment for your terrible stew," a voice called out to the pear-shaped, blubbery man who was pushed toward the gaping hole.

"Catch a few extra! You can cook up a batch of fried creech," another taunted.

The man was sobbing, begging Warmond to reconsider, even though it was plain the Master of Apprentices was enjoying the cook's distress.

"I can't climb ropes like a Zealote," he wailed.

"No doubt you'll learn quickly," Warmond said.

The crowd jeered but kept a good distance from the pit, seemingly reluctant to even look into the dark depths.

Four men held the rope, and the cook awkwardly took hold of it, his slack face bright red from weeping.

Calla didn't think he'd be able to climb back up, but the crowd grew silent in anticipation. She didn't know whether they were hoping for his success or his failure.

His cries grew blood-chilling, but Warmond stood patiently waiting, the rope that held Calla captive wrapped around his hand.

Dobner emerged from the hole in a panic, scream-

341

ing as though caught in a bone-crushing vise. The rope holders gave him a boost, then retreated in haste, leaving him alone beside the hole.

"Take it, take it, please, master, take it!"

He held out his hand, blood streaming down his fingers, but Calla had to strain to see the cause of his distress.

A greenish blob, shiny like a worm but with dozens of hair-like legs, fell to the ground, and Warmond prodded it with the toe of his boot.

"A creech," he said with satisfaction. "Bloated now with Dobner's blood, but such a little creature to cause so much pain."

"Teeth like rusty nails," the cook blubbered.

"He's not entirely wrong," Warmond agreed. "A creech only bites once, but its saliva is a caustic acid that burns into the skin while the beastie takes its fill of blood. One bite won't kill; several hundred will, and each little feeding will burn like the fires of the mythical Hell!"

"Please don't put Logan in there!" Calla threw aside all vestiges of pride and begged Warmond. "I'll be your slave! Just let him go!"

His laugh was so chilling, the crowd became silent. She hoped for an instant his followers might rebel at his insane barbarism, but all she saw on the faces of the men was mindless acceptance.

"Do it now!" Warmond ordered. "You two, and you." He singled out six men who stepped close to Logan. "Untie his hands, then lower him down. Be careful. If he escapes, you'll take his place."

"No!" Calla cried out.

"Don't think you can escape, Master of Defense.

My steel is the best on Thurlow. You'll never break the grate, and none of my people are foolish enough to remove the bar that holds it in place."

"Why free my hands?" Logan asked, straining against the hold of the six men.

"To prolong your agony! You'll kill many creeches, but you can't kill all of them. They'll keep coming, biting, weakening you. You'll get thirsty, hungry. You'll despair, and your 'love' will be learning how to please a real man."

The unbearable was happening. She would never see Logan again, but she'd relive his torment in her imagination for the rest of her days. Horrified as they lowered him into the pit and slammed down the grate, Calla slumped to the ground in a deep faint.

Calla woke up in a small cubicle with unpainted plaster walls and a dark flagstone floor. She was lying on her side on a narrow cot, staring at a wooden chest large enough to hold all the clothing and possessions she'd left behind at her father's freehold. Ornately carved with a large burnished lock, the chest was too fine to sit in a prison cell. There was no comfort in knowing she wasn't in Warmond's dungeon.

Her dreams had been horrible scenes of Logan in the pit, but waking was even more frightful. Although she couldn't understand his failure to seize the girl as a hostage, she loved him beyond reason. Staggering to one of the two doors opening onto the room, she tried to shake off dizziness and find a way to reach Logan. Removing the bar that held down the grate would be easy for anyone standing above it, impossible for a person in the pit.

It was no surprise the first door was locked. The other one opened easily, but only a windowless water closet lay beyond it. To her surprise, a metal tub was filled with fragrant water and a plush towel was laid out on a stool beside it. She dipped her fingers into the water and found it lukewarm. Was that an indication of how long she'd resisted consciousness?

"Get in it and be quick about it!"

Startled, Calla whirled around to face the girl who'd let them into the fortress when she was driving out the woolies.

"Take me to him!" she begged.

"We'd both end up down there with him if we tried to free him." She didn't sound cocky or shrewish now, and her expression softened when she talked about Logan. "He's a fine man—his death is a great waste."

"He can't be dead yet!"

"No, not him. He'll last for days, poor soul!"

Instead of feeling jealous of the girl who so obviously admired Logan, Calla remembered that all females were slaves in the fortress and felt a measure of compassion.

"What's your name?" she asked. "Where do you come from?"

"Mayme," she answered, sounding surprised anyone would want to know. "Kric bought me in Bordertown. I don't remember anything before that—I was little more than a babe when he brought me here."

"He's your master?"

"He was until he died of a fever. Sometimes the mists rise off the marsh and bring the sickness. The people here can't wait to start living in the Citadral."

"Is that what Warmond promised you?"

"I can't waste more time," she snapped impatiently, suddenly changing moods. "The Master orders that you bathe yourself and dress as females should. Now hurry before he punishes both of us!"

With nothing to gain by resisting, Calla stripped off her soiled clothing, the shapeless smock and shirt, and climbed into the comfortably large tub. Her naked body only reminded her of the pleasure it had given her in Logan's arms, and big tears mingled with the bathwater on her cheeks.

"Hurry!" Mayme urged several times, even though Calla wasn't trying to delay.

She came out of the water closet wrapped in the strip of white toweling and carrying her travel-worn boots.

"Leave those," Mayme ordered. "This is what you're supposed to wear."

Calla's jaw dropped; she'd only seen such garments once before, and the memory of them wasn't pleasant.

"Do they belong to Warmond's mistress—the woman he rejected?"

"They're clean," Mayme said defensively. "It's my job to care for her clothing—and the slut hasn't been able to wear this size for many moon-cycles. Since Warmond stopped coming to her chamber, she's done nothing but stuff sweet morsels into her mouth."

"But I can't wear them!" Calla felt petty, worrying about her garb when Logan's life was in jeopardy, but she didn't even know how to get into the pile of gauzy yellow material.

"You have no choice, and you'll only get me a beating if you don't hurry. Here, this goes on first."

Mayme slipped a sleeveless silky gown over her head. It billowed loosely around Calla, but the caress of the fabric was disturbing.

"Now these," she said, helping Calla into a scarlet gauze and another over it of rich sunny yellow.

Material swirled around her like a tent, but Mayme fastened a girdle of gilded leather around her waist and insisted she wear a pair of red hide slippers that caressed her feet like down.

"This is all for Warmond, isn't it?" she asked, not trying to hide her fear and loathing.

"He ordered it, yes, but I don't think he'll do more than amuse himself with you."

There was a smugness in Mayme's words that arrested Calla's attention.

"Someone will take Xanthe's place," Mayme said less surely. "She taught me many tricks to please a man."

"He's evil!"

"He owns me! Better to be his bedmate than his servant."

Calla couldn't make Mayme see that she was a slave in either role, but she vowed to die before giving in to Warmond's cruel demands.

"Is it still day?" she asked. "How long did I sleep?"

"Not long. It would be daylight if this hellish green glow didn't hang over us."

A key rattled in the door, and Calla realized Mayme was locked in with her. She froze, expecting to see Warmond, but the head mistress from the nursee stood there instead, a large woven basket at her feet.

"I should be the one to go," she said resentfully. "You dare not touch the babe. Only carry the basket, and the Master will see to his needs."

A small wail rose from the depths of the basket, and Calla nearly made the fatal mistake of rushing to comfort her nephew. Just in time, she remembered and backed away, perplexed by what looked like a child prepared for travel.

If she were forced to leave the fortress, Logan's only chance of survival would go with her. To free Logan she would submit to Warmond, hoping to gain an opportunity to slip away while he slept. Now it appeared Warmond was going on a journey with Fane. Was she included in this plan?

The indignant older woman left them, and Mayme picked up the basket, urging Calla to follow her. Calla's only thought was to escape, so she stepped through the door into the eerie green light desperately looking for an opportunity.

Two ferocious renegades were waiting outside the door, and they fell into step behind the women. Calla reached for the handle to help Mayme carry the basket, but the slave girl curtly refused her assistance, insulting her for the benefit of the guards.

Was there an unwritten code that women should demonstrate nothing but hostility and loathing toward their own gender? Mayme's attitude changed as soon as men could hear, and Calla suspected that the girl's scorn was only a way of ingratiating herself with the ex-Zealotes. Calla didn't admire such devious behavior, but she could understand it.

They entered a building set aside from all the others, not far from where Logan was imprisoned underground. The barren field was deserted; to her surprise not even the vicious lads who'd whipped Logan with sticks were keeping vigil over the grate to mock his suffering.

She was taking careful note of all she saw, hoping against hope she'd have an opportunity to return the same way and free Logan. The low narrow door wasn't locked; Warmond's people seemed too fearful of him to trespass where they didn't belong.

"The Zealotes don't use locks, and I see most doors here lack them. Why was there one on the chamber where I slept?"

"Xanthe's doings. She was afraid someone would steal from her precious chest—silly bovine. As if theft could pass unnoticed in this place."

With one guard leading and the other following them, they went down a steep flight of steps carved in the bedrock of the planet. Slow-burning torches were fastened to the wall above them with metal brackets. Calla asked why metal was so common in the fortress, but Mayme had lost all patience with her questions and refused to answer except to command silence. The men spoke not at all, making her wonder if casual talk between males and females was contrary to custom.

The air grew frigid as they descended another steep flight of stairs and then a third, and Calla shivered under the billowy layers of gauze. She worried that Fane wasn't warm enough but didn't dare check his covers. For Logan's sake as well as the babe's, she couldn't provoke Warmond or his men into killing her.

Why had he failed to take the girl hostage? Her mind was boiling with recriminations, disappointment, and frantic fear.

They were walking down a long tunnel past cell-like cavas with barred doors.

"The slaves who built the fortress lived here," Mayme whispered. "If they'd only known how close they were to freedom!"

"Do slaves ever try to escape?"

"There's only women left, and none would risk what's at the end of this route."

Calla saw a few pathetic remnants of human habitation: a bit of rotted cloth, a battered cup, a pair of manacles left to rust beside a cell. She couldn't believe so much evil existed unknown to the Outsiders who had loved and nurtured her.

They went down another flight of steps, and it felt like they were going into the bowels of an evil netherworld. The stairway was so steep and narrow Mayme grudgingly accepted Calla's help with the basket. Neither of the men offered assistance, but one of them urged haste, slapping his rope against the steps as though he'd prefer a more yielding target.

Mayme followed one guard, and the other prodded Calla from behind, giving her a shove to start her down a narrow, foul-smelling tunnel. The rough-hewn corridor through solid rocks seemed endless, but at last she heard a faint sound: water lapping against rock.

The tunnel had a confusing number of curves and twists, but there was only a single route to follow. She wouldn't get lost if she ever had an opportunity to retrace the route.

They descended a short flight of steps into a more spacious area, and Calla began to doubt her senses. Had Warmond's blow addled her brain? Her nostrils rebelled at the pungent odor, and she could swear the walls of the cavern were glowing with an eerie incandescence.

The guard leading them turned to berate Mayme for lagging behind, and Calla was able to edge closer to one rock wall. She touched a luminous patch on the surface and pulled her hand away in distaste. The walls were slick with petrolia. They were under the Marsh of Misery!

She hadn't imagined the sound of water. Ahead of them the tunnel ended in a river of petrolia-blackened water with several small craft rocking gently to and fro on the surface. Now she knew the secret route from the Citadral to Warmond's hidden fortress, but was it too late to save Logan?

Warmond stepped forward from the murky shore of the water and issued a rapid series of orders to his two men.

One of the guards climbed into the open wooden craft and reached out for the basket, stowing it carefully between two of the wooden planks that served as seats. He offered his hand to Mayme, and she gracefully boarded, eyes averted, raising her coarse cotton skirt more than was necessary to step into the boat.

Warmond's silent sneering was a goad to Calla, and she turned to gauge her chance of reaching the narrow steps and outdistancing pursuit. As though he read her mind, Warmond barked another order and the burly renegade who'd followed them grabbed her and lifted her into the boat, dropping her on a seat without regard for the place where she did her sitting.

The basket was at her feet, and both men stepped onto solid ground for a last-minute confab. The only light came from the glowing walls, and Mayme was intent on watching the three men.

Calla reached down and caressed Fane's soft little cheek, savoring the baby-sweet smell of her dear nephew. She let him grasp her finger, warily watching Warmond so she couldn't be detected. Under her breath she whispered a promise to the babe: She would return him to his mother! Let Warmond try to sacrifice him now. Her touch had defiled his sacrifice—she hoped—and saved the last of her father's line.

Warmond climbed into the boat alone, and one of his followers cast them adrift on the slow-running river. The Master of Apprentices was in the stern, intent on some contrivance that protruded above the back of the craft.

Calla wondered how this route could be a fast way to the Citadral. There were no oars, and the lazy current wouldn't carry them very swiftly.

Suddenly a terrible racket came from the back of the craft, and they were propelled through the water at an amazing speed. Fane cried out in protest, and Mayme hugged Calla in terror.

Warmond laughed at the girl's distress. "See what the use of metal and a little borrowed technology can do!" he boasted. "The men who work my forge have learned well. One day men will soar over this planet as they do on Mother Earth. And they'll worship the great leader who made it possible!"

"I've never seen such a thing," Mayme said, sounding suitably impressed, but Calla refused to give him any satisfaction.

They moved down the underground stream with smooth, if noisy, speed, and the power source even rocked Fane to sleep.

With success so near, Warmond was less reticent. He seemed almost eager to share his cleverness with his captive audience.

"I discovered this underground stream many years ago," he said. "It begins at the Citadral, and now that I have real power to propel the craft, it's only a matter of a few hours before we're there."

Calla had questions—many questions. Why was he telling her this, and why was she wearing an outlandish costume? Why did he leave his men behind? She feared it meant he had other followers planted among the Zealotes. Knowing

352

he was unlikely to tell her anything she really wanted to know, she asked a question to keep him talking, hoping to glean some clues about his plans.

"The steps were chiseled by men. Did you have them built?"

"I can't take credit there," he said with a tone suggesting everything else redounded to his glory. "I discovered long-unused cells below the Tower of Penance when I was searching for means to impress the ways of the Order on wayward apprentices. I found steps way below the level then in use and followed them to this waterway. I believe the ancient Zealotes designed an escape route in the days when they had enemies."

He laughed, the cruel sound echoing in the eerie tunnel.

"Now, at last, the Zealotes have a new enemy, but they don't know it yet. With the creeches feeding on the Master of Defense, our arrival should be a complete surprise."

"Do duck your heads now," he said with mock concern. "There's a low passage ahead, and I don't want Calla's pretty garb spoiled by blood."

When the tunnel roof rose safely above them again, Calla slumped against Mayme, emotionally exhausted. She considered jumping overboard and trying to swim back to the fortress, but running her hand through the water convinced her it was folly. The stream was thick and oily; it would drag her under and suffocate her; then no one would stand between Fane and the horrendous sacrifice.

353

She slept, and Logan was in her dreams as he had been a lifetime ago when she'd been an innocent girl. His eyes were soft and compassionate, and he reached out for her with loving tenderness. Then, to her horror, a vile creech crawled out of his mouth, and she awoke screaming.

Mayme patted her head and murmured comfort, for once not courting favor with her master, who laughed uproariously at the evidence of Calla's troubled spirit.

The first creech bit him just after nightfall, crawling undetected to the back of his thigh and sinking vicious teeth through the leather of his breeches. Logan reacted instantly, knocking away the repulsive blob and crushing it under his heel. He kicked the remains aside as he had so many others since his imprisonment in the pit began. His Zealote training kept him from crying out, but the acid injected into the bite burned into his flesh like a hot coal, making him gasp in agony.

"Great Power, let me die before the pain drives me mad," he prayed, knocking another invader off his sleeve and crushing it.

He'd tried scaling the gritty wall, but it collapsed wherever he planted his foot or hand. All he accomplished was to stir up a nest of the vicious bloodsuckers.

Already his throat was parched and his stomach rumbled. How long would it be before he grew weak and exhausted, unable to maintain constant vigilance against the loathsome little attackers.

He could shorten his suffering by not resisting, and part of him wanted the ordeal to end as quickly as possible. One thing kept him from giving up: his love for Calla. The thought of Warmond enslaving and raping her was greater torture than a barrel of creeches. If there was one chance in a billion he could escape and save her, he had to will himself to live as long as possible.

He tried again to scale the wall of the pit, choosing a new area with the same results. Segments of dirt broke away, and this time the darkness made him more vulnerable. A creech attached itself to his grasping hand, sinking teeth into his left thumb with a bite every bit as vicious as a lepine's.

Logan pulled the bloated body from his flesh and threw it against the wall, stunned by the intensity of the pain.

A grating sound made him alert for added danger; he expected nothing but the worst in the hellhole that held him.

Staring upward, he probed and found human fear even greater than his own.

"Who's there?"

The only answer was a rope end thrown down with ease—because the grate was gone.

"Climb quickly," a soft whisper urged. "I tied the other end through the bracket that held the rod."

He didn't need urging. Biting back the pain in his thumb when his hand grasped the rope, he pulled desperately, quickly gaining the surface because the pit was only twice the height of a man.

Joy flooded through him as he stood to face his rescuer, expecting to see Calla. He went slack with disappointment when he realized his mistake.

"Who are you?"

"Not now. Follow me!"

He was following a female, hurrying along the dark wall at a pace that seemed maddeningly slow. After covering a short distance, she veered away from the wall to a nondescript structure that stood by itself.

The door opened under her touch, and he was surprised to see torches lighting the windowless interior.

"Why are you risking your life for me?" he asked, stopping her at the head of a flight of stone steps.

"You could have used me as your shield. That you didn't is the first kindness I've received since I came here. You gave me the courage to try escaping."

"You're the girl who's carrying Warmond's child."

"Yes, I'm Delia, but I hate him! I won't let him have this child. Please help me!"

"So far you've done all the helping. We'll talk when we're safely away."

"Come quickly. They're all intoxicated, celebrating the coming eclipse, but someone might miss me."

He went first to block her in case she stumbled, ponderous as she was with the weight of a new life.

The air was dank and foul-smelling, but Logan continued to descend, coming to the corridor of barred cells and finally to the walls with the luminous glow. He touched it and knew they were under the marsh.

"Don't delay," Delia begged. "It's forbidden for a female to be here."

"If they find you with me, we'll both die," he said, sharing her sense of agony.

He heard the lapping of water and found a boat moored for the use of traveling renegades.

"I don't know where this river goes," she said, "but I've watched men go through the door above and not return for many days."

"I think I know," he said, realizing how easy it would be for a renegade Zealote familiar with the Citadral and wearing the robe of the Order to enter and leave the grounds at will just by pulling a cowl over his face.

He understood the use of boats, but the contrivance on the back was one he'd only seen in books.

"What is it?" she whispered, even though they'd heard no sound of pursuit.

"A device to move things—an object of power."

"Can you make it help us?"

"I can try. I know the principle."

He examined every part of it, even reaching into the water to handle the submerged blades. At last he determined that he needed to pull a cord. The contrivance made a sputtering sound, then stopped. A second and a third try produced the same results. Not seeing any oars and angry at his failure to make it work, he furiously pulled the cord, and a great roar propelled the boat away from the docking place and into the current.

Chapter Sixteen

The walls lost their luminous glow, and Warmond maneuvered through the dark cavern with only the echo of the craft's mechanism to guide him.

Fane was quiet after Warmond slowed the boat to feed him from a bottle. The babe slept so soundly Calla suspected the milk had been laced with some calming drug, which added to her fears for his welfare.

She needed to plan, to focus on what was ahead, but the image of Logan being bitten to death by vicious bloodsuckers was too horrific to push aside.

For the last part of the trip, Warmond stopped the contrivance that propelled them forward at a fast speed and let the current carry them to their destination. When Calla saw the light of several torches in the distance, she knew her guess had been right: Warmond had conspirators in the Citadral. She shivered with dread, waking Mayme who was sleeping with her head on Calla's lap.

The sight of black-robed figures standing under torches set in wall brackets brought back memories of her narrow escape from execution at the hands of Zealotes. Was it part of Warmond's plan to see the judgment of death carried out?

The boat drifted toward a mooring spot, and Warmond threw a rope to one of his followers.

"The time is at hand," he said, stepping off the boat and embracing first one and then the other Zealote. "Brother Wyatt, go alert the others and have them meet me in the Grand Elder's audience chamber."

The man hurried off without questions, a sure sign that a well-organized plot was about to unfold. Calla squeezed the handle of the basket, trying not to give in to despair.

"Brother Abner, your loyalty must be rewarded. Take the girl and the babe to my quarters. She can tell you how to tend him if the need arises, but under no circumstances allow her to touch him. Only you can lay a hand on him—a single tender touch will spoil the sacrifice. The Dark Power demands an innocent unspoiled by that profitless emotion, love. I used a female at the fortress who was incapable of that sentimental folly, but I saw more use in bringing this slave with me. No doubt you'll agree." He cupped Mayme's chin, squeezing so hard he brought tears to her eyes.

"I gave the babe a loving touch!" Calla cried out, climbing from the boat unassisted.

"You're lying!" Warmond said. "You heard how I've kept him pure, and you're only trying to thwart my plans."

"No, it's true! I stroked his cheek and fondled his tiny hand."

"Liar!" He cuffed her face, making her stagger to keep her footing. "You're full of tricks, and I'll have none of them. Did you see her touch the babe?" he asked Mayme, his face contorted with rage.

"No, Master." Her voice trembled, and he seemed satisfied that she was too frightened to lie.

"Brother Abner, take yourself, the babe, and the slave to my chamber. Wait there until a messenger comes to summon you."

"Yes, Master."

"The Power of Darkness will have a sacrifice right after the eclipse of the three moons, and neither Logan nor his whore can stop it." He glared at Calla, a look which was more unnerving than his backhanded slap.

"When will the eclipse begin?" she risked asking.

"Very soon! Thurlow will throw its shadow over Primus, Secondus, and the favorite of the Power of Darkness, Amoura. The Earth ship will be able to pass into our atmosphere, and by the time their representatives arrive, they'll have to deal with me! When I control the Zealotes, the government will fall into my hands like overripe fruit falling from a tree."

His laugh echoed in the subterranean chamber, and Calla shook with a chill more violent than a seizure. She recognized his hunger for power for what it was: evil run amuck.

She looked with longing at the boat, wondering if she could reach it quickly enough to escape his madness. Torn between giving up all hope for Logan and abandoning her nephew to a lunatic, she hesitated an instant too long. Warmond grabbed her arm and propelled her forward with more force than she could resist.

He pushed her ahead, knocking her to her knees twice on narrow stone steps when she didn't climb fast enough. The gauzy skirts tripped her up, and the slippers fit too loosely with the slippery soles finding little purchase on the damp rock.

They reached a level where a torch burned brightly, and he made her stop. Reaching for a robe folded in waiting on the floor, he shook it out and ordered her to put it over her gaudy costume. When the tips of the slippers showed below the hem, he made her abandon them and proceed barefooted down the rough cold corridor floor blasted out of solid rock.

On the next level they passed a cell with a barred door, and Warmond walked over to stare at two occupants huddled on the floor.

"You're both still alive!"

"The Grand Elder has had other things to concern him," a defiant voice answered.

"Expect a change for the worse very soon, Brother Perrin. I count myself lucky to be here to peel your living skin from your bones!"

He rushed her up a series of rough-hewn stairs connecting levels of confinement cells. When they left the dungeons behind and walked out into the sweetly scented air of the Citadral grounds, Calla wanted to scream warnings about the monster who held her captive.

"Remember you're a fugitive under sentence of death," he warned, as though reading her mind. "Keep the hood pulled low, or you're signaling your own death."

"As if I care!"

"Some ways of exiting this existence are less pleasant and more interesting than others."

The grounds were deserted; they didn't pass a single brother, and it disturbed Warmond enough to make him mutter to himself.

"Fools! Why aren't they waiting in meditation for the eclipse? My rule won't be so lenient—so slack."

Calla recognized the anteroom of the Grand Elder's audience chamber, but she was surprised by the dense crowd occupying every bit of space.

"Make way for the Master of Apprentices," Warmond sharply ordered, but no one moved aside.

"No one can enter the chamber," an elderly brother volunteered.

"Fool! Of course I can."

"Don't you know? The Grand Elder is dying. We're gathered to hear his final words and learn his successor, but the physicians have the doors blocked. All anyone can do is wait."

Calla heard Warmond's sharp intake of breath

and wondered how the Grand Elder's death would affect his plan.

By trial and error, Logan learned how to coax the maximum speed out of the craft. This was a technology only a few government engineers had mastered, and he began to understand the full extent of Warmond's quest for power. If he really expected to seize control of the Earth vessel, he must have cohorts within the government—and the Zealotes!

"Rest as best you can, Delia. I don't know how long this trip will be."

"Do you know where this river leads? Females were told it ends in certain death for our gender."

"Don't worry." He didn't want to add to her fears by mentioning the Citadral. "I pledge my life to your safety. If you hadn't been so brave, I'd be dead by now."

The bites on his thumb and thigh were like heated daggers in his flesh, but the physical pain was nothing compared to his fear for Calla. Delia had seen her leave with Warmond and his followers. If he had the audacity to take her to the Citadral, he must intend to use her as a pawn in his deadly game. Would he use her execution as a distraction while he took over the Citadral? Or would he hide her away for his private pleasure?

Cold sweat beaded Logan's forehead, and he suffered agonies beyond pain at the thought of Warmond abusing his beloved.

The river ended abruptly after a time that

seemed endless to Logan but was amazingly short compared to the distance by land. After securing the craft and helping Delia ashore, he tried to get his bearings.

Two torches were burning in wall brackets. Had Warmond's men left them there in their haste to execute his orders? The light was reflected on wet rock walls, and he located a stairwell without any difficulty.

He wanted to race up the stairs two at a time and begin his search for Calla, but Delia's condition made haste impossible. He eased her climb as best he could, controlling his impatience with great effort. He couldn't desert the terrified girl who'd overcome her fear to rescue him.

Probing ahead, he at last reached a level where he could sense life. Here, too, a torch was still giving off some light, and he felt Warmond couldn't be too far ahead.

He knew where he was: the level where he'd been confined.

"Who's there?" he softly called out.

"In here! Turnaby and Perrin!"

"Thank the Great Power! You're still alive!"

"Half-alive, but delighted you're here, Master of Defense," a weak voice cried out.

Opening the cell door was much easier from the outside than when he'd been confined behind it. He soon embraced his friends with great relief, but there was too much to do for a joyful reunion.

"Warmond passed by—" Perrin began.

"Was Calla with him?"

"I think so—but Logan, who is this?" The big man looked down on Delia, his eyes wide with surprise.

"Delia rescued me from a place that makes this cell seem like a sanctuary. She's carrying Warmond's child—through no fault of hers. But there's no time for talk."

"Logan, if you know a way to leave here, do so. Your life is forfeit if you're seen in the Citadral," Brother Turnaby warned.

"My life means nothing. I have to warn the Grand Elder. Warmond plans to take over the Zealotes and the government. He covets the technology on the Earth vessel."

"Go quickly and leave these old bones behind!" Turnaby begged.

"No, I may need you. I never expected to find you alive with whole skins."

"It's strange," Perrin agreed. "We've languished here without so much as an interrogation. No one will speak to us, but we've been fed well enough. They gave Brother Turnaby a warm robe. Something's wrong. The two of us can warn the Grand Elder. We've nothing to lose. Take this lovely lass and flee while you can."

"I can't do that."

The upward climb was steep, and Perrin swept Delia into his arms and carried her like a babe.

"Go ahead. I'll catch up," Brother Turnaby wheezed. "Climbing at this pace will kill me."

"We'll go slower," Logan offered.

"No, I must rest. Don't worry. I'll follow you to the Grand Elder's chamber if it's the last thing I do before I gasp my final breath."

The rest of the climb went fast, and not a single monitor was there to challenge them as they left the Tower of Penance.

"The grounds are deserted too," Perrin said, expressing the puzzlement both men felt. He pulled Delia's hood low over her face and wrapped her small hand in his huge paw.

"I expected the paths to be crowded with brothers in meditation. The eclipse isn't far off."

The three of them hurried toward the Grand Elder's audience chamber.

Warmond had elbowed his way through the crowd to the white and gilt door of the audience chamber, but his threats didn't sway the monitors blocking the entrance. He lapsed into a gloomy silence, but he didn't give Calla a chance to slip away. He didn't relax his viselike grip on her arm.

At last the door slowly opened, and the Master of Physicians, white-haired with an unlined, cherubic face and the skills to merit his position, stepped forward to address the assembled Zealotes.

"I regret my news isn't good. The Grand Elder's time is near, but he's conscious and able to make his wishes known. The members of the council may enter first, then all senior brothers. Youngers and Apprentices are to remain in the anteroom, but the Grand Elder's words will be repeated so you'll miss nothing."

With quiet haste, those allowed into the huge audience chamber passed through the door. Calla tried to hang back, but Warmond dug his fingers into her arms until she winced in pain.

The Grand Elder's bed had been carried into the audience chamber and elevated on supports so all the brothers could see their leader by the light of the three moons streaming through the windows. He seemed very small in the massive bed, the gold and white headboard of carved cherubs and foliage soaring toward the ceiling. He was propped up on ivory silk cushions, and warmed by a coverlet embroidered in a hundred different shades of purple, red, and blue.

Even in the dim light, his skin was pasty-white tinged with gray, and his arms rested on the coverlet like broken sticks.

"My brothers," he said, tapping his last reserves of strength to give his voice authority. "I must bid you good-bye. I have loved each of you as my own flesh, and I thank you for your loyalty and trust. Before I go, you must have a new leader." He coughed weakly and paused to rest.

"Beloved Master," Warmond said, stepping forward with Calla still in tow. "I know you'll rest easier if the honor of the Order is restored. We've been betrayed, not once but over and over, and I've brought the proof."

Whispers of protest came from the crowd, but Warmond faced them down. He surveyed the assembly, then smiled with satisfaction when one of his followers called out, "Let the Master of Apprentices speak!"

The Grand Elder nodded weakly as a physician checked his blood flow and another held a cup to his colorless lips.

"The Master of Defense disgraced our Order by releasing a condemned female and spiriting her away. Worse, he made this creature his whore. Now he plans to usurp your power and keep this harlot within the sacred confines of the Citadral!"

Calla cried out in protest, but her words were drowned out by the din of outrage and surprise. Before she could resist, Warmond pushed her forward and ripped the robe from her back with an ease possible only because it had been cut down the front and only lightly restitched.

"Look at her! She's an evil temptress, and she's seduced a once-noble member of our Order into treason and deceit." He glanced over his shoulder and gave a signal to two of his followers to seize her.

The physicians and monitors only added to the uproar by trying to silence the crowd, but at last curiosity accomplished what they couldn't. The brothers quieted, eager to hear what would happen next.

The Grand Elder tried to sit up, and two physicians quickly propped another pillow behind his back. He fought for breath, so weak he couldn't wave his hand for attention.

Behind her back Calla heard sputters of outrage that a female had once again defiled their sacred place. She was frightened beyond reason, but defiance fueled her courage. She wouldn't let these bigoted males see her cringe or beg for mercy!

"What is the purpose in this intrusion?" the Grand Elder managed to ask.

"To protect you and your sacred office, Master," Warmond said, not bothering to use the Zealotes' secret language. "Even as we speak, Logan may be on his way here with a force to seize the Citadral by force. I've marshaled my most trusted brothers to your defense." Warmond gave the signal for his followers to separate themselves from the crowd and step forward.

Calla regretted Logan's horrible death with all her heart and soul, but she knew this disgrace in the eyes of the Order would have been a worse torment to him than any physical pain. Death had spared him terrible degradation.

"For the good of the Order, you must pronounce me Grand Elder! I'm the only one who can defend the Citadral against its enemies!" Warmond beseeched, his voice rising so the lowliest Apprentice in the outer chamber could hear his appeal.

His followers cheered and tried to raise a cry from the others, but those in the rear saw something that made assent stick in their throats.

Calla nearly collapsed with joy when she saw Logan walk toward the bed flanked by Perrin and a small hooded figure.

"Beloved Master," Logan said, going down on his knees, "it's never been the way of the brotherhood to condemn a man without a hearing."

"Do you have proof to back your charges, Brother Warmond?" the Grand Elder asked with a feeble show of strength.

"He has none," Logan quickly said, "because none exists. A long time ago, Master, you gave me a mission. Today I offer my findings. This female can shed light on the truth. I beg you, hear her story."

He slipped off Delia's hood, revealing the sleek, dark hair and enormous frightened eyes of the woman he'd refused to take hostage. Calla's joy drained away, and she felt wrenched with confusion and doubt. Why had Logan brought the girl with him?

"He will listen to the female with Brother Logan," one of the physicians said, overruling Warmond's outraged protest by repeating what the Grand Elder whispered to him.

"This is a great blot on the honor of the Order!" Warmond insisted, stepping toward Delia and scowling to intimidate her.

"Let her speak!" Perrin made himself a human shield, protecting Delia from the sight of her tormentor.

"The Master—Warmond—planted his seed—" She started weeping, but every ear in the room strained to hear her soft voice. "I carry his child, but it's a great curse to me!"

"Where did he ravage you?" the physician asked on the Grand Elder's behalf.

"In my cubicle—at the fortress. I was stolen from my father's freehold and made a slave in the place he built with male slaves. He forced me to—" Her weeping overcame her words, and Perrin took her tiny hand in his, squeezing encouragement.

"These are lies! All lies!" Warmond protested, perspiration giving his cruel features the look of wet granite.

"There's more proof!" Logan shouted. "Warmond has stolen summoned babes for many years. The female condemned to death by the Order was only searching for her infant nephew. He was one of many spirited away on an underground river running from below the Citadral's dungeon to Warmond's secret retreat beyond the Marsh of Misery. The proof is all there waiting to be found: a fortress housing stolen and illicit children, enslaved females, and renegade Zealotes, the runaways of two decades!"

"I have the final proof!" a female voice cried from the back of the room.

Mayme walked forward carrying a basket. "I thought I cared nothing for babes, but I can't let Warmond go through with the grisly sacrifice he has planned for this babe. He brought me here with the child. His man took me to a chamber and tried to ravish me. I was his reward for faithful service to Warmond and the Power of Darkness!"

"This is proof of nothing!" a voice called out.

"Then go find my attacker. I hit his head with a pitcher and escaped. That old man brought me here." She pointed at Brother Turnaby, stooped and slack-faced but smiling with his half-mouth.

"You miserable bitch! You could have bred a future soldier for my army!" Warmond shouted, lunging at the slave girl who'd betrayed him.

From the recesses of his robe, he produced a razor-sharp dirk, and the light of the three moons shone on the lethal blade. He held it at Mayme's throat.

Perrin and Logan both moved toward Warmond, but he tightened his grasp on the terrified girl.

"Steel!" a furious voice cried out.

"He'll use metal on a human!" another called.

An outraged murmur spread through the chamber, the Zealotes shocked by the sight of steel against flesh, an outrage against one of their most sacred rules.

"I'll use it, you fools!" Warmond screamed. "I've planned too long, worked too hard! This Order can't live for the past anymore! I'm the only one who can lead it to future glory! Declare me Grand Elder, Zachary, you imbecile! Now! Or this chamber and every brother here will be forever polluted by her blood."

Cries of horror and outrage turned the room into a bedlam of protest. Shedding the blood of a female in the Grand Elder's chamber would taint every soul in the room. The sanctity of the Zealotes and the hope of life in the hereafter were in grievous jeopardy, and no one dared push Warmond into this unthinkable act by trying to stop him.

"I refuse," the Grand Elder wheezed, the power of his lungs ebbing away but the ring of authority still in his voice.

"Do it! Do it!" the brothers urged from all corners of the chamber.

"If he spills her blood with a metal weapon in our sight, we'll all lose our eternal souls!" a powerful councilman cried out.

The Grand Elder rose up on his own power, shocking his physicians whom he impatiently waved

373

aside. "Hypocrites!" he boomed with superhuman effort. "Is this all the Order means now? A passport to another existence? I've been blind, but now I see!"

The brothers held their breaths, seeing a miracle in their leader's burst of strength.

"Come close, Logan, Master of Defense, son of my heart," the Grand Elder commanded. "My first instincts were right when I saw you as a child. I gave you a mission and thwarted it myself by wrongly letting the female be condemned. The Zealotes must change to meet the needs of the future. I pronounce you my successor as Grand Elder of the Sacred Order of Zealotes."

In the shocked silence of the audience chamber, he spent his last reserve of strength slipping the insignia ring from the withered third finger of his left hand.

Logan knelt beside the man he'd loved as a father and mentor for so many years and submitted when the Grand Elder slipped the heavy, burdensome ring on his finger.

"Noooo—" Warmond's scream of protest was drowned out by the mournful keening of the Order's faithful, grieving as their beloved leader slipped peacefully away into his next existence.

"Release the girl, Warmond," Logan ordered, giving his first command as the new Grand Elder.

The room, illuminated only by the glow of the triple moons, was plunged into darkness. As the Grand Elder breathed his last, the moons slipped into the shadow of the planet. The long awaited eclipse was upon them, a single bloodred disk burning in the sky.

"I won't be robbed of everything!" Warmond screeched, shoving aside the slave girl and grabbing the babe still deep in a drugged sleep in the basket. "The Power of Darkness will restore my power if I carry out the sacrifice!"

Without thinking, Calla raced for the child, seeing a glint of Warmond's blade as a sliver of moonlight reappeared on the surface of Amoura. Before she could get there, a rope whistled out of the darkness, snapping the steel instrument of death from Warmond's hand.

A wise hand found the switch for the power source that illuminated the spires and the audience chamber on sacred occasions. Golden light flooded the room and illuminated the new Grand Elder. He had seized a coil of rope from a monitor's waist and reduced Warmond to a raving, impotent monster.

Perrin made a high-pitched whistling sound, and Youngers loyal to the Order rushed into the room, surrounding the men who had cheered on Warmond's behalf.

"Take them all to confinement cells," Logan ordered.

Four husky youths surrounded Warmond, taking him away shrieking threats of vengeance.

"Take the women and the babe to my former chamber," Logan said, his eyes filled with pain and regret as they met Calla's. "Treat them well; see that no harm comes to them. We've pressing matters to deal with. I want messengers dispatched to warn the government. Warmond's men must be questioned to learn the identity of other traitors. We must deal with the renegades and slavers in his fortress."

He watched as a pair of Youngers led the women away, his heart constricting when Calla looked back, his eyes swimming with tears of regret.

"Now," he said, gently pulling the embroidered coverlet over the face of his departed mentor, "we must act. Later we'll grieve for a man who loved the brotherhood more than his own life."

He led the council members and his faithful friends into an inner chamber, fighting his own tears as the keening in the audience chamber grew in volume and intensity. The new Grand Elder didn't have the luxury of time to mourn— or to love.

Calla fingered the bindings on Logan's books, but her eyes were too teary to focus on titles. Fane was sleeping at last after a lusty session of wailing, seemingly none the worse for the drug Warmond had given him three days ago. He no longer lacked love; Delia and Mayme showered him with attention, vying with each other to win a smile.

The four of them had been confined to Logan's chamber since the night of the eclipse. They were treated with kindness, offered any foodstuff they desired, and supplied with clean clothes of the type worn by Apprentices. Mayme was used to long days of grueling labor, and she blossomed with ample rest and idle time. She delighted in dressing up in the gauzy robes Calla no longer wore, making Calla and Delia smile when she did imitations of Xanthe.

Delia was a quiet companion, spending long hours holding Fane even though his active squirming made him an uncomfortable armload for a woman so advanced toward birthing.

On the second night Calla awoke on her cot and found Delia crying in the bed she shared with Mayme.

"I'm so afraid my babe will be a monster like Warmond," she admitted.

Calla did all that she could to comfort her, but she was mired down in gloomy thoughts herself.

Until the moment Logan accepted the Grand Elder's ring, she'd harbored a secret hope that he was her soul mate. Even though death itself separated them, they were meant to be together through all eternity.

She admitted to herself that she'd even been jealous of poor Delia, who'd so bravely risked her life to save Logan. Now she knew losing him to another woman wouldn't be as painful as being separated by his loyalty to the Order. She could compete with another female, and if she lost, solace herself by hating Logan.

He hadn't come near her, hadn't sent a message, in all the long hours since he'd become Grand Elder. She no longer feared death; no doubt Logan would arrange a way to send his unwelcome guests to safety. She did fear a lifetime of loneliness and longing, unable to forget him but prevented by the rules of the Order from ever contacting him.

She had to return Fane to his family, but there was no place for her in their lives. No matter how her father tried to persuade her, she would never marry Gustaf, not even if it meant being banished from her family.

Smiling with bitter irony, she realized her only option might be to apprentice herself to Doran and learn the arts of the midwife. How could she spend her life pulling newborns from their mothers' bloody wombs knowing she'd never give life to a child of her own?

She went to the long, narrow window and stared up at the sky, intrigued by the silvery form of the spaceship. It hovered above their massive planet like a child's lost toy, and yet it represented a connection with Earth that shaped all their lives.

What would it be like to leave Thurlow, to soar above planet-bound beings, never to return? Given the chance, she knew she wouldn't go. The only world that mattered to her was one she shared with Logan. He might never stand in her presence again, but he'd always live in her heart.

Logan watched the Earth ship, snatching a few moments from his schedule of nonstop work. The government, in gratitude for his timely action in safeguarding the visitors from Warmond's followers, had invited him to meet the visitors, but the Grand Elder of the Zealotes never left the Citadral's sacred ground.

Had Brother Zachary's burden been this great during the long years he'd served as Grand Elder? Logan wished he could have his mentor's counsel and understand what he'd meant by change coming under Logan's leadership.

Four times four days had passed since he accepted the ring of office, and he knew a decision about the women had to be made. The council agreed that none deserved death, and the brotherhood was still too shocked by Warmond's betrayal to care about their fate.

Still he delayed, giving as his reason the imminent arrival of Delia's child. No female in her condition could be expected to travel. The council argued that Warmond's child belonged in the Order where wary instructors could watch for signs of his father's lust for power. Logan agreed to ask Delia, but in his heart he was resolved that no infant ever again be summoned into the Zealotes unless his parents wished it.

Warmond's followers would be tried, but the council shared Logan's hope that some would be found worthy of rejoining the Order after a suitable period of penance. There was still much evidence to gather, but Warmond had used many means of controlling his men, some involving drugs that whittled away their will to resist.

As for the Master of Apprentices, he was still confined to a cell and watched day and night by the most reliable monitors. The Master of Psyche doubted he'd ever be rational enough to face a trial, and the council was considering permanent confinement at a rural retreat under constant guard.

The fortress surrendered without resistance to a force of Zealotes who went there on the underground river. When the renegades heard of Warmond's failure, many of them slipped away in the night, reluctant to live under the rules of the Order again.

The Order needed recruits; the children in the fortress needed homes. No Zealote would object to making room for the male children, but Logan had to be concerned with female babes and the many enslaved women.

Frowning deeply, Logan didn't allow himself to think of the aching hollow in his heart, the emptiness of a life filled with duties and devoid of love.

"Send for Brother Perrin," he gruffly ordered a Younger who stood in attendance.

Logan had appointed Perrin as his counselor, the only Zealote who could still address him by his name. Now he wearily wondered what words of wisdom his new counselor had for a Grand Elder whose heart was dying day by dreary day.

Calla placed Delia's infant at the new mother's breast, watching as the tiny rosebud mouth hungrily suckled. The babe was a dainty replica of her mother with great brown eyes and silky dark hair, but she was a greedy feeder, draining her mother dry at each nursing. Calla fervently hoped it wasn't a sign she'd inherited her father's nature, but Delia seemed content. She had a female child who bore no resemblance to her wicked father. Soon, when she was strong enough to travel, she could return to her family. For now, Delia was happy, several times expressing her strange reluctance to leave the Citadral.

Mayme busied herself with Fane, but Calla felt numb, unable to believe a full moon-cycle had passed without a glimpse of Logan. It seemed like a lifetime, and she felt ill, sure it was dread for the future that was draining her health.

Below her on the spacious grounds a makeshift platform had been erected on a broad sweeping lawn. Since the eclipse, the days had been warm and balmy, a gentle wind making the garden blooms dance in a kaleidoscope of colors.

First she noticed the Apprentices milling around the platform; then a hoard of Youngers shooed them to a patch of grass farther from the stand. Others came, and before long the entire membership of the Order seemed to be assembled, a sea of dark robes waiting for something to happen.

Calla's heart beat faster, and she leaned out the window to better watch the platform. Such a large gathering must mean important news. She hoped against hope she'd finally get a glimpse of Logan.

She was too far away to hear anything being said, but there was no chance she could sneak down to the grounds. A pair of Youngers watched their door by day and night, willing to provide them with anything but freedom to move about the Citadral.

*   *   *

He wore his white robe, letting his sable hair stream over his shoulders and down his back. He looked like a holy man but felt like a fraud. How often had Perrin denied him the opportunity to do penance, insisting he had nothing to regret. Had he made a mistake in choosing his closest friend as his spiritual guide? Did Perrin's high regard for him make him blind to his faults? No matter. After today he might not need a counselor.

They were all assembled, every Zealote in the Citadral except two elderly men who replaced the Youngers watching over the females. Logan looked down at their trusting faces and understood the love Brother Zachary had felt for the brotherhood during his long term as Grand Elder.

"My brothers," Logan began, slowly phrasing the thoughts in his mind. "Our Order was formed to benefit the people of Thurlow in their darkest hour. When our great mission was completed, we withdrew to the sheltered life that has nurtured all of us.

"I've called you together to tell you the Order has a new mission. For too long, we've looked inward. We haven't seen what's happening to our beloved planet."

He pointed upward at the speck of silver rapidly moving away from Thurlow's atmosphere.

"We've been ruled by Earth's needs. Because of their greed for energy, the men of Thurlow go into the bowels of the planet and come out unable to father healthy children. Even as I speak, hoards of defectives are massing, generations lost

or severely handicapped without help in realizing
their potential. I owe my life to a defective lad,
and it's not a debt I take lightly.

"We must throw off our dependence on Earth
and build a new society based on the needs of
those who live on Thurlow. But to do this, legions
of children are needed, healthy, creative offspring
that only Zealotes are capable of fathering!"

The silence was so complete, he could hear the
hum of an insect on the fringe of the crowd.

"We Zealotes must establish a new Order. We
must mate and share our seed, accepting women
as equals to nurture and train a new generation
of Thurlowians."

He braced himself for the reaction, whether it
be silent scorn or vicious stoning.

Calla heard a rousing cheer, a boisterous, full-
throated boom so unlike the Zealotes she couldn't
imagine the reason for it.

Logan was only a tiny dot on the distant platform, but he was unmistakably the reason for the
jubilation. Youngers and Apprentices were frol-
icking like spring woolies. There was a confused
milling, and Logan's white robe disappeared in a
sea of black and gray. She wondered if this was
the last she'd ever see of him.

Logan paced the audience chamber, illuminated
now by sunshine streaming through the tall windows. He didn't know where to put his hands,
locking them behind his back, folding them across
his chest, letting them swing loosely at his sides. He
twisted a strand of hair, then tossed it impatiently

over his shoulder, combing his fingers through the strands swept back from his forehead.

He muttered threats against his slow-footed messenger, then opened the door and shouted at one of the Youngers in constant attendance, ordering him to see what was delaying Brother Perrin. When the young man ran off like a school lad, Logan felt foolish and stormed back into the room, compounding his display of temperament by slamming the door.

When the entry chime sounded, he was weak-kneed and dry-mouthed with hardly enough strength to open the door.

"Calla." He nodded at her escort to leave them and close the door.

He was going to send her away; she loved him too much to make it difficult for him. Bowing her head, she vowed no tears would fall in his presence.

"Look at me, Calla. Please."

He stepped so close, she could see the texture of his gleaming white robe.

She couldn't look into his face, not without crying.

"I couldn't see you all those days—"

"A moon-cycle!" she interrupted, suddenly struck by her own words. A moon-cycle had passed, and before that how long had it been since her last flow? Perhaps she could keep part of Logan forever. . . .

"Forgive me."

"Forgive you?" Please, please, please, she wanted to shout, don't be nice to me before you send me away! Make it easier! Give me a reason to hate you!

"I'm Grand Elder now."

As if she didn't know!

"Today I spoke to all the Zealotes in the Citadral. You see, Calla—" Where was the skill with words that had convinced his brothers to give up the old way? He felt as awkward as a new Apprentice.

"Please," she begged, "no long good-byes between us! Logan, I can't bear it."

"Oh, no, no! Not good-byes, my darling. I just can't find the words to ask you to be the wife of a Grand Elder!"

"Wife . . . Grand Elder?"

"Brother Zachary chose me to bring change. I never suspected how welcome it would be to all but the most conservative brothers. Calla, the Zealotes have a new mission: to rebuild Thurlow—with their seed. I want you to share in this mission—as my mate and mistress of the Order."

"I can't believe it!" She threw her arms around his neck, afraid so much happiness would stop her heart. "Logan, it's too good to be true!"

He scooped her into his arms and carried her into his inner chamber, the bedchamber of the Grand Elder. In the place where Brother Zachary's bed had been, a plain bedstead of heavily grained pere wood was waiting for them, a dark green coverlet folded back over woven white sheets.

"So many nights without you," he murmured, lowering her to the bed and covering her mouth with his.

"Does the Grand Elder's wife have to wear boys' clothes?" she asked, teasing him with the tips of her fingers.

"I'll decide later." He tried to kiss her again, but she rolled away, evading him on the far side of the bed.

"Will the Grand Elder make every decision?"

"Females!" he said in mock horror. "Do you like the robe I'm wearing?"

"Very much. It's soft and white and—"

He pulled it over his head and tossed it at her.

She pressed her face into the folds, loving the texture and the clean masculine scent, loving that the Grand Elder stood before her as he had been when the midwife brought him into the world.

"No more boys' clothes," he promised, walking around the bed to pull her into his arms.

The dull gray robe flew across the chamber; her rope sandals landed on a carpet so plush it nearly swallowed them. Their bodies came together, two parts of a whole: warm, pulsating flesh. She was caught up in the rhythm of his thrusts, slow, hard, undulating, until her breathless moans became soft screams.

The ripples of pleasure didn't stop, and she surrendered to mindless joy, mashing her mouth against his, riding a pounding surf until they collapsed together, complete, whole, united.

"How do Zealotes marry?" she whispered, lying in his arms and examining the raw scar on his thumb.

"We'll have to decide."

"The Grand Elder should bless the couple."

"I already have, my darling."

"It's too soon to have the Zealotes dance on the lawn."

"Agreed."

"Clasped hands, a vow to love forever, two friends as witnesses."

"No honeyed drink, no dress of shimmering cloth, no weeping family or giddy girls hoping they'll be next?" he asked, bemused by the vision.

"Not for mothers-to-be."

He sat up, staring at her in stunned disbelief.

"You are—"

"I am!"

She had her dance, a rowdy, raunchy, noisy round that tore up the room and left the bed a shambles.

Later, much later, Perrin was summoned into the audience chamber, his face scarlet with agitation.

"By the Great Power, Brother Logan, do you think I have nothing to do but cool my heels? Has your exalted status turned you into an inconsiderate lout? I change my mind about penance! An unlearned lad knows better than to keep the Grand Elder's counselor pacing and—"

"We worked out the details of the ceremony, Brother Perrin. And until you witness our vows, you do not have permission to . . . to court Delia."

"Court?" the red-haired giant roared.

"A word I once read in an ancient poem. As good as any for what you intend."

"Perrin?" Calla looked at him in astonishment. "You're willing to raise her babe?"

"The Grand Elder," he said, giving Logan a disdainful look, "has already warned me to be wary of Warmond's offspring, but I believe a young twig can be bent toward the sun. It's a chance I'm willing to take."

A Younger was summoned, entering with a sheepish expression and just a tinge of envy in his eyes.

Calla gathered the folds of the Grand Elder's white robe around her and put her hands in Logan's.

"I vow eternal love," she said.

"I vow to cherish you through all eternity."

Outside the Zealotes gathered on the grounds, eyes sparkling with dedication to their new mission.

LOVE SPELL

THE MAGIC OF ROMANCE
PAST, PRESENT, AND FUTURE....

Dorchester Publishing Co., Inc., the leader in romantic fiction, is pleased to unveil its newest line— Love Spell. Every month, beginning in August 1993, Love Spell will publish one book in each of four categories:

1) *Timeswept Romance*—Modern-day heroines travel to the past to find the men who fulfill their hearts' desires.

2) *Futuristic Romance*—Love on distant worlds where passion is the lifeblood of every man and woman.

3) *Historical Romance*—Full of desire, adventure and intrigue, these stories will thrill readers everywhere.

4) *Contemporary Romance*—With novels by Lori Copeland, Heather Graham, and Jayne Ann Krentz, Love Spell's line of contemporary romance is first-rate.

Exploding with soaring passion and fiery sensuality, Love Spell romances are destined to take you to dazzling new heights of ecstasy.

COMING IN OCTOBER 1993
HISTORICAL ROMANCE
DANGEROUS DESIRES
Louise Clark

Miserable and homesick, Stephanie de la Riviere will sell her family jewels or pose as a highwayman—whatever it takes to see her beloved father again. And her harebrained schemes might succeed if not for her watchful custodian—the only man who can match her fiery spirit with his own burning desire.

_0-505-51910-0 $4.99 US/$5.99 CAN

CONTEMPORARY ROMANCE
ONLY THE BEST
Lori Copeland
Author of More Than 6 Million Books in Print!

Stranded in a tiny Wyoming town after her car fails, Rana Alcott doesn't think her life can get much worse. And though she'd rather die than accept help from arrogant Gunner Montay, she soon realizes she is fighting a losing battle against temptation.

_0-505-51911-9 $3.99 US/$4.99 CAN

LEISURE BOOKS
ATTN: Order Department
276 5th Avenue, New York, NY 10001

Please add $1.50 for shipping and handling for the first book and $.35 for each book thereafter. PA., N.Y.S. and N.Y.C. residents, please add appropriate sales tax. No cash, stamps, or C.O.D.s. All orders shipped within 6 weeks via postal service book rate. Canadian orders require $2.00 extra postage and must be paid in U.S. dollars through a U.S. banking facility.

Name_____

Address_____

City _____ State _____ Zip _____

I have enclosed $_____in payment for the checked book(s). Payment <u>must</u> accompany all orders.☐ Please send a free catalog.

COMING IN OCTOBER 1993
FUTURISTIC ROMANCE
FIRESTAR
Kathleen Morgan
Bestselling Author of *The Knowing Crystal*

From the moment Meriel lays eyes on the virile slave chosen to breed with her, the heir to the Tenuan throne is loath to perform her imperial duty and produce a child. Yet despite her resolve, Meriel soon succumbs to Gage Bardwin—the one man who can save her planet.

_0-505-51908-9 $4.99 US/$5.99 CAN

TIMESWEPT ROMANCE
ALL THE TIME WE NEED
Megan Daniel

Nearly drowned after trying to save a client, musical agent Charli Stewart wakes up in New Orleans's finest brothel— run by the mother of the city's most virile man—on the eve of the Civil War. Unsure if she'll ever return to her own era, Charli gambles her heart on a love that might end as quickly as it began.

_0-505-51909-7 $4.99 US/$5.99 CAN

COMING IN SEPTEMBER 1993
TIMESWEPT ROMANCE
TIME REMEMBERED
Elizabeth Crane
Bestselling Author of *Reflections in Time*

A voodoo doll and an ancient spell whisk thoroughly modern Jody Farnell from a decaying antebellum mansion to the Old South and a true Southern gentleman who shows her the magic of love.

_0-505-51904-6 $4.99 US/$5.99 CAN

FUTURISTIC ROMANCE
A DISTANT STAR
Anne Avery

Jerrel is enchanted by the courageous messenger who saves his life. But he cannot permit anyone to turn him from the mission that has brought him to the distant world—not even the proud and passionate woman who offers him a love capable of bridging the stars.

_0-505-51905-4 $4.99 US/$5.99 CAN

LEISURE BOOKS
ATTN: Order Department
276 5th Avenue, New York, NY 10001

Please add $1.50 for shipping and handling for the first book and $.35 for each book thereafter. PA., N.Y.S. and N.Y.C. residents, please add appropriate sales tax. No cash, stamps, or C.O.D.s. All orders shipped within 6 weeks via postal service book rate. Canadian orders require $2.00 extra postage and must be paid in U.S. dollars through a U.S. banking facility.

Name _____

Address _____

City _____ State _____ Zip _____

I have enclosed $_____in payment for the checked book(s).
Payment <u>must</u> accompany all orders.☐ Please send a free catalog.

Futuristic Romance

Cosmic love and passion on distant worlds!

Daughter of Destiny

JACKIE CASTO

Never in his life has Raul known sensations like those he discovers when holding Esme's delicate body. Yet the mastery he craves is missing, for the weapons he commands cannot compare to Esme's telepathic powers. Not until love transforms his heart will he understand his true place beside the daughter of destiny.

__3046-2 $3.95 US/$4.95 CAN

Futuristic Romance

The New Frontier

JACKIE CASTO

Love in another time, another place.

Raised to despise all men, Ashley has no choice but to marry when she is sent to the New Frontier, man's last hope for survival. Surrounded by women-hungry brutes, Ashley chooses the one man she is sure will refuse her. But before long, she begins to wonder if Garrick will set her free from his tender grasp...or if she'll lose herself in the paradise of his arms.

_3201-5 $4.50 US/$5.50 CAN